AND THEN IT APPEARED.

The shadow seemed to build from the floor upward, a low murky shape that stood out from the darkness with a definition all of its own. Drew staggered back. As it rose, first to the height of Drew's waist and then taller, it seemed to grow outward at the same time, filling the gaping hole that had once been the bay window. Drew stumbled, the strength in his legs failing him, almost losing his footing as he backed up. Wood and glass clattered to the floor around the creature as the remains of the window fell from its frame.

Outside, the lightning flashed, adding a brief glimpse of illumination to the scene. Upon seeing the beast, Drew's first thought was that it was a bear of some kind, but who had ever heard of a bear being bold enough to walk up to a farmhouse, let alone leap through its windows? It quickly became clear that the creature was far removed from anything that he'd ever seen, sharing little in common with the animals that inhabited the Cold Coast.

DEVOUR ALL THE WEREWORLD BOOKS!

RISE OF THE WOLF

HC: 978-0-670-01330-2
PB: 978-0-14-242108-6

RAGE OF LIONS

HC: 978-0-670-01389-0
PB: 978-0-14-242202-1

SHADOW OF THE HAWK

HC: 978-0-670-78455-4
PB: 978-0-14-242192-5

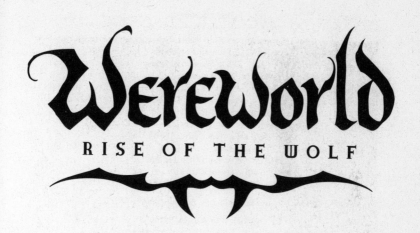

Wereworld

RISE OF THE WOLF

CURTIS JOBLING

PUFFIN BOOKS
An Imprint of Penguin Group (USA) Inc.

PUFFIN BOOKS

Published by the Penguin Group

Penguin Young Readers Group, 345 Hudson Street, New York, New York 10014, U.S.A.

Penguin Group (Canada), 90 Eglinton Avenue East, Suite 700,

Toronto, Ontario, Canada M4P 2Y3 (a division of Pearson Penguin Canada Inc.)

Penguin Books Ltd, 80 Strand, London WC2R 0RL, England

Penguin Ireland, 25 St Stephen's Green, Dublin 2, Ireland (a division of Penguin Books Ltd)

Penguin Group (Australia), 250 Camberwell Road, Camberwell, Victoria 3124, Australia

(a division of Pearson Australia Group Pty Ltd)

Penguin Books India Pvt Ltd, 11 Community Centre,

Panchsheel Park, New Delhi - 110 017, India

Penguin Group (NZ), 67 Apollo Drive, Rosedale, Auckland 0632, New Zealand

(a division of Pearson New Zealand Ltd.)

Penguin Books (South Africa) (Pty) Ltd, 24 Sturdee Avenue,

Rosebank, Johannesburg 2196, South Africa

Registered Offices: Penguin Books Ltd, 80 Strand, London WC2R 0RL, England

First published in 2011 by Puffin UK.
First published in the United States of America by Viking,
a division of Penguin Young Readers Group (USA) Inc., 2011
Published by Puffin Books, a division of Penguin Young Readers Group, 2012

5 7 9 10 8 6 4

THE LIBRARY OF CONGRESS HAS CATALOGED THE VIKING EDITION AS FOLLOWS:
Jobling, Curtis.
Wereworld: rise of the wolf / by Curtis Jobling.
p. cm.
Summary: When a vicious beast invades his father's farm and sixteen-year-old Drew suddenly
transforms into a werewolf, he runs away from his family, seeking refuge in the most out
of the way parts of Lyssia, only to be captured by Lord Bergan's men and forced to battle
numerous werecreatures while trying to prove that he is not the enemy.
ISBN: 978-0-670-01330-2 [hc]
[1. Werewolves—Fiction. 2. Action and adventures—Fiction. 3. Fantasy.]
I. Title
PZ7.J5785 We 2011
[Fic]—dc22 2010049517

Puffin Books ISBN 978-0-14-242108-6

Book design by Jim Hoover
Typeset in Elysium Book

Printed in the United States of America

To my pack:

Andrew, Evelyn, Scarlett, and Constance,

and mummy wolf, Emma. We made it!

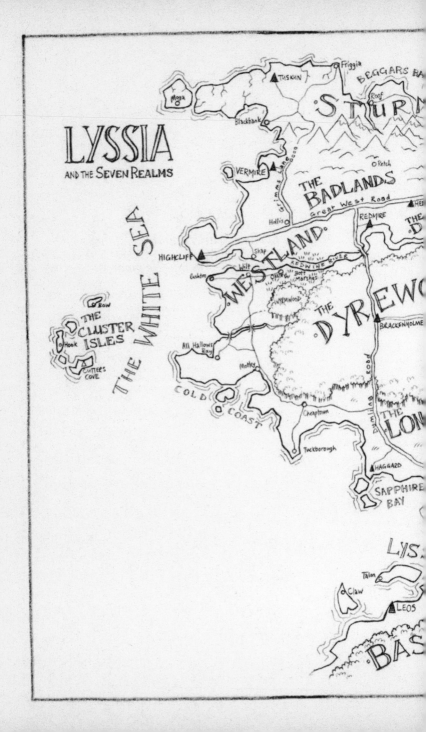

CONTENTS

ACKNOWLEDGMENTS

THERE ARE A FEW people who've played their part in my writing of *Wereworld*, either knowingly or unwittingly, so it's only right that I briefly mention them now.

I fell in love with storytelling via a misspent youth engaged in role-playing games, more often than not running the things. Thanks to all the guys I've gamed with down the years, in no particular order (and I'm bound to miss someone): "our kid" Mark, Andy J., Big Stu, Doctor Andy, Kinnon, Jesus Joe, Nick, Wayne, and all the gang from art college who stayed up playing *Cthulhu* when they should have been partying, including Ian, Bru, Ed, Ron, and Sparky B. Of course, my folks thought I was studying when I was at college as opposed to pulling all-night gaming sessions, so I also need to mention the incomparable and always supportive Kath and Mel.

Cheers to Andy Glazebrook for fiddling with my map (I shouldn't be allowed near PhotoShop), and Jon Hancock, the most passionate (and hairiest) children's book specialist I've ever known. Also thanks to my awesome test-readers who gave me the earliest feedback: Rich Dolan (he's lost friends with his critiques), Tom Martinek (read between blowing things up 920T_pre.indd vi 29/09/2010 09:16 for ILM), Patricia Brennan (should have been painting puppets), and my darling Emma (be gentle with me!), plus the children of her various Internet weirdo friends who were the target audience. Cheers, chaps!

Thanks to my brilliant agent, John Jarrold, for believing in this crayonboy and taking me on, and a massive debt of giddy thanks to Shannon Park, my editor. Without Shannon's unwavering belief and constant advice, a great deal of which she sent my way before Puffin even picked this up, *Rise of the Wolf* may never have happened.

And special thanks to my brothers from another mother—Ian Culbard and Niel Bushnell—who have followed my attempts to break into novel-writing every step of the way, providing varying degrees of support and ridicule when needed (suicidal sheep, anyone?). They even fashioned the spiffing *Wereworld* teaser trailer between them, with the help of the lovely Tanya Rich and the gang at Qurios.

One last thumbs up to Ian—the man who gave a name to the series: *Wereworld*. Cheers, buddy!

Curtis, September 2010

PART I

AUTUMN, COLD COAST

I

PARTING WORDS

DREW KNEW THAT there was a predator out there.

He looked out over the barley field, mottled shadows racing across it, and the crops swaying rhythmically as storm clouds flew by overhead. Behind him his father and twin brother continued to load the wagon, backs bent as they hauled sacks of grain onto the wooden boards. A heavy gray shire horse stood harnessed to the front, tugging with its teeth at tufts of grass it found at the base of the tethering post. Drew stood on the roof of the rickety old toolshed, scouring the golden meadow for a telltale sign, of what he wasn't entirely sure.

"Get your idle bones down off that shed and come and help your brother," shouted his father. "We need to get this loaded before the rain hits."

"But Pa, there's something out there," Drew called back.

"Either you get yourself down from that thing or I come over and knock you down," Pa warned, pausing momentarily to glare at his son.

Begrudgingly, Drew searched the barley field with narrowed eyes one last time before jumping down onto the muddy, rutted surface of the farm's yard.

"I swear you'd rather do anything than a bit of hard work," muttered his father, hefting a sack up to Trent.

Drew snatched up his own load, struggling for purchase against the rough hemp as he hoisted it up to his brother. Their father returned to the barn to haul out the remaining grain destined for the neighboring market town of Tuckborough.

Tall, broad, blond-haired, and blue-eyed, Trent was the very image of Mack Ferran. Shorter and slighter in build than his brother, with a shock of black hair that tumbled over his finer features, Drew was an exact opposite in all aspects. Though the twins were now on the verge of manhood, Drew knew it would be clear to the most casual observer which of the two had eaten the bigger portions of porridge at the Ferran breakfast table. But, different as they were, they were as close as any brothers could be.

"Don't mind him," said Trent, taking the weight of the sack and dragging it across the wooden boards. "He just wants to be off so he can get to market on time." He slammed the bag down as Drew pulled forward another to the foot of the wagon. Trent rarely had any trouble believing Drew—if his brother said something was amiss when they were in the wild, nine times out of ten he'd be correct. "What do you reckon it is?" he asked.

Drew paused to glance back at the fields surrounding the Ferran farm. "Can't say. A wildcat? Dogs maybe? Possibly a wolf?" he guessed.

"At this time of day, so close to the farm? You're mad, Drew. I'll grant you it might be wild dogs, but not a wolf."

Drew knew he wasn't mad. Trent might have been strong, athletic, and a natural horseman, but he knew little about the wilderness. Drew, on the other hand, was a born outdoorsman and with this came the gift of an innate understanding of the countryside and the creatures within it. Since his first trip out into the fields as a boy with his father, he'd taken to shepherding with an uncanny ease. He found he was completely in tune with the animals, his senses seeming to match theirs. From the smallest field mouse to the largest (and, thankfully, very uncommon) bear, Drew could usually recognize their presence readily, be it from the reaction of the other animals or the tracks and signs they left behind.

But today's feeling vexed him. Something was out there, watching them, stalking them, but it was unfamiliar. He knew it sounded crazy, but he could pick up the scent of a predator when the air was clear. This had proved invaluable on many an occasion, saving several of the family's sheep and cattle. Although today was blustery, there was still the faint hint of a creature that was out of place, foreign to these parts. A large animal was out there, looking in, and it irked Drew that he couldn't figure out what it was, much less spy it.

"You think it's the thing from last night?" asked Trent.

That was exactly what Drew had been wondering. For the last few nights Drew's shepherd watch had been unusual. The sheep had not been themselves, and all the while Drew had been consumed by an awful sense of foreboding. Ordinarily the sheep would be very receptive to his commands and calls but, bit by bit, they had become more erratic. This had coincided with the waxing of the moon, which often spooked the animals and had even caused Drew to grow ill with worry. It wasn't a pleasant sensation, the feeling of being stalked by a predator in your own backyard.

Toward the end of last night's watch he'd gathered and penned the majority of the flock and picked up the stragglers that had wandered farther afield. Only one had remained—the ram, naturally—and it had managed to find its way up onto the bluffs that towered over the coast below. The Ferran farm was situated on a rocky promontory of land that reached out from the Cold Coast into the White Sea, cut off on almost every side by the rock walls that surrounded it. He'd found the ram in a state of panic.

It had bucked and started, throwing its head back in fear. Drew raised his hands, which should have calmed it down, but it had the opposite effect. Shaking its head from side to side, mouth open and gulping at the salty air, the ram had backed up a step. Then another. Pebbles had tumbled over the cliff edge, dislodged by frantic hooves, as it struggled for purchase. One moment it was there, an eye fixed on him in stricken terror, the next it was gone, disappearing off the cliff.

Drew had scrambled the remaining distance to the edge, white-knuckled fingers clutching the earth as he peered over. A hundred feet below, heaped in a broken mass, the sheep lay unmoving, its life dashed away on the sharp rocks.

As the moon shone down Drew had looked about, convinced he wasn't alone, sure beyond reason that whatever had startled the animal was still nearby. He'd raced home through the sickly moonlight, heart thundering, not stopping until he'd hit the farm's front door with an almighty crash. Now, on this stormy morning, Drew had the same familiar feeling. He'd be keeping the sheep penned in tonight, close to the farm where he could keep an eye on them.

"Drew!" His father pointed in the direction of the remaining sacks that were lined up outside the heavy timber doors of the barn. "Get a move on. I want to get to Tuckborough while there's still daylight, lad." Drew trudged to the barn, speeding up when he caught sight of his father's glower.

His mother, Tilly, stood on the doorstep of the farmhouse, drying her hands on her apron.

"Try not to be hard on him, Mack," she said as her husband approached, reaching out and brushing the sweat-soaked hair from his brow. "He's probably still raw from what happened to that ram."

"*He's* still raw?" said Mack incredulously. "It's not him who has to fork out for another animal. If I don't get there before noon, the best on show will be gone to some other bidder." He saw his son dragging the last two sacks across the farmyard to the wagon. "If you tear those sacks, then it'll come out of your wages, lad!" he shouted.

Tilly had to bite her lip, mother's instinct telling her to jump in and defend the boy, but she thought better of it. Mack's mood was bad enough without one of their rows darkening it further.

Drew stopped to throw one of the sacks over his shoulder, looking back to his parents, who stood talking beneath the farmhouse porch. His father was pointing his way, his hooked thumb gesturing, while his mother shook her head. A few choice words to her husband and she walked indoors in annoyance. The boys' father looked back toward them, shaking his head wearily before following his wife indoors. Drew trudged over to the wagon.

"Are they arguing again?" asked Trent, positioning the final sack and binding them to the timber hoardings with a heavy length of rope.

Drew nodded, aware that the words his parents had exchanged were probably about him. It always seemed to be about him. It felt as though they were keeping something from him, but he didn't know what.

Times were undoubtedly changing at the farm, and Trent was biding his time before he finally left home to join the military. Under duress, their parents had agreed to their son's constant badgering to allow him to become a soldier, something he'd wanted to do since childhood. As a matter of routine, their father had trained both his sons in skill at arms from an early age, teaching them things he'd picked up himself a long time ago. Mack was a member of the old king's Wolfguard, and there were very few places across the continent of Lyssia that he hadn't visited. With Leopold the Lion on the throne, it was a very different monarch Trent would serve if he pursued his dream. This part of the Seven Realms was a changed place from days gone by. Leopold ruled with an iron paw, and it was rumored that many of Lyssia's people had fallen on hard times. Their father would mutter that the Lionguard were now little more than glorified tax collectors, a shadow of their former selves. He had done his parental duty in basic self-defense, with both boys now proficient with a sword, but there was only so much he was prepared to teach.

Regardless of his own skills, Drew had no desire to travel to Highcliff with his brother and join the Lionguard. His home was on the farm, and he felt no need to see the world. He knew his mother found his homebird nature heartwarming and loved the fact that her young boy would always be around. Drew suspected that his father found his lack of ambition disappointing, but the old man never spoke of it if he did. It seemed that his father had written him off at a young age, and if he were to stay around here for the rest of his life then so be it. After all, as Mack Ferran often said, another pair of hands was always needed on the farm, so the boy was good for a few things. It was as close to a compliment as he was likely to get.

Straining against his harness, the great gray shire horse kicked his hooves into the earth, keen to be on his way. He threw his head back and took a couple of forceful steps, almost causing Trent to fall off the back of the wagon.

"Whoa there, Amos," called Drew, slapping his hand against the wooden side. The horse relented, stepping back gingerly and dipping his head by way of an apology. "He wants to set off," said Drew, looking up at the gathering storm clouds. "Can't say I blame him."

Trent jumped down, and Drew followed him indoors to say farewell. They found their parents standing in the kitchen, embracing.

"Right, then," said their father. "I guess we're ready. Trent, get that basket off the table, lad. It's our lunch in there."

Trent picked up the basket and sidled past, back to the front door and the waiting wagon. They always took it in turns to accompany their father on the road to market. Tuckborough was some ten or so miles away from them, the nearest spot of civilization. By horse it was a brisk gallop, the coast road skirting the edge of the Dyrewood, weaving one way and the other along the cliff top past bays. By wagon it was a far slower affair. With a number of shops, watering holes, and other more diverting interests, it was usually a welcome break from mundane life on the farm. Come autumn, however, it was decidedly less enjoyable. Cold winds and sleeting rain seemed to instinctively appear on market days. Even the prospects of a sly sip of ale with their father or a flirtation with a pretty girl proved lean enticements.

Their mother cleared up the breakfast pots from the kitchen table. Drew reached up and unhooked his father's heavy hooded cloak from its peg, handing it to him as he made for the door.

"We should be back around nightfall, depending on the road and weather," Mack said as he fastened the brass clasp of his cloak under his chin. "You may want to see about keeping the flock a little closer to the homestead today. After yesterday and all, yes?"

Drew nodded his agreement as his mother squeezed by, looking to say her good-byes to her other son. Beyond the doorway, a light rain had started to fall.

"Try not to lose any more of them. And look after your ma," his father added as she passed.

The old man patted his hip, checking his hunting knife was at home in its sheath. Drew handed his father's longbow to him before picking up the quiver of arrows that lay at the foot of the stairs. He'd rarely had to use any of these weapons on the road, certainly not in recent years anyway. There had been a time, when the boys were toddlers, that bandits had stalked the coast road, and bows and blades were a necessity for travelers. Eventually the local farmers and road traders had come together to form a makeshift posse that dispatched the brigands. Those who weren't slain or hanged in Tuckborough had fled to pastures less feisty. Now the most dangerous encounter they might face would be a boar, big cat, or wolf. Still, old habits died hard for the ex-soldier. Trent followed his father out into the drizzle, wrapping his scarf tightly about his face and pulling up the hood of his cloak.

They both climbed into the cart, and Drew followed them to pass up the quiver of arrows. Amos gave a whinny of excitement, feet stepping in anticipation, aware that they were about to be off. Drew stepped up to pat the horse's nose with an open hand, but the beast pulled back, uncharacteristically arching his neck with a nervy snort. Clearly the horse was also on edge, and Drew guessed he was picking up on the same unsettled atmosphere.

"Gee up," called Mack Ferran, snapping the reins in his hands and spurring the old shire horse on. With ponderous footsteps the horse stepped out, pulling the great long wagon behind him. Drew stood clear of the vehicle, the huge wheels cutting up the mud as it went. As the drizzle slowly turned to a downpour and a storm rumbled overhead, the wagon disappeared into the rain.

2

THE GATHERING STORM

THE AX HOVERED briefly in the air, poised for the drop, its blade glinting in the lantern light. With a thunderclap and a simultaneous flash of lightning, it flew down, cracking the log in two. Drew returned the ax to its bracket on the barn wall, picked up all the firewood from the floor, and set off back to the farmhouse through the sleeting rain.

Once his father and Trent had left, the day had been one of the most miserable Drew had ever experienced. The storm had been relentless, windowpanes rattling and shutters clapping as rain and wind battered the farm. The yard was a quagmire of mud and water, great dirty pools clogging the ground underfoot. He could hear sheep bleating from their shelter beyond the barn, where he'd moved the flock earlier in the day.

Hoping his bad luck with the animals was behind him, Drew had been disappointed to find the hex still firmly over his head. The sheep had proved skittish and unpredictable, almost impossible to herd when he took them to the field. A week earlier the flock had come to him when he called, happily gathering around him. Now they were different animals, the arrival of this invisible predator leaving them edgy and out of sorts. After trying to coax and cajole them for an hour, he had eventually turned to shouting to scare them into obeying his commands, something he'd never needed to do before. All the while he'd watched over his shoulder for any clues as to what was out there. By now there was no doubt in his mind that, whatever it was, it was something to be afraid of.

A day alone with his thoughts had not been the best rem-edy for Drew's mood, which was darker than ever. Whatever had upset the sheep had also played havoc with Drew, leaving him sick and fevered, and unable to eat his supper earlier. El-bowing open the front door, he stumbled into the hall, shaking the wet cloak from his shoulders and hopping about on one foot then the other, kicking off his boots. Barefoot and shiv-ering, he trotted into the living room, where his mother sat knitting in the armchair by the dying embers of the fire. He tipped his armful of kindling and wood into the scuttle on the hearth with a noisy clatter, placing a couple of pieces on the coals of the fire. Crouched on his haunches, Drew remained at his mother's feet, hands held out toward the fire.

"How are you feeling, son?" asked his mother, putting down the needles and wool. She leaned forward, stroking his damp hair affectionately. She laid the back of her hand against his forehead, checking his temperature. He knew it was up.

"Not too bad, Ma," he lied, fighting back the cramps that rolled and shot through his belly. He looked up at the mantelpiece. Below his father's Wolfshead blade was a brass carriage clock. It was almost half past ten in the evening, well beyond the time that his father and Trent would normally be home. He had to assume that they had fallen foul of the weather.

Standing, he managed to smile to his mother. "Do you fancy a brew, Ma?" he asked, making for the kitchen. A hot drink seemed to be the only thing he could keep down at the moment.

"That would be lovely," she called after him. Filling the kettle with water he placed it over the big old stove. Whereas his brother clearly followed in his father's footsteps, Drew took after his mother, sharing her peaceful demeanor and easygoing nature. He always figured his mother must have been wasted in her youth as a scullery maid in Highcliff serving the king; her sharp mind and quick wit could have made her a great scholar if the opportunity had been there for her.

Leaving the kettle on the stove, Drew wandered back into the sitting room, settling cross-legged on the rug by the fire.

"Still not hungry?" his mother asked, concerned again.

"No, can't eat anything, Ma. Sorry," he replied, aware that his mother had spent hours preparing the evening meal earlier.

14

Unable to eat, he had lain in his bunk in his bedroom, leaving his mother downstairs to eat her meal alone. The table still remained set, the cutlery for Pa and Trent laid out, plus his own.

"There's no need to apologize, my dear," said his mother. "I know how it is when you feel ill." She looked intently at him, as if reading his thoughts. "And I hope nothing else is troubling you." She put a reassuring hand on his shoulder. "I know you didn't mean to lose that sheep."

Drew nodded. It was true he'd been worried about that, but now something else was disturbing him. He'd attempted during the day to unravel what had been going on with his parents' heated arguments, but his mother had proved adept at dodging his subtle lines of questioning. Although she'd provided no answers she had, however, revealed some clues.

To his relief, it didn't appear to be his fault. He knew his father was annoyed at the loss of a prize-winning ram, but his mother had just made it clear that he had done nothing wrong, and he believed her. She would sooner stay silent than tell a lie to either of her boys. Nor was it something that stemmed from a disagreement between his parents. Whatever it was, the clues suggested that it had something to do with the flock's strange behavior, but that was all he could work out. With his father dismissing his theories earlier, Drew was surprised to find out that he also thought something was wrong.

Drew was pulled back from his thoughts by the rapid *rat-tat-tat* of the rain on the windowpanes, making it seem as

15

though the glass might shatter at any moment. Picking up an-other log, he threw it into the fireplace. The flames leapt high, the fire burning hungrily now, spitting, hissing, and popping. Drew walked across to the huge bay window. Over the storm he could hear his sheep bleating, wailing with worry. Should he go outdoors to check on them? Surely they'd be safe in the pad-dock? The moon, full and bloated in the night sky, broke through the storm clouds, casting an eerie light over the farmyard.

Drew suddenly felt the fever take him anew, as never be-fore. A wave of dizziness washed over him as the blood rushed from his head. He grasped the heavy curtain with a trembling hand to stop himself from falling. His breathing rasped in his chest, labored and shallow, as rivulets of sweat rolled down his face and into his eyes. Drew wiped his forearm across his face and his sleeve came away sodden, clinging to his flesh. What kind of illness could have this effect on him?

He fixed his eyes on the moon, trying to focus, trying to clear his head of the painful sensations that now assaulted his body. His skin crawled, a fevered itch spreading its way over every inch of his flesh like wildfire. Nausea assailed him, his chest heaving, his lunchtime meal threatening to make a break from his stomach. The world turned around Drew, spinning on the bright white axis of the moon. Focus on the moon.

Focus on the moon.

His body seemed to calm, the pains passing as quickly as they had come. His flesh cooled; the sickness passed. Outside the rain was subsiding, gentle now and almost tranquil. The sheep had quieted, suddenly calmed. Drew released his grip from the curtains, putting his hand to his clammy throat and massaging it softly. The peace he felt was unnatural, unnerving.

His mother rushed over. "Are you all right, Drew?"

"Not really," he replied. "I feel ill. I think it's the sheep being in distress. I'm picking up on it, and there's nothing I can do."

His mother chewed her lip, her brow creased as she stroked his cheek.

"Ma," asked Drew, taking a deep ragged breath. "What's wrong with me?"

"Nothing, my love. Nothing at all."

Her face looked so sad, Drew thought, her frown aging her before his very eyes.

He smiled.

"I know there's something you're not telling me, Ma," he said, then, as she started to protest, "Please don't deny it. I've seen you and Pa. There's something you're keeping from me. I know I'm right, but hear me out. I need to say this. I just want you to know that I trust you. Whatever it is, whatever you and Pa are worried about, I know you'll do the right thing. I just hope, whatever it is, there's something I can do to fix it."

He was surprised to see tears stream down his mother's cheeks at his words, rolling freely as she smiled and sobbed.

"Oh, Drew," she said, her voice breathless. "Always so thoughtful, so understanding. Please believe me when I tell you

17

that no parents ever loved their child as much as we love you."

Drew was slightly taken aback, and with a sadness in his heart doubted she genuinely spoke on behalf of his father.

"I wish I could be strong like Trent, and let Pa see that I'm worth something more. Are there two twins more different in all of Lyssia?" He smiled weakly. "But I never meant to upset you, Ma," he said. "Really, I didn't!"

His mother laughed at his words, hugging him. "I know you didn't, you silly boy, I know you didn't." She squeezed him tight. The storm outside seemed to stop, fading away for the moment. The rumbling of thunder had gone; even the rain had subsided. The world seemed silent.

"Don't try to be like Trent," she added quietly. "There will come a time when your pa and I need to tell you more. But you do need to know . . . that you're not like your brother."

Drew's eyes queried the strange statement, although the full understanding of her words was totally beyond his reach and comprehension. Just then the kettle began to whistle on the stove in the kitchen, low and slow at first before building toward a crescendo. The hairs on the back of Drew's neck stood on end. His mother wasn't finished.

"You *are* different."

He wanted to know more, to ask her what she meant, but as he opened his mouth the small panes that made up the bay window suddenly shattered in a hail of flying glass as the frame buckled and exploded into the room.

3
THE VISITOR

THE STORM RAGED with a renewed fury, bellowing in the sky over the tiny farmhouse. As the curtains whipped about, caught and torn on crooked shards of broken glass, wind roared in through the gaping chasm of the demolished window.

Turning his back into the glass while dropping to the ground, Drew had sheltered his mother from the explosion as best as he could.

"Are you all right?" he called over the din.

His mother nodded quickly, eyes shooting toward the window. She looked shaken and scared, but beyond some scratches on her face, seemed unharmed. Drew slowly helped her to her feet, surveying the situation.

The great bay window now blanketed the floor with hundreds of tiny pieces of splintered wood and shattered glass. The odd piece of timber swung from its brackets attached to the window frame, broken and ruined. The bookcases that had flanked the window lay on their side, empty and smashed, their far-flung books flapping as the wind clutched at their pages. Rain continued to drive into the room, harsh cold spittle that spattered Drew's face.

Helping his mother back in her chair he began to step over the damaged furniture, making his way toward the window. The fallen bookcases would be best put to use as a temporary hoarding over the hole until the morning came. He'd have to dig out his pa's toolbox from the cellar, but once his father and brother returned they could all set about putting things back to normal. Still, the situation unnerved him.

His eyes searched the room, an important piece of the puzzle missing. The hairs on the back of his neck trembled, a shiver still coursing down his body and making his whole frame tremble. Something wasn't right. Squinting into the darkness, Drew couldn't see what had caused the impact. He had expected to find a great tree branch jutting into the house, but the lack of any obvious cause both surprised and worried him. Surely the wind alone couldn't cause such damage? He took another step toward the window, still searching for evidence. The fire roared against the storm before suddenly giving up the ghost, chased from the room.

Then it appeared.

The shadow seemed to build from the floor upward, a low murky shape that stood out from the darkness with a definition all of its own. Drew staggered back. As it rose, first to the height of Drew's waist and then taller, it seemed to grow outward at the same time, filling the gaping hole that had once been the bay window. Drew stumbled, the strength in his legs failing him, almost losing his footing as he backed up. Wood and glass clattered to the floor around the creature as the remains of the window fell from its frame.

Outside, the lightning flashed, adding a brief glimpse of illumination to the scene. Upon seeing the beast, Drew's first thought was that it was a bear of some kind, but who had ever heard of a bear being bold enough to walk up to a farmhouse, let alone leap through its windows? It quickly became clear that the creature was far removed from anything that he'd ever seen, sharing little in common with the animals that inhabited the Cold Coast.

A thick coat of oily black hair covered its heavy frame, a foul-stinking pelt that bristled with muddy rainwater. Heavy forelimbs swung down from its hunched shoulders, viciously clawed hands scraping the splintered floorboards around it. Smaller legs were bent double below, supporting the body, threatening to spring the great mass forward at any moment in a mighty bound. What appeared to be a long, fleshy tail wound out from the base of its torso, snaking back through the rubble toward the window. It stood some eight

21

feet tall in all, dominating the darkness of the room.

Whatever horror the body of the beast had created in Drew and his mother paled in comparison when the fearsome head rose slowly from the black nest of fur on its chest. The long snout came into view, tapering toward the end where a cluster of long, sharp teeth jutted out from curling blood-red lips. Its breath rolled into the room before it, making Drew gag at the stench. The foul air carried the scent of rotting flesh and disease, the stink of death and decay, sweet and sickening. Its ears were small and pinned back to its head, almost hidden in the glistening dark coat. Two pale red eyes flashed from pitch-black sockets, narrowing with wicked glee as it stared back at its prey.

It opened its mouth wide, throwing its head back as it bared its teeth, a long black tongue lolling and snaking from its maw as saliva spattered down to pool with the rainwater.

Drew's stomach was in turmoil as he stared at the monster. His heart raced, the burn of the fever still gripping his body but now fueling something, feeding his will. Spurred into activity he leapt to the fireplace between the beast and his mother, reaching up and unclipping his father's Wolfshead blade from the chimney breast. It felt heavy and awkward in his hands, but he held it wavering before him, palms gripping the hilt of the sword. He felt his mother's trembling hand on his shoulder, her fear passing over him as she stood up to shelter behind him.

The creature seemed to chortle, loud, low, and guttural, as it clambered over the overturned furniture and farther into the room.

"Get out!" cried Drew over the wail of the wind, swinging the sword before him to try to ward it off. The beast raised a hand, batting the sword aside, stepping ever closer. Drew's bones and muscles burned, a sudden sharp pain racing wildly through his body to clench his heart. Losing control he lashed out with the sword, lunging toward the monster blade-point first. The sword disappeared beneath its arm, hitting home somewhere in the monster's midriff. It recoiled, staggering. Lowering a clawed hand to its bloodied side, it examined the dark black liquid with no small degree of concern, before glaring back at its attacker. A huge hairy arm scythed out, quick as a flash, arcing across the room to tear Drew's chest. Blood flew from a trio of razor-sharp cuts as Drew collapsed against his mother, the sword tumbling from his grasp with a clatter onto the floorboards.

"Drew!" called his mother, but the cry was in vain.

His body shook violently, picking an unfortunate moment to seemingly give up its battle against the fever that had haunted him. Tilly Ferran let out a scream of despair as her son tumbled from her arms to the hearth, his poor body convulsing. She snatched up the blade.

"You've killed my boy!" she cried, waves of a mother's grief exploding from her.

The monster raised a thick black claw, waggling it in a show of disagreement, before pointing it at her. Its voice gurgled, a malevolent laugh that belonged to the dark places of the world.

"For you. Came. For you . . ."

Tilly's eyes widened. She staggered forward, sword flailing wildly, but the creature powerfully swung out its arm, claws meeting her as she ran, the sword tumbling from her grasp. The impact sent her flying through the air toward the kitchen. She landed on the table with a sickening crunch, sending crockery tumbling to shatter on the tiled floor.

Twitching and shuddering, Drew could only watch as the monster sent his mother crashing into the kitchen. As it followed her, all he wanted was the strength to rise and attack the beast, bring it down, tear its throat from its body. But he was paralyzed by an unfathomable weakness that had now consumed him.

The creature slowly advanced into the kitchen, drawing out the inevitable. It stepped through the chaos, wind cloaking it with rainwater as it shambled up to the table. A huge clawed hand trailed playfully along the wood, blood dripping onto the surface.

Tilly Ferran whispered the word "no" over and over, again and again, but she knew this was her end, knew there was nothing she could do to stop the monster. The beast shook its head, stinking drool falling onto the table beside her head.

"I thought . . . I thought I was safe from you," she mouthed, though the words found no volume. "I thought you'd never find us."

The animal snarled a grin, leaning in toward her and mouthing a single word as it opened its mouth.

"Never."

Then it closed its jaws around her throat.

Indescribable anger and fear raged through Drew's body as he watched the nightmare scene unfold. He closed his eyes, willing his limbs to move but was instead assailed by a feverish spasm.

It started in his guts, as before, but worse. Much worse. He felt his insides tearing now, not fighting to pull free from his body but twisting about and finding fresh homes. His bowels seemed to rise from the pit of his belly and shift farther back, while his lungs grew threefold, great gasps of air racing into his chest. As the lungs grew, so did the rib cage, straining at first before cracking and popping. His chest expanded as his ribs took a new shape. The pain was unbearable. He wanted to yell out loud against it, but nothing came other than a silent scream.

He gritted his teeth as he felt a pressure grip his skull like a vise. The strain increased; Drew thought his eyes might burst from his sockets. He felt his gums beginning to tear as his teeth seemed to work themselves free. His arms came up before him, but he could only stare in horror as his hands distorted, stretched, and elongated, with his nails tearing from his fingers into great long claws. Hair shot from his flesh, up his arms, from his chest, and he felt his mind threatening to slip away. His skull cracked under the pressure, and his jaw dislocated when a muzzle broke out.

His eyes hazed over, yellow and baleful, as he looked up from where he crouched. A semblance of Drew's mind remained, locked away inside, unable to fathom this horrifying transformation. He was looking on, a witness to what unfolded, as if suspended from the ceiling above. Fur bristled along his spine as, hackles raised, he watched his enemy, the intruder's back turned.

He let out a low growl, almost inaudible over the sound of the storm, but the monster heard him. It turned, slowly, blood staining its muzzle as it looked back into the sitting room. Disbelief appeared on the monster's face. It faced the boy, or what had been the boy, warily.

Before the creature could move Drew instinctively leapt forward. He cleared the distance between them in one bound, crashing into the beast's chest, and the two tumbled to the floor in a ball of flailing claw, tooth, and fur. The monster tried to defend itself from Drew, but the beast-boy was taken by a furious hunger, a rage that was unstoppable. The monster, though clearly stronger and a seasoned killer and fighter, let slip its guard in the panic, and Drew's jaws snapped over its skull. He yanked the beast's head back in a sharp savage motion, and with a ragged tear the flesh came with it. Letting loose a screech of pain, the monster struck back, a clawed fist hitting Drew hard in the chest. The force of the blow sent the boy tumbling back, crashing into a dresser in an avalanche of crockery. His strength escaped him when he tried to get up, the jangling pain of broken ribs adding to the shock of being winded.

Looking up from where he lay in a heap, Drew saw the creature rise from the floor, towering over him again. Ragged breaths escaped from its mouth as moonlight streamed in through the kitchen window, illuminating the damage Drew had dealt it. The right-hand side of its face was missing, revealing torn sinew and cartilage slick with black blood. Bare skull caught the light, a crescent of bone that arched around the eye socket like a bright white sickle. Flesh hung in tatters from the side of its mouth, the teeth in all their glory vanishing into the shadows of its jaws.

Snarling, the monster let the remainder of its lips peel back, emitting a gurgling growl. Raising its hands, it let its claws play against one another, long black talons that clicked and clacked with anticipation. It hunched its shoulders as it took a step closer, its legs crouching, muscles flexing, as it prepared to pounce on the boy. A noise from the front of the house made the beast stop, its head twitching up, bobbing, as it listened intently. It looked back at the strange helpless creature at its feet, spitting blood at him in anger before turning and diving through the kitchen window. Sheet glass fell from the frame as the beast vanished into the stormy night.

Struggling to regain his composure, Drew fought to get to his feet, grasping a leg of the kitchen table with one clawed hand over the other until he stood tall. While he climbed he could feel his body shifting, twisting again, as his human self returned. The hairs that covered his body receded, disappearing beneath his skin, and his bones and muscles reverted back to their natural state. Last to crack back into position was his muzzle, and he felt his face slowly return to normal as he looked down on his lifeless mother.

Laid out as if on a mortician's slab, Tilly Ferran stared up at the ceiling through dead eyes, blood spread from her throat over her chest. Unable to hold back the tears, Drew bent low, taking his mother in his arms and lifting her head until they were cheek to cheek. Tears streamed down his face as he sobbed in silence.

When Mack Ferran stepped through his house a short time later, it took him only a moment to register what had happened. Turning the corner of the upturned living room he looked through the archway into the kitchen. His wife of twenty years, the only true love he had ever known, lay sprawled on the table. His son stood hunched over her, her head in his hands, limp as a rag doll. She was dead, her throat torn ragged. The boy's jaws and hands were slick with blood, and when he looked up to face his father he had a wild, animal look that cried of madness and murder.

Mack's eyes glanced to the Wolfshead blade on the floor. Crouching slowly he let his right hand slip around the hilt, his fingers feeling their way before clenching into an all too familiar grip. All the while he fought back his fury, keeping his composure. He straightened as Trent dashed into the house, skidding to a halt behind his back.

"Put her down," said the old soldier, raising the sword out before him, the blade motionless as the wind and rain still whipped through the ransacked house.

Drew trembled, his head shaking, uncomprehending. Why was his father holding the sword to him?

"Father . . ." he gasped. His voice came out low and bestial, struggling to escape through his still-twisted throat. His face twitched and spasmed as his dislocated jaw grated back into place.

"Put. Her. Down." His father stepped closer, two, three steps.

Drew looked from his father to his mother, trying to comprehend his father's actions. Surely he couldn't think that Drew was responsible for this? Tears streaked down his face. His eyes darted toward Trent, his brother's face a mixture of fear and confusion at the scene before him. "But Father . . ." Drew said, bloodstained lips trembling.

"Stop saying that," the older man screamed, his sword beginning to quiver in his hand now as he struggled with his rage.

Drew wanted to be sick, wanted to collapse. What should he do? He tenderly released his grip and laid his mother's head back on to the table from the cradle of his arms. "An animal . . ." he started to say, but could not complete the sentence.

His father leapt forward, covering the distance in a swift bound, sword scything through the air with deadly accuracy. The sword tore into Drew's shoulder blade, cutting deep and fast. Wailing, the boy stumbled back, scrabbling barefoot over broken glass as his father now stood before him and his mother. Trent watched the drama unfold from the archway into the living room, jaw slack as the horror played out.

"You're no son of mine," his father spat, eyes red with tears as he snarled and choked on his words. "Monster!" he screamed as he lunged forward once more.

Drew raised his hands in a vain attempt at defense, but the sword flew straight to his belly, sliding in and through his stomach, right up to the hilt. Father and son were face to face, eyeball to eyeball. Drew's eyes blinked in disbelief as his father's eyes narrowed, his grisly job done. He released his hand from the sword hilt and let his son stumble backward into the cold shadows of the kitchen.

Drew's fingers reached for the handle that sat flush to his stomach, stained dark with blood. He felt the tip of the blade scrape the brickwork behind him from where it extended almost three feet from his back. His fingertips played over the decorative pommel, a steel Wolfshead glaring up at him in an emotionless stare.

Mack stepped back to his wife, taking her still-warm hand in his own before dropping to his knees. It had come to this. This boy whom he had raised, this monster, taking the life of the most precious thing in his world. In his worst nightmares he'd never dreamed of this moment. The boy was an aberration, a monstrosity. Justice had been swift, but he could never forgive himself for allowing this to happen. He looked at his wife, her ivory skin coated crimson with her own blood. They had known, and still they had been unable to stop it.

Trent stepped forward and patted his father's shoulder, just once initially and then repeatedly, more insistent. At first Mack thought they were pats of consolation, of shared grief, but he quickly realized as the pats became frantic tugs that the boy wanted his attention. He looked up.

Trent stared wide-eyed across the kitchen, his hand stretched out and a trembling finger pointing toward his brother, who stood silhouetted by the shattered kitchen window. Still stood. The wind whipped around him as he teetered, bloodied, blade firmly lodged through his midriff.

Mack rose, knowing what had to be done. How could he have forgotten? All those years in the king's service and his mind had slipped. He turned to his son as Drew looked on, speechless and stunned.

"Boy, go fetch me the poker," he said. Trent simply stared at his brother, who by all rights should have been dead but stood wobbling on his legs like a newborn lamb. His father grabbed him by the coat, shaking him. "The poker from the fire, boy. Fetch it. And be quick about it!"

Drew watched his brother dart into the living room. The whole thing was surreal, all of the night's events escaping explanation, a twisted dream. The beast, his mother, the transformation that had taken him. His own father had run him through with a sword. Surprisingly the pain from the sword seemed diminished somewhat, dull compared to the bone-breaking injuries the monster had dealt him. He should have been lying on the floor in a pool of his own blood. Yet somehow he still lived, the Wolfshead blade slicing him like a stuck pig, and now his father wanted the old poker from the fireplace. Drew used to play with that poker as a boy, fascinated by the fancy metalwork that ran the length of it up to the now-banned silver handle.

But this wasn't a dream. Drew fought the nausea that welled up inside him. His father had attempted to kill him once already tonight and looked determined to try again. The next time he was bound to succeed. Drew's decision was made.

He clambered up onto the window frame before looking back just the once. His father stood there, obscuring his mother from his view.

"Hurry, boy!" yelled Mack Ferran as Trent snatched up the poker from the cluttered chaos of the living room.

32

Drew hovered on the glass-peppered windowsill, half-naked in tattered clothing that flapped in the wind. His eyes glinted as his father stared at him with an unfaltering gaze.

"Give it to me," Mack called as Trent stumbled through the broken furniture and thrust the poker toward him. He grabbed it by the pointed end, raising the silver pommel over his head before turning back to the boy who used to be his son. Drew had killed now, would kill again no doubt. He had a taste for blood.

But it was too late. The window was empty, now simply framing the rain that lashed in. Mack Ferran slowly lowered the poker and shoved it through a loop of leather on his belt. His other hand settled onto the hunting horn on his hip, palm closing over the cool ivory as he crossed over to the window. He peered through the rain that flooded the muddy yard outside. Beyond, in the black night sky, the moon stared down, full and white.

The boy was gone.

PART II

SPRING, THE DYREWOOD

I

THE STORYBOOK SCOUT

THE WOODS WERE quiet but for the snapping of twigs beneath the horse's heavy hooves. Hogan bowed low in his saddle, hands resting on his horse's neck as hanging vines disappeared over his head. He watched them as he passed beneath, a canopy of green tendrils that reached down toward him, tantalizing and tempting to touch, their sweet scent intoxicating. He knew better, though. For almost forty years he had been a scout in the Dyrewood. He was the oldest working ranger in Duke Bergan's service, in times of war leading troops through the Bearlord's lands as swiftly and discreetly as possible. He was not one to make mistakes. Once clear of the veiled curtain of vines, he sat upright in his saddle, surveying the way ahead across the forest floor.

Hogan reined his horse to a halt. Squinting into the half light of the woods, the horseman peered through the gloom. Here and there a shard of sunlight would break through the masses of huge trees, finding a way between the leafy branches to the mulchy ground below. Rock and root made their passage slow and treacherous, and deep banks of fallen leaves concealed boulders and fallen branches in the most unexpected places. Combined with the murderous curtains of wych ivy, the woods were a place for any man to fear. Hogan was unconcerned by these dangers, though. Today there was something else in the Dyrewood that was far more deadly.

Twisting in his saddle, he looked back the way he'd come. He waited. Gradually a figure on horseback appeared through the hazy light of the dark, dank forest. The youngster was slumping in the saddle, paying little attention to the path ahead, letting the mount follow the horse in front and bring the novice rider ever nearer the hanging trails of wych ivy.

Hogan rolled his eyes for a brief, exasperated moment. Through gloved hands he clicked his fingers twice. His apprentice's head whipped up at the sound, and not a moment too soon. Hogan pointed upward with his index finger, indicating the deadly ivy. The young rider tugged back on the reins, stopping the horse, and stared up at the plant with dread recognition. Satisfied that the danger had registered, the master set off once more, spurring his horse on with heels to its flanks.

Whitley stared at the trailing ivy with wide eyes. Gulping

hard, the apprentice hunkered down low in the saddle and patted a hand against Chancer's neck. Wych ivy was deadly to the
touch, as any scout knew full well. Tiny needles peppered the
emerald vines, each one laden with fast-acting poisons. Once
the poison had worked its magic, the wych ivy snared its victim and recoiled into the dark boughs above to slowly digest it.
The regular diet of this plant was any number of birds or small
mammals; a scout's apprentice would make a fine and rare meal
indeed. Tentatively the horse trotted forward, the rider hugging him tightly as they passed beneath the green tendrils.

The scout and his apprentice had been in the woods for a
week now, searching for their prey. Admittedly, Whitley had
little to do besides watch and learn from Hogan. In a perilous
place like the Dyrewood, daydreaming was a potentially dangerous distraction. Ancient and vast, the great forest was the
greatest in the Seven Realms of Lyssia, three hundred miles
long in all and half as wide in places. It was widely considered
haunted, and few dared enter the woodlands, tales of the monsters and terrors within dissuading most. Wizened black trees
lined the edge of the forest, gnarled and twisted ancient trunks
that splintered into the ground as if driven there like great
stakes, marking the borderlands where civilization ended and
the wilds began.

Beyond where they now traveled, the lusher trees of the
Dyrewood thrived, creating the leafy canopies that blotted out
the sun. The occasional road wound its way into the forest, but

they had remained virtually untraveled in recent years, routes that had once been well used now becoming overgrown and impassable. The apprentice had heard the stories about strange creatures within the Dyrewood, but these seemed to be no more than fairy tales for little ones. The Wyldermen, however, were no such fantasy. Whitley couldn't imagine why anyone would want to live in such a forsaken place. Hogan had revealed some of the Dyrewood's mysteries to his apprentice in their training, but for Whitley it didn't mean the place was any more inviting.

As a child, Whitley had always felt destined for great things, craving adventure like the heroes in the storybooks. Save the villagers, kill the enemies—the apprentice loved those tales of the old knights. Whitley's mother had said that they were just stories, myths, and folklore, but the youngster had known otherwise. Whitley was remarkably well read, and the names of some of those old heroes popped up in history books from all over the Seven Realms. Those characters were real. Heroes were real. The apprentice's heart had been set on a path of adventure ever since.

Chancer stopped suddenly in his tracks, whinnying and taking a nervous step backward. Whitley's fists clenched around the horse's mane, looking up the trail ahead for Hogan: no sign. The beast snorted, agitated. His eyes rolled in their sockets, a fearful terror gripping the poor animal. Whitley looked all about as the horse began to jostle and back up, retreating from some unseen threat. Time and again he threw his head back, dark brown mane swatting the apprentice in the face. The youngster kept hold in a white-knuckled grasp. The woods seemed to spin as the mount began to circle randomly, leaving Whitley little chance of seeing what it was that had spooked the horse. Chancer was a sturdy fellow and, as Hogan had said time and again, had to be treated with respect. "Lose control of your mount, lose control of your life," had been the mantra. As such, and as with all scouts, the bond between beast and rider was a special one.

"Whoa, calm, boy," called the apprentice, craning down close to Chancer's pricked ears. Releasing one hand, Whitley patted the horse's neck heavily, desperate to calm him down, but the animal flung his head back with a whinny. The back of the beast's skull impacted hard with Whitley's head in a mighty crack. The apprentice tumbled from the saddle like a sack of bones, seeing stars as the forest floor rushed up swiftly.

The moss-covered earth provided Whitley with a thankfully soft landing. The youngster's right shoulder blade took the brunt of the tumble, and the shooting pains that followed brought Whitley back to full consciousness instantly. Struggling up, the apprentice had just time to see Chancer's dark brown tail swish in the shadows as the horse vanished into the Dyrewood's darkness.

For a moment, Whitley wondered what the sound of drums was that thundered through the woods, before realizing it was the sound of blood rushing through both ears and a hammer-ing heart. The apprentice's eyes darted about nervously. What had scared the horse? Was it the Wyldermen? Or maybe the beast: their prey? Was it still out there, or had it gone after the poor animal? Whitley hoped it was nothing, hoped Chancer was just spooked. Maybe the horse would return when he had calmed down. The apprentice looked over the undergrowth for Hogan but, after such a fall, the young rider couldn't tell north from south.

"Some scout you're turning out to be, Whitley."

"Master!" Whitley called out into the vast shadows, strug-gling to stand on an ankle that now hummed with pain. After attempting to apply pressure to it, the apprentice collapsed once more to the mossy floor. Sprained. Pulling up dirty breeches and rolling down a sock, Whitley looked at the ankle—it had already started to swell up.

Whitley was about to shout a complaint to Hogan but instead stopped suddenly, sensing something awful. The ap-prentice looked up in time to see the undergrowth part and a creature step out of the darkness. Whitley tried to call out in alarm, but a thin, reedy croak was all that came forth as the scout desperately scooted back, hands scrabbling in the mulch. Ahead, some kind of monster advanced.

The creature seemed almost human, walking on its hind legs. Its hair was dark, wild, and shaggy, hanging over its face and shoulders. Its hands twitched, long fingers revealing wickedly curved dirty claws that clicked against one another in anticipation. Its face was invisible in the shadows but for the glow of its amber eyes and the glistening of its sharp teeth, which seemed to flood its face with a cruel smile. A low growl emanated from its great heaving chest, muscles rippling beneath its dark skin.

Whitley's retreat halted suddenly as the young scout backed up into a tree trunk with a thump. There was nowhere left to turn. Where was Hogan? Surely it wasn't supposed to end like this? Whitley's life was an adventure just waiting to happen. The tale had only just begun. Tears flowed freely down the apprentice's face as the beast's mouth opened, arms outstretched and claws flexing. Whitley turned away.

It was at this moment the apprentice realized, with regret, that this was no storybook, and there were no heroes.

2

The Beast and the Apprentice

HOT BREATH SNORTED against Whitley's face, spittle spattering one cheek as the monster let out a feral snort. With the beast closing in for the kill, Whitley prayed for a swift end.

Still it had not struck.

Was it playing? Fighting nausea and blind panic, the apprentice needed every ounce of willpower to risk opening an eye. The creature loomed large overhead, blotting out those patches of blue sky that were visible above the treetops. Its arms were outstretched, hands open, clawed tips flexing. It swayed from left to right as it surveyed its prey, yellow eyes narrowing to slits. Whitley took it in, but could feel unconsciousness about to take hold. The apprentice stared into the beast's eyes, since little else of its face was visible. As the blackness began to draw in, the monster's eyes seemed to soften, almost relax, as its arms fell limp to its sides. It crouched on its haunches, head cocked to one side. The apprentice's last recollection was of the monster doing the strangest of things.

It folded its arms.

Drew wasn't sure how long he sat there watching the unconscious boy. Judging by his slight frame, the boy couldn't have been much younger than him, maybe a year, if that. And judging by the green and brown outfit he was probably a forester's son. *Someone's son,* he remembered painfully. To anyone arriving on the scene, the boy would have looked quite dead, what color there had been in his face now drained clean away.

Drew couldn't help but feel a pang of envy. The boy looked peaceful, as if enjoying some pleasant dream. It occurred to him that this was the first civilized person he'd seen in ... well, he didn't know how long. He didn't count the Wyldermen as civilized, let alone human. He'd tried keeping track of the days when he'd first stumbled blindly into the Dyrewood, but after the first month of chalking off days with flint on the cave wall that had become his home, he'd lost track. That seemed a very long time ago, and certainly the harsh winter weather had come and gone since then. It hadn't been his intention to find refuge in one of the most godforsaken and feared parts of Lyssia, but when he'd heard his father's hunting horn as he released the dogs that night, he'd had little choice but to go where he knew they wouldn't.

Somehow he'd stumbled from the farm at Cold Coast to the edge of the Dyrewood forest, with the Wolfshead blade still embedded firmly in his stomach. Although the wound ached, a scab had already formed over the top of it. The cut itself, where jagged inches of flesh had been torn apart, had already begun to knit itself back together again. How this was possible he might have pondered a while longer, had the sword in his stomach not demanded his attention a little more urgently. What should have been a fatal wound now held about as much discomfort as a severe case of gut rot.

Drew had grasped the hilt between both his hands and pulled, once. The sword flew out, a fresh gout of blood following. A new pain struck him as the wound reopened, a dizzy spell washing over him. But before long a strange healing overcame him, and the blood stopped flowing. Then he'd heard the horns and instinctively run toward the dark cover of the forest, the Wolfshead sword now his only protection.

He'd used what moon he could see as a guide. But it held a spell over him, enthralling and sickening him at the same time. His flight had been staggered by bouts of spasms, attacks that had repeatedly ravaged his body. None had been as extreme as the remarkable transformation that had taken him in the house, but each of them had been debilitating. At times he had dropped, poleaxed with the pain, as the cramps had hit him. On other occasions, slight changes had threatened to run away with him as claws and teeth had grown and elongated before slowly returning to their natural state. His body seemed to be in a constant state of flux, battling with the monster that raged within wanting to break free. He couldn't remember when he had gained some sort of control over himself—his memory was as tattered as the clothes in which he'd fled. But now, seemingly months later, he was here.

Drew hadn't meant for any of this to happen. He'd stumbled across the boy while hunting; with his bloodlust up, it had been all he could do to actually resist attacking him. The boy must have had a weak constitution if the appearance of Drew had caused him to black out. Unless his appearance really was that threatening. . . .

Drew unfolded his arms and looked at his hands. The skin was cracked and filthy, his palms grubby and soiled. He looked at his fingertips. Yellowed, cracked nails had hardened and grown through his time in the Dyrewood. The hair on his head and body was matted and clung to his skin with mud and dirt, concealing any skin beneath as a wild animal's would. When he hunted, he felt his whole body change, adapting to the chase. His senses heightened, his muscles grew, and his nails became claws. He was built for the hunt.

His own appearance was in marked contrast to that of the

forester's boy, who was decked in a hardy outfit for life in the woods. He certainly wasn't a wild man, and that came as a relief to Drew. A leather jerkin was buttoned up to below his chin, a woolen scarf keeping the cold from his throat. Drew put his hand to his own throat. Bare. He ran his hand over his chest. Also bare. He looked down at the rest of his body. Not a scrap of clothing remained, bar a thong of leather over his shoulder that held the Wolfshead blade.

He must have looked monstrous.

He would apologize to the boy when he woke up. It then occurred to him that he couldn't recall the last time he'd spoken a word. He'd resorted to growling as a form of communication when warning wild animals away from his cave or his kills. He mouthed his name, feeling his throat with a hand as his voice cracked and strained.

"Drew."

It came out as barely a whisper. He coughed, his chest wracked with the unfamiliar exercise. A memory flitted through his mind. He dropped a hand down to his side and picked up a clump of damp moss. He reached calmly over to the boy, brushing the moss against his brow. His mother used to do this when Drew was sick. He remembered that. It was locked away, but he remembered it. And other things, too, things he didn't want to recall.

He patted the boy's brow. He would make things right. . . .

A wooden staff came cracking down with such lightning ferocity that Drew didn't stand a chance. The heavy pole smashed into his forearm, knocking it clear away from the boy and no doubt breaking it in the process. He let out a roar of pain as he turned to his assailant.

The pole was already swinging once more, arcing through the air and hurtling back at Drew. He pulled back, scrambling, but wasn't quick enough. The attacker had taken him completely by surprise. The last few inches of the staff connected with his forehead with a sickening crunch. He felt his head spin as he cartwheeled back onto the forest floor, temple torn and bloodied.

Quickly, Hogan stepped over his prone apprentice, between Whitley and the beast. A lifetime spent tracking quarries through the most inhospitable terrain had enabled the old scout to catch the creature completely unawares. He noticed Whitley stir on the ground. Relief. He turned back to the beast.

What kind of monster was this? When he'd spied it hulking over his apprentice, he thought it was a wild dog or wolf. But now he realized it was humanlike, walking upright on its back legs. It was with dread realization that he figured out what he was facing. Hogan had ranged and tracked through most parts of the western woods for Duke Bergan. He was charged with keeping the city of Brackenholme safe from harm, so there was little he hadn't come across. On this occasion he'd assumed they were just hunting a simple wolf or wildcat, hence suggesting to his master that he take young Whitley. He wouldn't have dreamed of bringing along his apprentice in light of what they'd now encountered. He had to think quickly. The monster staggered against a tree, catching its bearings, turning its head in his direction, seeking him out through a blood-soaked gaze.

Take no chances.

Hogan wasted no more time, leaping forward with his huntstaff raised over his head like an executioner about to bring his ax down. It whistled through the air, catching the beast square on the top of its head. The beast collapsed to the ground in a heap.

Hogan heard Whitley stirring behind him as he crouched to better examine the creature. To his side, a Wolfshead blade lay in the earth. With increasing alarm the scout brushed the shaggy mane of hair away from the monster's face and grabbed a clump of leaves from the floor to wipe the blood aside.

An icy chill spread along the scout's limbs, raising the hairs on the back of his neck. Beneath the bloody mask were the unexpected features of a young man.

"Fetch my ropes from my horse, Whitley," he called back. "The good ones, mind. The strong ones."

3

THE WYLDERMAN'S WORDS

HOGAN GLANCED AT the sky. Thunderclouds seemed to shadow the trio, a brooding gray canopy of rain and ill winds, as they made their way slowly through the Dyrewood, cutting a path for the Dymling Road. Bearing east, they were sure to hit the main woodland road before too long.

As the rain hammered down, his faithful horse, Argo, showed no sign of distress with the unusually heavy load. Hogan looked over his shoulder. Whitley sat huddled on Chancer, trying as best he could to hide from the rain. The youngster had shown a resilience of character that, up until their encounter with their captive, Hogan hadn't been sure existed. At no point in time had Hogan pandered to his apprentice on account of the other's privileged upbringing; they were out in the woods now, Hogan's woods, where he was the boss. But when all was said and done the youngster was an accomplished tracker and scout in the making and, if the apprentice's already proven woodlore could be matched by field abilities, Whitley would make a worthwhile addition to Duke Bergan's forces.

The scout looked down to survey their prisoner, who was being pulled along the forest floor behind him. The wooden stretcher he'd fashioned from saplings and branches was still holding strong, the young Wylderman strapped firmly to it. Vines around everything from his ankles and thighs to wrists and throat kept the prisoner secured. The first day of travel had been a painful affair for all as the lad had fought and struggled to break free of his bonds. Indeed, at times, he had raged so fiercely that Hogan had feared even his master knots might loosen and fray under the strain. Fortunately they had held firm. From thereon in, Hogan had seen to it that their captive's water was laced with a mild sedative derived from an abundant ground ivy. The Wylderman was going nowhere.

Hogan didn't know what to feel about the stranger, beyond a burning desire to get him into the custody of Duke Bergan. The Bearlord would know what to do. Since Hogan had discovered that the beast was actually a young lad, his perspective had shifted somewhat. He felt a sense of remorse for having broken the boy's arm in the melee three days ago, but at the time he had honestly felt that Whitley was in danger. Furthermore, this was no normal boy he had come across.

The Wyldermen of the Dyrewood were a reclusive tribe of men who lived in the darkest and most inhospitable parts of the old forest. Their society was violent and bloody, as far as the civilized folk such as those of Brackenholme could see, and it was an agreed fact that they were more beast than man. Dealings were nonexistent between wild men and other forest folk, as previous attempts at diplomacy had led to bloodshed. Duke Bergan would be pleased to have one in his custody.

Pulling gently on Argo's reins, Hogan spied the night's campsite up ahead. Barely touched by the rain, a large expanse of moss and bark stretched out before them beneath the boughs of a great spruce tree. He gave Whitley a quick call and they both dismounted with a thump. Hogan handed the youngster his reins while he surveyed the terrain.

They'd traveled ten long and arduous leagues since coming across the wild young man those few days back, managing only short distances each day due to both the awful terrain and the laden stretcher that they dragged along with them. Hogan believed they were out of the Wyldermen lands now. At least he hoped that was the case. A distant peal of thunder added to his already grim mood. Unhitching the stretcher from Argo, they set about making camp.

Dinner consisted of stewed strips of rabbit meat and root vegetables that the scout had foraged nearby. Whitley watched on as Hogan fed the Wylderman, spooning the stew into the young man's mouth. They'd dressed the prisoner in a pair of Whitley's spare breeches and a heavy winter cloak.

Hogan remained crouched on his heels as he held a waterskin to the boy's mouth. He gulped at it, his Adam's apple bobbing against the ropes that bound him about the throat, struggling to swallow as much water as he could. The scout let him have his fill. No need to be barbaric. He glanced down at the arm that had been smashed in their fight. At the time the flesh on the forearm had been contorted where the splintered bone had threatened to break free from the skin. It had turned Hogan's stomach, but he'd had no choice but to bind him. That injury alone had caused the boy no end of pain as they'd traveled, but his growling complaints had gradually ceased. The old ranger had suspected that gangrene might have begun to set in by now, and he figured the arm would be lopped off when they got to Brackenholme. The scout pulled back the folded cloak. His jaw went slack.

It would be clear to anyone looking at it that the arm had been recently injured but was on the mend. It was bruised and discolored, but one wouldn't have guessed that it had been broken only a few days previously. Hogan tipped his head to one side, running his free hand the length of the bound arm. The boy didn't flinch, just kept drinking greedily, gulping at the waterskin. No pain, no injury—what kind of powers of healing did the boy have? Hogan glanced back at Whitley, who was finishing off the stew, and then quickly covered the arm with the cloak. It was unnatural but not inexplicable. The healing combined with the bestial outbursts he'd witnessed already on their journey made him eager to get the boy to Duke Bergan at once.

The old scout went and sat by Whitley, both of them on the opposite side of the fire from their captive guest. Reaching into his saddlebag, he grasped the Wolfshead blade by the pommel and pulled it out in a smooth motion. He held it to the dim light of the campfire before driving it into the earth, blade first. Rummaging back through his bags, the scout withdrew a tatty, bundled notebook, tied around the middle by a length of cord. Leafing through the pages to the latest entry, the old man set about updating his journal, adding to his notes on the captive boy with a sharpened piece of charcoal.

The young Wylderman sat staring into the fire, unblinking.

"Do you think he speaks the king's tongue?" asked Whitley, watching the boy.

Hogan packed tobacco into a thin reed pipe before taking a light to it from the fire's embers. "Doubt it," he replied. "You can keep on trying to speak to him, if that's your wish, but I fear it's wasted on him. He's a wild man, Whitley; they have no need for language. There's little that you or I have in common with his kind."

"What's he really going to do to us, though, Master Hogan?"

"You'd like to cut him free and find out? He nearly skinned you the other night, child, so I'd resist any further foolish talk if I were you, you hear?"

"I've already said, Master, he had his chance and he didn't kill me," protested the apprentice. "He just watched me. He could have killed me as easy as blinking if he'd wanted to!"

Hogan drew hard on his pipe before letting a trio of smoke rings drift over the camp. "Whitley, it simply isn't worth taking the chance. I believe you when you say he held back from attacking you, but what we have here is a most unusual young man. When the blood gets up in him—you saw it yourself—he takes to changing, and you and I know only too well what that means. If it comes down to it, he's more like Duke Bergan himself, although a different breed altogether, and more mongrel than noble for that matter."

The young Wylderman still sat staring at the fire, apparently in a world of his own.

"When I was a lad, there were more of them about, but they're fewer in number these days thanks to Wergar's campaigns." Hogan chewed his lip, thinking back to times long gone. "Not entirely sure whether that's a good or a bad thing, mind you, but that's another story." Hogan was aware that Whitley knew all about the Wolf's exploits, they being a topic of conversation rarely far away back home in Brackenholme. Duke Bergan made sure that all the children of the woodland realm were well versed in the history of the Werelords. Not surprisingly, Whitley had been a more than attentive student.

"Anyway," Hogan continued, "if anyone will know what to do with this young fella, Duke Bergan's the man."

"Let me free."

Both scout and apprentice looked up, startled. The young Wylderman had spoken. Not just a word, either, but a sentence. Hogan was on his feet in a flash and reaching for his huntstaff. He skidded up to the feet of the bound young man, staff at the ready.

"Silent for three days and you speak now. You expect us to cut you loose? Is that it? Good lord, lad; you have got a tongue, but it appears you're witless."

"Let me free," the boy repeated, this time looking up at the scout. "Please, sir."

The manners of the prisoner caught Hogan off guard. At the most he was expecting a primitive command of the king's tongue, but this was remarkable.

"What makes you think I'm going to cut you loose? I saw what you are, remember? You may not have harmed my apprentice, but I don't doubt for a moment that you could tear strips from the pair of us if the mood were to take you. Even if you didn't kill us, you'd no doubt go scurrying back to your filthy brethren to tell them of our whereabouts. No. Sorry, lad. You're staying put. Your freedom is out of my hands, and instead in Duke Bergan's paws."

"You don't understand," said the boy, his voice fragile and cracking. "If you want to live, you'll cut me free."

"Lad, that blow to the head you took must still be ringing some," said Hogan, crouching down to the boy's side. "Threatening me in your position is a tad slack-brained, don't you think? I don't care much for whatever you are, but I know my knots can hold the wildest animals. I say it again: I'm sorry, but I'm taking you in."

The boy strained, his eyes flitting this way and that as he looked into the darkness. "I swear, sir, it's not me you need to fear!"

From the deep, dark depths of the woods, faint at first, the call came: a wild cry like an animal in trouble. Hogan spun about, listening intently. Then it repeated, clearly distressed. Another broke from the forest, now a frantic, screeching caterwaul. The cries were getting nearer.

"What does he mean, Master?" asked Whitley, more than a little concerned now, looking about the woods, head twirling and eyes darting from side to side as the calls kept coming.

Hogan remained silent as he listened, but Drew replied for him.

"They're coming," he whispered. "The Wyldermen are coming."

4
Fight or Flight

IT TOOK ONLY the briefest of moments for Hogan to make up his mind. The stretcher that they'd been dragging the young man along on had slowed them to a crawl. Being pursued would make such travel impossible. He'd heard what happened to those captured by the Wyldermen in the Dyrewood and had no intention of experiencing such a gruesome ordeal firsthand. Dropping to his knee, he pulled a dagger from his boot, cutting the bonds that kept the boy captive.

"Whitley, see to the horses," he called to his apprentice as he worked at the ropes. Whitley didn't move, frozen in fear, listening to the bloodcurdling calls of the approaching Wyldermen. "Now!" the scout shouted. Whitley jumped before snatching up Argo's heavy saddle and stumbling over to the mounts as quickly as possible.

"Listen, lad, and listen good," said Hogan under his breath, his mouth inches away from Drew's forehead as he sawed at the ropes. "You get one chance and one only. You let me down in any way, shape, or form, and I cut you down. If I suspect you're with them, I cut you down. If you threaten my ward, I cut you down. I think for one moment you're wolfing out on me—"

"You cut me down," interrupted his prisoner, eyes wide with realization. "And my name is Drew, sir."

Hogan nodded, cutting the last rope. "Looks like you and I have come to an understanding, young Drew." He ventured a hard smile that cracked his leathery face, then gave the neck of his short bow a rub before slinging it over his shoulder.

Drew recognized that the man was good for his word and nodded his agreement, rubbing his throat with freed hands.

The scout and his apprentice had turned the camp over in moments, remains of the stew being tipped over the fire, dirt and soil kicked up and putting the last embers to death. Drew looked back the way they'd come. He hadn't ventured this far east in his time in the Dyrewood, so this was all new to him. The chilling calls of the Wyldermen, however, were not.

"Can I help?" he called to the old man, following his footsteps as he finished saddling his horse, the young apprentice taking care of his own steed. The calls seemed strangely more distant now. Either that or they were quieter. Drew kept one eye on the woods.

"Pick up your sword, lad," the man said without looking.

"You trust me with it?" he asked in surprise.

"I wouldn't go so far as that," said the scout grumpily. "Best you've some protection if things get personal, though."

"I've never really swung it in anger," said Drew, pulling it out of the ground.

"Then if I'm wrong about you that may be a blessing," finished Hogan.

The scout's apprentice slung a backpack over one shoulder, giving the straps a short, sharp tug. The rain still hammered down onto the treetops overhead, the pattering providing a constant accompaniment.

"Whitley, isn't it?" asked Drew, trying to catch his eye. The boy seemed nervous and did all he could to avoid his gaze. Drew persevered. "Thanks for looking after my bumps and bruises, is all I wanted to say. I appreciate it."

Whitley glanced over. Drew could see a fear in his eyes, the cause of which stretched back to their first meeting in the woods. His recollection of what happened was a haze, as if a red mist had descended before him. The nightmare had thankfully lifted before he'd caused Whitley any real damage. He couldn't help but feel remorse.

"No need to thank me," said the scout's apprentice, finding

a way past him to his master. Drew didn't blame the boy for his distance. He'd have done the same if the roles were reversed. They both stepped up to the scout, who had finished preparing his horse. All three realized that the cries of the Wyldermen had apparently ceased.

"This is how we do this," whispered Hogan, patting Argo's saddle. "You two are up top on the horses; I'll be on foot. Argo and Chancer are smart horses and if anything should happen to me they'll be all right to take you to Brackenholme. We'll be on the Dymling Road before we know it, and that takes us home. They know the way. I'll keep up just fine. If anything untoward does happen, you push on. Don't stop—whatever you do."

He took Drew's hand and started to help him up onto the horse, when Argo bucked, objecting. Drew raised both his hands defensively and took a step back from the startled beast. Hogan quickly got the horse back under control, bringing his face to the horse's head and whispering into his ear. The horse steadied and they tried again. This time, Argo relented and let Drew clamber on. He was quickly followed by Whitley, who hopped onto Chancer.

Without another word, they set off, Hogan leading the way, huntstaff in one hand and Argo's reins in the other. Drew crouched low into the saddle as overhanging branches swung and parted before them, and Whitley ducked likewise behind on Chancer.

The faster they moved, the more distance Hogan put between him and the horses. Letting out the reins as their pace quickened, was the best way of avoiding being trampled underfoot. Drew was impressed by the nimbleness of the older man as the scout hopped over logs, skipped beyond ditches, and deftly avoided rabbit holes and roots.

Uneasy, Drew looked about as they pounded a march through the Dyrewood, checking over his shoulder again and again, searching for a sign of pursuit. Something wasn't right. The boy glanced to his left and then right, eyes narrowed as they flitted across the undergrowth. Back to the left. There! Something moving alongside them, only yards away. Tracking them. Fast.

He had to warn the scout. He faced front once more, about to shout, but instead got a face full of conifer branch. By the time the branch had sprung clear and he'd spat the needles from his mouth, it was too late.

Hogan was already falling, tumbling forward toward the forest floor with the shaft of an arrow buried deep within his left shoulder blade. Not a fatal blow, but certainly enough to knock him clean off his feet. The reins flew from the old man's grasp at the moment of impact, leaving Argo loose. The big horse kicked and reared on his hind legs, letting loose a shrill whinny at the sight of his master crumpling to the ground.

Drew spun from Argo's back like a leaf from the surrounding trees. His fall turned into a roll as he tucked himself into a ball and tumbled to safety. Strapped safely across his shoulder, the Wolfshead blade flat against his skin felt cold as the world turned around him. Whitley fared worse, as Chancer danced back to avoid the panicked Argo, who bolted into the forest. The horse sent the apprentice flying from the saddle to land on the ground with a crunch.

Springing to his feet, Drew fell into a run, bounding into the darkness of the trees, seeking the safety of the shadows. His time in the Dyrewood had honed his survival instincts. He'd hidden and fled from the Wyldermen before—he could do it again. He ducked and scrambled as he ran, putting space between himself and the chaos he'd left behind. Instinct said run. Instinct said save your skin. That's how you survived in the forest. That's why he was still alive. Only the strongest beasts of the woods lived. He bounded on, on all fours now, leaping and tearing through the bracken, low to the ground.

Drew skidded to a halt, panting. He rubbed his eyes, blinking, shaking clarity back to his mind, to his head. What had gotten into him? This wasn't him. He wasn't some self-serving opportunist, a selfish turncoat who only looked after himself. He heard Whitley cry out behind in the dark.

Why are you stopping?

An inner voice, low, almost growling at him.

Run, fool.

He thought back to the care the young apprentice had shown in tending to his wounds. And the scout's kindness in sharing their provisions. He might have been their prisoner, but they'd looked after him. Made him feel human again.

No, he would not run. That wasn't him. He was no animal, no matter how long he'd lived among the beasts of the Dyrewood. He began to sprint back.

Whitley had hit the ground with a paralyzing impact. Having landed heavily, the apprentice could no longer feel either leg, and shooting pains raced up the youngster's spine. Bright lights played before Whitley's eyes, and a deafening high-pitched note that blotted out the noises all around rang in both ears. The apprentice looked about.

Chancer stood close by, hooves hitting the floor skittishly as he danced on the spot, spittle rising to his lips as he fought panic. Beyond the horse Whitley could see Hogan on the ground, some ten yards or so away. Argo was nowhere to be seen, nor was Drew for that matter. The old scout rolled over, snapping off the broken shaft of the arrow that emerged from his shoulder. Through gritted teeth he shouted something at the apprentice, but Whitley couldn't tell what it was. Hogan began to struggle to his feet.

Seconds later a figure leapt out of the darkness, barefoot and blackened with dirt. It was a man, short and heavyset, with a small hunting bow grasped in his hand. He wore a ragged animal skin over his torso, torn and tattered around the edges. A small quiver hung across his shoulder, and his free hand reached back toward it.

Whitley watched him as another arrow emerged, short of shaft with a wicked barbed flint blade on the end. Sharp black capercaillie feathers made up the flight. The Wylderman turned to face the apprentice, slow and menacing. His face was black with mud and inks, and his chest rattled with necklaces made from tiny animal skulls. He threw the youngster a bestial smile, revealing rows of ritualistically sharpened, filed teeth. Whitley felt burning tears as the villain began advancing. Behind him, Hogan leaned against the tree, groggy and unable to find his balance. Seeing the danger his apprentice was in, he pulled his dagger from his boot and lurched forward, holding it before him and calling out. He stumbled as he went, feeling waves of nausea wash over him, his vision blurring. The arrow, had it been poisoned? That would have been true to form for the Wyldermen.

Laughing, the bowman turned to the ranger and pulled back on his bow, aiming at the old man's belly. Whitley cried out, breaking the silence the trauma had induced.

"No!"

What followed happened so fast that Whitley would later struggle to recall it properly. One moment, the Wylderman was standing there waiting to loose his arrow into Hogan; the next he was flying backward through the air, the lithe figure of Drew having tackled him around the torso. The boy hadn't so much run into the clearing and taken the man down as exploded from the undergrowth like a wild animal, hitting his target square in the chest. The bow had tumbled from the Wylderman's grasp, snapped in two by the collision.

Both rolled in the earth, wrestling for dominance. The Wylderman snarled, taking Drew in a headlock, twisting the boy's arms beneath his back with his free arm, pinning him down. Although Drew was slightly taller than the attacker, he lost out to the man's superior physique, squat and heavyset. The boy kicked at the ground to prize himself free, but the Wylderman had him in a firm hold.

The hunter cried out into the night, a whoop of victory, hollering like a crazed bird. His call was met by others in the forest, different animal calls but each distinctly belonging to another huntsman, not nearby but closing. The woods now seemed alive with the noise of Wyldermen, their chase drawing to a close.

Whitley saw the Wylderman bare his sharpened teeth, and the apprentice's eyes widened in horror. It was no secret that the Wyldermen possessed a hunger for flesh of all kinds. The tribesman bore down on Drew, biting him in the neck.

It was the wrong move, judging by what followed. There was a sharp, cracking noise as the boy arched his back, a sudden, violent movement. This was enough to send the Wylderman bouncing up and off him, crashing to the ground. Drew jumped to his feet, shoulders hunched, arms outstretched. Whitley could make out the yellow of the boy's eyes beneath his mop of shaggy hair, but the rest of his face was lost in shadows. His fingers flexed, nails clicking.

"Nobody bites me," Drew growled at the Wylderman, revealing his own pointed teeth. Quick as a flash he darted forward, slashing at the other with his hands. Whitley caught a glimpse of Drew's fingertips, nails like sharp claws, tearing and ripping.

Drew was aware that his senses were heightened. His blood was up, racing through his body like lightning. Every nerve was on fire; he felt better than ever before. He recognized the feeling burning within, the animal that was coming to the fore. As tempting as it was to give in to it, he knew there would be no coming back if he let go now. He was far from master of his own actions while he was transformed, still struggling to understand what he became, let alone control it. He might even be a danger to his companions, never mind the Wylderman who now backed away from him in fear. It took all his discipline to contain himself as he closed in on his enemy.

Curling his fist, he launched a fierce punch at the man, catching his opponent on the chin. He heard a crack as knuckle connected with jaw, saw the man go down, poleaxed. He stooped over him, waiting for him to try to rise. Instead the Wylderman lay unmoving on the ground, unconscious, his chest laced with clawed ribbons.

The other tribesmen were almost upon them. Cries like

dogs, cats, owls, boars—all kinds of animal calls—closed in.

Drew shook his head, trying to clear his vision. The rage within began to subside as he reached down and helped Whitley to his feet.

"How are you?" he asked, checking the young apprentice, who wavered from side to side.

"Not good," he replied, "but I'll live."

"Well, quick now, get on Chancer while I see to Master Hogan," Drew whispered. As Whitley grabbed the horse by the reins, Drew scrambled over to the scout, who lay slumped in a bed of bracken.

"Get gone," said the old ranger, barely audible. The color had drained from his face, and his lips were pale and bloodless. Whatever poison had been used, it was working its dark magic on him. His breathing was thin and reedy as he fought to get the words out. "Slow you down. Get onto the Dymling Road. Chancer do rest. Go."

Drew nodded. Then, struggling with his weight, Drew picked the scout up, ignoring his protestations, hefting him over his shoulder before slinging him across the saddle in front of Whitley. The apprentice grabbed his master's belt buckle with one hand and snatched a clump of the horse's mane in the other. Taking the reins from the younger boy, Drew set off back along the trail, following their original route, pulling Chancer behind him as swiftly as he could.

5

THE DYMLING ROAD

IT WASN'T LONG before they hit the Dymling Road. As it happened, they had only been a half league away when they'd set up their fateful camp. Their clumsy escape through the forest had been thankfully brief. The screams and calls of the Wyldermen on their heels had given Drew and Chancer all the encouragement they needed, forcing them on in search of safety. Once on the road they were able to break into a forced run, the horse slowing enough to allow Drew to keep pace with it.

The Wyldermen had chosen not to give chase, much to their relief. After a stumbling run that must have lasted an hour, Chancer had slowed to a trot and then an exhausted walk. At the first opportunity Whitley had suggested they set up camp to address their predicament.

Hogan was in a bad way. With Drew as his assistant, Whitley had seen to his injuries, starting with the remains of the arrow that was buried in Hogan's shoulder. The young scout told Drew he had seen the arrows the Wylderman had used up close, and remembered all too well the barbed flint arrowheads. Such arrows were outlawed in the kingdoms of so-called civilized societies. A good archer could take out a target with a sure shot. To leave a barbed arrow in there that would tear the flesh loose if the victim tried to remove it was brutal in the extreme.

Taking the old man's dagger, the apprentice had to cut around the wound, working at the flesh until there was room for fingers to be hooked deeper and around the flint blade. The two blanched, Drew keeping the scout still while Whitley struggled to prize the head out. By now discolored veins and arteries crisscrossed away from the wound as the poison found its way into Hogan with ease. His skin was cold to the touch, his throat and neck mottled with blotchy red patches, inflamed and sore.

The scout had passed out in agony as the arrowhead was removed, and had yet to reawaken. Cleaning the wound with water, Whitley bandaged it with a strip of cloth torn from the scout's jerkin. But even without an exchange of words, both Drew and Whitley knew that the treatment Hogan needed was beyond the apprentice's limited knowledge.

They'd gotten the scout back onto Chancer then, using

what ropes they found remaining in his backpack to tie him into his saddle, slumped forward like a drunk. From that point they'd set off on their march in silence, leading the horse along as they walked through dawn and onward toward midday.

Now, hunger gnawing at their stomachs, they chose to stop and rest. Drew had discovered that Whitley's life a few weeks ago had been at a more relaxed pace, safe within the boundaries of Brackenholme as he went from tutors' lessons to wild craft class. This trip with Hogan had been a first foray into the woods for the young apprentice and was intended to be a simple training trip to teach him awareness of his surroundings and what life as a scout would consist of. The dramas that had unfolded had taken Whitley completely unaware, and the youngster was struggling to keep up.

Whitley rummaged around in the backpacks for the remains of the dried rations. There were a couple of strips of dried salted bacon, and one roll of rye bread left. He tore the roll in half and handed it to Drew along with a piece of bacon, and the two sat on the ground eating hungrily while Chancer stood over them, snorting softly. Drew tossed Whitley the waterskin and the apprentice took a couple of big gulps.

"I think we could be in Brackenholme by tomorrow if we keep to this pace until nightfall," said Whitley. "It's another ten hours' ride from here."

"We'll be there before midnight," returned Drew, picking crumbs from his cloak.

Whitley looked puzzled, staring up at the faint sun through the low clouds for bearings. "Not sure how you work that out," said the apprentice. "I reckon we're ten leagues away—there's no way we can make it before sundown."

"I never suggested we'd be there before sundown," corrected Drew. "Midnight and you'll be at the gates of your city," he said. "We're not setting up camp and breaking the journey tonight."

Whitley obviously wanted to protest but thought better of it. If Hogan was going to stand any chance of survival, they had to get him to safety as soon as possible. That meant marching on until they got there.

"At least we're on the Dymling Road now, anyway," said Whitley. "That should speed up our progress. I just hope the Wyldermen don't come after us."

"I doubt it tonight, Whitley. We've put some leagues between their territory and us already. The night is when they like to hunt, and we're way beyond their borders now. We'll get you to this Brackenholme place tonight, I promise you."

Whitley nodded solemnly. "Oh . . . and thank you," he added. "It was very brave, what you did back there. You saved our lives."

"It was nothing, really," said Drew sheepishly. He wasn't used to compliments, and felt uncomfortable. Particularly when he wasn't even sure himself what it was within him that had saved them all.

72

"I owe you my life, and I'm indebted to you," continued the apprentice, head bowed in gratitude.

Drew rose, wrapping the winter cloak around his torso. He looked down at his bare feet. Living in the wilds for heaven alone knew how long had left him with toughened feet, but the exertions of the last few days had done some damage. The soles of both were scratched and pitted, lacerated by rocks and branches. Whitley spied his examination.

"You know, you should wear Master Hogan's boots. He has no need for them at present."

"No, I'll make do without. The damage is already done."

"You'll get a pair of boots soon enough when we get to Brackenholme," said the apprentice, untying Chancer from where he'd been tethered.

"I don't intend to go into Brackenholme," replied Drew, joining him.

Whitley looked puzzled again. "What do you mean? Of course you are. We're going there, with Master Hogan."

"I'll accompany you to the gates or whatever border you have to your territory, but I won't enter. I don't belong in there. I belong in the Dyrewood."

"Sorry, but that's just rot," said Whitley. "These woods are dangerous, and I don't care how long you've been roughing it out here, you need to rest and recover in a safe place."

Drew sighed. The problem he faced was whether Bracken-holme would be a safe place for him. After what had happened back on his family homestead, there was probably a warrant out across Lyssia for his arrest, possibly even for his execution, regardless of his innocence. There could be soldiers looking for him across the realm. It wasn't worth risking. He'd take his chances in the great forest.

"Like I said, I'll help you get there, but we'll part on the border, Whitley. Please don't press me on this," he went on, patting the apprentice on the shoulder and looking into his eyes. The younger boy chewed his lip as Drew gave him a squeeze. "My mind is made up." He turned and set off along the road with Chancer in tow.

Whitley followed, deep in thought. After a few minutes, he found his voice, striding a few steps behind Drew as he caught up. "You do realize that Master Hogan was taking you in, don't you? You were his prisoner. Our prisoner."

Drew didn't stop walking, just kept on along the path, leading the horse.

"By rights," the apprentice went on, "I should turn you in to the Watch."

"But you won't," said Drew. "You won't do that, Whitley, because you understand that I'm not an enemy. Not to you, Master Hogan, or even your people. Whatever misunderstandings we've had are behind us. You'll let me go and that'll be the end of it."

"I'm not sure that's what Master Hogan would want me

to do," Whitley continued, troubled by perceived loyalties. "He mentioned that you were to be taken to Duke Bergan. He was going to sort things out, decide what was best for you."

Drew turned and glanced back at the other boy, a look of anger on his face.

"My will is my own. I decide what's best for me, not some stranger or lord."

"But you're a prisoner!"

Drew stopped, letting go of the reins. He held his arms out, exasperated. "Whose prisoner am I?" he asked incredulously. "I don't see any manacles, any ropes that bind. I see a man, possibly mortally wounded, strapped to a horse, and a boy who is scared of his own shadow. Am I your prisoner, Whitley?"

The apprentice's blood rose in his cheeks as he was stared down. He held his gaze, staring right back at Drew, jaw clenched and teeth grating. Finally he looked away. Drew sighed, shook his head, took the reins, and set off again.

They marched in silence awhile longer. The atmosphere was cool, not a word passing between them for the next few hours. The fog banks and mists remained, causing no end of stumbling and slipping as the boys failed to see the terrain clearly. Thankfully, there was no missing the old Dymling Road itself as it cut a great straight line through the woods, with other road traffic being nonexistent but for squirrels, birds, and boars.

As the day drew on, the quiet time allowed Drew the first chance he'd had in some time to gather his thoughts. Over the few months living in the forest he'd been able to lose himself, get away from the terrible things he'd witnessed back home. He'd almost managed to forget the awful events that had followed with his father. Occasionally those memories had crept back in, niggling at the back of his mind as he remembered his mother and brother, but his life in the wilds had allowed him to disengage from that past life. Now he was being forced to face those demons head-on once more, and he didn't like it, not one bit.

Continuing their swift pace in silence, he was also able to consider his traveling companion in a little more detail. Whitley certainly looked younger than Drew, maybe by a couple of years, his face being smooth, without the telltale signs of puberty. Drew suspected that life as a scout was going to turn out tough for Whitley. Like Drew, the other wasn't a particularly well-built youth, and his traveling gear hung from him in a way that suggested there wasn't much meat on his bones. He'd have to fatten up and find some muscles if he was going to survive in the Dyrewood, Drew reckoned.

Hours went by and the daylight faded as dusk drew in, a chill appearing in the forest air as they continued their arduous hike. As they'd hoped, they heard no signs of pursuit from the Wyldermen, that danger long gone.

"I'm sorry about what I said earlier, Whitley," said Drew,

over the shoulder of Chancer as they flanked the horse.

"Eh?" replied the other, stirred from the lull he'd fallen into.

"The things I said back there today. I was out of order and I apologize. I should never have said those things about prisoners and the like; it was foolish of me."

Whitley shrugged, shaking his head. "You might have a point. I'm not going to turn you in when we get to Brackenholme. If you hadn't come back and helped us, my master and I would have been in the cooking pot at the Wyldermen village."

Drew grinned. "I don't know about that, Whitley. I'm sure if push had come to shove you'd have fought back. You should have more faith in yourself. You've got a backbone—it's just unfortunate you landed on it back there!"

The two boys laughed, big belly guffaws that they struggled to hold back. It felt good to find something to smile about after all they'd been through.

"Believe me, Drew, I have a backbone. You should ask my father—he'd testify to that. I just like to pick my battles carefully is all."

"Not get on with your pa, then?" asked Drew.

"I guess you could say that I've had a privileged upbringing, and that choosing the life of a scout is a bit of a step down. My training has been . . . discreet to save face for my father. It's difficult," explained Whitley, frowning. He changed the subject quickly. "So what are your plans? Do you have family in the woods?"

Drew didn't answer immediately. He didn't really know what to say; it was the first time the question had been fired at him, and he hadn't considered it.

"No family, no. They're gone. I'll probably just head back ..."

"I'm sorry, Drew. I didn't realize." The younger boy stared over Chancer's mane, Hogan's pale face hanging low over the saddle, the ranger hunched but secure. "Back to where, anyway? Where's home?"

Drew thought for a moment. Home had been a cave in the Dyrewood, a shelter from the elements. Home had been a cold floor and no door. He doubted he'd even find that place again if he tried. And the farm at Cold Coast certainly couldn't be considered a safe place now. He had no idea where home was anymore.

"I don't know, Whitley," Drew whispered. "I really don't know. The forest I guess. The Dyrewood is my home now."

"Drew of the Dyrewood," said Whitley thoughtfully. "It's got a nice ring to it, like Bergan of Brackenholme. You sound almost noble," said the apprentice, winking at the other to try to cheer him up. "Almost ..."

"Drew of the Dyrewood it is," Drew replied smiling. "Welcome to my kingdom!"

Their conversation was interrupted by a voice.

"Who goes there?"

Six hooded figures stepped out of the darkness on either side of the road, three on each side of them. Drew reached for the sword but had second thoughts. Making a move against one man was dangerous enough. Inviting combat with six was a death wish.

Each man was dressed in a woodland green cloak with a heavy cowled hood that concealed his face. Beneath the cloak trim Drew could make out brown leather armor that was studded with metal. Even in the half light, Drew spied five of the men with longbows to hand, arrows drawn and pointing at the boys. Instinctively Drew put his hands in the air. Whitley didn't.

"Well met, sir," said the scout's apprentice, addressing the figure who'd spoken. "My master has been terribly wounded and we're trying to get him safely back to Brackenholme." He nodded toward Hogan, who sat still on the horse. "Please, you must help. He's gravely ill and I don't know what to do with him."

The men relaxed their bows and rushed forward to the party. Two of them helped the old scout down from the horse as Whitley continued to explain their predicament. Half of the contents of Hogan's saddlebags spilled to the floor with him, his heels still tied to the leather. Drew watched on, his hands now lowered but still wary of the men as they lay Hogan on the ground gently.

"Wyldermen attacked us," Whitley explained. "With arrows, poisoned I believe. I only hope you can save him."

The man who had challenged them helped rearrange the

scout's saddlebags, gathering up the personal effects from the road.

"Don't worry. You've done exactly as anyone would have. You may just have saved his life." He picked up the scout's journal and thumbed through it briefly. "The Wyldermen are well known for using poison on their arrowheads. You're lucky they didn't nick you while they were at it."

Drew sidled up to Whitley, whispering to him, "Looks like you're all right here with these men. I should get going, now that you're safe."

"Of course," said Whitley, shaking hands with his friend. "And thank you. For everything. I owe you my life, remember? Look after yourself on the road. That is, if I can't persuade you to stay?"

"No, thanks and all," said Drew. "It's been good to meet you and even better to travel with you, but I should be going." He gave the other boy a hug and patted his back. All the while he watched the soldiers, but they seemed more concerned with Hogan and his condition. He wanted to leave quickly and quietly and with a minimum of fuss. "Take care, Whitley," he whispered. "Take care."

"You, too, Drew of the Dyrewood," Whitley replied.

Drew turned to walk away.

"Young man," said the soldier who spoke on behalf of the others, his voice clear and loud. "If you'd like to hold it right there, I have some questions for you."

80

Drew cursed under his breath, stopping in his tracks. He didn't turn.

"I won't be able to assist you, sir," he called back. "I was just helping your folk get home, that's all. Can I go now?"

"No, lad, you can't," replied the soldier. "But you can turn around slowly."

Drew felt that familiar dryness in his throat. What now? He turned on his heels to face the men.

Three of the men had their bows trained on him. Two of them finished seeing to Hogan and hoisted him back onto Chancer. Whitley looked on slack-jawed as the soldier standing beside him glanced up from the scout's journal.

"And while we're at it, lad, you might want to drop that sword and pop on these handcuffs." He threw a pair of solid steel manacles onto the forest floor at Drew's feet. He held up Hogan's notebook. "The old man was right. Duke Bergan is most certainly going to want to meet you."

6

CAGED

DREW HAD BEEN right about one thing; he'd got Whitley and Master Hogan to Brackenholme before midnight. But, surrounded by the four walls of a prison cell, he didn't feel quite the triumph he should have. Sitting on the bunk cross-legged, he contemplated his arrival in the city.

The men whom they'd encountered on the Dymling Road yesterday evening had turned out to be the Woodland Watch. They were a part of the City Watch, although their territory included the surrounding forest within twenty leagues of Brackenholme. Drew had gleaned that there were some three hundred of them in all, a small army.

The groups like those they'd come across were known as a "branch," with five soldiers and one captain in command. The captain's name was Harker, and when all was taken into account, Drew reckoned the man had been pretty fair with him. As his prisoner, Harker had allowed Drew to talk while he walked, had even allowed him to converse with Whitley, but always with the big captain within earshot.

Harker was about six feet tall, and lean rather than muscular. When he'd dropped his hood to read the stars that night, he'd revealed a mop of curly black hair that was tied away from his brow in a thick braid. His face was dark and leathery, a similar complexion to Hogan's and no doubt also achieved by a life outdoors. The longbows weren't the only weapons the men had carried. Harker had a broadsword hanging from a scabbard on his weapon belt, with a leather loop on the opposite hip providing a resting place for Drew's Wolfshead blade.

Although the captain had been holding Drew captive, the young man couldn't help but warm to him. Though maybe "respect him" would have been more appropriate. Whatever the captain had read in the scout's journal had obviously given him reason enough to have Drew clapped in irons, but that was where any show of force had ended. The soldier had tried repeatedly to extract information from Drew by conversation, to no effect. At no point did Whitley mention Drew's monstrous appearance the other night. Judging by the looks and line of questioning the sergeant had taken with Drew, he suspected Harker already knew about it. He'd have given his eyeteeth to know what Hogan had written in that journal.

Harker had taken Whitley to one side and talked at length with the scout's apprentice. Once the captain had recognized that the scout in question was Hogan, he'd gone out of his way to be as accommodating to Whitley as possible. Drew had figured that the scout was well liked by the Woodland Watch if they treated the man's apprentice so generously. Whatever the two had discussed it had been out of Drew's earshot, but he could only pray that Whitley held some kind of influence that might help him. After all, the boy's father worked in the court with Duke Bergan, so there was hopefully something he could do. Indeed, their exchange had become quite animated as they'd discussed the prisoner, Whitley standing his ground with the captain as the two debated how they would proceed to Brackenholme. Drew had surmised that the captain was concerned about Whitley's safety and proximity to the prisoner, but it had been clear that the apprentice was going to get his way. If Drew hadn't been too exhausted to be sure, he could have sworn he'd seen Harker bow in agreement.

They'd trudged on for what must have been a further three hours that night, with both boys in the middle of the marching order, again alongside Chancer. Harker had walked at Drew's shoulder, while three men stayed up front and the remaining two kept up the rear. Compared with the pace that Drew and Whitley had been keeping, which the boys had felt was pretty intense, this had been even tougher, with the men jogging at times. If Whitley hadn't been fit before this journey into the woods, then he was certainly getting in shape now, Drew had reckoned.

The first hint they'd had that they were nearing Bracken-holme was twinkling lights in the depths of the woods. These came from homes, Drew had surmised, dotted around the feet of the great trees. The regular trees they'd passed were dwarfed now by enormous behemoths with trunks that must have been ten to twenty paces around the base. Lights had occasionally flickered in the treetops, and with a sudden realization, Drew had figured out there were guard posts up there.

Soon the road had shifted from being a dirt track into rocky paving beneath their feet, great slabs of puckered, yellowed stone that bore the scars of passage and time. The Dymling Road broke from the cover of the Dyrewood eventually, where a meadow of bracken stretched out before them. Although it had been the dead of night, Drew was in no doubt that he was entering a realm more fantastic than any of his wildest imaginings. Not one tree had risen from this enormous field, the inhabitants of Brackenholme clearly taking great effort to keep the outskirts of their woodland city clear—all the better to view an oncoming attack, if any fool felt so bold as to attack Duke Bergan's home. Drew's education had covered little detail of the world outside his immediate surroundings on the Cold Coast, beyond his parents' occasional reminiscing about their past in the old king's service. But he'd known that any territory in Lyssia was hard won, and the precautions in

Brackenholme made that clear for all to see.

The party had traveled apace until, as if some great beast loomed before them, an enormous wooden palisade wall had emerged out of the darkness and shadows. Drew reckoned the walls were maybe fifty, sixty feet high, with enormous tree-trunk stakes driven deep into the earth. Immovable. Impenetrable. High up, guards walked the battlements, and their voices had suddenly become audible from below as they peered down and shouted instructions.

A pair of tall wooden gates had opened slowly before the group as they'd approached, the mechanical grinding of cogs and the creaking of pulleys accompanying their motion. A pair of soldiers holding lanterns and pikes stood to either side of the gates as the party passed through, Harker's branch exchanging a few words and nods with them as they'd strode on. Drew had noticed that the City Watch wore a different uniform from the Woodland Watch; instead of long green cloaks, they wore lighter green capes that hung from the shoulders. Again, studded leather armor had been visible beneath. If he'd been a visitor rather than a prisoner, he might have marveled at how splendid they looked. The street ahead was lit by lanterns that sat atop tall posts, the Dymling Road still keeping its path true and straight. Small one- or two-story buildings had lined either side of the road, but they were quite unremarkable compared with what else Brackenholme had to offer.

Drew had counted five Great Trees that sat within the

walls of the city, visible at night thanks to the lights that were dotted all over their trunks and suspended high up within their boughs. What starlight had managed to creep through the heavy clouds overhead revealed their silhouettes. Great wasn't really the word for it—these were gargantuan oaks. Drew had felt the dig of a soldier's palm in the small of his back as he'd realized he'd stopped to stand slack-jawed at the sight.

"This is where you say your good-byes," Harker had said to Whitley and Drew. Again, the boys had parted company with a few brief words.

"Come find me, Whitley," he'd said to the apprentice. "Speak for me to your father, if you think it might help?"

The other boy had nodded vigorously as he, too, was led away by two of their guards, along with Chancer and the injured Hogan. Harker had gone on to mention that the scout was being taken to the temple. Herbalists there would see to his festering wound and try to draw the toxins from him. If it wasn't already too late.

The remaining soldiers had led Drew to one of the Great Trees. When they'd neared it, he'd seen that the bark was blackened and the trunk seemed wizened, twisting one way and then the other. Pockmarking its entire length as it twisted up into the sky were windows. It must have been hollowed to allow passage through the trunk and up, Drew had mused. As he'd pondered this, he was led up to a huge gate that stood open, lights from the carved hall beyond illuminating his path.

When they'd passed through, Drew had noticed a great sign carved above the door, the black bark revealing white lettering beneath: GARRISON.

Harker had taken a moment to speak with his superior officer, who had come out to meet them. This fellow had worn black leather armor with a silver tree emblazoned on the breast-plate. The two men had spoken for a few moments. There had been much muttering and many glances his way, before Harker had finally come back to Drew, leading the boy toward the armored man. The officer called out, and from a nearby guard-room two more black-suited guards entered the hall.

Harker had patted Drew on the back. "Lad, it's been my pleasure to bring you here—I wanted you to know that. I'll check in on you, you have my word, and I'll watch with interest how things play out for you. Don't look so frightened, boy. We ain't Wyldermen here." He'd leaned in close at the last. "This is for your own good." The guards had taken him by the manacles and led him up a flight of stairs, Harker staying to watch on as the boy was led out of sight.

They had taken him to the room in which he now resided, thinking about what fate awaited him. He felt exhausted, having hardly slept. He hadn't been used to sleeping on a bed, for starters, the hard boards being "too straight," if there was such a complaint. He'd slept on the floor, using Whitley's cloak as a blanket. When the first rays of sunlight had drifted through the barred window, he'd risen and paced the chamber, itching to be free from his confinement. The door to the room was a heavy timber affair, strapped with metal for reinforcement. It was firmly locked. A small shuttered window sat in the center of it. He'd called for a guard, but nobody had come. That had been hours ago.

Standing on the bunk he peered out of the barred window. He could see the ground below beyond the tree-trunk walls of his cell, some fifteen feet down. It must have been nearing noon as he looked at the city of Brackenholme. In daylight it was even more remarkable. The streets immediately around the Garrison Tree seemed quiet, with little traffic to speak of, but back down toward what he figured was the Dymling Road he could see there were crowds bustling. The shouts of shopkeepers and stallholders told him there was a market on, and the smells that drifted up to his windows were intoxicating: pastries, meats, cheeses, all manner of foodstuffs. His mouth watered. He still hadn't eaten since his arrival.

Drew could clearly spot the green capes of the City Watch, who mingled freely, chatting with the traders and citizens of Brackenholme. He also noted that there were other soldiers present, though their uniform was unfamiliar: breastplates that bore the image of a rampant lion and floor-length red cloaks. They were gathered outside the doors to a tavern, having spilled out from within, mugs in hand, bringing their merrymaking to the street. Travelers on the Dymling Road gave the soldiers a wide berth, as they lurched into one another, singing and laughing boisterously. It surprised Drew that the men still wore their uniforms off-duty and, judging by the reaction of the men of the City Watch who looked on with disapproval, he wasn't alone.

From this vantage point he could also see the largest of the city's five Great Trees. It was maybe three or four hundred feet tall, with huge branches that spread out over the rest of the city, keeping vast districts in its shade. Within the boughs at the heart of the tree, sitting atop the central column of the trunk, a huge hall had been built, and even from this distance he could make out signs of activity up there. No doubt the home of Duke Bergan, he reasoned.

A key turned in the door. Drew jumped back from the window and dropped to the floor. The lock went quiet for a moment, and Drew stared toward it expectantly before the door swung open.

The man who stepped in dwarfed Drew. He was at least six foot four with a full head of thick red hair that tumbled over his face, and a long beard to match. His clothes consisted of a brown leather vest and hemp trousers tucked into heavy boots. Unless you counted the knife and fork that sat on the tray of food that he brought with him, he had no visible weapons. Moving the tray to one hand while closing the door carefully behind him, he then clattered it onto the small table, before moving to sit on the bunk. Drew heard keys moving in the lock once more, as someone in the corridor secured the door. The heavy clunk set his nerves on edge.

"Eat," was all the visitor said.

Drew needed no more instruction, moving to the table swiftly and setting into the meal: boiled ham, new potatoes, carrots, and a large hunk of bread that was slathered in butter. Drew devoured it quickly, hungrily, not pausing to use the knife or fork. All the while he kept an eye on the man, darting glances his way as he watched. He was probably in his fifth decade—on closer inspection his hair was peppered with gray streaks. While one heavy hand rested idly in his lap, the other played with his beard, his fat thumb twining in and out of the thick hair.

Drew licked his fingers and then licked the plate, polishing off every last scrap. "So you're my jailer, then?" he asked, instinctively stepping back from the table to lean against the wall of his cell. With something solid behind him and the stranger in front, Drew felt as safe as he could under the circumstances. The man carried himself with a confidence and authority that Drew wouldn't have expected to find in a jailer, so Drew could only assume his experience was vast and well respected, perhaps due to unscrupulous tactics.

"You could say that, I suppose," said the man after surveying the youth long and hard from beneath his bushy brow.

A chorus of shouting outdoors caught their attention, and the big man strode past Drew and up to the window. Drew stepped to one side as the jailer looked out through the bars, then he hopped back onto the low bunk so he, too, could see.

An altercation between a stallholder and a trio of red-cloaked soldiers had taken place, and tempers had flared. The stall sold cooked meats, and the youthful owner was shouting angrily as two of the soldiers held him back. The third soldier chortled as he chewed contentedly on a freshly cooked drumstick before throwing the stripped bone at the young vendor. As they released him, he took a swing at one of them, resulting in a flurry of blows from all three as they threw him back into his stall. With a crash the stall collapsed in on itself, the meats and sausages showering the stallholder as everything came down. All the while the men of the City Watch looked on nearby but did nothing.

"Who are they?" asked Drew, his lip curling with disgust.

"The Lionguard," said the jailer, shaking his head with dismay. His deep voice was tinged with sadness.

"Why don't the City Watch do something?" asked Drew. "How can they just stand there?"

"That's why," said the man, raising a finger to point toward the tavern. A further ten of the red-cloaked soldiers lounged against the wall of the building, watching as their companions tore the stallholder's business down. They laughed and stared gloatingly at the ineffective City Watch. Indeed, Drew could now see that the soldiers of the woodland realm looked angry and anxious, but they were grossly outnumbered.

"But isn't Duke Bergan the lord of Brackenholme? Why does he stand for this?"

"Perhaps it's not as easy as that, lad," muttered the bearded man, stepping back into the center of the room and turning his back on the melee outdoors. "Who knows what stresses and strains King Leopold has put the Bearlord under?"

Drew remained at the window, glowering, anger rising within. He saw the soldiers swinging at the prone man on the ground, raining punches and kicks down on him as he lay help-less. He clenched his fist, struggling to control his rage. Where had these feelings come from? Was this his father's principles coming to the fore? Mack Ferran had never been a man to stand idly by as another was bullied or harmed.

"Somebody should do something," hissed Drew. "This is so wrong." Frustrated by his inability to help, his thoughts re-turned to his own predicament. "I don't know why I'm being held here," he said, turning from the barred window to face the jailer. "I helped your men get home last night, and your city rewarded me by taking me captive."

"I need to thank you for that, boy," said the man. "Master Hogan is gravely ill, but he will recover, and that is in no small part down to you. His apprentice, Whitley, made a special ef-fort to inform us of the part you played when the Wyldermen attacked."

"Then why am I being held prisoner?" challenged Drew.

The other man reached behind his back to untuck a book from his belt. Drew recognized it immediately as the old scout's journal.

"This," said the man, planting a fat finger on the leather cover, "is the reason you're being held. What can you tell me about the words within? Master Hogan says that you were a beast when he found you, more monster than man. He writes that you have some kind of accelerated healing that enables you to recover at an unnatural rate. What's the story, boy?"

"I've nothing to say to you," said Drew petulantly, folding his arms and looking sulkily toward the window. "If he is the only one who can free me, then I'll speak only to Duke Bergan."

"Then speak on. You're in his company," replied the heavy-set man.

Drew's head jerked back in surprise as he looked at the stranger with fresh eyes. Despite his rough appearance there was an aura about the man that inspired respect. Drew tried to recover himself.

"M-my . . . lord," he stammered, bowing awkwardly, not knowing what to say or what to do in the presence of nobility. It occurred to Drew that he'd been disrespecting the Bear-lord moments earlier. "What I said, about the soldiers, and the Watch . . ." he began.

Duke Bergan waved his hand dismissively. "Don't bother with all that," he said. "We don't have time. Besides which, I'm sorry to say you're right, lad. Something should be done. But for now you have to listen to me carefully. Drew, isn't it? It's imperative that you tell me exactly who you are, do you understand? There are others in Brackenholme on their way to this very room who have far less benign intentions toward you. As hard as it may be for you to believe me, I'm your best hope. I need to know, who are you? What are you?"

Drew looked to the door anxiously. "Others?" he asked. "Who? Who wants to see me?"

"You're wasting time, lad. Those soldiers? What you saw beyond that window pales in comparison to the behavior of their masters. Tell me everything, and leave nothing out. Where did you get the Wolfshead blade? Where have you come from?"

Drew had to make a decision, and make it fast. Was he to trust this Duke Bergan? The manner in which Sergeant Harker, his men, Master Hogan, and Whitley had spoken about him suggested he could. And, assuming the man before him was indeed whom he claimed, what was there to lose? Taking a deep breath, Drew began to tell his tale to the Lord of Brackenholme.

He unloaded his past six months on the man, sparing no details. His peaceful life on the farm. He told of the attack by the beast, his mother's death, and his father's reaction. Then his fearful flight into the Dyrewood, wounded and terrified. As quickly as he could, he described his time in the great forest, living wild, turning feral as autumn shifted into the icy grip of winter. He told of his encounters with the Wyldermen, starvation and survival, his battle to control the animal urges within him. When he finally finished, his shoulders slumped with exhaustion. Duke Bergan reached into his pocket and pulled out a handkerchief, passing it over.

Drew wiped away the tears that streaked down his face, the square of cloth coming away wet and grimy. "I'm sorry," he said. "I didn't mean to cry."

"It's all right," replied Bergan. "There's nothing wrong with crying. You're young, after all. But a word of advice: Let those be the last tears you shed for the foreseeable future. As healthy as it is, it will be seen as a sign of weakness by your enemies."

"What enemies?" asked Drew. "I have no enemies. I'm just a farm boy. I shouldn't even be here. This is all a huge mistake; can't you see that?"

"None of this is a mistake, Drew. It's fate that brought you to Brackenholme, lad, fate that brought you to me. Your life as a shepherd boy is over; you can't go back to it. You have to realize that you're different from normal men. You have a gift, like my own."

"I don't understand."

"You'll come to. I wish I could help you, show you how to master it, but there's no time, and it's time and patience that you need to control the beast within."

"The beast? That thing I was in the Dyrewood?" asked Drew, struggling to understand.

Bergan stared at him, and Drew could see sympathy in the big man's eyes. "Look, we don't have long for me to explain. . . . Drew, you are a therianthrope, a shape-shifter. It's got nothing to do with the Dyrewood; it's who you are. You can acquire the shape and form of a beast, at will if you've trained hard and mastered it. There's so much more to it than that, but we don't have the time. He'll be here shortly."

Drew's head thundered and his vision blurred. It was all too much for him. A therianthrope? He was a monster, just as he'd feared. Duke Bergan had mentioned that this "gift" was like his own.

"You're a . . . shape-shifter too?"

"Yes, my boy," replied Duke Bergan. "I'm a Werebear, Drew, like my father was before me and his father before him. And whoever your father was, you're just like him—"

"I will never be like my father," Drew interrupted, his temper flaring at the thought. His stomach muscles twitched at the memory of the Wolfshead blade piercing flesh. He realized it was in fact easy to believe his father was more beast than man, after all.

Bergan stepped forward and looked Drew square in the eyes. He moved the boy's shaggy hair from his face with one hand, then grabbed his jaw and turned it this way and that. There seemed to be a glimmer of recognition from the older man.

"What is it?" asked Drew, motionless in the man's surprisingly gentle grip. "What are you looking at?"

"You have the look of someone I knew a long time ago," said Bergan, chewing his lip. "But it can't be. It's impossible." Bergan looked at the door, nervous.

"Who is coming?" Drew asked.

The sound of the key turning in the lock interrupted them, then the door swung open and a procession of men walked into the room. At the front of them was Captain Harker, who gave his commander the briefest of nods as he entered. Behind him came a man whose youthful face seemed a year or two Drew's junior. Younger though he clearly was, already he had the same height, physical perfection, and strength as Trent, Drew thought. Groomed blond hair tumbled around his face, landing elegantly on his shoulders. He was strikingly hand-some, almost ladylike in appearance and manner, and like no one Drew had ever seen in his life. A red surcoat with a long honey-colored cloak was fastened around his throat by a gold, jewel-encrusted clasp in the shape of two animal paws. Drew spied Duke Bergan bowing slowly as the boy looked around the cell with an expression of repulsion.

"What a vile little room you're keeping him in," said the young man. Two more figures entered behind: a crooked-looking man in a long black robe and a pasty-faced youth of a similar age to Drew. The man in black was the opposite in appearance to the golden boy. He was middle-aged, with leathery skin stretched too thin over his face, revealing every jut of his jaw and hollow of his cheekbones. His receding hairline left his straggly, greasy black hair to tumble down his back in oily ringlets. A thick black animal fur hemmed the top of his robe and his cuffs, further emphasizing the ghostly skull that was his face.

The youth at his side kept his head bowed, standing to the side of the man in black in a way that indicated he was in service to him. His master coughed, wheezing, and gave the boy a dig with an elbow. The youth reached into a satchel that was slung over his shoulder, withdrawing a vial of liquid that the other downed in one swift gulp before tossing the empty bottle back to him.

"It's very good of you to accommodate my prisoner like this, Bergan," said the boy with the golden hair.

"Your Highness," replied Duke Bergan, rising from his bow, "your prisoner?"

Highness, thought Drew. Who was this?

"You heard me right, Bergan," replied the other, settling his gaze on Drew. "I had orders directly from my father to bring this creature to Highcliff if and when he was . . . captured. We all know he's been running riot in those wretched woods of yours; there have been sightings aplenty."

"Surely it would make more sense for us to question him here, Prince Lucas?" asked Bergan. "The boy only arrived here last night and has scarcely had a moment to recuperate. Taking him on such a long journey to Highcliff so soon could severely harm his recovery."

"Recovery?" The prince laughed. "If, as we believe, he is blessed like you and me, then what does he have to worry about?"

Quick as a flash the young prince whipped a slender dagger from within his cloak, slashing swift and sure at Drew and leaving a bright red bleeding cut across his cheek. The boy at the side of the man in black gasped, and both Bergan and Harker struggled to hide their own horror. Drew raised a hand to his cheek, gritting his teeth in pain and anger. Bergan flashed him a look that told him to stay his hand.

"Was that entirely necessary?" asked the Bearlord.

"Stop your worrying, Bergan," the prince sneered. "He'll be good as new in no time, mark my words. There'll be nothing there in the morning."

"And if he is mortal? If he isn't a Werelord?"

"Then he's scarred for life," replied Prince Lucas arrogantly. "But we all know that's not the case. And please don't bandy around the term Werelord. There's nothing noble about this creature; anybody with an ounce of perception can see that. He's from the Dyrewood, a freak, an anomaly. Still, my father will want to better inspect him and discover precisely what he is. Can't have him running amok, flashing tooth and claw at every woodcutter he bumps into now, can we?"

"I have to strongly protest, Lucas—" started Duke Bergan.

The prince raised a warning finger to the Bearlord and shot him a chilling glare. "You forget your place, old Bear," he said. "Refer to me as Your Highness, or call me Prince by all means, but don't dare to address me simply by name. Do we have an understanding?"

Bergan visibly bristled with discomfort but held his anger in place. "Yes, Your Highness. I apologize. But please, Prince

Lucas, leave him with us for a further week while we unravel the boy's origins."

The prince stepped up to Drew and regarded him in much the same way as Drew had witnessed his father inspecting cattle. He snatched at Drew's bloodied face roughly, turning him this way and that before releasing his grip.

"What have you got out of him thus far, Bergan?" he asked, all the while glaring at Drew with cold, cruel eyes. Drew averted his gaze and stared at his feet.

"Nothing, as of yet," replied the Bearlord. "But I was hopeful we could start questioning him in the morning after a full day's rest. That's if he isn't mute."

"Mute?" snapped Lucas.

"Possibly," lied the Bearlord. "We're unsure currently; he hasn't said a word since he got here." Drew saw Harker pass Bergan an almost imperceptible glance. "If he can speak, surely it's better to gently cajole such delicate secrets from him. Just look at him—he's almost feral!"

"No," snipped the prince, turning and making for the door. "I return to Highcliff this afternoon and shall be taking him with me. Lord Vankaskan here will be able to extract whatever information the creature has on our way there. We'll have him speaking in the common tongue in no time at all. Vankaskan is very . . . adept at persuading folk to part with secrets—had you heard?"

The man in black smiled thinly at Duke Bergan before a

cough rattled his skeletal frame. He brought his sleeve to his mouth to wipe thick, dark bile across it.

"I'm well aware of how the Rat King operates. Each of the five brothers has a reputation that spreads to the farthest corners of Lyssia's Seven Realms. What a wonderful skill to have mastered," said Bergan sarcastically.

Vankaskan hissed at the bigger man, baring his yellow-stained teeth at the Bearlord. "Mind your mouth, Bergan, or I shall be asking questions of you, if you'd prefer?"

"Stop bickering now, gentlemen," cut in Prince Lucas. Taking a pair of gloves from his belt he tugged them on, flexing his velvet fingers as he made for the door. He waved his hand toward Drew. "So, see to it that the boy is bound, secured, and transported to my caravan. We depart this afternoon as agreed, yes?" He turned to Duke Bergan, seeking a response.

Bergan bowed low and clicked his heels in the affirmative. "As you wish, Your Highness," he replied. "I shall make preparations immediately."

"Now," said the prince, turning back to the door. "Come walk with me back to your delightful tree house. I need to look over your ledgers one final time and we'll be out of your red hair at last, I promise. I hope we can expect to see you in Highcliff for the wedding?" he went on as he disappeared into the corridor.

"Yes, Your Highness," confirmed Duke Bergan, following after him.

Vankaskan afforded Drew the briefest of smiles, widening his eyes with gleeful anticipation. "Rest while you can, boy," he said. "You and I have a long journey ahead of us. Come, Hector," he commanded, turning and disappearing out of the door, his young aide following hot on his heels.

Last to leave the room was Captain Harker. He shrugged his shoulders in a hopeless expression that spoke volumes to Drew. And with that he left the room, closing the door behind him, and the lock clunked into place once more.

7

THE HEALER

EACH BUMP THAT the wagon made over rut and ditch brought fresh new waves of pain to Drew's already broken body. The wagon came to a shuddering stop. His head swam with dizziness and his mouth was slick with the taste of blood and vomit. He looked down at the bonds that held his wrists and ankles together—lengths of silver twined rope that were knotted tightly in place, his hands behind the small of his back, his feet bound in place, legs buckled at the knee. A further rope attached both sets of bindings to one another behind his back, leaving him as helpless as a trussed pig destined for the fire.

The Ratlord had worked on him three times now since they'd left Brackenholme. He'd been bundled out of the Garrison Tree unceremoniously and shoved headlong into the waiting wagon. Bergan, Harker, and his men had been there to see them off and escort them from the city, and Drew had the briefest of moments to spy the old Bearlord as he watched ashamedly, his head hung low. No sooner had the caravan of wagons left the outer palisade than Vankaskan had joined him in his mobile cell, stripping Drew bare and unpacking his various instruments of torture before setting to work.

Naked as he was, Drew could inspect the wounds and injuries with which Vankaskan had adorned his body. Protracted cuts marked each of his ribs, where the Ratlord had scored the flesh with his long knife. His back was ripped and tattered where he'd been whipped with the studded flail that his torturer had wielded so expertly. Bruises marked the length and breadth of his body.

Drew bit his bloodied lip, coughing as he lay there on the floor of the wooden wagon. It occurred to him that he'd like to take the Wolfshead blade and drive it into Vankaskan's heart. But that merely reminded him that the sword was gone. Even with the bitter memories it held of his father, it was the only thing he'd truly owned. Now it was probably being used for sword practice at Brackenholme by one of Harker's men.

If he could be pleased about something, it was that throughout his ordeal he'd remained silent. Living wild in the Dyrewood had taught him great resilience. A tiny voice at the back of his mind kept telling him to endure, endure; that no matter what the man did to him he would heal, he would revive. And he had. Whatever magic it was that coursed through his veins, allowing his body to repair itself, Drew felt thankful for it. It left him with the satisfaction that the pain was temporary. He had no doubt, however, that the mental scars the Ratlord was dealing out were anything but.

Under the duress of constant questions and punishment, clenching his teeth and holding his tongue, the only time Drew betrayed himself was when the torture reached such sickening heights that his body had begun to change. His jaws had thrust outward, his teeth had snapped, his eyes had yellowed. Vankaskan had needed no more proof that Drew was a werecreature, a therianthrope, but what kind? He couldn't yet tell, but he had the time, methods, and means on his side to find out.

Drew couldn't be sure, but thought they'd been traveling for two days and two nights. There had been three wagons that made up their convoy; that much he'd noticed when he was transferred to his own. A large, opulent-looking vehicle stood at the front of the company, obviously the carriage of Prince Lucas. There were maybe three dozen mounted soldiers who made up the Princeguard, their horses flanking the wagons. Even if Drew had been able to escape, the soldiers would have cut him down in moments. He'd given up on plans of escape. Now he was concentrating on survival.

The only respite he'd had from the Ratlord's constant experimenting and extraction techniques had been the intermittent arrival of Hector, Vankaskan's aide and apothecary. It was clear the youth had been sent under strict instruction—he wasn't applying salves, ointments, and balms to Drew's wounds out of the goodness of Vankaskan's heart. The Ratlord wanted to use the boy's skills with herbs and drugs to help speed up the healing process so he could set to work once more on Drew as soon as possible. Though Drew realized the purpose, and what fresh pain would inevitably follow, he was still grateful beyond words for Hector's care and attention.

Hector wasn't present during the actual questioning—he was left to ride on the footplate at the back of the wagon, beyond the locked door of the cell. Whenever Vankaskan's sickly wheezing became too much for him, he called the boy to prepare him another dose of medicine, which he promptly knocked back before ushering Hector away. When his work was finally done and Drew was bloodied and close to unconsciousness, he summoned the boy in and left him to work his magic on the prisoner, only to return when Drew was on the mend once more. Then the horror started all over again.

Drew noticed the bolt on the door of the wagon opening. Squinting through bruised and blackened eyes he looked up to see who was entering. To his relief it was Hector. The youth entered, the door slamming and being bolted behind him. His satchel was slung low on his shoulder, bottles and balms clinking against one another as he settled on the floor beside Drew.

Hector opened the satchel and started his ritual of unpacking jars, packets, and porcelain tubs, unbundling packs and mixing pastes with his pestle and mortar. He didn't look at Drew and the work his master had carried out, instead concentrating at the job at hand.

"Hector," said Drew quietly, through cracked lips.

Hector's eyes widened, clapping straight onto the captive before darting a glance to the door.

"You can talk?" he said, leaning close.

"I'm not an animal," replied Drew, coughing.

Hector moved forward, unstoppering a bottle and pouring a milky liquid down the other's throat. Drew choked, spluttering, as the fiery cream rolled down his throat, instantly warming his insides.

"My master said he suspected you were indeed mute, as he's had no luck getting you talking. Speak to him, for goodness' sake. If you answer his questions, he'll stop his investigations."

"Investigations?" Drew managed to exclaim. "You call this an investigation? Who are you trying to fool, Hector? He's torturing me within an inch of my life, then sending you in here to patch me up. He's a monster. He's the animal."

"Please, you mustn't speak that way," said the youth nervously, looking back to the door.

"Will you go and tell him I've spoken now, then? Is that how it works?"

Hector shook his head furiously. "No, no, no. That's not my place. I'm simply here to look after you once my master has carried out his investigations."

"Stop calling it that," said Drew. "It's torture. And you're helping him." He flexed his broken fingers, which were already beginning to set and repair themselves. "And you're doing a good job of looking after me. I'm very grateful," he said sarcastically.

"Please don't," said the apothecary, color flushing his cheeks.

"Why do you work for him? What on earth possesses you to stay in his service?" Drew craned his head so he could secure eye contact with the boy, but Hector was doing his best to avoid his gaze. Drew realized he had hit a nerve and now had to see this through and get some questions of his own answered.

"I have no say in the matter. The king ordered me into Lord Vankaskan's service. Believe me, this brings me no pleasure whatsoever. However, I'm bound to my master now, and must do his bidding regardless of how unsavory it sounds."

"Why you, Hector? Why does he need you? And please don't say, 'I was only obeying orders.' You have free will. No man should be a slave."

"You really know nothing of how King Leopold runs his court?" gasped Hector, astonished. "What the king says is law. You step out of line, you're gone."

Drew scoffed. "Now, now, Hector, that sounds like rebellious talk to my simple ears."

"I'm in his service," the youth went on, ignoring him, "because my family are renowned as healers and herbalists. I, too, am a Werelord," Hector explained. "My father is the Lord of Redmire; his lands border the edge of the Dyrewood—indeed he's an old friend of Duke Bergan. The knowledge is passed on through the family from father to son, mother to daughter, and as such we have been physicians to the Royal Court since before recorded history. As my father is too ill to travel anymore, it's been my duty to take his place in Highcliff. It didn't take long for the king to appoint me to look after Lord Vankaskan."

"And Vankaskan?" asked Drew, intrigued by the new information. "What's his story?"

Hector stopped what he was doing for a moment, obviously considering whether he'd already said too much. He looked at Drew once again, taking in his injuries. "As you heard Bergan say earlier, Vankaskan is one part of the Rat King," he conceded. "Not a real king, you understand. It's an ironic title they were given by the old king, Wergar—you'll find 'rat kings' in most any sewer, where a mass of rats have gathered and a number of them get their tails in a tangle. They're forced to live out their lives bound together as a feuding cooperative. I think that's how Wergar viewed Vankaskan and his siblings, and the name stuck. He and his four brothers share the title in Vermire, a city to the far northwest of here. I've been there a few times and a harsher, more inhospitable place you'd struggle to find anywhere."

Drew had indeed heard of the city from his father as a boy, but hadn't paid a great deal of attention. He only knew from what scraps his pa had passed on that it wasn't a place you wanted to visit in a hurry.

"So the Rat King is the collective name for the five brothers. There's Vankaskan, the eldest; Vanmorten, King Leopold's right-hand man; the twins, Vorjavik and Vorhaas; and Vex, the youngest, who isn't much older than you or I. They rule their lands together, which sounds democratic but isn't. They bicker and fight like the worst of siblings, and often betray and change allegiances with one another."

"They sound great," sighed Drew, shifting on the floor to try to get into a more comfortable position. Hector pulled a blanket down off the bed, rolling it and placing it against the small of Drew's back, affording him a touch more comfort. This brief show of kindness had a profound effect on Drew, but he kept silent. His trust could not be given so easily under these circumstances. Hector finished mixing his salves and, taking a flat wooden spoon, started to scoop and smear the ointment onto Drew's wounds. Drew shivered at the contact, icy against his raw skin. The warming liquid he'd swallowed earlier was still burning his insides, reminding him of the feeling of drinking his father's rum on rare family get-togethers. "So if you're a Werelord," Drew went on, "what kind are you? This is all new to me."

"I'm a Boarlord," replied Hector, raising his right hand before Drew to reveal a gold signet ring on his middle finger. It shone with the image of a boar's head. "Like all of my family.

Admittedly I don't have the power or control to fully transform, although my father used to be able to in his youth. Not all Werelords are in command of their abilities. It tends to be those of the purest stock who can fully transform into their wereselves: the king, Duke Bergan, and the like. I don't mind one bit. I'm not an aggressive person, and I think you need that kind of essence to trigger the change in the first place before you can have a hold over any animal instincts."

"Fascinating," said Drew, genuinely amazed. He wondered what loyalties connected the Werelords, if any. Perhaps his best hope of escape would be to appeal to possible allegiances with his own confession. "Duke Bergan said I was a . . . therianthrope?" he admitted.

"You spoke with Duke Bergan?" asked Hector, surprised.

Drew cursed himself. Had he betrayed the Bearlord? "Yes, but only briefly," he admitted. "Just before you arrived in my cell in the Garrison Tree. I don't believe he was intentionally trying to mislead the prince or your master. You do believe me, don't you?"

"Don't worry," said Hector. "If I can promise you anything, it's my silence. I give you my word."

"And Prince Lucas? I noticed he hasn't been back here to join in Vankaskan's questioning. Is he in the fancy carriage up front?"

"Indeed," replied the young Boarlord. "You won't find him back here until you start supplying answers to my master.

112

The minute you're talking, don't worry—he'll be present."

"He's a Werelion, like his father the king?"

"Yes, very much the image of his father in most all aspects. Possibly a little more volatile and used to getting his own way. He's not to be crossed. His temper is terrifying. He beat me so hard once that I blacked out. He calls me 'Piggy' and, believe me, it's no term of endearment."

Drew wanted to say he felt for him, but, despite the trust he'd displayed, Hector was still his captor, allowing him to lie bound in agony. "Are we out of the Dyrewood yet?" he asked instead. Strangely, so long as they were under the great boughs and branches of the ancient forest, he felt protected. The idea of the open road to Highcliff chilled him to his core.

"Nearly," said Hector, giving Drew one more draft of the warming elixir. "I think we'll be out of here in the morning. We'll be setting up camp for the evening in a couple of hours. I'll see about bringing you some food, though I can't promise anything."

The wagon came to a halt once more. The two could hear booted footsteps making their way down the road toward them from one of the carriages in front. It was Vankaskan, returning. Hector quickly started to pack his components away in his satchel. Drew sighed, trying to mentally prepare himself.

"Good luck," whispered Hector.

"See you in a few hours' time, I guess," managed Drew, but he couldn't smile. He felt sick with dread at what was coming.

Before Hector left he turned back. "What's your name?" he asked.

"Drew," the bound youth replied. "It's Drew."

Hector nodded, smiling sadly. As the bolt went on the door, he stepped to one side. Vankaskan hauled himself up onto the footplate at the back of the wagon, wheezing as he came. He carried his instrument case with him, pushing it ahead and sliding it across the floor along the boards. Clambering into the wagon he looked his apothecary up and down.

"Move it, boy. I want hare stew for dinner. Get to it." Hector bowed low and hopped out the door, as a member of the Princeguard stepped forward and slammed it shut behind him, the bolt slamming into place on the other side.

The Ratlord shambled forward, towering over Drew on the floor. Reaching down he gripped the rolled blanket that Hector had placed in the small of Drew's back for comfort. Giving it a swift tug he yanked it free, throwing it into a heap in the corner. He unclasped the locks on his case, reaching in to withdraw a wicked serrated knife.

"Now," he said, "where were we?"

8

Bonfires and Bandits

HECTOR LAY BY the fire, curled up in his bedroll, staring into flames as the burning logs crackled, popped, and hissed. Tiny sparks fluttered up into the air, high into the night sky, escaping embers dying out as the wind whisked them on their way. He could not sleep. Try as he might he couldn't shake from his thoughts the image of Drew lying in the wagon. Clambering out of his blanket he rose and stretched, picking up his satchel. A soldier who was standing on watch nearby looked across. Hector tried throwing him a smile, but the man stared straight through him, as if he didn't exist. To these soldiers he was Vankaskan's puppet, his lapdog, nothing more.

The Ratlord was not prepared to share his caravan with the apothecary, noble or not. The young Boarlord was left to sleep rough outdoors in the shadow of his master's great, long wagon. With eight wheels, it was the same size as Prince Lucas's, although it wasn't adorned with the same over-the-top finery that the boy insisted should decorate his. The king's son wouldn't travel without his luxuries, so his forty-foot royal carriage cut a most unusual sight in the darks of the Dyrewood. Carved lions painted in gold rampaged along the sides, rising up over the wheel arches, rampant and roaring.

Vankaskan's carriage was a fortified monstrosity: thin arrow slits as opposed to the prince's ornate windows, and a sturdy, studded metal frame holding it together, in contrast to the choir of trumpeting angels that danced along the prince's roof. They were as dissimilar as one could imagine, the Ratlord's "battlewagon" a truly frightful sight.

Hector's master had joined the prince in the royal carriage for drinks that evening. Although the men did not have a great deal in common and would surely avoid each other's company in court, they each recognized that out here, on the open road, miles from civilization, they were about as kindred as spirits could get. They shared brandy and tobacco, and traded stories about the gossip and goings-on behind the throne that they were privy to. Hector shuddered. They both repulsed him, but he felt almost as trapped as Drew was. This would not end well.

Hector wanted away from this world, away from the foul acts he'd been forced to assist in. A life in servitude to a wicked master was no life worth living. Treating Drew and listening to the wild youth's words hadn't simply struck a chord with the Boarlord; a bell was now pealing in his soul as his conscience cried out at him. He was born to heal, born to help. What he was doing went against everything the lords of Redmire stood for, all that he'd been taught to honor. But what hope was there for him? He'd been a coward all his life, and he'd remain so until his death.

He walked up to the wagon that Drew was in. The night grew even darker as clouds passed over the half moon that hung in the sky. Two members of the Princeguard stood talking by the footplate. He recognized one as a captain of the guard; Perry was his name. They looked at Hector as he approached.

"A pleasant evening, is it not, gentlemen?" he offered, searching for any kind of conversation to spark his mind into life. The two men looked to each other, then fixed him with a cold stare. These men were hired to the prince's staff directly from the army. They were as cherry-picked as the king allowed—the very best soldiers were directly recruited into the Lionguard, the king's own personal infantry and body-guard. As such the prince's men were a varied bunch: less noble than the Lionguard, more unruly and capable of random acts of cruelty. With the prince as their commander in chief, this came as a surprise to nobody.

"You might want to stay by the fire, my lord," said Captain Perry as politely as he could manage. The soldier didn't respect him, the boy knew that only too well, yet at the end of the day the grizzled old campaigner still knew his place. "We're still in Wylderman country until we get out of the Dyrewood. I'd hate to have to see your coffin shipped back to Redmire." The threat in his voice was barely disguised. Nodding, Hector turned to walk away.

An arrow hit the wagon only a yard away from his face, splintering the weathered wood with the impact. Before he could react, the air filled with the sound of missiles in flight, as the night sky rained an attack from all directions. Two more arrows hit the wagon, and Hector stumbled back into Perry's shoulder. The captain's sword was drawn as he leapt from the side of the second soldier, who now lay on the ground, an arrow protruding from deep within his hip. The man screamed with pain, gripping the shaft with bloodied knuckles.

"Wylderman attack!" Captain Perry barked out an order as his men leapt into life. Some of them immediately ran straight for the woods where the sounds of the ensuing melee broke through the darkness. Others ducked for cover, unslinging their crossbows and returning fire at an invisible enemy. Wounded men crawled along the ground toward the caravans, seeking safety.

Despite the chaos, Hector felt a pang of something. Hope. And not just for himself. Stepping over the fallen soldier he jumped up onto the footplate, tugging the bolt back from its holdings.

"Stop that," gurgled the soldier. "Stop!" he shouted. Hector ignored him, flinging the door open and rushing inside. Drew lay curled in his forced fetal position on the floor, looking up from beneath a blood-matted fringe.

"Hector?" he gasped. "What's going on?"

"No time to talk," whispered the young Boarlord. Reaching around Drew's back, he worked feverishly at the knots binding his wrists. Soft fingers that had never done a hard day's labor struggled for purchase, nervously bitten-away nails finding nothing to grip. Pulling a knife from his belt he worked at the rope, sawing hard until finally it began to fray, allowing him to rip the last of it apart. Drew's arms collapsed forward, taking his weight as he rose to a kneeling position and then onto his back, tearing at the bindings on his ankles. Hector rose and pulled the naked prisoner to his feet. Drew wobbled, crashing into the wall of the wagon. Outside the noise of combat echoed in the night, swords and screams filling the air. Hector took Drew's weight, allowing him to lean on his shoulder.

"I'm getting you out of here, but we need to move quickly. The camp has been attacked by Wyldermen; this is our only chance." The Boarlord clambered down the steps, helping Drew behind him as he went. Before they could take another step Hector froze. Standing in the shadows of the wagon was Captain Perry, a snarling look of hatred playing across his face.

"Well then, Piglord. Seems you've just crossed the line. I'll take great pleasure in explaining this to your master." He raised his longsword, ready to strike a blow. Drew, exhausted, was helpless. All Hector could do was close his eyes and wait for the impending blow. Nothing came.

Opening his eyes he saw Captain Perry standing stock-still, his face captured in a snarl, eyes wide and wild. The sword slowly dropped from his grip as he fell to his knees in the mud. Directly behind him stood a figure in a hooded black cloak, his own longsword lowered to his side after its killing blow. The figure raised a hand to his lips within his shadowed hood, imploring the boys' silence before beckoning them toward him. He lifted the injured Drew across his shoulders with ease. Setting off at a jog he disappeared into the woods, away from the sounds of fighting, Hector following after him. The Boarlord looked back to see the wounded soldier watching them go, his captain's lifeless body slumped beside him. Farther back he could hear the roar of Prince Lucas as the young Wereprince joined the fracas.

The trio ran some way, stumbling over hidden roots and along little-used animal tracks as they put distance between themselves and the campsite. Even though the hooded man was carrying Drew, Hector still struggled to stay alongside, and the man had to stop occasionally so that the Boarlord could catch up. Finally they emerged into a small, moonlit clearing, where the man promptly lowered Drew gently to the ground.

"Who are you?" Hector asked breathlessly. The figure loosened his hood, revealing the lean features of Captain Harker.

"We couldn't leave you to him," came the voice of Duke

Bergan from the edge of the clearing. The Bearlord emerged from where he'd been obscured in the shadows, leading a saddled horse by his side as he came. He wore a studded leather breastplate and carried an ax at his hip, a simple woodland green cloak hanging from his shoulders. A younger emerald-clad man sat behind him on his own steed, high in his saddle and scanning the woods for any pursuit.

Duke Bergan stepped up and removed a backpack that he'd been carrying, handing it straight to Hector.

"There should be a week of provisions in there for one man, although it'll last the pair of you at a stretch if you're smart. Have you had a change of heart, little lordling?" he asked Hector. "You've picked a dangerous ally here. You know there's no going back, don't you?"

"Perhaps they'll think I was abducted in the attack. I hope so, anyway."

"If we can retrieve any of our fallen men from the battle, then to the unsuspecting eye it should look like a Wylderman attack, as you requested, my lord," whispered Harker. "They didn't know what hit them, and with the cloud cover they'll be even more unsure who their enemy was."

"Splendid work, Captain," said the Bearlord, clapping his man on the back. He looked down at Drew, who lay naked on the ground, shivering and shaking. "By Old Brenn, what did they do to you?" he gasped. Bergan unhooked his modest cloak, crouching to fasten it around the youth's shoulders.

"This is the most I can do for you, Drew. I can help you this once, and that's it. You never saw me tonight. I can't have news of my aiding you getting back to the king. It would be too grave for my people. They depend on me, and I keep the peace wherever I can. You understand, don't you?"

Drew nodded, struggling to find words. He bit his teeth and set his jaw.

"Why?" he asked eventually.

"Why what, lad? Why do I help you?"

Once more Drew nodded as the Bearlord stepped up close, his voice quiet beneath his bushy red beard.

"I owe you a great favor, Drew. You may not know it, but you saved the life of someone very dear to me, and for that I was indebted. Consider my actions tonight as payment in full."

Drew didn't understand what the man meant, but could only assume that his returning Hogan safely to Brackenholme where the healers could see to his wounds had struck a chord with the Werelord. He'd certainly got the impression that the two were close and that Bergan thought highly of the old ranger.

"And the king?" asked Drew. "What of Leopold, my lord? Will you stand up to him now? Somebody needs to, and it strikes me that you aren't afraid of him."

The Bearlord chortled a deep, throaty chuckle. He shook his head from side to side.

"No, lad. Whether I'm personally afraid of him is neither

here nor there. I have to think about those in Brackenholme who look to me to provide safety and security in the Dyrewood. I don't care about what he'll do to me, but my people . . . ?" Again, a shake of the head.

Drew pressed his point home. "It seems your people are already suffering, Duke Bergan. The stallholder in the market? Your men let him get attacked and did nothing to stop it!"

The Bearlord growled, and Drew caught the flash of bared teeth within the dark red beard. He shrank back, suddenly terribly aware not only of the power of Duke Bergan but also of the line he'd just overstepped. Hector stumbled away, acting on instinct. The young Boarlord had been on the receiving end of enough beatings to recognize the warning signs.

"Don't push me on this, boy," he said. "We all do what we can to get by. Times are hard for everyone across Lyssia."

"I'm sorry, my lord, I didn't mean to offend you. It just pains me to see innocent people suffer that way."

"Get used to it, Drew," sighed Bergan, his face softening suddenly and a great sadness replacing the anger that had flashed moments before. "There isn't a corner of the continent that hasn't experienced hardship at the paw of Leopold." He clasped a hand on the youth's shoulder, squeezing to emphasize his words. "Listen. You need to get out of here, and fast. My men are already withdrawing—Lucas's Princeguard will start searching the woods at first light. You have to be long gone. Stay low. Stay hidden. Stay safe."

Drew and Hector could no longer hear the noise of battle. Instead voices shouted out as the Princeguard began to regroup. Bergan rose again, nodding to Harker to get ready to move out.

The cloaked captain reached down to shake Drew by the hand. "Good luck, Drew of the Dyrewood. I wish you well on your journey and pray Old Brenn watches over you. I'm glad to have met you." And with that the captain was gone, leaping back into the woods to ready the route home for his master.

The rider who remained behind turned his horse about. "Father, if I may take my leave, I want to sweep for my men. We need to be away from here before the Princeguard recover."

Duke Bergan waved his hand agreeably to the other.

"Be quick, Broghan. Remember, we leave no one behind, injured or fallen. I want no clue as to who it was that attacked them."

"As you wish, Father," said the rider, and spurred his horse into the shadows.

Drew clambered to his feet with the help of Hector, who was already fumbling through his satchel for a medicine that would help Drew regain his stamina.

"Oh," said Duke Bergan, stopping in his tracks as he was about to set off. "I almost forgot. You'll be wanting this." Reaching around the other side of his horse, he unfastened something that was strapped to the saddle. He reemerged carrying a sword in a scabbard, and passed it across. Drew grabbed the

Wolfshead pommel in one hand and the attached weapon belt in the other.

"I know this blade," confessed the Bearlord. "I fought with your father, and I'm sure he'd want you to have this, just like all the soldiers in his Wolfguard. I betrayed that man many years ago—I broke a promise to him and I'll live with that guilt until I go to my grave. If this in any small way begins to make amends, then I hope he's looking down on me now." He looked up to the heavens.

"Dead?" whispered Drew. Pa Ferran had been very much alive the last time he'd seen him. How could Duke Bergan know him? "My father's alive. I told you, remember? He tried to kill me with this sword."

"Not the man who raised you, Drew," said Duke Bergan, pulling himself up into his saddle. "I'm speaking about your real father. My friend, the king: Wergar the Wolf."

Drew's head swam, and Hector moved to hold him upright as his body swayed.

"You are the last of the Werewolves, Drew. Don't fight it, son; embrace it. Conquer it. It may be the only thing that keeps you alive." The Lord of Brackenholme kicked his heels into his mount's flanks and they thundered off into the night, leaving Drew and Hector to gather their senses.

PART III

THE REDWINE RIVER

I

THE ROAD TO REDMIRE

HE SAW THE deer standing motionless, ears pricked and head upright. She sniffed at the air, searching for a telltale scent that might drift downwind. Skittishly she took a couple of steps, shifting her position and dancing nervously, ready to bound away at the slightest sign of trouble. Her fawn skipped about her feet, happily oblivious to the fact that they were being stalked. The open meadows were silent but for the distant cawing of a crow. Shadows raced over the tall, shifting grasses as clouds sped across the blue sky overhead. The deer looked up, briefly distracted by the cloud formations. It was at that moment he struck.

Bursting out of the long grass, Drew sprang onto the animals. The mother leapt away clear of danger, but the fawn was not so lucky. After a brief struggle and swift snap, its neck was broken and the evening meal was in Drew's arms.

Drew took great pleasure in hunting and even more in the fact that he could do it without having to rely on the bestial nature that lurked inside him. From a young age he'd been excellent at stalking animals. In the Dyrewood, wild and alone, he'd embraced what he now knew to be the Wolf, and let it take him over, opening himself up to the killer instinct in his heart. Now, thriving on human companionship once more, he'd brought along the skills he'd learned in the wild and made use of those which meant he could retain his humanity. His senses were keener than ever; he felt fitter, stronger, and faster than he ever had in his life.

Heading the short distance back to the makeshift camp, he stayed low, scanning the horizon as his head bobbed intermittently over the swaying fronds of tall grass. In such wide expanses of grassy plains, his view was unimpeded for miles around, but anyone else might see him with equal ease. All it would take was one scout from the Princeguard to spy him and they'd attack in no time at all.

Hector sat by a small fire, feeding branches and small logs into the flames to keep it alive. He smiled when he saw Drew approach with the deer, and shuffled to one side to let him take over. The two youths worked well as a team, Drew realized. Hector's life had been spent cozied away in libraries, courts, and council chambers, and this journey through the wilds was the greatest adventure the boy had ever experienced. He was observant and attentive, and any tasks Drew showed him, such as gathering firewood and tending the fire, he'd mastered immediately. The Boarlord's scholarly mind clearly made him a quick learner.

Saying nothing, Drew crouched on his knees as Hector handed him a knife from his satchel. With a sure cut Drew slit open the belly of the fawn and set to work disemboweling and skinning the animal. Hector sat back, clear of the mess that inevitably began to pool and, taking a book from his satchel, began reading. Drew glanced over at him now and again as Hector quickly became immersed in the book.

Hector was out of shape. He'd probably never been *in* shape, Drew figured. As a privileged Werelord, he'd been used to having things fetched for him, leading a life of luxury compared with Drew's existence. Drew didn't begrudge him; far from it. Instead he looked upon his new friend with a large degree of awe. People such as Vankaskan and Prince Lucas may have treated Hector like a fool, calling him names, but Drew saw beyond Hector's physical frailties. The boy had placed himself in grave danger by freeing Drew a week earlier, and his previous life back in the court of Highcliff was now an impossibility. Drew saw a brave heart in the young medicine man and was pleased to have him by his side as they fled.

Moments after Duke Bergan had left them they'd made a forced march out of the Dyrewood, not stopping until they'd cleared its edges. After they had hiked right through the following day and night, it seemed the prince's men hadn't pursued them, but that wasn't to say that their enemies weren't out there looking for them. *Caution* had been their watchword. Since then they'd traveled at night and camped during the day, trying their best to avoid any roads or paths that might cause a meeting with anybody. They had followed the banks of the wide and fast-running Redwine River that ran down from the northeast. It was used as a trading route by Hector's people, winding its way through the countryside all the way to the sea south of Highcliff. Its source lay high in the vast and treacherous Barebone Mountains that straddled the eastern edge of the Dyrewood.

The previous night Drew and Hector had been forced to briefly take the Dymling Road as it bore north from the Dyrewood, cutting through the grasslands. The large stone-constructed Dymling Bridge joined the north and south banks of the Redwine at its thinnest point for miles upriver and down. Drew had scurried across, Hector close behind, all too aware that it was used frequently by travelers, even at night. Finally they left the Dymling Road to slip into Redmire proper on the other side. The remainder of the path headed north for many more miles before hitting the Great West Road.

Hector had explained to Drew that this ancient thoroughfare was one of the main arteries of the Seven Realms. Hector's homeland of Redmire lay nestled beside these two huge roads, north of Duke Bergan's woodland realm at Brackenholme. Farther north Drew could make out the realm of Sturmland and its snow-capped mountains, the Whitepeaks, shrouded in distant clouds. Somewhere up there was Icegarden, home of the White Werebears, high in the frozen heartland. As Hector provided Drew with a commentary on the land and people, the young man became aware just how far from home he was. Being a peasant, Drew knew so little about the Werelords that he couldn't help but feel embarrassed by his ignorance. The wider continent of Lyssia was all new to him. A look back south had shown the Dyrewood in the moonlit distance, its threatening outline filling the horizon as far as his eye could see. Far beyond lay his home on the Cold Coast, the market town of Tuckborough a world away, and after days of allowing himself easy conversation with Hector, Drew found himself missing his brother deeply. He'd become immune to those feelings during his time in the Dyrewood, but gradually some of his more human instincts were returning. While he wondered about Trent, he still couldn't bring himself to consider his mother's horrific fate. There was a wound in his heart that would never heal, forever home to her memory. After all that Duke Bergan had said, he didn't know if Trent was even his true brother—their differing looks had always been something to joke about, and Trent had shown none of the primeval rage that had exploded in Drew. But after a lifetime together they were bound by friendship, if not by blood. He wondered where Trent was at that moment. Was he still at the Ferran farm? Or had he left to join the army, as he'd always threatened to? A great rider, Trent had always dreamed of making the light cavalry. As Drew walked along listening to Hector, he just hoped his brother was safe.

Finding a safe place to make camp that morning, the two boys had settled down to sleep. Now, as the evening approached, Drew trusted that the fading light would hide any sign of their small campfire. Having finished preparing the fawn he took a makeshift spit, fashioned from a branch, and passed the carcass along its length. Suspending it on upright branches over the fire, he settled back while the meat began to cook.

"How many kinds of Werelords *are* there?" he asked. "I know there are the lions, the bears, the boars. There's me . . . a *wolf*." It still seemed unreal, but deep down he knew it to be the truth.

"The world is covered in therianthropes," his friend replied. "I'm sure there are some in distant lands we aren't even aware of that have taken a different path from our own and live in quite, quite different societies. But the Werelords of Lyssia are made up of the beasts that you or I might expect to see if we traveled these lands. There's Duke Manfred, Lord of Stormdale, the Werestag. He's an old ally of Duke Bergan's from Wergar's campaigns, his lands lying in the foothills of the Barebones. I don't think he'd have taken too kindly to our offerings if he'd joined us for dinner this evening," he said, smiling. Drew chuckled with him. "Also the late Earl Gaston of Hedgemoor, the Werefox, one of the wealthiest of the Werelords. There are lesser Werelords, too. They rule over the smaller lands that cover the Seven Realms: the badgers, the otters and the like."

Drew laughed at the idea of a Wereotter.

"Don't scoff, Drew," said the other seriously. "You'd do well to remember your place if we come across any of them."

"And do the Werelords stick to their own kind?" asked Drew. He felt color in his cheeks, embarrassed by the question. He struggled to explain. "By that I mean do the wolves stick with the wolves and the lions stick with the lions?"

"Oh, no; any Werelord may wed another. How else would they stay strong? If they interbred too much, this would weaken the species. No, almost all the Werelords will take a bride or husband from another noble house and race. It's very rare that such marriages take place out of love—we're talking politics here, Drew. The marriages of Werelords are inevitably arranged to strengthen unions between noble households."

Drew scratched his head, struggling to follow.

"So if, say, a Bear were to marry a Boar . . . what would the children be?"

"That depends entirely on the paternal line. If the father is a Bear, then almost invariably so shall be the children. Occasionally an anomaly might arise, where the maternal animal comes to the fore, but that's tremendously unusual. There have been times throughout history when a Werelord has taken a mortal mate. Offspring from these unions can also be shape-shifters, but not therians in the truest sense. They're wilder and more bestial, more often than not, with limited control over their abilities." Hector watched Drew as he shook his head in amazement. "There's a lot to get your head around here, isn't there?"

"And Vankaskan? The Wererat? What's his place in all of this?"

Hector sucked his breath through his teeth, shaking his head. "The Werevermin have made a place in the Seven Realms as diplomats and courtiers, but at the end of the day their business is subterfuge. They're spies for the powerful, assassins for the wicked. They have mastered their ability and taken it to a level that no other Werelord can. Some say they can shift their shape into whatever human form they desire, hence their usefulness in matters of spying and espionage. They're not to be trusted."

"And yet you worked for one," said Drew, immediately regretting the comment.

"I know." Hector looked bitterly disappointed—though in himself or his master, Drew couldn't tell. "But until I met you I thought I had no choice in the matter. You showed me that no man should be enslaved, and I'm forever in your debt, Drew."

Drew raised his hand to silence Hector. "I owe you my life for helping to break me free and for restoring me to health, so let's just say we're even."

2

COURT OF THE BOARLORD

ONCE THE FOOD was eaten Drew and Hector buried the fire with dry earth, killing the flames and dousing the smoke. Packs on, they set off across the grasslands, the stars twinkling overhead and the moon once more lighting their way along the Redwine River, pressing on toward Redmire. Along with everything else, Drew was grateful for the spare pair of breeches that Hector had stowed in the bottom of his satchel. They fitted loosely around Drew's lean waist, but provided him with more dignity than wandering around naked would have. With Duke Bergan's cloak he had ample protection against the weather. He'd lived as a wild animal for six months—a brisk northern wind was nothing.

Their path took them close to the outskirts of a few of the

outlying villages that dotted the land around Redmire town, small farming settlements that provided sustenance for the Boarlord's people and precious goods for export. Being of farming stock, Drew couldn't help but notice that all the fields were barren, and the few sheep on show looked underfed and scrawny.

"I don't mean to offend, Hector, but the farmers of the Cold Coast could teach your people a thing or two about looking after their land. Where are your crops? Where's your livestock?"

His friend sighed. "As Duke Bergan said, Drew, there are few who haven't suffered at the hands of the king." He looked over his shoulder, unused to speaking out of turn about his monarch and fearful of being overheard. Then, realizing how ridiculous his reaction had been, he continued.

"The people of Redmire don't have it as bad as others. But the raised taxes for the military that the king has levied have hit our farmers hard. Most of the grain has been seized by the army, and they've devastated our livestock. The king says we should be proud that the good folk of Redmire feed the Lionguard. What a joke." Hector shook his head miserably.

"I'm sorry," muttered Drew, all too aware of the inadequacies of his words. "It seems that so much has been going on in the world outside of Tuckborough. We were just so . . . unaware."

Drew thought back to the history lessons his mother used to give him. They were sketchy, and they were invariably about the years before the rise of the Werelion, but times certainly seemed happier back then. Was there nobody who would make a stand against the king?

Just before dawn, the two young men found themselves at the low palisade wall that marked the perimeter of Redmire town proper. As Hector had explained to Drew, his people were peaceful and, for the most part, neutral in dealings with neighboring states and Werelords. As the Boarlords were famed as masters of healing, it didn't make sense to choose a fight with them. Furthermore their lands were rich with medicinal herbs that were found nowhere else in Lyssia, and only Hector's family held the secret of how to harvest, prepare, and apply them.

The gates were open, and Hector told Drew that wasn't unusual. Nevertheless Drew felt anxious. He half expected to see the red cloaks of the Lionguard at any moment. Keeping their hoods up, the two travelers made their way up the main thoroughfare into the center. Townsfolk passed them by, heading out to work. They paid no special attention to the two cloaked figures, offering greetings of good morning before carrying on their way. Instantly Drew felt at home. He recognized that the people here weren't dissimilar to those back on the Cold Coast. Drew felt a pang of sadness for a life that was long gone.

Before long they arrived at Redmire Hall, the home of Hector's father, Baron Huth. It looked like a grand hunting lodge, modest compared to how Drew had imagined it might be. There were no walls or gatehouse at the front, only huge, great double doors where two guards with pikes stood to attention. They wore chain-mail surcoats that stopped at their knees, with a green tabard over the top emblazoned with the image of a charging white boar. It was the biggest building in the town, but had only three stories. To the rear Drew could see the Redwine River rushing past, long jetties and launches reaching out into the water where boats were moored and tethered.

Hector walked up the wooden steps to the guards, who crossed their pikes to bar his way. As he pulled the hood of his cloak back the men instantly stood at ease, and neither could hide his surprise at seeing the young Boarlord.

"Lord Hector," said one, bowing low. "We were unaware that you were returning home, my lord. If message had been sent it never came through, or we would have met you at the border to escort you on your passage."

Hector waved his hand.

"Don't worry about it, Gerard—my return is unexpected and should not be broadcast beyond the walls of Redmire Hall. This is of the utmost importance."

Both men nodded, understanding implicitly the young Boarlord's words. Gerard stepped forward and rapped his knuckles on the door. A slat of wood slid to one side, revealing another guard within who took one look and slapped it back into place. A heavy lock turned and the doors shuddered, swinging inward. Hector marched in, with Drew close behind. Drew kept the hood of his cloak up.

The entrance hall was a large, open-plan affair, with leather seats that ran all around the edge of the chamber. Two more guards stood to attention just inside the doorway, eyes widening at the sight of Hector. A large double staircase ran up to the first floor opposite the doors, beautifully polished yew balustrades curving at either side. Hector unfastened his cloak as a maid scurried into the room from an antechamber. He smiled as he folded it and handed it over.

"Thank you, Marie," he said warmly. He looked to Drew, gesturing for him to do the same. Drew didn't move. "It's quite all right, Drew. You're safe. Nobody knows we're here."

"If it's all the same with you, Hector, I'll keep the cloak," he said. Drew pulled the cloak back briefly, revealing his state of undress—he was standing there bare-chested with a pair of slack, tattered trousers, and a sword, scabbard, and weapon belt the only things that stopped him from being nude. He felt the color in his cheeks, pulling the cloak shut as the young serving girl tried to look away from his naked torso. It came as small consolation that she was as embarrassed as he was. Hector nodded, finally understanding.

Hector set off up the staircase and Drew followed after. Crossing the wooden landing they headed toward the back of the house, where the first floor opened up onto a large, open-air balcony some fifty feet wide. The view over the Redwine was breathtaking. As the first rays of the rising sun hit the water, it seemed to glow like deep red claret, making the naming of the river unmistakably obvious.

An elderly man reclined in a huge oak chair, nestling among a mass of scattered cushions. A breakfast tray of half-eaten eggs and cheeses lay on the floor beside him. On the other side a portly young man sat in a smaller chair. When the old man saw Hector, he rose from his seat in disbelief. He covered the distance to the youth in a short time, although a pronounced limp made it a less than graceful affair. Arms open wide he took his son in a deep embrace.

"My lord," said Hector, hugging him back fiercely. "I am so sorry to visit you without warning."

"Nonsense, my boy, absolute nonsense. Since when should you worry about arriving back to your home unannounced?" It was at this moment that the old man noticed the half-naked, long-haired, wild-looking companion who was standing in the open doorway. "Who's this?" he asked.

"This is Drew of the Dyrewood; he's my friend and I've promised him a roof over his head for a while. Can we accommodate him?"

The old man stared hard at Drew, taking him in. Drew was painfully aware of his shabby attire.

"You must trust me that his appearance belies his . . . true origins, Father," Hector explained quickly.

But the old Boarlord wasn't looking at Drew's outlandish dress—instead straight at his face. Drew raised a hand over his jaw, looking out from under the curtain of matted hair that made up his fringe. He felt a mess and couldn't hide his shame in the presence of the elderly Werelord. The old man suddenly snapped out of it.

"Certainly," said Baron Huth. "I see no reason why he can't stay with us. A friend of my son is a friend of mine."

At this the other young man rose from his chair. He hugged Hector, although Drew sensed reluctance.

"Brother," said Hector, kissing him on the cheek.

"Brother," replied the other youth. He was almost the exact double of Hector, although life on the open road with Drew had left Hector in leaner condition than when he'd found him.

"How is life in Redmire, Vincent?" Hector asked. "It's so good to see you," he added slightly awkwardly.

"Life in Redmire is as you'd expect," replied Vincent. "Pedestrian. How is life at the king's court in Highcliff? It's very gracious of you to honor us with a visit like this."

"Please, dear brother," said Hector. "Don't be like that. I am not in Highcliff of my own free will. I would trade places with you in an instant."

"Then why don't you, dear twin?" replied Vincent frostily.

Twin? thought Drew. Hector hadn't told him he had a brother, let alone a twin.

The three youths pulled chairs up toward the wooden throne, sitting down only when the Boarlord took his seat. Baron Huth was about to speak when footsteps across the landing disturbed him. He looked over just as a young woman strode through the open door. She stopped, taken aback.

"Is that dear cousin Hector?" she said with surprise. She stepped into the dawn light as Hector rose from his seat, a boyish grin of nervous anxiety exploding across his face.

Drew felt the breath rush from his lungs. She was the most striking young woman he'd ever seen. She was a few years younger than he, with wave after wave of red hair that rolled down her back. Braids held the hair in place around her brow, and her trailing scarlet dress was embroidered with tiny dancing birds in flight. She strode forward to take Hector's hands.

"Lady Gretchen," gasped Hector, bowing clumsily. "It's so lovely to see you! What are you doing here?"

Drew stayed put, feeling further embarrassed about his appearance in the presence of such an elegant lady.

"She is staying with us ahead of her impending nuptials, Hector," answered Baron Huth on her behalf. Did Drew detect a hint of displeasure in the Boarlord's voice? "The king wants her to travel by ship to Highcliff. He intends to send a flotilla of yachts up the Redwine to escort her to the wedding."

Gretchen grinned with impish pleasure.

"Indeed. Kindly Uncle Huth has been a most gracious host," she said, skipping over to plant a kiss on the old man's cheek. "Your poor father has had to endure my chattering ladies-in-waiting for two weeks already. It would drive a sane man quite mad! I don't know how he does it."

Baron Huth rolled his eyes, as if in agreement.

"It has been my pleasure to look after you this past fortnight, my lady, and I and my house are at your service for as long as you need us."

"Don't worry, Uncle," she said. "I shall be out of your hair in no time. Highcliff awaits, and as delightful as your little town is I'll admit I long for the city and my place in the royal court by Prince Lucas's side."

Hector shifted nervously at the mention of Prince Lucas. Drew remained seated, trying to avert his gaze from the young woman. She noticed him suddenly, as if he'd been invisible.

"Father, did you say the king is sending ships here?" questioned Hector.

"Yes, in a little over a month," replied the old man.

Hector turned to Drew. His look was grave. "I don't think we can stay here for long," he said to his friend.

"And tell me, cousin, who is this man and why has he remained seated in front of his future queen?" said Lady Gretchen sharply. Her face was a mask of horror, as if Drew had committed the most appalling act. He rose quickly, bowing clumsily, the dirty cloak falling open.

"And why on earth is he almost naked?" She looked Drew up and down as if he'd just crawled out of a sewer, and took a step back. "And when was the last time he bathed?" she gasped, holding her hand to her mouth.

"Father," said Hector, turning from Drew to the seated old man. The young Boarlord's face looked sick with worry at what was coming. "We need to talk."

3

THE FOX AND THE HOUND

BARON HUTH HAD taken Hector's news badly. Drew had left father and son alone to speak at great length of the previous fortnight's events, discussing everything from his arrival at Brackenholme to their appearance on the doorstep of Redmire Hall. They'd disappeared into the lord's private chambers to talk further, with Vincent close behind.

The maid, Marie, had escorted Drew to a guest room, filled a hot bath for him, and left him to his own devices. Drew had soaked in the soothing water for over an hour, dozing off as the heat worked its way through tired muscles to aching bones. When he finally got around to washing his hair, he was horrified to find it was in solid clumps, half a year living as a hermit having had quite a profound effect upon his appearance. Rooting through a dressing table he'd found a knife, which he used to cut the huge knots away. Grimacing, he stared at himself in a mirror. With his madman's hair he looked absurd. He sighed. There was nothing that could be done about it. Possibly a cunning hat might do the trick, he mused.

Drew found a closet that was hung with a variety of garments, from hunting and riding wear to outfits that he imagined wouldn't look out of place in the king's court. Choosing a simple brown shirt and breeches, he managed to squeeze his feet into a pair of stiff leather boots. Washed and dressed, he left the room and returned to the balcony.

It was midmorning, and with the terrace vacant it appeared father and sons were still in deep conversation. Finding a chair he pulled it up to the balustrade so he could look out over the river. He felt about as welcome as a dose of the pox in Redmire. If he could, he'd have left there and then. The sound of movement behind him made him turn. It was Lady Gretchen. Behind her, three girls, equally finely dressed and roughly the same age as her, stood in a huddle, giggling and whispering among one another. He rose to his feet quickly and improvised his very best bow.

"You're still here? What on earth are you wearing?" she said dismissively as she strode over to a table that was laden with a variety of fruit.

"I took it from the wardrobe in my room," said Drew innocently.

Gretchen rolled an apple in her palms, polishing it on the

length of her scarlet skirts. "I suppose it's got to be an improvement on the outfit you arrived in." A chorus of girlish laughter followed from the trio of ladies-in-waiting.

"My lady," protested Drew. "That clothing wasn't worn to intentionally offend you. I've been in the Dyrewood. I was—"

"Young man," cut in Gretchen. "I would be mortified to arrive at the doors of a Werelord of such importance as Baron Huth dressed in such inappropriate attire. I don't know how you do things in your Dyrewood, but in civilized society we find such crass appearances appalling."

Drew was speechless. Speechless with shock, embarrassment, and, in no small part, anger. Who did she think she was, speaking to him like this? She might be a noble lady, but that didn't give her the right to address a complete stranger in such a foul and abusive manner. But he held his tongue, remembering he was a guest of Hector's, and consequently of Baron Huth's. He wouldn't let her words upset him. He couldn't.

"I apologize if my appearance caused any offense," he said through gritted teeth. "I forget myself."

"You might also want to do something about the rest of your appearance," she continued, his apology unnoticed. "Which sheep shearer attacked your hair? Tell me, I'll see he's flogged." She laughed, amused at her little joke, turning to her companions who all giggled in appreciation.

Drew forced a smile back to her, bowing once more. *That's it,* he thought. *Humor her. She'll get bored shortly.*

"So tell me, ruffian," she went on. "What on earth is dear Hector doing in the company of such an unusual fellow as yourself? Are you some kind of manservant? Do you carry his luggage?"

"Lord Hector has shown great kindness to me," said Drew. "I would go so far as to call him a friend—that is if such a boast from someone as lowly as I doesn't offend you?"

"It doesn't offend me," barked Gretchen, "although I'm sure poor Hector would have issue with that claim. Whatever reason has brought the two of you together, I'm sure now that he's back home in Redmire your relationship has run its course. You could be on your way now, don't you agree? I can't really see what's keeping you here. Hector is home safe and sound now—I shall see to it that you're paid whatever reward you desire, but I think it's best that you're gone before he gets out of Baron Huth's chambers. What is it you need? Gold? Food? A barber?" Again the supporting cast laughed. A smile of satisfaction spread across Gretchen's face.

"If it's all the same to you, I think I'll just wait, my lady, until Lord Hector's business is finished with his father. I shall be off immediately after I've said my good-byes. I wouldn't want to overstay my welcome."

"Too late for that," she muttered with a bitter sigh as she took a bite out of her apple.

Drew considered himself a pretty good judge of character. How could he have gotten this girl so wrong? His first impression of her had been of a flighty songbird, uncatchable and captivating. Now, in such a short time, he saw her for what she was: a spoiled little rich girl who was used to getting her own way. Drew was just a plaything for her to poke at, like a cat attacking an already dead mouse until it grew bored. Prince Lucas was marrying his double. He ground his teeth, keeping his anger in check.

"Take your cloak and go now," Gretchen said, yawning. "I really do find you quite the most impertinent young man I've ever encountered. I'll pass on your regards to Hector and have the guards escort you out." She set off toward her friends, her job done.

"No," said Drew.

Gretchen stopped in her tracks, turning on her heels, her face white with horror. Drew thought he'd said smarter things in his life, but it felt good to make a small stand. She'd clearly never had anyone say no to her before.

"I beg your pardon, boy?"

"I said no. And I'm not 'boy.' My name is Drew."

One of the girls behind Gretchen started laughing, but swift looks from the other two quickly silenced her. The glances that passed between them were serious.

"You forget your manners, *boy*," said Gretchen. "You are speaking to your future queen, Lady Gretchen of Hedgemoor, and you will address me as such."

"I don't see a future queen before me," snapped Drew, no longer able to hold back. "I see an arrogant little girl who doesn't know how to speak with the humanity that Old Brenn gave her."

Her eyes popped. "Do not speak to me of humanity," she snarled, stalking toward him. The ladies-in-waiting shrank back as the very air around her seemed to darken. "Humanity is the curse that you and your kind must live with each day, a fleeting lifespan and a fear of death. In a blink of an eye your life is over, snuffed out by a misplaced step or a common cold. I am blessed with something greater than humanity. I am therianthrope, boy—a Werefox. I am *better* than you, and I'll make sure you never forget that." She raised a hand to strike him, bringing it down swiftly toward his face.

He caught her by the wrist with an even faster hand.

"That's where you're wrong," he whispered. "You're no better than me or anyone in this world. You are rotten, Gretchen, and you and *your* kind stand for all that is wrong in this land."

"You *dare* to insult the Werelords?" she gasped.

"I dare to insult anyone who would trample beneath their feet those whom they see as less than human, simply on account of what hand life and chance has dealt them. I judge people as I find them, and I find you to be a very suitable bride for that nasty boy Prince Lucas."

"You will *hang* for these insults," the Werefox snapped, trying to tug her hand free, but Drew held it firm. One of the girls behind her ran off down the stairs, calling for the guards. "You know nothing of my prince!"

"I know he's a vile and cruel child who was content to beat

Hector and let his pet Ratlord cut and carve me to within an *inch* of my life." He couldn't hold his secrets in now as he felt the animal growling in the pit of his stomach. "I have only Hector's intervention to thank for being free this day. I'm sure you and the Lion cub will be very happy together; you make the perfect couple."

"Get off me, you dog," she cried, slashing at him with her free hand. Her fingertips were now clawed, he noticed, as they tore livid red strips along his cheek. It seemed she was struggling to hold the Fox in check.

"That's where you're wrong," he growled, tugging her closer. His eyes shifted from green to a deep golden yellow as, to her horror, she looked into the eyes of a fellow Werelord. "I am no dog." With that, he let her go, striding back toward the balustrade.

Gretchen staggered back into her companions, who caught her as she stumbled, rubbing her wrist with anxiety. The guards arrived at the top of the stairs with the third lady-in-waiting, lowering their pikes as they advanced onto the balcony. Drew paced along the far side of the wooden decking, hands flexing, claws showing. He glanced down over the side to the rushing river.

"Seize him!" Gretchen cried, pointing at him with a trembling hand.

Before the guards could move a voice boomed from within the building.

"Halt!" cried Baron Huth, limping from his private chambers

with his twin sons by his side. "There shall be no blood shed here today, nor any day. This young man is my guest and you shall all do well to remember that. I am sure whatever has just occurred was a misunderstanding, nothing more than that."

"But, Baron Huth," gasped Gretchen in disgust, "he manhandled me! He threatened me!"

"My dear," went on the aged Boarlord, embracing her, "you don't realize how tightly wound you are with the upcoming wedding and all the drama that accompanies it. And young Drew here has been traveling in the wilderness, bringing my boy Hector safely home. I am sure he is still exhausted from his journey, and any offense he has caused is solely down to having been away from civilization for such a long time. Isn't that right, boy?" said the old man, indicating clearly that this was Drew's one and only opportunity to back down.

"My lady," said Drew, gathering himself, "I apologize unreservedly. I forgot my place and have disgraced myself. Please forgive me." Again, he bowed, but this time it was less low.

Lady Gretchen looked from Drew to Baron Huth and, in a furious swirl of scarlet cloth, strode swiftly from the balcony and toward her bedchambers, with her ladies in hot pursuit.

Baron Huth limped up to Drew, stopping by his side to clutch the balustrade with gnarled and liver-spotted hands. He grimaced. "Young man," he began. "I can provide you with a roof over your head, warm food in your belly, and a bed in which to sleep in for a week, no more. In this time you must stay within the confines of my house. My son has told me everything I need to know."

"My lord . . ." Drew started, wanting to apologize.

"It's fine, boy, you don't need to say it. She's difficult—I understand. But I made a promise to her father on his deathbed to look after her, and so I shall until the king sends his men to retrieve her for this wretched wedding. We all have our little penances to endure. Mine comes in the form of a fiery young Werefox."

"Are you not worried she will tell the king of whom you have harbored?" asked Vincent.

"She wouldn't do that," said Hector. "She's hotheaded and used to getting her own way, but she would never put Father or anyone else here at risk. Our two households have known each other for too long, are too firm friends. No, she may dislike Drew, but I'm sure she'll stay silent as to our involvement in helping him. For the time being, at least."

"But you must not be here when the king's men arrive to collect her," said Baron Huth. "You must be gone, beyond my borders and as far away as your legs or a fast horse can carry you. I thank you for helping bring my son home, but I also resent you for what shame you have brought upon him. He can never go back to the life he had, can never take his place on my throne here or in Highcliff's royal court. That life is dead to him now, and he must go into exile, like some common criminal. My people here can be trusted—they're loyal and faithful to me—and I even believe Lady Gretchen will keep her cousin's fate secret from the Lion. But the king has to believe my son died that night in the Dyrewood at the hands of bandits. And I must mourn his loss as if that very thing happened."

Baron Huth's head sank to his chest. Hector put a hand on his father's shoulder and gave him a reassuring squeeze. His brother looked on coldly from a distance, eyes locked on Drew.

"But I shan't be dead, Father. I shall be alive, safe from harm and retribution. Only not here. Not with you."

The old man placed his cheek against his son's hand.

"Drew," said Vincent quietly, beckoning. "Come, we should leave them alone. They still have a great deal of business to discuss, not least where my brother's exile will be. Let me walk you to your room so we may become better acquainted."

The brief journey back to Drew's guest quarters in the old hall provided little time for the two to discover a great deal about each other. Vincent's questions were pointed and pre-dictable, the youngest Boarlord keen to know where Drew orig-inally came from and how it was that he could be a Werelord. Drew was unable to answer this, still not entirely convinced he was one himself, and when he arrived back at his room he was relieved to be able to close the door on Vincent's queries. He lay back on the bed, staring at the beamed ceiling, wondering how he managed to keep getting himself into these situations.

4

PREPARATIONS

THE FOLLOWING DAYS were for the most part uneventful for Drew. He kept his head down, steering clear of Lady Gretchen whenever possible, only sharing her company in the evening for family meals. The iciness between them was palpable in the very air of the room; hardly a word passed between the two of them for the remainder of his stay. She would make the odd pointed remark that was meant to belittle Drew, but he continued turning the other cheek.

On one occasion, she'd managed to surprise him, though. He had been in the library late one evening and had heard a woman quietly singing on the balcony. It was a sweet, lilting tune, a folk ballad not dissimilar to the kind his mother would sing to him when he was a child and had trouble sleeping.

Following the sound, expecting to find one of the staff singing while carrying out chores, he'd been shocked to discover Gretchen as the source of the pleasant music.

She stood with her back to him, palms flat against the balustrade and facing out to the night-shrouded Redwine. She was alone; no ladies-in-waiting present, no audience but for a hidden Drew. A warm breeze floated over the open landing, sending ringlets of red hair fluttering as she opened her heart to the lullaby. It was melancholic and clearly very personal. Was she crying as she sang? Drew suddenly felt terribly intrusive, more so than on any occasion during his stay at the Boarlord's hall. He'd backed up quickly, slipping away before he was noticed.

Lying in bed later he could still hear her gentle song playing through his head as he'd drifted off to sleep. She confused and angered him, but would not for much longer. Before the week was out he intended to be back on the road.

His time in Redmire Hall allowed him time to reflect, something he'd barely had a chance to do since encountering Whitley and Hogan in the Dyrewood. His thoughts inevitably returned to the Ferran farm and the events of that fateful night. He couldn't get the image of his mother out of his head, her eyes glassy and body broken. She might not have been his birth mother, but she was the only mother he'd ever known, and he had adored her. The nightmares that had haunted him back in autumn also returned, and Drew awoke each night, drenched with sweat, convinced the murderous black beast was in his room. His fingertips would move to the three scars that marked his chest, sore to the touch at the memory.

Occasionally the monster was Mack Ferran, grinning wickedly as he thrust the Wolfshead blade into his son again and again. Trent would stand there beside his father, watching impassively as Drew cried out for help with each sword blow. Down came the sword, down and down again. He couldn't decide which night terror he feared most—the beast or his father.

The only respite he had was during the waking hours, where he allowed himself to think back to happier times with Ma and Trent. He couldn't help but compare his own childhood with that which Hector had experienced. Different as their lives had been Drew felt an affinity with the young Boarlord that brought a smile to his face. He was going to miss him.

Baron Huth had expressly said that he didn't want Drew and Hector to travel together. If one were to head north, then the other must head south. On the off-chance that Hector was found by somebody while traveling to his planned destination, there was a slight possibility that he might yet be able to explain his disappearance from Prince Lucas's convoy in the Dyrewood. If he had the fugitive Werelord with him, then all hope would be lost. These final few days would be the last the boys would spend in each other's company. The Boarlord decided that his son was to head north to Sturmland to stay with Duke Henrik. The White Bear of Icegarden owed him a good deed and, with no love lost between Henrik and Leopold, he expected the favor to be happily repaid. With their fate decided, the two young men were left to spend their remaining time together.

Drew also had a chance to get to know Vincent a little better. He readily admitted he might have misjudged the younger twin somewhat upon their first meeting; he'd seemed cynical and haughty, and there was an edge of disdain and envy in his voice when he spoke to his older brother. Drew knew all about what it meant to have a twin brother—Bergan's revelations didn't change his bond with Trent, which had been as close as any brotherly love he could imagine. Not so with these two. Seven brief minutes might have separated them at birth, but they were a world apart from each other in personalities. Vincent was a more political animal, aware of all the comings and goings within the royal court. Drew had sensed his envy at the fact that, as the second born, he would never taste the power that his brother might have as heir to the seat of Redmire. Since he'd discovered that his brother was preparing to take flight into some remote and far-flung corner of Lyssia, his attitude had appeared to lighten considerably. The fact that he now stood to inherit his father's title probably played no small part in this, Drew thought.

If anything, Vincent was going out of his way to be accommodating to Drew for the rest of his stay. The two brothers had pulled out all the maps and scrolls the library had to offer and, with their father and Drew looking on, had devised the perfect plan for where Drew should head. Many miles southeast of the Dyrewood, beyond the Barebone Mountains, was an arid desert region known as Omir. It was here where the nomadic Doglords came from, the Werejackals. Inhospitable as the place sounded, it also appeared to be the only place where King Leopold and his allies wouldn't follow. A man—or a therian—could get lost in such a vast place. And stay lost. Nearly two decades earlier, King Wergar had led his army into Omir, engaging the Jackals in a long, bloody, and expensive war. Leopold might have the crown now, but only a foolish king would willingly return to the desert realm.

The tales of Wergar's deeds cast long shadows over Lyssia and the whole of the Seven Realms. Time hadn't healed; the Lion's animosity toward the Wolf was as strong as ever. Another Werewolf who could challenge his throne? That simply would not do. They were under no illusion: the king would want to see the last Werewolf put to the sword, and would not rest until he'd done so. In all of Leopold's conquests and victories he had faced countless Werelords, but only one had truly ever dared stand in his way, and that had been Wergar. His hatred for the lycanthropes knew no boundary; he would want Drew captured and killed.

In moments when he was alone, Drew reflected upon his plans to flee. His father had always taught him never to run from a fight, instilled in him a belief that he should stand up for his fellow man. But surely even the Mack Ferran he used to know wouldn't have questioned Drew's choices under these circumstances? He was all too aware that the men and women of the Seven Realms were oppressed, struggling under the king's harsh taxes and brutal Lionguard. Lyssia needed someone to speak out for the people, to put an end to the injustice of Highcliff. But what could Drew do? If he stayed to face the king, he would be killed, without a shadow of doubt. No, he had to go, had to disappear east. Son of the Wolf or not, he was just a boy, and a helpless one at that. Someone else would have to take up that fight.

The Boarlord's tailors fitted new traveling clothes for Drew, which he immediately fell in love with. The only clothes he'd ever known had been tattered hand-me-downs from his physically bigger brother, Trent. This was the first time he could remember that he'd had clothes of his own, and he felt like a new man in them. A brown leather affair with a studded breastplate, his suit had been designed in such a way that if he were to change suddenly the buckles holding the armor would separate from the outward pressure, allowing the clothes to fall safely to the ground. They could be donned once more when he had returned to normal shape. On top of this, he'd taken to wearing Duke Bergan's green cloak everywhere, with the Wolf-shead sword in its sheath at his hip. The cloak, though well made, was nondescript and certainly wouldn't connect him to the Lord of Brackenholme, but it felt good to wear it, a gift as it was from the old Werebear. He was beginning to actually feel like a Werelord, even if he was never going to truly be one.

On the subject of shape-shifting, even Baron Huth got in on the act, providing Drew with precious pointers on how to control and master his gift. He gave him suggestions and notes on mental and physical exercises he could carry out that would help him control the beast. Early each morning they would go through simple meditations, safely concealed from prying eyes in the private gardens to the rear of Redmire Hall. The moon was to be respected by Drew; it was an additional source of power and strength for a Werewolf. Although Drew was only an apprentice, and the old man had only scratched the surface of what it meant to truly control his lycanthropy, he had taught him well in the basics.

Gerard, the head guard whom he'd met when he'd first arrived, took it upon himself to show Drew a thing or two with the sword, allowing him to train with the young guards in Redmire Hall's small barracks. As master-at-arms and a veteran of Wergar's crusade, he had fought alongside his liege, Baron Huth, in the few battles the Boarlord had been directly involved in. It wasn't entirely clear to Drew whose side the old man had fought on, the Wolf or the Lion, and Drew decided that now probably wasn't the appropriate time to ask. Gerard was a fantastic swordsman. He quickly taught the youth a great deal about the craft, from guards and stances through the full gamut: blocks and parries, **balance**, evasion, cuts, and strikes, every move Drew could dream of and then more besides. Mack Ferran's lessons from Drew's childhood stood him in good stead now and were a credit to the old soldier's skills with a blade. Drew was able to hold his own and even match the skills that most of the young guards already had, men who'd been taught to fight since they were born. Only Gerard was his superior.

The days went by, and Drew was beginning to feel a gnawing anxiety in the pit of his stomach. It was going to be difficult to leave the place behind, and not least his best friend. Redmire Hall was starting to feel like home to Drew, with or without the shrewish Lady Gretchen.

5

STRANGLEHOLD

DREW STOOD OVER the foot of his bed, surveying all his worldly possessions. He'd been given a backpack by Gerard, into which he'd safely stowed various essentials: two weeks' worth of rations, a change of clothes, a lightweight bedroll, and various handy tools and implements that might help him on the road. There was a tinderbox, a superior quality rope, and a small metal cooking pot containing a tin plate and spoon. It lay on the quilt beside his cloak and the Wolfshead blade, which was safely sheathed in its scabbard. Fastening his weapon belt around his middle, the sword on his left hip, he draped the cloak across his shoulders, snapping the clasp shut at his throat. With a final look at his room, he hefted his backpack and set off out of the door.

Coming out onto the main landing that overlooked the entrance hall, he glanced down to see Vincent talking to a guard at the door. By the looks of the fellow he was an outrider, with a dusty coat that appeared battered from being on the road. Vincent looked up and caught Drew's eye, then quickly shepherded the man away from the front door, back out onto the porch. Drew was grateful to his hosts that, wherever possible, they endeavored to keep him out of sight of anybody visiting Redmire Hall. It would be grave for all if his presence were to be known beyond the four walls.

As the front doors closed, Drew made his way along the landing and out onto the open veranda. The large balcony was very much the heart of Baron Huth's house, as the aged Werelord took breakfast, dinner, and the evening meal there, retiring to his private quarters only for especially serious business or to sleep. Baron Huth was out there now as Drew stepped into the sunlight, leaning forward in his seat to speak with Hector, who crouched at his side. Lady Gretchen sat nearby in an area of the decking that was wreathed in shadow—the last thing the noblewoman wanted was a dark complexion, tanned skin being a feature that marked one as a peasant. Her ladies-in-waiting sat on cushions at her feet, chattering away as they cross-stitched. She didn't try to hide the look of disdain as Drew appeared, but he threw her his best winning smile. He didn't have to walk on eggshells around her anymore—he would be on his way in a matter of moments. Hector rose to meet him as he approached Baron Huth, stepping forward to shake his hand.

"You all packed, then?" his friend asked, a note of sadness in his voice.

"Yes, and please do thank your kitchen staff again for preparing those rations for me—I'm sure I'll be able to make them last a month if I can grab some provisions along the way."

"So you're ready to be off, my boy?" asked Baron Huth, nodding in approval. The old man had been a most gracious host throughout Drew's stay, but all knew it was time for the young Werewolf to leave. He'd stayed at Redmire for a week, already two days longer than he'd planned, and as the Boarlords were expecting the king's escort to arrive in a few weeks' time, there was no time like the present to strike out for Omir.

"I am, my lord, and again I cannot thank you enough for the kindness, generosity, and hospitality you have shown me," said Drew. Gretchen listened in over her ladies-in-waiting's chattering, showing no sign of displeasure in him for once. Was she actually impressed by his manners? wondered Drew. *Perhaps she'll miss me after all,* he mused.

Footsteps rattled up the stairs as Vincent arrived on the balcony, nodding to everybody in turn.

"You're going already?" he asked, surprised. "That came around awfully fast." He shook Drew's hand heartily.

"I have to get out of here—I've a long road ahead of me. And to you, Vincent, I am indebted for arranging such exact maps for the journey. You're making this so much easier than it might have been."

"Think nothing of it," said Vincent. "It was my absolute pleasure. Tell you what," he said, walking over to his father's wooden throne. "Don't go just yet—one more hot meal in your belly will serve you well on the open road."

"I don't know," said Drew, running a hand through his hair. That was another thing that had been taken care of—Marie, the maid, had done a fine job of sorting out his home-made haircut, and now it was smartly cut around his face, framing his sharp features very handsomely. Ironically, it made him look "wolfish," Baron Huth had said, as if he needed anything else to drive home his ancestry. "I feel I've already over-stayed my welcome." He glanced at Gretchen, who arched an eyebrow straight back.

"No, not at all," said Hector, stepping between Drew and his father. "He can stay for lunch, can't he, Father? Just one more meal before he leaves? You can do that, can't you, Drew?"

"My lord," said Drew, after thinking for a further moment, "if it does not inconvenience you, I would gladly accept the offer of one more meal in your house before I leave."

The old man smiled. "It pleases me," he said, clapping his bony hands. "Yes, stay. Eat well and be on your way afterward. If the Lionguard find you in a ditch sleeping off your meal not a hundred yards from Redmire, then you've only yourself to blame."

Laughing, the men hugged once more as Drew unhitched his backpack and lowered it to the floor. He sensed Lady Gretchen watching him, willing him out of there, and he took a small amount of delight in irking her for a while longer. Word was sent to the kitchens that there would be one more seat at the dining table. The butler brought out a tray of glasses and a bottle of vintage port, which Vincent proceeded to pour as Drew and the Boarlords went over his plans one more time. Hector fetched his satchel and selected a few choice bottles of herbs and potions, helping to stow them in Drew's backpack.

The table was prepared and Baron Huth and his guests all took their places for the meal. A hot tomato broth warmed them ahead of the main course as they dined in the spring sunshine, looking out over the fast-flowing Redwine. A freshly cooked haunch of venison was brought out to the table, and Hector rose for carving duties. His friend's appetite was a thing of wonder to Drew, who'd always managed to survive on frugal portions of food. The fat that had fallen away in their time flee-ing the Dyrewood was back in force now on the young healer's face.

As Drew leaned back to accept a slab of meat on his plate, he could overhear horses outside in the open courtyard to the front of Redmire Hall. He'd just reached over to take a scoop of minted potatoes from a steaming bowl when the front door slammed and booted footsteps ascended the double stairs. It was Gerard, and his face was ashen.

"My lord," he said, disregarding his usual bow in his master's presence, "it's the king's men. They're here!"

"What?" cried Baron Huth in horror. "Here? That's impossible! Are you sure?"

"Yes, my lord: Captain Brutus and twenty soldiers from the Lionguard. They're at the doors presently and demanding to be let in!"

No sooner had he said this than there was a crashing sound from down below as the ancient double doors were forced inward. Drew leapt to his feet, instantly alert. There was a second smash and the diners heard the doors buckle inward, hinges and locks splintering under the force.

Drew snatched up his cloak from a chair and threw his backpack over his shoulder.

"Go, my boy!" cried Baron Huth, pointing to the balcony's edge.

Already booted footsteps were racing up the staircase, and Drew could distinctly hear the sound of armor clinking and clattering. Before he could bound clear he'd stumbled into Vincent, who had risen from the table simultaneously, sending him tumbling to the floor clumsily.

"Halt!" boomed a voice on the landing. A procession of soldiers made their way through the open doors, their golden breastplates catching the sunlight in such a way that they glowed with an almost angelic radiance. Their swords were drawn and their faces were set, flanking the long veranda as they fanned out. Red cloaks swirled as three of them walked straight up to the hopelessly outnumbered Gerard, relieving him of his sword and leading him away. In the midst of them their captain stepped forward, a battle-honed heavyset man with a thick, black beard that was streaked with gray. His sword was slick with blood.

"Captain Brutus," gasped Baron Huth, rising from his chair, a look of outrage rising to his face. "What in Old Brenn's name is the meaning of this? How dare you enter my house uninvited!"

Captain Brutus never took his eyes from Drew, staring across the table at the young man as he rose to his feet beside Vincent. The blood from his sword steadily dripped from the blade, pooling in a tidy puddle at his feet. The blade reminded Drew of his own, only the pommel featured the head of a roaring lion instead. Faintly scored runes like those of the Wolfshead blade marked the length of it, red with gore.

"Baron Huth, you have been found guilty of harboring a fugitive, an enemy to the king and to the free peoples of the Seven Realms," he growled.

"Preposterous," cried the Werelord. "I am entertaining guests, each and every one of them loyal to the king. Need I remind you that Lady Gretchen is in our company, if you needed further proof of our love for the king?"

"That boy," said Brutus, raising his sword toward where Drew stood, "is an enemy of the king. You have willingly and knowingly taken this villain under your roof."

"He is a scout from Brackenholme, nothing more," said Baron Huth. Drew looked back at the Lionshead sword, the blood now all but gone.

"He is the last of the Wolves," barked Brutus.

From across the table Gretchen let out an involuntary gasp.

"The king has ordered that he be taken presently to Highcliff to await trial."

"Trial?" cried Baron Huth. "What kind of trial can this poor boy expect?"

"Father," said Vincent, stepping forward. "I think it is for the best if we hand this man over to Captain Brutus, no? The king will understand, I am sure. He is a forgiving man, remember that."

Drew's jaw fell slack, and he wasn't alone. Baron Huth turned to his son, disbelief in his eyes.

"You?" gasped Baron Huth incredulously. "You brought them here! You turned against your own blood!"

Hector shook his head, unable to hide the dismay at his brother's betrayal.

"I am merely protecting our interests," said Vincent, stepping past his father and over to Captain Brutus, who grinned triumphantly. Baron Huth was trembling with fury. Hector put a hand on his father's shoulder, restraining him.

"If I had not alerted the king to this folly, then the consequences would be grave not just for us, but for our people," Vincent went on. Drew glanced about. He could still leap out of here, a quick hurdle over the balcony and he'd be away.

"You come here, swords drawn, attacking my household staff," roared Baron Huth, turning once more to Captain Brutus, "and you expect me to comply?" He snorted, his face distorting as his back began to arch.

"Father!" cried both his sons at once.

"Control yourself, my lord," said Vincent. "For Old Brenn's sake, control yourself!"

But the old man would hear none of it. He tossed his walking stick to one side, tearing at the robes that fastened at his chest. His rib cage snapped and thrust forward as old bones and the beast within him came to the fore. His mouth cracked as tusks appeared, rising from his jaw as it shifted shape.

Drew glanced over to Captain Brutus, who looked not in the least intimidated by the metamorphosing Werelord before his eyes. Why so unafraid? wondered Drew. Baron Huth was indestructible, immune to the men and their weapons. Then he looked back to the Lionshead sword. The rays of the sun glittered across the runes as the embedded silver caught the light. Drew's mind flew back to the Ferran farmstead and the silver-handled poker by the fireplace. Silver had been banned by the Werelords because it was dangerous to them. Deadly.

"Baron Huth," cried Drew raising a warning hand, but it was too late. Brutus took two steps forward and thrust the sword deep into the old man's belly, catching him midchange. His roaring and snorting stopped immediately as the king's captain twisted the blade once, twice, before pulling it free, the old Boar's lifeblood flowing from the wound.

"No!" screamed Hector, reaching for his father as he collapsed, but with his grasping hand Drew caught him and pulled him back. Baron Huth landed on the wood with a sickening crunch, dead in an instant. Lady Gretchen screamed in terror, rising from the table and staggering back to the balcony's edge.

"Father!" cried Vincent, dropping to his knees in despair. The blood pooled around him as he cradled his dead father, his body having returned to its human state. "Why?" he sobbed, looking up at Brutus. "Why, you monster?"

"You do well to remember your place, Vincent," said Brutus, wiping the blade across his red leggings. "You are spared only by the king's blessing. He thanks you for informing us of your traitorous family, and assures you that you are to take your father's place effective immediately."

"This was never what I agreed to!" screamed Vincent. "You were to take the Wolf away, nothing more. My father was an old man, misguided and confused. What threat did he hold to the king?"

"I would hate to see another pig slaughtered today," Brutus snarled, raising a warning finger to his lips. He turned to Drew. "Now, boy. Unhitch that dog's sword at your waist. You're coming with us. Quietly."

Drew had to think quickly. He was under no illusion that surrender wouldn't lead to death, either on the road or as soon as he got to Highcliff. Hector stood by his side in a shell-shocked trance. Drew knew that his friend, too, would be executed for his part in Drew's escape and sheltering. As for Vincent, he deserved whatever he got, betraying his family to further his own gains and curry favor in the king's court. He would have to live with his father's death firmly on his conscience. That was no life for any son.

Drew looked around, backing up to the edge of the balustrade and glancing down to the launches and jetties below. A number of boats were moored to posts, held tight against the rushing Redwine's pull. Could he make it? Could he kick Hector into life?

"Don't even think about it, boy," warned Brutus, beginning to walk around the long table toward him, sword held before him. Drew might have favored his chances but for the outlawed silver runes that decorated the blade. A blow from that sword would be the death of him, regardless of his lycanthropy. Lady Gretchen stood a couple of feet away, eyes still wide in shock at the events that had unfurled.

"I'm sorry," he whispered to her, then moved fast.

Reaching over, he grabbed her by the arm, yanking her toward him. She swirled as if she were dancing in a ballroom, before landing in his arms. He raised a hand, a clawed hand, to her throat and she squealed with fright. If they wanted a monster, they'd get one.

"Stay back!" he shouted. "Or so help me I'll take your

precious princess's throat clean out!" This did the trick. Not only did the men and Brutus stop advancing, but Hector suddenly stirred, awakened by his friend's voice and the gravity of the standoff.

"Leave the lady alone, boy," said Brutus, raising a hand to keep his men back. "This doesn't need to be any messier than it already is."

"Unhand me, you dog!" cried Gretchen, wriggling in his grasp. He let the claws close round her windpipe, his hot palm flush to her tender throat.

"I'm afraid I can't do that," said Drew. "Hector, how are you at jumping?"

The other looked incredulously at him, as if he were speaking in another language.

"Jumping," Drew repeated, motioning over the balustrade with a nod of the head. "Get a boat ready, and quick."

Some of the soldiers began to unhitch their crossbows, loading their quarrels into place. Hector picked up his satchel, slinging it over his shoulder. He looked over at his father's body in his brother's arms, and then back to Brutus. Pointing at the brutal captain, he struggled to find words of anger and revenge to throw at him. At the sound of crossbow strings drawing tight to their triggers, he instead clambered over the side before dropping with a crunch to the jetty below.

"You won't get far," said Brutus to Drew. "Where do you

think you can run to? We'll follow you down the riverbank and catch you in no time."

"It's a wide river," said Drew. "And fast. We'll take our chances." He lifted Gretchen in his arms, still keeping a hand tightly around her neck. Then he kicked a chair against the balustrade and with a quick step jumped onto it before leaping over the side. He landed awkwardly in a tumble of limbs and red dress, his right foot splintering through a timber plank and hitting the cold water beneath. Yanking it free while keeping Gretchen in his grasp, he rolled clear, looking up to see all twenty men with their crossbows aimed toward him. He shrank behind the Werefox, keeping her in front of him as a shield.

It was a huge gamble. He would never hurt her, and he only hoped that Brutus was under strict instruction not to harm her either. That seemed to be the case, he reasoned, as he backed up to a small sailing boat that Hector was readying. Already it was fighting against the current. Brutus's men might be on horseback, but the speed with which the river was racing gave Drew a small window of hope. He saw there were two other boats moored there. Whipping out his sword he slashed at their holding ropes, cutting them free to float out into the river. Still holding the struggling Gretchen, he stumbled onto the boat as Hector set about untying it.

All the while they were shadowed by the bowmen, some

of whom dropped down onto the jetty to get closer. Resolutely, Drew held the young Werefox before him. Hector finished with the ropes and took to the tiller.

"The king will have your hide, dog," spat Gretchen.

"The king? Is this the same king who just butchered your dear uncle?" he whispered into her ear. "He's a monster. A killer. And yet you still choose not to see it. Don't worry," he added. "I'll get you to your wedding on time. . . ."

The boat quickly took to the currents. Hector, an adept sailor who'd spent many occasions on the Redmire in his youth, steered it into the fastest waters.

"What are you standing around for? Ten of you, follow me to your horses!" shouted Brutus in a fury, slamming his sword into its sheath.

Vincent knelt on the floor beside his dead father, eyes blank and soulless.

"The rest of you, burn this foul hovel! Burn it to the ground! Let these pigs know their king's displeasure. . . ."

Once the boat was out of range of the crossbow bolts, Hector let out the sails, which billowed and flapped as the wind took hold. Tears streamed down his face as they raced away from his home. Moments later a flaming Redmire Hall was visible behind them. It lit the spring afternoon sky with a ravenous red glow, a smoking, black cloud billowing overhead.

6

FLIGHT ON THE REDWINE

THE WIND REMAINED strong behind the small boat as the trio cut through the water at breakneck speed, leaving the torched town of Redmire in their wake. Hector manned the sails and tiller, and stared toward the horizon, lost in grim and grisly thoughts. Gretchen had lain down in the prow of the boat, sheltering against the chill winds that chased them on their way. Drew had offered her his cloak to keep warm, but she'd snarled at him and turned away.

He could hardly blame her. Gretchen's life had been on its leisurely path toward impending queenhood until Drew had arrived on the scene. In a matter of days he'd upset her, offended her, insulted her, and now manhandled and kidnapped her. Up until the abduction he'd felt he had the higher ground, morally speaking, but now he would be the first to admit that he might have stepped over a line. The balance had tipped. He was the villain now, certainly in the Werefox's eyes.

Drew shuffled to the back of the boat where Hector stared off into space, his knuckles white as he gripped the wooden tiller and held the boat steady. They'd passed under the Dymling Bridge earlier that afternoon, hitting great speeds as they whistled beneath its ancient stone arches. There had been no sign of Captain Brutus or his men, and the bridge was sure to throw a stone into their hooves. They would be forced to split there, to follow the river on both sides in order to avoid losing the boat on whichever bank it alighted. This gave Drew hope, as it meant fewer soldiers to contend with, although they would still be armed and seasoned men from the king's personal guard. Even with Drew's natural ability with a sword, he would be tested to his limits against such opponents—and very probably defeated. He hadn't considered whether they, too, had the same silver blessing applied to their swords as their captain had. He didn't want to find out.

The plans they had made back in Redmire were now in pieces. Hector should have been planning for his hike north to Icegarden, and Drew had intended to camp in the hills of the Dalelands this evening. Instead he was hurtling downriver in the opposite direction, his route taking him west toward Highcliff and the man who wanted to see him dead. If any of the king's men were on the river, then he was playing right into their hands. The sooner they were off the boat the better Drew would feel.

He wasn't entirely sure what his next move should be, other than getting Gretchen to safety. His gut instinct was still to head east as he'd originally intended, strike out for Omir at the first opportunity and not stop until he felt the desert sand under his feet. Only he'd been betrayed by Vincent—the king would be watching that passage now. Where else might he run? His options were limited by the small amount of knowledge he possessed. For a brief moment he considered his chances against the king. He'd seen the oppressed people of Westland and the Dyrewood firsthand, and they didn't seem like the rebelling kind. It was unlikely they would gather behind someone brave and noble like Duke Bergan, let alone a lowly farm boy like Drew.

It was getting well toward dusk, and mists were beginning to appear over the surface of the water. Still Hector held his position at the back of the boat.

"Hector," said Drew, drawing closer. "How much farther are you planning to take us? I've seen no sign of the Lionguard. I think we're as clear as we can be. Shouldn't we be looking to cut over to the bank now?" His friend said nothing, and just leaned against the tiller, his face stern.

"*Hector,*" repeated Drew, tapping his shoulder with an open palm. Hector's head turned to face Drew. His eyes were bloodshot, dark-rimmed, exhausted from crying, and his face was a mask of pain. The look he gave Drew was chilling.

He blames me, he thought. *He blames me for all of this: his father's death, our escape from his home. It's all my fault.*

But as suddenly as the awful look had appeared it dissipated, whatever hateful feelings had been bubbling beneath the surface now blown away. Hector's face softened, and he looked to Drew with familiar eyes.

"I'm sorry," said the Boarlord, "I was miles away." He sniffed and cleared his throat. "We need to stay on the Redwine into the night, I fear. If we're on the river, we can't be tracked. The minute we hit land there'll be a trail for them to follow. I'd rather hold that off for as long as I can. If we can make it to the edge of the Wyrmwood, we may be clear of them; it's mostly marshland down there and I can't imagine they'll willingly send their horses in, not unless they want to see their legs broken." He shuffled to one side. "Here, take the tiller."

Drew replaced his friend at the rear of the boat, taking the wooden handle in his novice grasp.

"Keep her straight and steady," said Hector as he rummaged in his satchel. He pulled out a small book, its cover scored with a compass design. Opening it up in the failing dusk light, he started to thumb through a series of maps. "I've had this gazetteer for years, and it's got most of the thoroughfares, roads, rivers, and highways in this part of Lyssia marked out." He hit the map with his forefinger. "Here, this is where we are." He handed the book over to Drew and took the tiller once more. Drew shifted to one side and began to examine the map.

"The Wyrmwood is far removed from Brackenholme. It's the Dyrewood's sickly younger cousin, if you will. Traditionally it was the home of Vala the Wyrm, the Wereserpent. If she's still alive, which is unlikely, she holds the Wyldermen of the region in her thrall. Legend has it she chose to take the form of a great serpent, the Wyrm, ignoring the human half of her life. She was a sorceress, and didn't just embrace her shapeshifting ability, she indulged it, preferring it to the limitations of her human form. Vala accepted the human sacrifices of the Wyldermen, who worshipped her as a living god. She spent so much time in her wereform that she forgot how to change back. The Wyldermen still worship Vala the Wyrm, or at least the myth of the Wyrm."

"So she wasn't a god?" asked Drew, trying to keep up.

"No," replied Hector. "Just a wicked creature. She's long gone now, but the Werelords stay well away from the Wyrmwood out of a healthy degree of fear, respect, and superstition."

"And that's where we're going?" chimed in Gretchen from her curled-up position at the front of the boat. Drew thought she'd been asleep, and started at the sound of her voice.

"Old Brenn, no!" exclaimed Hector. "We're going to moor the boat in the Bott Marshes and make our way on foot from there. There are a few human settlements dotted along the paths where we might find shelter away from the Dyrewood and the Redwine. The Lionguard won't have reached out that far in their search for us—they'll be sticking to the main highways, I would imagine. Trust me, nobody will be expecting us to come ashore within the Bott Marshes."

"Can't you leave me on the boat and let me take it farther downriver, Hector?" asked Gretchen earnestly. "I can sail this thing, I'm sure, and I'm bound to run into river traffic as I get to the mouth of the Redwine."

"I'm afraid not," answered Drew, immediately receiving a glare. "We need you to stay with us until we get to somewhere safe to leave you. Hector tells me that bandits run the Redwine, so it wouldn't be wise for you to be alone."

"I wasn't *speaking* to you, dog," she snipped.

"No, but I needed to answer," said Drew.

"You just want to hold me hostage for as long as you can, use me as a bargaining tool. You call Prince Lucas a monster and you're no better than him!"

"I apologize *again* for my actions back in Redmire," said Drew as Hector looked away once more. Drew and Gretchen had done nothing but bicker from the start of the trip, and Drew was uncomfortably aware that their fighting was taking its toll on his friend, still mourning the murder of his father. "I can only tell you that at no time did I intend to harm you, Gretchen."

"There you go again, dog," she said. "Forgetting your manners. Call me 'my lady' or don't bother calling me anything at all. And what if those soldiers had fired? What then?"

"It was a gamble I had to take, *my lady*. Besides which, I was right. They didn't fire. They couldn't. The king and his son need you alive. Am I right in thinking your father is wealthy beyond my imagination?"

"What's that got to do with anything?"

"The king *needs* his son to marry you," he answered. "This is a political marriage, one of convenience and gold."

"You know nothing of marriage, boy," she said, turning away and shivering. "Prince Lucas is marrying me because he loves me—he could have had his pick of brides across the whole of the Seven Realms. Do not talk about things you cannot fathom or understand. You know nothing of love."

"As you say, Your Majesty," he said, sighing. "Will you at least take my cloak?" he asked, unfastening it and offering it to her once again.

"I have an aversion to fleas," she said. "Keep it—I want nothing from you."

She was impossible. Drew left the cloak on a wooden seat and returned to Hector's side. He chose to continue the conversation in whispers now, away from the Werefox's ears and jibes. She looked up when she realized they were whispering, made a sound of great annoyance, and then threw herself back down into the prow.

"Where *are* we going to let her go, Drew?" asked Hector.

"Believe me," said Drew, "I'd happily kick her overboard now. She's unbearable. But I got her into this mess, so the least I can do is get her somewhere safe from where she can easily reach the authorities. I only hope that when that time comes she doesn't send the troops after me. Maybe she'll have cooled off by then," he added halfheartedly, not really believing it himself.

Hector nodded in sympathy. "In that case I would suggest we try to get out to the coast," said the Boarlord. "There are any number of small ports and seafaring towns dotted along the Cold Coast where we can secure a room on a ship. I have gold with me," he added, patting a leather pouch on his belt. "Certainly enough to cover the two of us on a boat heading south. Once we have passage secured, we can send my dear cousin on her way."

"The sooner the better."

"Give her a bit of space, Drew. Our fathers were very close. Though not blood relatives, they were close enough that we were encouraged to think of one another as family when we were growing up." He leaned closer to Drew. "I lost my father today, but Gretchen also lost a dearly loved uncle. She's hurting, too, right now, so if you're sparring with her she's bound to lash out. Just let her be, please."

Drew was shocked. He didn't realize that his words had been so combative, but Hector was right. He'd wasted no time in arguing with Gretchen when they were on their way, forgetting the fact that she had indeed been very close to Baron Huth. He looked across to her. She was still. His thoughts trailed back to the evening in Redmire when he'd overheard her singing. It wasn't a spoiled child he'd heard that night, but a young woman who wasn't half as frightful when she was without her audience of giggling girls. Had he felt sorry for her? Was it sympathy her song and mood had evoked in him? She didn't seem like a confident future princess that evening, quite the opposite. She'd seemed anxious and a little scared, just like now.

7

KING WERGAR THE WOLF

OVERHEAD THE SKY had darkened quickly, stars lighting their way as they progressed into the night. The moon was only a third illuminated, but it still held a draw to him. He stared up at it, embracing its glare as it gazed down at him like a giant, lidded eye.

"You do that a lot, you know," said Hector.

"What?"

"Court the moon," he said, smiling. "It's understandable; you're a wolf, after all."

"Is it that obvious?" asked Drew, looking a little embarrassed, feeling as if he'd been caught peeping at something he shouldn't.

"We all have a fascination with the moon, Drew, all the

therianthropes. The moon is, after all, the eye of Brenn looking over the world. Only with you, understandably, that attraction is a great deal stronger. They say the most focused lycanthrope can draw additional strength from the moon. Your father could do it, apparently."

Drew turned to his friend. It was the first time Hector had openly referred to Duke Bergan's revelation that Drew was a direct descendant of the old monarch, and Drew had been wary of mentioning it himself.

"What do you know about Wergar, Hector?" he asked, seizing the opportunity. "The truth, I mean, not the rumors and tales that one hears across the realms. Did your father know him?"

Hector's eyes lit up, as they always did when he was sharing knowledge, be it geography, language, magicks, or history. It obviously provided distraction from thinking about what they'd left behind in Redmire.

"What have you heard about him?" Hector asked.

"That he was a tyrant, a monster. They say that he would eat the children of his vanquished foes and leave their bones for the vultures."

Hector shook his head.

"My father was the magister and court physician in High-cliff when the Wolf reigned. You must remember that it is the victor who gets to write the history books; what actually happened was quite different."

Hector's words filled Drew with hope. He noticed out of the corner of his eye Gretchen shift in the prow, her head rising from where it rested on the planked seat. Was she eavesdropping?

"Wergar was a warmonger, there's no shadow of doubt," Hector went on. "He lived to fight, and would throw his men into battle wholeheartedly the length and breadth of Lyssia. He would lead them, though, right at the front line, inspiring great faith and courage in those who followed. His soldiers loved him. The people did too. He would seek out conflict with those who intended to harm his people, striking before they had a chance to strike first. If you were an ally to Wergar, you were safe. If you were an enemy, you had better look out. The Wolf was coming."

Drew sighed inwardly. He'd hoped that his blood father had been misrepresented.

"Duke Bergan fought alongside your father, as did many of the other Werelords, until Wergar chose one campaign too many. Word had reached him that one of the Doglords, Faisal, the Werejackal, was assembling an army of the other Doglords to stand against him and form a separatist kingdom with Faisal as king. Wergar trekked across the continent to face Faisal, without the aid of his staunchest allies, and in the burning deserts of Omir waged a fierce war with his distant neighbor."

Again, Gretchen shifted where she lay. She was certainly listening to the Boarlord's history lesson. It seemed to Drew that whatever events had followed clearly must have cast a long shadow over the Werelords of the Seven Realms.

"But Wergar had left the Seven Realms open to attack should anyone choose to strike. And that threat came in the form of forces from the south, led by the then-unknown Leopold. The only Werelord who stood in his way was Bergan, but the Werebear was defeated. Leopold took Highcliff, the keep, the throne, and Wergar's wife and family. He gave Duke Bergan one option: surrender, and bring the Wolf to him. Only then would the king, his family, and his people be spared.

"When Wergar returned victorious but with a battle-weary and exhausted army, Duke Bergan rode out to meet him, telling him the grave news. In order to see his wife and children once more, he was to surrender and hand over the crown before being sent into exile. The king's first response was retaliation, but Bergan pleaded with him to dissuade him from attacking for fear of what might befall the royal family."

Hector's voice was low now, his head bowed as his delivery slowed. Drew nodded, encouraging him to go on. Gretchen had turned where she lay now, making no attempt to hide her interest in their conversation. Hector raised his head and continued.

"Betrayed by those closest to him, Wergar saw no choice. My father was there to witness this. Bound in silver manacles, the Wolf was taken back to Highcliff and delivered to Leopold. What happened then . . . well, it's almost unthinkable." Hector shook his head.

"What?" asked Drew. "What happened?"

Before the Boarlord could answer the trio felt the boat shudder, as it hit something below the surface of the water. Reeds began to whip past them as, still at speed, they found they were cutting into the skirts of the marshlands. Hector moved quickly to drop the sail, gesturing for Drew to take the tiller. Gretchen ducked down in the prow, peeking over the top of the boat like a guard on a parapet.

"Where are we?" she gasped.

"The Bott Marshes, Gretchen, or certainly the beginning of them. Drew, try to steer the boat between those islands of reeds, would you?" Hector asked as he struggled to lower the sail.

Gretchen scrambled clear as the boom swung about, the sail bunching along its length as the Boarlord took it down. This slowed the craft's speed, but the boat was still going too fast for a novice yachtsman like Drew. Hector took over the controls and began to navigate the inlets and creeks that criss-crossed the marshes. Steadily the little islands became more numerous, and the boat slowed as it weaved between them, the main current of the river releasing them. Before long the boat was drifting idly, gradually nearing what appeared to be a larger expanse of land.

Hopping from the boat, Hector landed in muddy water that came up to his waist. Taking the mooring rope and wrapping it over his shoulder, he began to wade through the midge-infested waters toward the bank. Drew picked up a long oar that lay in the belly of the boat, shoving it into the water until it hit the bottom, and then pushing with all his might, punting the vessel closer and aiding his friend in the process. Soon Hector was scrambling up the mud bank, hauling the light-weight boat after him. Drew jumped across to join him.

"We need to drag this into the reeds so it isn't visible from the river," said the Boarlord, straining with the rope.

Drew joined him and the two slipped and struggled against the treacherous sucking mud, gradually bringing it ashore. Once Gretchen realized she was being no help by sitting in the boat while they worked, even she summoned the courage to hitch up her dress and underskirts and leap onto the mud bank with them. She landed with a deep squelching sound that Drew found tremendously satisfying. He tried not to let her see him grin.

Once the boat was clear of the shore and ditched within a heavy nest of reeds, the boys grabbed the backpack, swords, and satchel, and the three of them set out into the marshes.

It was arduous going, the stinging and biting insects worrying them all the way, and the sound of feet squelching in mud and the constant buzzing and slapping of skin disturbing even more mosquitoes from their hideaways. They were grateful for the moon's light to illuminate their immediate surroundings;

however, it was impossible to get any bearings beyond that. Both Drew and Hector half expected Gretchen to begin a fresh round of complaining, but she kept her own council. After an hour's trudging, wading, falling, and struggling, they found the land seemed to toughen up underfoot, the mud pools getting fewer and farther between.

Ahead they could make out the faint lights of what appeared to be a village. Before moving closer, Hector inspected his map book by moonlight. They reasoned that it was the small town of Oakley, right on the edges of the Bott Marshes.

"So what's the plan?" asked Drew. "Can we try to get a roof over our heads for the night?"

"Certainly," said Hector. "There's no way word of our misadventure will have gotten to a backwater village like Oakley yet. Let's just keep our heads down, find a room, and get moving early in the morning. We want to remain unnoticed," he said, "so let me do the talking, all right?"

Drew nodded in agreement, while Gretchen finished looking at the map book before handing it back to Hector. The three of them marched on into the marsh town. A low dyke circled the settlement, acting as a defense against hostiles as well as the floodwaters. A single guard stood inside the shelter of a timber-constructed watchtower, a burning brazier within keeping him warm. He looked down as they passed, not responding to the friendly wave Hector threw his way.

There were maybe forty or fifty houses in Oakley that the travelers could see, which Hector said actually made it quite large as small towns went in this part of the Seven Realms. An inn sat in the square center of town, the muddy thoroughfare outside lit up with pallid yellow lights that shone from within dirty windows. A sign over the doorway read THE MERMAID INN, and a poorly depicted picture of a buxom mistress of the sea adorned the timber below it. A wooden staircase ran up the eastern wall of the building, heading up to what they could see were rooms on the next floor.

Stepping up onto a covered porch that ran the length of the building, the three of them were about to walk in when Hector stopped Gretchen, insisting she wear his cloak. As she was dressed in her royal finery, it was a wise idea if they were to avoid drawing attention to themselves. She took the cloak appreciatively, affording Drew a dark glower in the process. Drew rolled his eyes as he followed the other two inside.

8

MERMAIDS
AND MILITIAMEN

DREW LOOKED AROUND. A pall of pipe smoke filled the air of the Mermaid Inn, gathering in swirling clouds above the patrons' heads. Chairs and tables were situated haphazardly throughout the room, occupied by townsfolk intent on drinking, gambling, and, in some quarters, arguing. A huge open fireplace occupied the west wall, the tattered armchairs that sat before it clearly prized by the two old men who sat in them, drawn close to the flames for extra warmth. A circular bar filled the center of the room, where a huge middle-aged man with an expansive belly was busy filling pint pots. He looked up as the three travelers walked in, but for the most part they appeared to enter unnoticed.

Hector made his way straight to the bar, the others at his shoulder, and held a hand out to attract the innkeeper's attention. The man finished serving the ale, dropped some copper pieces into his apron, then sidled across to the young man.

"How can I help you, young sir?" he asked.

"Two rooms for the night please," said Hector, flashing a bronze coin in the palm of his hand. "One for two gentlemen and one for a lady."

"'Fraid we ain't got no separate rooms; just the one left tonight, sir, a twin one. But I can see about rolling out a cot on the floor if it suits?"

Hector looked over his shoulder, and Gretchen nodded wearily.

"That will be fine, thank you," he replied. "Are you still serving meals? My companions and I have been on the road for some time now and I'm sure we'd all benefit from something hot in our bellies."

"The missus might have stew left. I can rustle up a few bowls and some bread and butter. How's that?"

"What kind of stew is it?" asked Hector.

"Pork and vegetable."

The Boarlord blanched. "Just two bowls and a few extra rounds of bread, if you'd be so kind."

"May I take a bath, innkeeper?" asked Gretchen, only a hint of her previous haughtiness audible in her voice.

"In the morning, sure," he said gruffly. "Won't be heating

any water until tomorrow, missy, I'm afraid." He handed a key to Hector, gesturing upstairs with his thumb. "Room six."

Drew could see Gretchen bristle at being referred to in such a way, but she forced her best smile by way of response.

"Then I shall bathe in the morning," she said, before turning to her companions. She held out her filthy dress from under her cloak. "Gentlemen, I'm going to retire to our quarters to clean up—I'd appreciate it if you could resist the temptation to disturb me for the next hour while I see if I can wring the Redwine out of my frock."

Both Hector and Drew nodded vigorously. She took the room key from her cousin, and the innkeeper passed her a flickering candle in a ceramic holder.

"Your stew?" asked Drew.

"Bring it up later," she said in a quieter voice. "I don't intend to spend another minute down here with this rabble of marshmen and bogtrotters." With that she turned and made her way back to the door, heading for the external stairs.

"She's really mellowing," said Drew. "I'm liking the new Gretchen."

Hector smiled. "I know, this is hardly what she's used to, is it? She'll be all right. With a good night's sleep she'll be in finer form in the morning, you just mark my words."

The two youths found a table with high-backed wooden benches affording them a bit more privacy. As the innkeeper brought over two bowls of stew and a plate of bread and butter,

Drew scanned the dingy room in more detail. Hector pushed one of the bowls away, a look of disgust at the stewed swine showing on his face.

For the most part the locals appeared to be fishermen and farmers, judging by their clothing and the subjects of conversation Drew overheard. The innkeeper seemed a popular, if somewhat gruff, fellow, who knew all of his regulars' names. All the while the big man kept an eye on his two visitors, glancing over intermittently to see how they were getting on. Drew kept his head down, trying not to attract unwanted attention.

"Have I really got her so wrong, Hector?" asked Drew.

"What?"

"Gretchen," he replied. "I see her with you, with other people, and she's fine, pleasant, charming even. Leave her with me for one moment and she's ready to swing for me in no time at all."

Hector swallowed down a hunk of buttered bread.

"She's . . . complex," said the Boarlord. "You have to remember she's been groomed for this role throughout her childhood and adolescence. This is all she knows. She's used to barking out orders and expecting people to follow them, telling a joke and seeing everyone fall about laughing. She meets you and . . . well, you might as well be from another world. You don't conform to her views and you're not likely to either." He bumped two crusts of bread together. "You clash."

"She can't be all bad," said Drew, tasting the stew.

197

"Oh, she's not," said Hector. "You just have to know how to handle her. I've had practice, I guess, but after recent events I'm not sure you'll ever win her over."

A small group of people made their way from the bar, and Drew caught sight of a sword hanging in its scabbard from one man's hip. As the crowd moved away, he saw that four men, all armed, sat at the bar drinking and smoking. He and Hector hadn't noticed the soldiers when they'd walked in, and it appeared the men were unaware of their presence. They were a rough-looking foursome, and the locals were clearly giving them a wide berth. Drew nudged Hector, nodding in the direction of the men-at-arms as the Boarlord scraped a huge slab of butter onto a hunk of bread.

"Militia, by the looks of it," said Hector. "They're not wearing army issue clothing, but they're certainly soldiers. Probably the town guard, by the looks of it."

"Should we be worried?" asked Drew.

"No, I don't think so. Don't stare at them, eat your meal, and we'll head off to the room. Let's not go looking for trouble, eh?"

Drew relaxed, confident that his friend was able to read the situation better than he. If Hector saw no danger, that was good enough for Drew. He calmed and set about polishing off his stew, stopping only briefly to apologize for tucking into one of Hector's distant relatives. The other managed a halfhearted smile back before taking another big bite out of his stale loaf of bread.

From the bench that backed onto his own, Drew could overhear a conversation that captured his attention like a moth to a flame.

"It's like I told you," said the voice, "the Werewolf is back."

Drew nearly choked on his stew, reaching for his goblet of mild ale to wash it down. The voice continued.

"My cousin Farr in High Sankey said that there were soldiers in their town asking questions. Serious like, even roughing some people up. They say the Werewolf has returned."

"I hear it's old Wergar's ghost," said another, "back for revenge. He's brought an army of dead Wolfguard with him, too, and he's going to march on Highcliff to take back his throne."

"Don't talk such rubbish," chimed in another voice. "The Wolf is as dead as my mother, may Old Brenn bless her soul. They're old wives' tales, naught more."

"I don't care what you say," said the first man. "I hear the king is looking for the Wolf. Make of that what you will. My cousin ain't no liar!"

Hector was listening in now as well, also keenly aware that the same conversation was going on elsewhere around the inn. The gossip was spreading like wildfire, but it was clearly just hearsay at the moment from a group of uninformed villagers. Only the two young men knew the truth behind the story. Nevertheless Hector could see Drew visibly shrinking in his seat.

They could hear raised voices at the bar as one old fellow slammed his tankard onto the counter.

"It's not before time, I says! We need Wergar back, and if it's his ghost that's comin' then it has my blessing!" he jeered, taking a swig of his ale. The innkeeper leaned toward the old-timer, acutely aware that militiamen stood down the bar. They, too, were now listening in on the old man's tirade.

"Quiet now, Ebert," said the burly barman. "Mind your mouth or you'll land yourself in trouble." But the old man was having none of it. He had things to say, and the alcohol he'd downed was only fueling him. He was a wiry fellow, with straggly white hair that was scraped across his balding head.

"You quiet yourself, Jonas," he wailed. "That Lion has done nothing but bring misery to this town. Higher taxes and for what in return? He sends his hired help here to keep us in our place, taking our crops and catches whenever their will takes them. There's a store full of our grain out there that we'll never get to see!"

"Ebert," warned the innkeeper, clearly concerned as the militiamen rose from their stools on the other side of the bar.

"They ain't even soldiers," said Ebert woozily, "just robbing mercenaries out for a quick coin. I fought in the Wolf's army—I know what it means to be a man of honor. These villains would fill their britches if they ever came across a real soldier."

"So you'd be a real soldier, then, old man?" said one of the militiamen as the other three surrounded Ebert. Those sitting nearby moved clear, an uncomfortable silence settling around the room. The townsfolk, honest laborers every one of them, exchanged worried glances as the four armed men circled one of their own. The drunk old man hardly seemed to register their presence.

"Don't mind him," said Jonas. "He gets like this when he's had too much ale. Pay him no attention; he doesn't know what he's saying."

One of the guards raised a hand to silence the barman, who instantly stopped talking, twining his hand towel between his fingers nervously. The leader of the men was obvious, a sergeant's insignia on his right shoulder marking his rank apart from the others. He was bald, with a drooping black mustache that ran right down to his chin. Broken yellowed teeth splintered into a tobacco-stained smile as he patted Ebert on the back.

"He knows perfectly well what he's saying," said the sergeant. "Looks like we've got ourselves a little rabble-rouser here, eh, lads?" The others laughed in agreement. "Any of you peasants agree with what this old boy has to say?" he barked, looking around the room. Each and every face turned away, avoiding eye contact, as the sergeant scanned the room for any more disgruntled locals. Many in the room wanted to step in, help poor Ebert out in his moment of need, but the militia would make their lives miserable.

Ebert said something under his breath, barely audible.

"What's that, old fella?" said the sergeant, clipping him around the ear. It was enough to send the old man bouncing into one of the other soldiers, who promptly shoved him into another. The soldiers jostled the drunk man between them, until he stumbled into a stool, holding on desperately for balance. Jonas raised a hand, wanting to reach out across the bar to grab Ebert's sleeve, but one of the guards snarled at him, daring him to make his move. He brought his hand tentatively back and watched on, miserable. The sergeant kicked the stool legs away, sending seat and man crashing to the floor. The soldiers laughed heartily, one even congratulating the officer with a clap on the back.

Ebert looked up from where he lay on the ground, blood streaming from a deep cut on his head. "You're bullying scum, the lot of you!" he spat. "You're not fit to wear a tabard. Look!" he cried to everyone in the bar. "Look at the Lion's men! Look at our noble king's army!"

Jonas was shaking his head fretfully behind the bar. "Please," said the innkeeper. "Let him be!"

The sergeant turned to him, scowling. "He has dishonored me and defamed the king. I'll punish this fool as I see fit. All of you—outside!"

9

THE WOLF REVEALED

THE SERGEANT STRODE out of the inn, followed by the other soldiers, who dragged Ebert with them. A crowd of scared villagers led by Jonas gathered on the porch, the light of the inn spilling out behind them. Hector and Drew joined the crowd on one side, hearts thumping with a combination of anger and dread.

"Let this be a lesson to you all, peasants," said the sergeant. "Any of you mongrels get ideas of spreading idle gossip about King Leopold, you'll end up with more than a beating. I'll have your heads on a pike!" He rolled up his sleeves as his three men dragged the old man into the street. Ebert's legs trailed in the mud behind him, his head slumped to his chest. Some of the locals tried to retreat into the inn to avoid the inevitable scene.

"Get back!" screamed the sergeant. "You all need to see this!"

With one soldier each taking an arm and the third grabbing the old man by his bloodied white hair, they held him in place as the sergeant stepped up, pulling his fist back.

Before he could strike, a hand closed around his wrist.

"I can't let you do that," said a voice.

A chorus of murmurs went up from the crowd. What madman would endanger his life for the sake of poor Ebert? These soldiers were killers; there was no doubt about that. The sergeant craned his head around, a look of bewilderment upon his grizzly face. A boy in a dark green cloak was standing there, holding his fist in his own viselike grip.

"What do you think you're doing?" snarled the soldier.

"Stopping you from hurting this poor man and preventing you and your men from making bigger fools of yourselves than you already have," replied Drew, his jaw set and his eyes narrowed. Inside, his heart was pounding even faster than before, as if it were threatening to rip free from his chest. His stomach lurched, his head swam; fear gripped his every nerve, but he stood his ground. The crowd watched with a mixture of awe and anxiety. Who was this fool who would risk his life for one of them? Was he mad?

The sergeant struggled to pull his hand free, eventually tugging clear and spinning to face the boy. The other three soldiers dropped the old man facedown in the mud, spreading out until the four of them faced off against Drew. The sergeant reached for his sword, pulling it out of its battered scabbard, his men following suit. Their blades were pitted and rusted, uncared for by the lazy militiamen.

"I wouldn't do that," warned Drew. "Put your weapons away and return to your posts. Nobody needs to get hurt."

Hector scrambled forward to roll the old man over, pulling his face free from a filthy puddle. He began to drag Ebert back toward the stoop of the inn, Jonas coming down from the steps to help him.

"Nobody needs to get hurt?" laughed the sergeant. "I have a pike in my tower that shall suit your pretty head," he said, stepping forward.

Drew swirled his cloak clear of his hip and in a flash the Wolfshead blade was out and held forward. There was a gasp from the crowd. Some recognized the blade from long ago. The soldiers saw it as well, two of them wavering for a moment until their sergeant urged them into action.

"At him!" he yelled. His men rushed forward, past their commander, as he hung back to join the melee in his own good time.

Drawing on all that Gerard had taught him at Redmire, Drew met the first man with a simple feint, sidestepping him and sending him flying into the mud with a well-placed trip. The second was better prepared and their swords clashed with a clang. Two quick trades and Drew was able to slip around the soldier, bringing the flat of his sword down onto the man's head with a dull crunch. He fell to the ground in a heap. Drew had left himself open, though, something Gerard had warned him against. The third soldier lunged in swiftly, a deft thrust finding its way into Drew's back. Only the studded leather jerkin beneath his cloak prevented the blade from finding his flesh, but it was enough to send Drew cartwheeling forward.

Stumbling, he unhooked his cloak, throwing it clear toward the steps of the inn. The crowd watched on, hope rising among them. The sergeant and his remaining man closed in on Drew, while the soldier who was still conscious struggled to pull himself from the muddy ruts in the road.

Hector was watching, helpless to aid his friend. It was moments like these when he wished desperately for the control of his father. Although he was a Boarlord, he'd never bothered to try to channel the ability, instead busying himself with medicine and magistry. While Vincent had dabbled in shape-shifting, it had been alien to the peaceful, book-loving Hector.

Drew had provoked this battle, and he knew it was his responsibility to finish it. But he couldn't do it as himself. As the soldiers approached, he began to change.

He seemed to gain six inches in height before the men's eyes. His shoulders filled out; his arms seemed to thicken, muscles straining within his clothes. The dark hair that fell around his face became shaggier, more animal-like. He snarled at them, revealing sharp teeth that gnashed. And his eyes, bright gold, glowed from beneath a darkening brow.

"It's the Wolf!" came a cry from the inn.

"Wergar lives!" shouted another, to a cheer.

"It can't be," gasped the sergeant, blinking in disbelief. Grabbing the soldier who stood to his side he hurled the man toward the Werewolf. The man roared a futile battle cry as he charged, sword dipped and tucked in both hands like a lance at his chest. Drew leapt forward, meeting him as he ran, striking him in the face with the pommel of the Wolfshead blade. The man fell, unconscious in an instant. The soldier who had struggled to raise himself from the mud now staggered toward the monster before him. Drew turned to roar at him and the man collapsed beside his comrade in a dead faint.

The sergeant darted forward, sword swinging down in a slashing blow.

But Drew was too fast, too aware. He thrust out his clawed hand, catching the man by the throat, lifting him high into the air in one clean motion. The soldier dropped his sword into the mud as he struggled for breath. The crowd went silent.

Drew pulled the sergeant close, his lupine teeth grating and hot breath and spittle showering the man's face. "If you or your men harm *any* of these people *ever again* I shall personally return to this town and seek vengeance on each and every one of you." With superhuman strength he threw the soldier twenty feet down the street to land spread-eagled on a parked hay wagon.

The crowd of townsfolk cheered, waving and clapping with joy. Hector and Jonas helped Ebert to his feet as Drew shifted back to his human form as quickly as his body would allow. The change was uncomfortable as bones and muscle reset themselves, but within a minute the reversion was complete. He raised a hand to the people to quiet them.

"Do not let these men bully you," he shouted. "They are here to serve you. You number many more than they. Remember that, and find courage in it."

"Wergar!" called a voice. "You've returned!"

"No," shouted Drew over the cacophony. "I am not—"

"The Wolf! It's true!" cried another.

"Hail Wergar!"

"Hail the true king!"

"No!" shouted Drew over them. "I am not Wergar, I am not your king, and I am not a Wolf. I am just a boy!" The crowd quieted a bit.

"But you're one of them!"

"You're a Werelord!"

"I have a curse," cried Drew. "I'm a common man with an uncommon illness, and that is my burden. Nothing more. I am not who you think I am." The crowd didn't appear convinced. *"You* must stand up to your oppressors. You don't need me to do that when you have free will." With that he walked over to Hector, who had collected his cloak and now passed it back. Awkwardly he took it and fastened it around his throat once more. Ebert stared at the sword on his hip.

"You might be able to fool them," he muttered, "but you don't fool me, my lord. That there's a Wolfshead blade and they don't just give them to anybody. I fought for Wergar. I saw the great man." He whispered now. "And I'd recognize a son of his *anywhere*. . . ." He bowed to Drew, which wasn't missed by those who still stood about them, and staggered indoors.

Drew watched the villagers head back inside. He felt a warmth in his heart that hadn't been there before. It had felt good to help these people. But at what cost?

"I'm going to go and clean him up," said Hector, nodding after the injured old man. "It may be worth you checking in on Gretchen, seeing if she's all right."

Drew nodded as his friend followed the crowd into the inn. He stood there, speechless, as the townsfolk filed past, nodding to him as they went, others also bowing. The last to go in was Jonas.

"You ever need a roof over your head or a belly full of food, my lord," he said, smiling, "then look no farther than the Mermaid Inn. But remember your currency's no good here." He also bowed, before following the stragglers to the bar.

Drew shook his head. What had he done? His instincts told him to protect the innocent man, to stop the tormenting guards, nothing more heroic than that. But he'd underestimated the impact the sight of the Werewolf would have on the villagers. Thinking clearly now, he realized that the evidence of shape-shifting among the Werelords was probably rarely seen by the likes of these people. He'd certainly never witnessed such a sight growing up on the Cold Coast. *Well*, he thought, *if I've inspired them to stand up against these brutes who are pretending to guard them, then I might have done some good. But I have undoubtedly ruined our chances of getting to the coast unnoticed.* He dreaded what Hector might say to him in private as a result.

Scaling the staircase at the side of the inn, he walked across the landing to room six and rapped his bruised knuckles on the door. He was surprised Gretchen hadn't come out to watch with the noise and commotion that had gone on. There was no answer from the room, so he knocked again. "Gretchen?" Maybe she would mellow a little if she knew he had stood up for the underdog, something he'd always wished he had the strength—both mental and physical—to do. Now he had that confidence, but she'd probably see his fighting as another blatant disregard for her king's authority. There really was no pleasing the woman. Still no answer, so he knocked again.

"My lady?" he called, hoping to encourage a response. Nothing. He tried the handle: locked. Something wasn't right. Taking a step back he put his shoulder to the wood, barging it once, twice, and on the third occasion the mechanism smashed and the door swung in.

The room was as he'd expected to find it. A candle flickered on a simple side table, beside two beds with clean towels folded neatly at the foot of each. In the corner sat an empty tin bath. The window was open and the cold spring breeze sent the curtains fluttering into the room, smacking the timber walls gently.

She wasn't there.

He rushed over to the window and looked out. A drainpipe ran the length of the wall to the ground below, the tops of trees and bushes obscuring anything more. Had someone taken her? What fools they'd been to leave her unguarded! They should never have left her alone. If anything had happened to her . . . he didn't want to think about it.

That's when he saw a note on the pillow of one of the beds. He snatched it up. A folded letter. On the outside, in red ink, it read:

Hector & Hound

He grimaced at her dig. She really couldn't help herself. He unfolded it to reveal the message within.

Have gone. Shall find own way to Highcliff. Do not follow.
—Gretchen

Drew curled the note up in his fist, his head full of fresh worries, before sprinting for the door.

PART IV

THE WYRMWOOD

I

THE SHAMAN OF THE WYRMWOOD

DREW AND HECTOR crouched low in the reeds, ankle-deep in foul-smelling marsh waters, staring ahead toward the bonfire-lit village. Drew held his sword in a white-knuckled grip, his other hand shifting tall fronds to one side to better view the village's layout. There was no wooden palisade surrounding it, no guards on patrol, no sentry they'd have to slip past. Twelve large wattle-and-daub huts, all looking like they might fall over in a strong wind, surrounded the blazing fire. One larger hut sat to the rear of the village, the skeletal branches of the Wyrmwood's blackened trees waving above it like ghastly puppeteer's hands. The shaman's hut, Drew reasoned.

The whole village danced around the bonfire: man, woman, and child. The Wyldermen were either naked or wore filthy animal skins, their decorative bone necklaces jangling musically as they hopped, skipped, and jumped around the inferno. The men carried spears or bows, shaking them up to the sky as they whooped and chanted. Three elders sat to one side, beating out a steady rhythm on animal-skin drums.

Leading the dance was a man who could only be the shaman himself. His body was painted black, and he was naked but for a capercaillie-feathered headdress, crowned with a ram's skull. The horns twirled away from his face demonically as he danced in his own little inner circle, closer to the flames, in the opposite direction of his dancing villagers. He waved a staff over his head with both hands, one end tipped with a mighty flint dagger, the other with a human skull.

Drew turned to Hector, who stood trembling by his side. He looked over his shoulder. Seven men from Oakley stood behind, looking even more terrified than his friend, swords, cudgels, and crossbows in their hands.

"How did we get here again?" he whispered to the Boarlord.

When Drew had dashed downstairs to find Hector in the Mermaid Inn, he'd quickly recounted the news of Gretchen's absence and the two of them had set out immediately. Jonas had insisted that some of the villagers accompany them—the marshes could be perilous in daylight, let alone the dead of night. The Oakley men had acted as guides, speeding up the search for Gretchen. By splitting into two groups, they were able to cover more ground. Jonas took a group while Drew and Hector accepted the kind help of the seven volunteers.

With Piotr, Oakley's best woodsman, alongside Drew, their group had begun tracing the path of Gretchen's escape. Piotr's knowledge of the land was a great help, and with Drew's natural—and unnatural—ability to track, the two of them had led their companions onto her trail. She'd been heading west, roughly the correct direction for Highcliff, when her trail was interrupted, five miles or so from the village.

Surveying the muddy ground where her footsteps abruptly ended, Piotr had surmised that she'd been ambushed. They searched the immediate area but found no trace of her body, giving Hector and Drew fresh hope that they'd find her alive. When Drew asked who might have abducted her, Piotr had suggested the Wyldermen of the Wyrmwood.

It wasn't unheard of for the Wyldermen to kidnap rather than simply kill humans in these parts, dragging them back to their village for whatever ungodly acts they planned on performing. There was nobody else out here who could have taken her, the townsfolk said. If it had been a bear, or even wolves, as one of them had chanced with a nervous glance at Drew, there would be at least some remains. As if further evidence was needed, after a few hundred yards Piotr found a discarded barbed arrow in the muddy marshes, not dissimilar to the kind that had struck Master Hogan when Drew had first been found in the Dyrewood.

As the group advanced upon the Wylderman village in the dead of night, they heard the drums first and foremost, and saw the sky lit by the fire. Nearer and nearer they stalked, stumbling through the grim bog, helping one another as they went. Drawing close, they saw the bare black trees of the Wyrmwood reaching up to the sky, looming above the village. All seven of the townsfolk whispered or mouthed prayers to Old Brenn, superstitious, and rightly so, about the haunted forest. This was closer than any of them had ever been in their lives, and their bravery wasn't lost on Hector and Drew.

The Boarlord turned to his friend. "My dear cousin does seem to make a habit of causing chaos wherever she goes," he said, trying to lighten the mood.

Drew didn't smile. He looked at the men behind them. "You need not follow us," he said earnestly. "You've already done more than enough, friends. You have families and loved ones waiting for you back in Oakley. You should turn back now."

Piotr watched the others to assess their reactions, his heavy crossbow cocked at his hip. They all shook their heads.

"No," he whispered. "We're staying with you. We found courage tonight where there was none previously. We owe you this, Drew of the Dyrewood."

If they accompanied them into the Wylderman village,

Drew could imagine a situation where one or two—maybe all of them—might be injured or even killed. Was he ready to take that grim responsibility upon his shoulders?

"Very well, then," he replied. "But stay behind me at all times. I will do my best to protect you . . . if I can." All seven nodded their agreement.

Hector leaned in close to Drew, speaking softly in his ear. "Er, what exactly is your plan?" asked the Boarlord, clutching his dagger in podgy, untrained hands.

"Plan?" said Drew, unable to hide the fact that he had none. "Like I said, let me take the lead. Just stay behind me, Hector, please." He beckoned with his free hand for the others to follow and the party waded forward.

The marshes slowly gave way to harder ground, as the men ascended out of the waters, slipping quietly and unnoticed behind one of the huts. Three of the Oakley men had crossbows; the rest of them were armed with melee weapons.

"It's the shaman you need to speak with," Piotr whispered. "He's the chief here. He's the one who'll know where she is."

Drew nodded his understanding. "Reveal yourselves only if you must," he instructed. And with that, he stepped around the hut and into the bright burning light of the bonfire.

At first the Wyldermen didn't notice him, so lost in their ceremony were they, chanting and shaking as they leapt around the flames. All of a sudden there was a shriek from one of them;

Drew had been spotted. The drums ceased immediately. The Wyldermen stood there, motionless, for a prolonged moment.

The shaman turned slowly. The young Werewolf pulled his sword from its sheath, launching the Wolfshead blade into the ground in front of him. He spread his arms, showing his hands as if to prove he was unarmed. The shaman opened his mouth to reveal sharpened teeth, which he snapped menacingly before running his tongue over their length. Then, raising his skull-headed staff, he barked a command in a guttural tongue, and the Wyldermen rushed to ambush Drew.

Arms wrestled him, hands grabbed at him, as they lifted him over their heads and carried him closer to the shaman by the fire. Drew floated along a sea of seething fury as spear points jabbed at him, tearing his cloak. Eventually they threw him to the ground, inches away from the flames, gathering around in a huddle, spears held toward him, daring him to move an inch.

Hector peered around the corner of the hut, trying to see what had happened. The Wolfshead blade still wobbled where it had stuck into the earth. Beyond, the crowd had parted to allow the shaman through.

Drew didn't waste any time, for fear of what might happen if he paused. "You have a friend of mine captive," he explained. "I'm here to take her back. Hand her over and I promise you there'll be no bloodshed." Drew's challenge was bold and, still pinned to the floor, he eyeballed the shaman.

The Wylderman opened his monstrous mouth and laughed wildly. The others followed his lead, howling and hooting until he raised a hand to quiet them. They fell silent instantly as he began to speak, his voice clicking as the filed teeth caught against one another.

"She is gone," he said. "She is offered."

"Offered?" said Drew, looking around at the empty mud huts. "What do you mean, *offered*?"

"She is given to the Wyrmwood. She is for Wyrm."

The crowd whooped with victorious delight, hollering to the heavens as the shaman mentioned the Wyrm.

"Tell me where she is!" demanded Drew, brushing a jagged spear point away from his face. "For the love of Old Brenn, before it's too late."

The shaman spat at him, kicking earth in his face. "Do not mention the false god here. There is only one god. Vala the Wyrm."

This was graver than Drew had expected. He'd hoped Gretchen was being held captive in a hut here, awaiting some awful ceremony with the Wyldermen, but it appeared they *were* too late. He tried to rise to his feet, but two of the Wyldermen warriors stepped forward, driving their spears into him. One weapon bounced off his breastplate, but the other found a chink in his armor, slicing deep into his shoulder blade. He let out a cry of pain.

"Vala has her offering," said the shaman. "Now we have ours. Blessed be Vala!" His men yanked Drew to his feet.

◼ ◼ ◼ ◼ ◼

Hector and the villagers began to move out from where they hid. They'd heard Drew's scream, and now realized they had to act quickly. Weapons raised, they fanned out, those with crossbows taking points of cover while the other men crept forward tentatively. Hector was shoulder to shoulder with a middle-aged fisherman named Joss. The boatman clutched a long gaff in his hand, a fishing pole with a wickedly curved hook and blade at its end. This was a tool of the water, not a weapon for war, but the man held it before him with fearful determination.

The shaman dipped his hand into the wig of feathers that sprang from the ram's skull on his head, withdrawing a long slender flint blade that had been concealed.

"The heart!" he cried to the crowd. They were in his thrall, in awe of the power he held over them. "The heart is mine!" And, with that, he plunged the knife into Drew's chest.

Complete chaos broke loose.

Three crossbow bolts found their targets immediately, cutting down the Wyldermen where they stood. Hector let out a war cry of his own, before bowling into one of the Wyldermen on the outside of the huddle, Joss thrusting forward with his gaff and finding the back of another. He yanked the pole, pulling the dying man clear before spinning to face another. The other townsfolk joined clashes of their own as the crossbows were reloaded, but they could already see they were greatly outnumbered.

To Hector's desperate relief, the other search party arrived at the village, rushing in to join their friends in the fracas. Jonas, the innkeeper, wielded a heavy woodsman's ax, finding one of the Wyldermen instantly. Beside him one of the Oakley villagers toppled to the ground, a short-shafted arrow buried in his throat. Nearby another of his companions fell as a trio of Wylderwomen beat down on him with rocks and knives.

The reinforcements might have arrived, thought Hector, parrying the blows of a savage spear, but the battle was still going against them.

Drew cried out as the shaman forced the knife through his breastplate, the leather splitting as the flint blade tore into his chest. It met resistance when it hit his ribs, grating against bone as the Wylderman tried to work it through to Drew's heart. The whites of the shaman's eyes shone with delight, and he licked his teeth with anticipation. Drew knew the knife would not kill him outright, but it would incapacitate him, and death would then be only moments away, with or without his lycanthropy. He thought back to Baron Huth's words and tried to focus while his body contorted in self-defense.

Suddenly, the shaman's knife worked its way back out of Drew's chest as his rib cage began to expand, muscle appearing on muscle and bones shifting shape. He threw his arms back, sending the four men who were holding him pinioned flying into the bonfire with a chorus of screams. His jawbone distorted as his muzzle burst to the fore, his eyes turning amber in an instant. Hair sprouted over his body and he pulled off his cloak as the leather armor tumbled away, the catches releasing as they'd been designed to.

The shaman didn't let up, stabbing wildly at Drew with his knife, hacking crazily at the changing beast before his eyes. In moments Drew towered before him, the Wolf leading the counterattack as he let out a roar. With one clawed hand he knocked the knife from the Wylderman's grasp, while the other shot forward, straight and true, disappearing into the man's chest. His hand clasped around the shaman's beating heart, and in a sudden, savage motion he squeezed it into a closed fist.

"Heart," he growled at the man as the light disappeared from his wild eyes. He dropped him to the ground, lifeless, and looked around to see if anyone else would face him. The Wyldermen had withdrawn, looking in horror at the still form of their tribal leader on the ground and the beast that stood over him. Shouting and wailing, the women and children ran to their huts, with their menfolk retreating shortly afterward. The look of shock on their faces was new to Drew. Shock at the death of their shaman, and shock at the appearance of the monster. Drew let out a chilling howl, raising his head to the sky. It felt good. The men fled, dashing into their huts and slamming their doors behind them.

Drew's humanity scrambled its way back into his mind as the Wolf reveled in the savagery of the moment. *Remember the mantra,* came the words of Baron Huth. *Take dominion over the beast.* Slowly Drew relaxed, his body shrinking back to normal size as the townsfolk gave him a wide berth. Fragments of the horror he'd just inflicted darted across his mind. He stared down at his bloodied hand.

Hector appeared by his side.

"Wh-what have I done?" Drew stammered, staring at the shaman's prone body, a wave of nausea rising in his throat at the sight of the man's bloodied chest.

Hector picked up the Wolfshead blade. "Drew, do not search for answers or explanations," he replied. "The Wolf inside you is inhuman; controlling it takes a lifetime to master." He picked up his friend's discarded clothes, handing them back to him. "You did what was necessary."

A bolt of fear ran the length of Drew's body as he realized the true implications of his inheritance. It was not something to disrespect—or unleash—without serious repercussions. A part of his human mind finally shifted as he accepted the uninvited responsibility that his lycanthropy brought. Things would never be the same again.

"We have to move fast," said Hector. Behind them, the men of Oakley tended their wounded and picked up their dead.

Drew buckled his weapon belt around his middle, the simple act bringing him back to the present. "They've sacrificed her to the Wyrmwood, to this Vala woman you mentioned," he said, dressing quickly.

"Vala?" said Hector as they walked toward the remaining

Oakley villagers. "She's just a myth, a folktale that the people of these parts tell their children. If they've taken Gretchen into the Wyrmwood, then it's something else that's going to take her, not some mythical Wereserpent."

"Regardless, Gretchen's in danger out there. We need to find her, and fast." Drew took a step over the body of the shaman, eyeing the huts all around, but there was no sign of the Wyldermen. They had clearly been completely terrorized by the sight of the Werewolf attacking their shaman.

"Jonas, Piotr," said Drew to the others, bowing. He saw the bodies of two of their men. "Thank you for aiding us. I can't tell you how sorry I am for what happened to your friends."

"Don't apologize, my lord," said Jonas heavily, insisting on using a title when speaking to Drew, no matter how uncomfortable the youth found it. "These men joined us knowing full well what dangers they faced. They died honorably, and the people of Oakley will never forget them."

Drew and Hector nodded their respect. "Hector and I are not done," said Drew. "Gretchen has been sacrificed to the Wyrmwood, and we must try to find her. You should return to your homes while these Wyldermen are still in hiding."

At this the men looked to one another. They needed no more persuading to return to their town. To face their old enemies the Wyldermen was one thing, but to enter the haunted forest was to seek out a swift and violent death.

"Very well, my lord," said Jonas, bowing to both Drew and

Hector. "May Old Brenn guide you to your friend and bring the three of you out of the Wyrmwood safely."

"Thank you," replied Hector. "Your bravery will never be forgotten by us or our people." With that, the men turned, backing up out of the village before heading off into the swamps toward Oakley.

Drew had noticed that three separate trails left the encampment, running into the Wyrmwood. Gretchen could be down any one of them. He turned to Hector.

The Boarlord had emptied his backpack onto the floor and was busily rooting through bottles, pots, and vials.

"What are you doing?" asked Drew, looking about nervously. "We've been here long enough; we should get moving."

"Where to? We don't know where she is," said Hector, concentrating on his search.

"All the more reason why we should start looking, then."

"Look where?" said Hector. "The Wyrmwood is huge. We don't know where they took her."

"And we've no way of finding out now," admitted Drew, staring forlornly at the dead shaman on the floor.

Hector examined the body beside him thoughtfully. "That's where you're wrong, Drew. I have an idea."

2

THE MAGISTER

AS I'VE TOLD you before," said Hector. "I've read of rituals that used to be carried out long, long ago, where elders would commune with those who had died suddenly and unexpectedly in order to discover their final wishes. I understand many of the basic principles of the old magicks. There are simple cantrips that I've already perfected, such as ventriloquism, smoke clouds, minor illusions, and whatnots . . ."

"What is it you're trying to tell me?" asked Drew.

"I believe I can commune. I can speak with the dead," Hector answered plainly. "Specifically this fellow here," he went on, pointing to the dead shaman. "Give me a minute—no longer, I swear—with this creature under my command and I shall have the whereabouts of Gretchen."

Drew shook his head, wanting to dispel this fresh madness that crashed over him. The thought that he and a select few "nobles" were therianthropes had been hard enough for him to handle. To now hear that his warm, compassionate friend was some kind of budding necromancer threatened to tip him over the edge. Whatever the Boarlord was planning, surely it was beyond anything he'd read about in his books. Surely it was dangerous.

"So long as you know what you're doing," said Drew worriedly. He wished he had the same faith in the magicks that his friend had. But the truth was plain to see: they were at a loss as to where Gretchen was. Maybe if there were the slightest chance that Hector could get the answer he needed from the dead shaman the risk would be worth taking. Drew tried to convince himself, but a dark cloud had gathered in his heart. Regardless, he had to help his friend. "What do you need me to do?"

"Stepping back would be a good start," Hector said, smiling, as he stumbled to his feet. In his hand he had a dark-green glass vial. Popping the stopper off he started to shake a line of yellow powder out onto the ground in a circle around the shaman's body. He smartly restoppered the vial and dropped it into his satchel. "I have to act quickly, though. We may have already lost our chance. The soul can only be dragged back for a limited amount of time. Knowing my luck our window of opportunity is already closed. Keep your eyes on those huts; I don't want to be interrupted."

Drew stood with his back to the fire, Wolfshead blade in hand, watching the Wyldermen huts as Hector settled on the ground in front of the body and the powder circle.

"What is that stuff?" asked Drew. "It stinks!"

"Brimstone, Drew. Now be silent, please."

Drew was taken aback by his friend's authoritative tone, but didn't argue. He stood over him, alert, as the Boarlord pulled a long black candle from his bag and held the wick to the bonfire, letting it catch. Then he closed his eyes and began to chant. Allowing the sleeves of his shirt to fall back he opened his left palm skyward before him, all the while quietly chanting ancient words. Drew looked over his shoulder nervously.

Tipping the candle, Hector let the wax drip from its end, pooling in a hot puddle in the palm of his left hand. Wincing at the pain, he didn't miss a beat, keeping his chant going while the smoking wax dribbled onto his skin.

Drew shivered as a chill breeze suddenly fluttered through the settlement. He looked about as the shadows from the fire seemed to shift and distort. The black wax now filled Hector's palm, dripping between his fingers and down onto his lap. He stopped chanting. Curling his fist into a ball, he brought it sharply down on to the earth and thumped it once. Twice. Three times.

The body on the ground seemed to shudder briefly.

"Did you see that?" gasped Drew.

"Quiet, Drew!" whispered Hector, concentrating.

The shaman's body was moving, trembling. Drew looked around to see if they were being watched, but still there was no activity from the huts. He felt his knuckles pop as they tightened around the handle of the Wolfshead blade.

"Rise, creature, and answer to your master's bidding," said Hector. The Wylderman sat upright on the ground, fresh blood pouring from the wound in his chest. His skin had a deathly pallor, and splintered bones were visible in his open rib cage. His neck was loose, his head hanging against the chest. The figure sat motionless for a moment before his head snapped upright, eyes open, revealing pearly white lights within. After a moment of stillness his mouth broke into a fractured, grotesque grin, exposing bloody gums and sharpened teeth. A low, guttural laugh emanated from within. It sounded like death itself.

"Pig boy," he said, raising a slack arm up in Hector's direction, black drool spilling from his hideous mouth. A splintered finger pointed accusingly at the Boarlord. It recognized the legacy within him.

"I'm here, Hector. I'm right by your side," Drew whispered. "Do what you have to do and be quick."

"Where is she?" asked Hector with renewed confidence. "What have you done with Gretchen?"

"Piiig boyyy," chuckled the risen shaman, head lolling to one side at an impossible angle while his tongue lolled out, black and swollen. "Pig boy," it rasped. "No answers!"

"I brought you back and I command you *now*!" shouted Hector, punching his fist to the ground once more. "Where is she?"

Drew looked about; he could hear movement from within the huts. A door opened, just slightly, but enough for the occupants to be able to peek out. He looked back at the horrific scene as it played out before him. The animated corpse looked at the Boarlord with newfound respect, the pale white lights of his eyes narrowing. Drew felt repulsed, watching the dead body's unnatural movements, his twisted limbs jangling and his broken rib cage grinding with each foul motion.

"What have you done with her?" repeated Hector.

The shaman's slack jaw grated as he spoke: "Wyrm take her. Vala feeds. Serpent teeth bite. Snip! Snap! Snick! Snack!" The corpse's fingers made cutting motions.

Hector gulped. "Where can we find her? One more answer and I will release you from your bondage."

The Wylderman's glowing eyes narrowed and a jagged smile reappeared on his painted face. "Goooooood. Pig boy release . . ."

"Tell us where you took her!"

The creature craned forward and raised his bony finger to his lips. "Follow third path into the Wyrmwood. Path forks right at stone. Find her. Find her at Serpent's Tree."

Hector let out a deep breath, as if he'd been holding it in the whole time.

231

"Good work, Hector," said Drew, clapping him on the back. "Now quickly get rid of this thing so we can go."

The doors to the Wyldermen's huts were opening now as the villagers got bolder. Drew shifted the Wolfshead blade in his hand.

"Now," said Hector, addressing the creature, "return whence you came." He opened his palm and slapped it to the ground in the black wax. The shaman began to recline onto the ground, his bones crunching and grinding against one another in his chest as he relaxed back into a death pose. The brightness in his eyes began to fade.

Hector made to get up, and Drew stood back, relieved that the encounter had gone as smoothly as he'd hoped. There was certainly more to his friend than he could have ever imagined. Climbing up from his knees, Hector's left foot trailed backward, and Drew noticed the tip of the Boarlord's boot cutting a dusty gap through the line of brimstone. They turned to walk away.

The astonished scream of a Wylderman afforded them the briefest warning and then the corpse was upon them. Drew stumbled and spun, sword raised, his eyes wide with horror. Hector felt the deathly cold grip of the corpse's hands around his throat. What was happening?

Drew wavered, unsure of what to do. How could the shaman's body have leapt back to life? Hector let out a squeal of terror, trying to pull his face away as the Wylderman's corpse brought its mouth down toward his scalp. This was enough to snap Drew out of his inaction. He leapt forward to Hector's aid, bringing his elbow straight into the face of the monster. The shaman's head flew back and he released his grip, Hector falling forward into a slump on the ground. In one fluid motion Drew whirled the Wolfshead blade about his head in an arc, bringing it scything around with a tearing slash.

The body of the decapitated Wylderman collapsed in an awkward heap, while his head landed beside it, the eyes dull, black, and dead once more. Drew kicked it into the bonfire, which hungrily consumed it.

"Let's not take any risks," said Drew, helping his friend to his feet.

The other Wyldermen were edging out of their huts now, advancing slowly, but with their spears lowered. Hector scooped his bottles and vials back into his satchel, and the two youths retreated toward the third path, to be slowly swallowed by the darkness of the Wyrmwood.

3

LAIR OF THE SERPENT

THE LOW HOOT of an owl overhead startled Hector, and he stumbled as he shadowed Drew deeper into the Wyrm-wood. The bird looked down at him, silhouetted against the crosshatched black branches that supported it, bright eyes blinking as it followed the boys' passage. Their path weaved between tree trunk and vine, zigzagging into the dark and misty depths of the woods. Drew wondered whether the Wyldermen had followed them, but he suspected they were mourning the death of their shaman, and possibly in no hurry to encounter the Wolf for a second time.

The ground was wet and mulchy, rotten mosses squelching beneath their boots and large beetles and grubs scurrying for cover. The mist was thickening, making the path less clear.

Before long, they found the ground obscured by a thick blanket of fog. It hung in the air like a giant, milky cobweb. Drew looked about, searching for any signs of Gretchen.

Ahead of them, a large, dark standing stone rose from the mist, marking the fork in the trail. Drew stepped closer, running his hands over its surface. It appeared to be an enormous slab of flint. Drew bore right as the dead shaman had instructed, feeling his way through the haze, with Hector following close behind.

Unlike the Dyrewood, where the steady and regular sound of wildlife floated through the forest, a deathly silence emanated from the trees here, bar the occasional birdcall. Few other creatures called this forest their home, only those that crawled and slithered over the swampy floor and its skeletal branches.

Thoughts of the shaman troubled both the young men. Whenever Drew closed his eyes, he remembered the fight with the Wyldermen, the image of the man he had killed haunting his every thought. The rational part of his mind told him to see things clearly: The Wyldermen were trying to take his life. They meant to murder him. It was kill or be killed and he had done what he had to do to survive. Still, it didn't sit easily with him.

He looked over at Hector. His friend wasn't at all himself, and Drew was worried for him. A thin sheen of sweat coated his face, and he mopped his brow and throat intermittently. Drew could see the livid red marks around the Boarlord's throat where the shaman had gripped him. When he wasn't rubbing his throat, Drew spied him scratching at the dark sore on the palm of his left hand where the black wax had pooled.

A sweet smell of decay thickened the air of the Wyrm-wood. Occasionally the squawk of a carrion crow floated out of the branches above. They walked on slowly, blind to what lay ahead, stumbling and tripping as they went. Hector leaned against a tree trunk to catch his balance. The bark came away in his hand, rotten to the touch, as an enormous foot-long milli-pede scuttled over his fingers. A nervous shiver jolted through him as he yanked back his hand.

Drew kept ten paces ahead of Hector, relying on his wolf instincts to lead them to Gretchen. He fought to find a scent over the stench of moss, damp, and death. One tree came into focus, slightly larger than the others with a thicker black trunk. Something drew him toward it. His heart pounded in his chest, his ears almost popping as the blood thundered through his veins. A small, cowardly part of him that up until now had re-mained hidden told him, *Turn back, turn back and flee. Gretchen is already dead. If you continue, you, too, shall die.* The tree seemed to hold him in its grasp, controlling his thoughts, and he strug-gled to overcome its power. Crushing the dark thoughts, he glanced back to see Hector was backing up, stumbling away from the clearing in front of the thick-trunked tree.

"Hector," he whispered. "Come back. Stay. It's an enchant-ment, nothing more!"

Hector stopped his retreat but would not follow. He stood just within Drew's vision, a gray figure in the mists. Drew stepped up to the base of the tree and looked about. The bark was pitted and peeling, like the others, but there were marks carved into it. He squinted to see what they were, but was blind to the details. Running his fingers over them, he thought they were surely manmade. His ears pricked suddenly.

He heard something.

It was low, barely audible, but it was a noise that didn't belong in the Wyrmwood. It came from higher up in the tree. Drew was about to start climbing when he heard a new sound from the woods, a splashing in the swampy waters beyond his field of vision, as if something heavy had fallen out of a tree. Looking about, all he saw was mist up to his waist and the black silhouettes of trees.

"Hector," he whispered, "don't go anywhere."

"I'll wait right here," his friend replied, the nerves in his voice obvious.

Drew shivered and turned back to the tree. Digging his fingernails in for purchase he started to climb. Although the bark was indeed rotten, the bare wood of the trunk beneath provided enough stability for him to get a grip.

About twelve feet off the ground he found a great hole gaping in the trunk, revealing itself to him as he rose higher and higher. Small insects scurried out of the way or sometimes into it. The hole was large enough for him to lean into the rotten chasm. What was stopping him? He craned forward, disappearing up to his waist.

The stench of death was strong in the hollow, his fingertips finding the corpses of small animals and birds piled up at the bottom, wriggling with maggots and buzzing with flies. Drew reached to grab a hold of the tree's innards for support, but found his hand close around something cold and hard. Taking a grip, he hauled it out, his fingers clenching around bony ridges. In his hand was what appeared to be a human skull. Recoiling, he dropped it out of the hole where it landed with a dull squelch in the mud. *If this is where humans have been held before . . .*

His hand searched through the gloom, this time connecting with something soft and clammy. Instinctively he pulled his hand back in shock. He reached forward once more and closed his hand around the soft flesh. It flinched at his touch.

"Gretchen?" he whispered. His question was greeted with a murmur of recognition. His hands continued up to find the girl's face. There was a vine around her mouth, tied tight to keep her gagged. Feeling around, Drew found other vines that held her fast.

"Wait. I'll get you free," he said in the darkness.

He strained at the vine that gagged her first, the fleshy membrane ripping as he tore it apart. Gretchen's head lolled forward, the young Werefox barely conscious after her ordeal. Drew continued to rip the others loose, every muscle straining as he struggled to free the girl. One after another, the vines split apart, sickly sap spattering the two of them in the process. Finally, Gretchen fell into Drew's arms, and the boy slowly began to climb out of the tree, mindful of his footing as he carried the Werefox over his shoulder.

Slipping and sliding, Drew's feet felt down into the mist for footholds as he used his free hand to grip the withered trunk for support. Moss and lichen came away under the weight of his step and he felt his legs go from under him. The two fell back into the mist, landing on the wet ground with a thump. Blind in the bank of fog, Drew felt for Gretchen, lifting her up.

In the pale light he looked her over. The Werefox's face was badly bruised around her left eye socket, the lip below bloated and broken. Hooking his thumb and forefinger, Drew scraped earth, bark, and vine from the girl's mouth, clearing her airways. She coughed, her chest heaving as Drew took her weight.

"It's all right, Gretchen. I've got you now."

The red-haired girl mumbled something inaudible, leaning heavily into Drew, her head falling forward. Drew winced as he saw two deep lacerations at the back of her neck where the top of her spine was visible through her torn and tattered scarlet dress. A thick ocher liquid oozed from the wounds, yellow and luminous against the girl's pale flesh. Venom?

Drew hefted Gretchen back over his shoulders. He had to get her out of here. Hector would have something in his satchel that would take care of her injuries. He started forward, wading through the fog as he stumbled through puddles and tripped over every root. Gretchen was a dead weight across his back, all arms and legs, limbs trailing against the young Werewolf.

He stopped.

His ears pricked at the sound of something in the darkness. He could see the silhouette of Hector waiting farther away in the mist, back the way he'd come, but this was something else. Only bare branches met his gaze as he scoured the area around him. He checked back to the huge petrified tree that Gretchen had been imprisoned in. What was the sound? Calling out to Hector would only alert whatever was out there to their presence.

He heard the sound again: a heavy, wet thump that trailed through water. *Splash!* There was something there, only it was *beneath* the mists. He looked about to get his bearings again. Hector was gone. There was no sign of him where he'd been standing only seconds earlier. Where had he disappeared to? Had the strange sounds spooked him into leaving?

Drew quickened his pace now, keen to be away from the grim, wooded swamp and back on firmer ground. His legs pumped as his stride lengthened, and he ignored the discomfort that carrying Gretchen brought with it. Gritting his teeth he waded into the mist, the thick blanket rolling in waves against his chest as he cut a path through it. His heavy breathing ruined any chance of hearing the sound again; he just hoped he was leaving it behind.

He cursed as a root caught around his ankle. As he pulled his leg to tear it free, what he'd assumed was a root quickly tightened its grip. Drew's eyes widened with horror. With a sharp tug, the boy was yanked back violently, Gretchen flying from his grasp as he was dragged beneath the fog.

4

THE ENEMY IN THE MIST

WHATEVER IT WAS that had a hold of Drew dragged him kicking and flailing at least ten yards over the forest floor before finally releasing him with a splash in the middle of a large, swampy puddle. Drew kicked at his attacker but connected with thin air as he struggled to right himself in the dirty water. Body jarring with pain, he rolled over and attempted to stand, still unable to see a thing in the blinding mist. Before he could rise he felt a heavy impact in the small of his back. He flew forward, spread-eagle into the puddle once more.

Drew felt the full force of his attacker's body weight on his back. He fought against it, his face submerged in the filthy, stagnant water. He choked as great gulps of liquid rushed down his throat and into his lungs. His enemy would not relent, bearing down, coiling and gripping around his waist as it arched and bucked against him. Trapped under the water, he felt tiny lights exploding before his eyes as his life threatened to fade away.

Not like this, he thought. *Not like this.*

With the last of his human strength he focused his energies into channeling the unnatural powers within him. The lycanthrope rose fast in response. His jaw strained as his teeth elongated, and his spine cracked, breaking his assailant's grip. With a mighty heave he thrust his shoulders back and his enemy tumbled loose, allowing Drew to snatch huge breaths of air. Leaping to his feet he spun about, clawed hands raised as he scoured the swampy forest for his attacker. Every sense tingled and his body trembled with anticipation. His blood was up. His yellow eyes narrowed as he snarled.

Rising out of the mist before him was the stuff of nightmares. A great serpent snaked up into the air, swaying one way and then the other as its black body coiled back on itself, revealing a ribbed, purple underside that glistened in the dim moonlight. From the tip of its flat, wide head to where its body disappeared below the milky fog, it must have been thirty feet in length. Drew could only wonder at how much more of the beast remained below the surface of the mist.

Its jaws opened, a blood-red tongue flicking at the air as its enormous fangs snapped menacingly. Drew jumped back as they slammed shut where he'd stood a moment ago. This was bigger than any living thing he'd ever seen before, anything he could even imagine facing. It rushed at him again and he leapt behind a tree for cover. The tree provided little defense as it splintered beneath the giant snake's impact. Drew rolled across the floor in a shower of broken timber, springing up to face his opponent. The monster's eyes flashed before him, like giant emeralds burning with a hateful inner fire.

"Vala?"

Her name was quickly out of his mouth, a bold challenge before he knew exactly who, or what, he was facing. The creature relented briefly, rising up again to survey its smaller enemy. Drew marveled at the size of it. If this was Vala, then whatever control over his shape-shifting ability he had, or indeed whatever control any of the other Werelords had, was far surpassed by what she had done. She had fully metamorphosed into her werecreature, not a single element of her human self still remaining. Except for her voice.

"Sssssso, little dog," rasped Vala, her voice steaming with venom, deeper and throatier than anything he'd heard in his life. "You crawl before my court, in my palace. Why do you ssssscurry to your doom?"

"I've come for Lady Gretchen," he explained, his own voice mingled with a deep growl. He strained to control his lycanthropy and remain calm at the same time, for fear that the animal would overtake and block his human judgment again. He needed to be able to reason with the Werelord. "Your Wyldermen mistakenly brought a Werelady to you as an offering. I

shall take her from here and be away from your palace immediately."

"Missssssssstakenly?" she hissed. "Meat isssss meat, little
dog. Human or therian flesh, it isssss all the ssssssame to me. It
appearsssss," she went on, beginning to raise a hidden coil from
the mist, "that I have an even bigger feassssst to enjoy now!"

Rising out of the bank of fog behind her came a length of
her shining black body, curled elegantly around the body of
Hector. His face was obscured, the coil firm across his face and
lower body, as his hands struggled in vain to pull and push the
monster away. Drew could only watch as the Boarlord's fingers
scrabbled against the serpent's skin, failing time after time to
catch a grip. He was suffocating.

"Let him go!" he yelled, pulling the Wolfshead sword
from its scabbard in a hairy, clawed hand. "You're a monster!"
The hackles on his neck rose up as his eyes searched her huge
frame, looking for any weak spot. Hector's arms were gradually
falling limp.

"We all are, darling," she cried back. "Only ssssome of ussss
know that'ssss no bad thing." She arched up, tongue flicking out
once more as her huge eyes narrowed. "Enough talk now, little
dog, little lordling. You die here tonight. Join your friendsssss
and fall before the Wyrm Goddessssss!"

"I'm no dog," snarled Drew. "And I'm no lordling." Throwing his arms back he leapt high into the air toward her, catching the Wyrm by surprise. He landed on her body beside Hec-

tor, slashing down with the Wolfshead blade and tearing a great rip into the coiled black skin. Pale white flesh lit up from within as dark blood welled out. Instantly Vala dropped the Boarlord, bucking her body to send her tail whipping around, striking Drew and sending him flying through the clearing. His sword spun from his grasp and landed with a resounding clatter against a tree trunk.

Drew was on his feet immediately and sprang forward, straddling the huge serpent around her underside, just below her jawline. As her mouth snaked down at him, trying to get a clear bite, he returned the favor, canines tearing at the ripe flesh of her underbelly. Try as she might her great jaws couldn't reach the Werewolf, narrowly missing his head as they snapped shut again and again. Gouts of thick, crimson blood sprang forth from the serpent's belly. She let out a wailing scream that seemed to make the forest shake. Her body convulsed violently, sending Drew bouncing off. He landed a great distance away on all fours, exhausted by his encounter.

The Wereserpent crashed and flailed around the misty clearing, disappearing beneath the surface of the fog momentarily before rising skyward to thrash in the air. Her tail came up, flicking and rattling as she spasmed and shook.

Her death throes, Drew hoped, looking about for Hector and Gretchen.

He combed the surface below the mist for bodies, instead

recovering his own cloak and armor, which had been discarded as he shifted form under attack from Vala. Finally finding the Werefox beneath the fog, Drew bent to pick the girl up, hooking his clawed hands under her arms and dragging her away to safety. When he'd hauled her clear, he returned to find Hector, who was already trying to scrabble free, having slowly regained consciousness. He was overjoyed to see Drew, who pulled him to his feet. As the pair stumbled toward higher and more stable ground, the cries that signaled Vala's demise disappeared into the background of the Wyrmwood. Reaching Gretchen, Drew lifted her onto his shoulders and they made their escape. Drew spared what energy he had to control his lycanthropy—it was too soon to relinquish the inhuman power it gave him.

"My sword," said Drew suddenly. "I dropped my sword!"

"You'll have to leave it," said Hector, rubbing his throat. "Find another one."

"I can't," said Drew. "It's my father's sword. I won't leave it." He hoisted Gretchen off his shoulder and placed her carefully on the ground. "Wait here."

"Drew!" cried Hector desperately, but it was no good. The Werewolf was running back to the clearing, stumbling through the mire.

Drew's alert eyes scoured the mists, looking for Vala. Her body would be beneath the fog, lying still in the brackish swamp. He spotted his sword, the blade buried in the rotten bark of a nearby trunk. Wading over, he grasped the handle and tugged hard. The Wolfshead blade came free, sending him staggering backward as a frighteningly chill wind blew through the clearing.

Momentarily, the mists recoiled, swirling out of the way to reveal the swamp that lay beneath. He could see now that the pool was littered with the bones and carcasses of hundreds of offerings, both animal and human. The surface shimmered, deep red blood spreading through the filthy waters. But there was no sign of the Wereserpent. Drew ran from the scene, away from the monster's lair and back to his companions. Hector was inspecting the wounds on Gretchen's back, his face grim. Drew lifted the Werefox in his arms and they continued their escape.

By the time the three arrived at the outer edges of the Wyrmwood, Drew was ready to collapse. Every muscle in his body cried out for rest, each and every step proving more exhausting than the last. He and Hector had taken it in turns to carry Gretchen's prostrate body, but his strength was fading at an alarming rate. Without instruction his body had returned to its human form.

As the sun slowly began to paint the sky pink in the east, dawn finally showing her face, Hector pressed on, urging Drew forward with words of encouragement. Drew could still taste the Wereserpent's blood in his mouth, the metallic flavor tinged with something else—toxins that made up Vala's poisonous bite. They were battling his efforts, sending dizzying waves of nausea that had him on his knees intermittently, his body weight seeming to quadruple as the venom took effect. He could hear the thundering of Hector's footsteps as occasionally his shadowy form passed before him, the bottles in his satchel clinking and Gretchen slumped across his shoulders. When Drew's body finally gave up on him and he slipped into uncon-sciousness, he could hear the sound of birds singing in flight as they raced across an open meadow.

PART V

WESTLAND

I

THE BOAR TAKES THE REINS

THE FARMER RAISED his scythe high in the air, about to strike a blow, and paused. The spring sun was high overhead, its refreshing rays beaming down onto the back of his neck and sweat-drenched shirt. He looked out over his crop of barley. An empty cart came trundling down the nearby Little Lane, pulled by a great gray mare that had seen better days. He and his son had been working the field since an hour before sunrise, and this was the first soul they'd seen all day. The boy stood up from where he was bagging the grain to follow his father's gaze. Was it someone they knew? Both father and son waved in the direction of the driver, a stranger, who returned their gesture in an instant. Smiling, the farmer raised the curving blade once more before slicing it down through the crops.

252

Hector glanced back as he passed the two workers in the field. His passage along the road in Westland had raised no suspicion, so he was still hopeful that the king had raised no hue and cry. If he had, Hector figured, it hadn't reached Merrydale. He gave the reins a quick crack in his hands and Esther, the old nag, picked up her pace.

He'd managed to buy the horse and accompanying cart from a farmer on the edge of the Bott Marshes. Hector had steered the old gray mare along the farmer's track, retrieving Gretchen and Drew from where he'd left them on the Little Lane.

There had been no option but to leave the two of them hidden in the reed beds at the side of the road. He was relieved to find that no predators or scavengers had found their bodies; at a glance, both appeared to be dead. Hefting them into the back of the cart, he'd checked their vital signs, wrapped them tightly in their cloaks, and then pulled a rough oilskin over them that he'd additionally persuaded the opportunistic farmer to part with.

The Little Lane ran all the way from the farmlands on the edge of the Bott Marshes through the heart of Westland. It was really only used by farmers and traders who needed to visit the small huddles of villages that populated the area. It had been almost a week since the trio had escaped the forest, and in that time Hector had only Esther for companionship. If Hector and, more important, his satchel had not been present when Gretchen and Drew escaped the haunted forest, they would both have been dead by now. Not only was Hector aware of how to treat poisons, he had the medicines and antivenoms with him, and was able to start administering treatment straightaway. Applying poultices to the bite wound on Gretchen's neck had been relatively easy, and it had drawn the poisons out while speeding up the healing of the savage wound, working alongside her body's superhuman ability to repair itself. Being a Werelord had a great many benefits.

With Drew it had been more complicated; the Werewolf had ingested some of Vala's poisonous blood, and there was no drawing the toxin from his system. All Hector could do was pour his potions down Drew's throat, keep him warm while he rode out the fever, and hope he'd pull through. He was then able to use some of his ointments on his own left hand, where the small wound from the black wax was still stubbornly refusing to heal. But it appeared he didn't have the right remedies for this particular burn.

The incident with the shaman's corpse still weighed heavily on his mind. His feelings of pride and achievement had quickly evaporated when the monster had leapt back to life. What had gone wrong? He'd read the books, memorized the manuscripts, and followed all the cantrips. The act of summoning the dead shaman had been smooth and problem-free. It was the release of the monster that had been botched. If he hadn't run his foot through the brimstone and broken the warding symbol, it could have been prevented. He was determined to learn from it, though, and didn't plan on making the same mistake again.

In the past day Gretchen's condition had improved rapidly, and now she was dozing next to Drew in the back of the cart. She'd been on her feet that morning, and had even helped Hector tidy the camp away before they'd set off. Though still sickly, she was through the worst of it, which was more than could be said for Drew. Hector looked back at the Werefox—she was curled up next to Drew, her head on his chest. Whether she knew it or not, her body warmth was aiding Drew's recovery, keeping his temperature steady as his body raged with the fever.

As the afternoon sun slowly disappeared beyond the hills and ocean in the distance, Hector guided the old horse from the lane, pulling up beside an abandoned barn that overlooked the Barleymow. Unhitching the cart, he let Esther wander down to the banks of the river to drink and graze upon the tall grass that flourished there. Gretchen stirred in the back of the wagon, and Hector watched her opening her eyes to see Drew's face next to hers, his eyes closed in a deep sleep. She didn't immediately jump up in horror; in the past, she might have done so. Instead, she took the oilskin and tucked it in around him where she had been lying before sliding off the back of the cart.

"Morning," said Hector, as he set off into the hedgerow, pulling loose branches, twigs, and dried dead grass from where they'd gathered around its base.

"Morning indeed," replied Gretchen, stretching with a great yawn. "How long have I slept?"

"Since midmorning. You went straight through lunch. I say lunch—it was just a couple of big fat reds that I pulled from a generous apple tree. You'll find one on the front seat if you're hungry."

The Werefox found the apple and tucked into it heartily as Hector continued to collect the makings of a fire. Returning to the front of the barn, he set about assembling it, trying to remember how Drew had done it.

"How are you feeling, Hector?" asked Gretchen, finishing the last of the apple. She came over to kneel by his side as he started to arrange the wood.

"Oh, I'm fine, cousin, fine," he replied, keeping himself busy.

"Do you need to talk about anything?" she asked. "Your father? There's no need to bottle anything up like those life-saving potions in your satchel. You can talk to me."

He couldn't hide from the fact that his own twin brother had betrayed him. His dear, beloved father had been murdered, and his killer was still out there. Hector wanted revenge, but he had nothing to say on the subject to Gretchen, regardless of the offer and her good intentions.

"No," he said, patting her arm. "I'm fine, really. I think I've got things straight up here." He tapped his forehead. Taking the tinderbox he started trying to light the fire, striking the flint with the steel.

"What are you going to do?" she asked.

"Light the fire, of course," he replied, smiling.

"No," she said, shaking her head. "I mean about the future. Where shall you go? I know what was going on back in Redmire. You were planning to head north, weren't you? To Icegarden?"

Hector's cheeks flushed with color. For her to acknowledge that he was a fugitive alarmed him. He was acutely aware that she was marrying into the king's family. If she wasn't to be trusted, anything he said might put his safety in jeopardy. He kept his eyes on the tinderbox in his fumbling grasp.

"I honestly don't know," he replied, and he was telling the truth. He hadn't figured out where he'd head to now that his and Drew's plans had gone up in smoke like his father's hall. At the inn at Oakley the two youths had briefly discussed the idea of boarding a ship from All Hallows Bay, but beyond that they had no solid idea.

"I just wanted you to know, Hector," she said, squeezing his hand to reassure him, "whatever you do, wherever you go, please don't worry. I shan't tell him. You have my word."

It went without saying that she meant the king. Gretchen had never lied to him in the past, and he didn't think she was about to start now. He squeezed her hand back in return, a silent thank-you.

"You were very brave, Hector, coming after me like that."

"Brave?" he asked, shaking his head. "No, I just followed

Drew. He's the one who bounded after you; it was all I could do to keep up with him. He's the one who saved you. Not me."

"Well, I don't care what you say, Hector," she said, leaning forward to plant a full-lipped kiss on his cheek. "You're my hero, and you saved our lives. If you hadn't known how to heal us, we'd be worm food of a different variety by now."

He blushed. She clapped him on the back before sitting back once more, drawing her knees up to her chin and looking at him pensively.

"You do realize the king will be searching for us, don't you?" she said. "Prince Lucas won't rest until he has me safely in Highcliff, and I suspect they're looking for the two of you as well."

"I know," said Hector, fear rising in his voice. "But what can we do? We have to keep running and just stay alert. I've decided that once we get to the coast at All Hallows Bay we can find passage on a ship and leave you there in safety."

"You could make things easier by letting me go now," said Gretchen. "They'll be looking for three of us, two young men and a woman. With a reward on top for information, it's only a matter of time before someone reasons who we are. How long have we been traveling now? Seven days?"

"But we can't let you go. It's too dangerous out here and we're too far from anywhere that would be safe to leave you. Please, Gretchen, just wait until we get to All Hallows Bay. The authorities there will have you whisked off to Highcliff and Prince Lucas in time for your wedding."

At the mention of her wedding she fell quiet, staring at Hector's hands as he repeatedly struck flint against steel pathetically.

He noticed her subdued look. "You know," he went on, "you could always come with us. That is, if you're having second thoughts about marriage?"

"No," she said, a little too quickly. "My place is in Highcliff. I'm betrothed to Prince Lucas, and I must not break that oath."

"But you know how cruel he is, Gretchen. I traveled with the prince. The man is a villain, a cruel and wretched fellow. What life are you going to have with him?"

"I shall be queen," she said, a glimmer of petulance rising in her voice. "Once I am queen I can set about righting any wrongs that have been done by Lucas and his father. He'll listen to me. I'm going to be his wife, his partner."

"You really think that?" Hector shrugged. "He may have feelings for you, but his father wants you to marry his son because of the great wealth Hedgemoor has at its disposal. The fortune your father accrued that sits in the vaults of your palace will be frittered away by King Leopold in no time at all."

"I resent that slur on my ability to protect what my father worked for, Hector," she snapped. "Regardless," she said, "my place is in the court of Highcliff, not running from one flea-ridden village to the next with a mongrel Werelord in tow."

He looked at her hard. "See. There you go again," he said. "After all Drew has done for us."

"I'm thankful that he saved me from the Wereserpent," she said. "But if he hadn't abducted me in the first place I'd never have *been* in a situation where I needed saving."

"He did what he had to do. It was impulsive, possibly rash. If he hadn't grabbed you, it wouldn't have just been him that was killed—it would have been me too. Drew has saved my life on more than one occasion already in the brief time I've known him."

"I just find it hard to trust him, Hector," she said. "There's something about him that makes me nervous. Perhaps it's the wolf in him."

"Duke Bergan has no trouble trusting him," replied Hector. "Would you say he is a poor judge of character?"

"What circumstances could possibly lead Bergan to trust him?" Gretchen asked.

"You won't have heard," Hector went on, pleased, "but Drew even saved Duke Bergan's daughter's life. She might have died in the Dyrewood if he hadn't been there."

"Whitley?" said Gretchen. The surprise was clear in her voice. "What was she doing in the woods?"

Hector waved his hand dismissively. "She's training to be a scout. It's not what her father wanted, but it's all she wants to do. Bergan's men are doing their best to keep it quiet, to protect her from any of his enemies who may see an opportunity."

"She always was peculiar," sighed Gretchen.

"She's strong-willed is all, an individual. Nevertheless," Hector went on. "Drew saved her life out there, and her master's too. Got the two of them safely to Brackenholme when they were being hunted by Wyldermen."

"It just seems he causes chaos wherever he goes," she said.

"Maybe out of the chaos he will bring order. There are prophecies that say as much, you know?"

"Prophecies about Drew?" exclaimed Gretchen, incredulous.

"I've not mentioned it to him, but some of the old predictions speak of a Champion of Light, a force for good. He'll come to the Seven Realms when all the usual portentous stuff supposedly happens—the realms broken, the dead walking the earth, brothers against brothers—you know the kind of thing. Now whether you believe *all* the prophecies or not, there are some that the magisters all agree on. A champion *will* come, Gretchen. And it might be Drew."

"It might be you, Hector, for all you know. I wouldn't hold too much faith in the ramblings of a bunch of long-dead elders."

"If more folk knew of his existence it could really change things in the Seven Realms. Imagine if people knew there was an alternative to Leopold? But how can I explain that to Drew? He isn't ready for that. I don't think he really understands how big a deal it is—not just his being a Werewolf, but being the son of Wergar. Maybe his appearance out of nowhere into our world will be the catalyst we need for change." The Boarlord shook his head. "I don't know, but he's a good man, be he the last son of Wergar or a simple shepherd boy."

"You really like him, don't you?" Gretchen said, not in a mocking tone but a thoughtful one.

"You know I do," he said smartly. "A life on the road with Drew as a companion has got to be better than a life of servitude to King Leopold and his court."

"Perhaps . . ." she said, searching for the right words. "Perhaps he and I got off on the wrong foot. I know I can sometimes be . . . difficult," she said.

Hector opened his mouth to object, but she raised a hand to silence him. "Thanks, cousin, but you don't need to keep walking on eggshells around me. I know I have a temper, and I realize I'm used to getting my own way. It isn't something I'm proud of."

Her head dropped and Hector found he was feeling sorry again.

"The idea of being a princess seems to come easy to you, Gretchen," he whispered, rubbing her back with sympathy. She smiled, wearily.

"It's my duty," she sighed. "I won't lie. I can tell you that a great deal of the time it's fun and exciting. But occasionally I long for the freedom that our friend there has had in his life." She gestured in the direction of Drew.

"See," Hector said, giving her a playful dig in the ribs with an elbow. "You're calling him your friend as well now!" He chortled as he carried on trying to get to grips with the tinderbox. Gretchen chewed her lip, deep in thought.

"How are you getting on with that?" she asked, after watching him struggle awhile with the flint and steel. Try as he might, he could not conjure a spark.

"Not terribly well," he grumbled. "There must be a knack to it."

"Let me try," came a voice over their shoulders. Drew was sitting upright at the end of the cart. How long had he been listening to their conversation? Sliding out of the wagon, he landed gingerly on the floor, his weakened legs buckling as he clutched a wheel for support. Hector rose instantly and dashed to his side. Gretchen remained where she was, watching.

Hector helped Drew as he wobbled over to the unlit fire like a newborn fawn. After gently lowering himself to the ground, Drew picked up the flint and steel in his trembling grip and started to strike them. On the third attempt a clutch of sparks flew through the air and landed on the dried grass that Hector had gathered at the fire's base. He silently leaned low to cup his hands around the smoking embers, shielding the breeze from it while he directed puffs of his own breath onto the fuel. Slowly it took the heat, the grass starting to smoke before a bright orange flame suddenly sprang into life. The other two watched on as Drew effortlessly repositioned the bundle of dried grass beneath the kindling. Hector wasted no time in getting the pan from Drew's backpack and dashing off to the banks of the Barleymow to fill it with water. It had been over a week since he'd had a cup of tea, and he wasn't going to miss this opportunity now.

"How are you feeling?" Gretchen asked Drew.

"Like death," he replied, sitting back exhausted. "What happened? The last thing I remember was getting out of the Wyrmwood and then . . . nothing."

"You'd ingested Vala's venom. Without Hector and his medicines we would both be dead."

"I owe him my life, then," said Drew, watching the Boar-lord as he bounced along the riverbank looking for a place to crouch and fill his pot.

"And I appear to owe you both mine," said Gretchen stiffly. Drew was taken aback, quite unprepared to hear such gratitude from the Werefox. "It was very good of you to come after me, Drew of the Dyrewood. Thank you."

He nodded his appreciation. "And I could do nothing less, having jeopardized your life in the first place, for which I apologize," he said eventually. "I'm sure you're keen to get to High-cliff and out of our company," he added.

"And what's that supposed to mean?" she said brusquely, folding her arms.

"You'll want to get to the court? For the wedding? Remember?" said Drew, unsteady with the tone of her response. His head still swam.

"Oh, the wedding! How could I forget? Because I couldn't possibly want to spend another minute in the company of a couple of outlaws, could I?" she exclaimed. "All I could possibly be interested in is Highcliff, isn't that right? I'm just a spoiled little girl, aren't I?"

She rose to her feet and stormed away from him, kicking up dust in her wake that settled about him, making him cough and cover his mouth. As Hector reappeared with his pot of water, he looked down at Drew incredulously.

"What have you said now?" he asked, exasperated. "I thought you were making a fresh start!" He watched her go.

"Nothing!" said Drew, startled by the change in Gretchen's mood. "Nothing at all. I simply said she'd want to be rid of us as soon as she could."

"You know," said Hector, "I despair with you two, I really do . . ."

Hector placed the pot of water on the fire and shuffled through his satchel to find some tea leaves. Drew craned his head around to see where Gretchen had gone. The girl was impossible. She'd clambered into the cart and settled down sulkily.

The night drew in and Gretchen wouldn't move again until Hector took her a mug of steaming hot tea. Following that she wouldn't say another word to Drew for a further two days. It was a long road to the coast.

2

THE DROWNING MAN

CLINGING TO THE EDGES of the turbulent White
Sea lay the bustling port of All Hallows Bay. Hector saw four
great, long piers running out into the choppy waters like
wooden fingers, grasping for purchase in the frothing foam
as the sea surged against them. Boats and ships of all shapes
and sizes jostled for room and, at the docks, sailors and fishermen milled about, eager to attend to their business. The town
itself crowded around the sickle-shaped bay; ramshackle timber buildings that huddled against one another flanked the
Tallstaff Road. Smoke billowed from chimney stacks, casting a
cloud over the port like a gray halo.

The cobbled streets were lined with stalls and carts as
farmers, tradesmen, and locals sold their wares to visiting mer-

chants destined for foreign lands. There was a lively mood in the town that was infectious—laughter pealed from inside taverns, and music carried out of inn windows into the streets below. All the shades and colors of the world could be found in All Hallows Bay, and it was no secret that, for the right price, a ship's captain could take a person anywhere.

They passed a number of soldiers who wore the red cloaks of the Lionguard. Patrolling in squads of four or five men, they stuck to the main avenues of All Hallows Bay, staring down everyone who passed, be it on foot or on cart. These weren't fit to call themselves protectors of the people; intimidation was a tactic for thugs. Drew felt his anger rising. Keeping their heads down inside their hoods, Drew and Hector piloted their wagon past without attracting attention. Begrudgingly, Gretchen had conceded to the boys' request to stow her away under the oilskin, thereby reducing their visible party by one. To the soldiers the two must have simply looked like a couple of farmers on a visit to town. Judging by the manner in which the men of the Lionguard strolled through the crowded streets and people quickened their step to give them a wide berth, it seemed the soldiers could act with impunity here. They weren't actively searching for the trio, it appeared. Perhaps the hunt was still concentrated along the banks of the Redwine after all.

Drew had asked a street seller where they might find a likely bar in which to negotiate passage across the White Sea. The heartiest recommendation had been the grisly-named

Drowning Man. Just off the main promenade, it was the largest tavern the town had to offer and was the first port of call for captains looking to pick up crew, commissions, and passengers. Navigating the bottom of the Tallstaff Road between a mountain of crates and barrels, Hector steered the horse onto the wide boulevard and followed the directions they'd received.

Though the darkening evening sky cast shadows over the town, the Drowning Man was unmissable. Four stories high, it was easily the tallest building in town, and each floor jutted out even farther into the street above its heavy, squat base. A huge, irregular slate roof hung down from above like a witch's peaked hat. Hector guided Esther up to a corner of the building, jumping down to fasten her reins to a hitching post. Drew craned his head into the back, tapping the oilskin and the shape that was hidden beneath it.

"We're here," he whispered, loud enough for Gretchen to hear.

Gretchen slid out of the wagon, the hood of Hector's cloak firmly up around her head, her striking red hair tied back and out of sight. Her clothes were torn and tattered beneath the unremarkable cloak, as were all of their garments.

Above their heads a large painted sign swung noisily from its iron ring brackets. The illustration depicted a hand reaching out of a stormy sea, the owner destined for a watery grave.

Briefly checking one another over, the three of them entered the tavern.

Two bars faced them upon entering the inn. Drew chewed his lip. To their left was a sedate affair that was the retiring room of any patrons who had secured one of the tavern's few rooms for the night. Through the warped glass panels of the door Drew could see serious-looking men sitting around tables, discussing trade routes and inventories while they downed ale by the tray-ful. To their right was the much rowdier public bar, with alcoves dotted about the wide walls of the room. A long counter filled the farthermost wall, lined with hardy-looking men throwing drinks down their throats. A huge open fireplace filled the mid-dle of the room, where a great copper-canopied chimney hung down, catching the fire's smoke and whisking it away.

Drew silently nodded right to his friend. Hector opened the door, and the three of them entered unnoticed.

A middle-aged woman wearing a white apron and bonnet bustled past the trio with a tray of foaming mugs held high over her head.

"'Scuse me, duckies," she said, edging past before delivering the beverages to a table full of sailors. She turned back toward the bar, and Drew stepped forward to cut her off.

"Excuse me," he said, as politely as he could. The woman looked him up and down for a moment, smiling.

"Bit young for in 'ere, ain't ya?" she said merrily. "How can I help you, petal?"

"Do you have any lodging?" he asked. The three of them had agreed that acquiring a room was probably the priority upon getting into town, as they weren't sure how long it would take to obtain the services of a ship.

"For the three of you?" she asked. "Certainly have, though you'll have to share. Nine bronze pieces that'll be," she said, holding her hand out. Hector rummaged along his belt, dipping into his money pouch and withdrawing two gold coins.

"Hopefully this will secure any further assistance we may need during the night, good lady?" he said. Drew rolled his eyes, all too aware of how noble the Boarlord sounded.

The woman smiled and threw him a wink. "I'll look after you, your lordship," she said jokily, clearly unaware she was speaking with a genuine Werelord. "Take yourselves a seat and I'll get you yer key."

As the woman disappeared behind the bar, the three travelers sat down around a table.

"Nice going, Hector," whispered Gretchen. "Very inconspicuous!"

"Actually I think she was just mocking him," chimed in Drew. He gave the blushing Boarlord a dig in the ribs with his elbow.

Hector sat at the table, gripping his left hand in his right, his thumb scratching circles into the middle of his palm.

"What's the matter?" asked Drew. "Why are you so anxious? We made it here at last. This is a cause for celebration."

"It's this burn," he said, revealing the small black mark in the palm of his hand, no bigger than an acorn. "It's not healed since our business with the shaman."

"Well, don't pick at it," said Gretchen, slapping his hands apart like a fussy mother. Drew couldn't help but smile.

"Have you nothing in your satchel that could take care of it?" he asked.

"Probably," said Hector, blushing. "I just haven't found the right cure yet; I've been too busy tending to you two. I'll be sure to get it sorted, don't worry."

Within the hour the three of them had enjoyed a hearty meal of roasted sea bass with mashed potatoes, as well as a pile of stewed green vegetables of indeterminable origin. After their nourishing feast Gretchen excused herself and rose to make for the bedroom.

"So soon to bed?" asked Drew, pulling a mock-sad face.

"I'd love to stay up and listen to more of your stories, Drew, really I would," she said, fluttering her eyelashes. "Alas, I fear another tale about big sheep, small sheep, and whatever other woolly creatures you kept on your farm might result in me falling asleep where I sit."

Gretchen smiled meekly and Drew played the part of the hurt suitor.

"Is my life story really so hard for you to endure?"

Hector leaned in close.

"To be fair to Gretchen, Drew, once you've heard one lost lamb story, you've heard them all. . . ."

The three of them burst into a chorus of laughter. There'd been a change in Drew's relationship with the Werefox in the last few days. Hostilities had visibly thawed. Of course she was still a kidnap victim—not the best footing for any friend-ship—but as they neared All Hallows Bay, and with an end to her ordeal in sight, she'd grown more relaxed and less combat-ive. Drew was almost growing fond of her company.

"Admit it," Drew said, smiling at her.

"Admit what?" she queried, straightening.

He leaned closer, keeping his voice low. "There's a part of you that's going to miss this, isn't there? The excitement, the drama, the open road. Held hostage by a handsome rogue Were-wolf and his cunning Boarlord accomplice. You'll miss me." He grinned as Hector chuckled at his side.

She bent close to him, whispering in his ear. "There's more chance of me missing your fleas, hound!"

Hector snorted, unable to stifle his laughter.

"Do we need to send anyone up to make sure you don't make a break for it again?" asked Drew. "Will we be rescuing you from the clutches of a kraken in a few hours' time?"

Gretchen smiled icily at him, eyes narrowed, before plant-ing a soft kiss on Hector's cheek. With that she turned and made her exit from the room. Drew watched her go, noticing that Hector was beaming with pleasure. He shook his head. She had so much spirit. It felt good that they'd be parting on better terms than when they'd met. The Boarlord rose from his chair, making his way toward the crowded bar, leaving Drew alone with his thoughts.

Now, so close to leaving on the next available ship, Drew found a small part of him felt like he was running away, abandoning his people . . . Ridiculous really. He might have accepted that he was the rightful king of Westland by birth, but it wasn't a role he could ever take to. He was a commoner, a farm boy—who would ever accept him as the man worthy to contest Leopold's position on the throne? Once in exile, he would simply fade into the background again, far from the drama of the Werelords and their courts.

Still, looking back at all he'd seen in the last year—the hardships the people of the Seven Realms were struggling with, the brutality with which Leopold and his Lionguard ruled—he couldn't help but feel he was betraying the people of Lyssia. He hoped that someone might make a stand, might speak out against the tyranny, someone stronger and more suited than a shepherd boy from the Cold Coast.

He was startled from his thoughts when he heard a chair being pulled up next to him. A gentleman who looked every inch the dashing sea captain had joined Hector at their table.

The stranger looked to be in his fourth decade, with a shock of thick black hair that was tied back in a ponytail. He wore a long seafarer's cape, black on the outside and red within, that hung three quarters of the way to the floor, and high-legged black boots rose to his knees. At his hip Drew could see the basket pommel of a cutlass. When he smiled, he revealed the most dazzling white teeth Drew had ever seen. The man held out a tanned hand to Drew, and Hector gestured with a nod that he should take it.

"Captain Cane," he said in a warm, smooth voice. Drew didn't recognize the accent, but it was unmistakably exotic and spoke of foreign lands and sunnier climes. "Your friend here says the two of you are looking for passage on a ship?"

"Indeed," said Drew, willing himself awake. He took the hand and winced at the man's viselike grip. "I presume he's already told you we're not fussy about where to. We think our fortune lies in the south, so were hoping to jump aboard a vessel that was heading that way."

Hector leaned forward, whispering. "The captain is setting sail south tomorrow morning; he's a Spyr Oil merchant, so his trade route takes him right down the Cold Coast virtually all year round. What luck!"

"Spice oil?" asked Drew. At that, Hector shook his head. "Forgive me," he said, turning to Captain Cane. "I've lived on a farm for most of my life and the only oil we had was the kind we'd use in a lantern."

"You wouldn't want to be using Spyr Oil in a lantern, my friend," chortled the sea captain quietly. "It's highly flammable, certainly, but it's of more value for its . . . let's say . . . euphoric qualities!"

"It's a drug," explained Hector cagily.

"You've secured us passage with a drug smuggler," said Drew flatly.

"Not a smuggler," replied Cane, grinning. "I can assure you, the wealthiest folk in all of Lyssia can be counted as customers of mine. Surely if I serve lords and ladies with this valuable commodity I can't be considered a lawbreaker? These people *make* the laws, young man." He smiled, again flashing his exceptional teeth.

"I'm not sure," said Drew to Hector. "Have you asked around thoroughly?"

The sea captain leaned back in his chair, ordering a tray of mulled wine, which the barmaid promptly brought over. As the man paid the lady and passed round the goblets, the two youths continued their whispered discussion.

"Believe me, I've asked around. This chap seems the most likely captain to take us, and he claims he knows his way around the White Sea better than any sailor who's ever sailed."

"Oh, they all say that," chided Drew. "Can we trust him? Do you think he's being straight with us?"

"Is your lady friend not joining us?" asked Cane, interrupting their conversation.

"No," replied Drew curtly. "She's retired for the evening."

"But you said you required passage for two, not three," went on the captain.

Hector leapt in. "Yes, she'll be staying here while we depart. She has family in the town with whom she'll be meeting up."

"Shame," said the captain. "A lovely young lady on board would really raise the morale of my boys." He took a large mouthful from his goblet.

"I'm not entirely sure a ship is the place for a lady," returned Drew defensively.

"Quite the contrary, young man," said Cane. "My old mother gave birth to me at sea, and she was as wonderful a lady as one could dream of meeting. No, it's a dangerous place for sure, but I've worked with enough lasses on my ship down the years to know that you're a fool if you discount someone on account of what's *down below*, if you know what I mean?" He winked at the two of them, nodding conspiratorially before laughing heartily, joined by Hector.

Drew felt slightly irked that Hector seemed to find the man tremendously entertaining. To Drew he was an overconfident loudmouth. "Really," he said, his nerves on edge, "I'm not sure about this. Maybe it's best if we wait a little longer, Hector. We're in no hurry and a couple of days in port won't hurt us." It was a lie, but he felt there was something not quite right. He didn't know whether it was the lycanthrope within, but warning signals seemed to be firing off in his brain in quick succession.

Was this smooth-talking captain to be trusted? Could they take that risk, knowing they'd be trapped on board a boat if Drew's instincts were correct? But whatever the reason for his distrust, it appeared Hector had no such worries.

"It's a bit late for that," said his friend, about to explain when Cane interrupted.

The sea captain waved a leather purse in the palm of his hand. "So, it's the five gold here now, and five when I get you to the Shanti Isles?" he said, clenching the purse as if to emphasize the fact that the deal had already been struck while Drew was lost in thought by the fire.

Drew sighed. It appeared the decision had already been taken from his hands.

"Sorry," said Hector, "but I think this is our best option, Drew." The Boarlord's mind was set. Maybe it was just Drew being overcautious. He'd never liked folk like this. Every man he'd ever met who'd liked himself that much had turned out to be a heel of one kind or another.

"Very well, sir," said Drew to Cane. "I apologize if I appeared to doubt your credentials. I'm just a little wary when it comes to deals like this." With this Drew focused a small element of the Wolf, allowing his shoulders to rise and broaden just a fraction, enough to appear intimidating. He also felt his eyes mist over a little, a hint of the Wolf appearing in an amber flash. "One hears stories about poor innocents being taken advantage of. Tricked. You understand?"

The man seemed to sober in his chair, reappraising the situation. Hector bristled with anxiety.

"You have the word of Captain Cane, young man," said the sea captain. "I shall grant you swift and direct passage to the Shanti Isles, may Sosha drag me to the depths if I say a word of a lie." The man looked back to them with the sternest and straightest of faces. Drew felt himself relaxing, and Hector breathed out an audible sigh.

"Marvelous," said the Boarlord.

"Let's drink to it," suggested Captain Cane, raising his goblet. The three of them downed their mulled wines and clattered the wooden cups into one another.

"What time do we sail?" asked Hector.

"At sunup," said the sea captain. "I have some further provisions to secure for the journey—bread, spices, fruit—but we'll be at sea with the sun at our backs."

Drew leaned back in his chair, edging closer to the fire and the warmth it was throwing out. He'd leave the rest of the conversation to Hector for the evening. He wasn't happy about the choice of passage, but it was passage nonetheless, and beggars couldn't be choosers. His body still ached with the exertions of recent weeks, and he wasn't yet fully recovered from Vala's venom. He could feel sleep approaching fast.

"I say again, it's a great shame the lady can't join us on this journey," said Captain Cane, withdrawing a cigar from a pocket within his cape and lighting it swiftly with a match. "It would have made for a far more pleasant journey with such an unusual lady on board."

Drew turned his head to look at the man, and noticed that Hector was also slumping in his own chair, head lolling as his temple drew ever closer to the table top.

"What's the name again?" said the sea captain, scratching his chin with a hooked thumb. "Gretchen, isn't it? Such an enchanting creature."

Drew's mind went blurry and he tried desperately to focus his thoughts. *How does he know her name?* He stared at the empty goblets and then to his drowsy friend. *Oh no.*

Cane leaned forward and patted Hector's right hand, stroking an elegant finger over the signet ring with the boar's head. "Which would make you, my portly young friend, Hector, would it not?" Hector's head slumped with a thump onto the tabletop.

Drew couldn't keep his eyes open. Though he fought the oncoming sleep with all his might, he couldn't resist the power of whatever sedative the captain had used to lace their drinks. He had just time to see Cane lean in closer, blowing smoke into his face.

"And you . . . would be the Wolf."

3

THE *MAELSTROM*

WHEN DREW CAME around it was to the motion of a pitching ship as it rolled with the sea. Raising his head, he winced. With each movement, each jostle, it felt to him that his brain was loose inside his skull, thumping with each shifting lurch as it hit the sides. His body cried with pain, and his eyes were clenched shut as if to keep the headache locked in place, but it was a hopeless gesture. He squinted, looking through the matted hair of his fringe.

He was suspended by a hook from a thick beam in the belly of the ship, his hands clasped in manacles, a link of chain keeping him secured in an uncomfortable slumping stand. His legs were buckled beneath him with the weight of his body. He stood up, taking the weight off his strained arms and letting

the blood course through them again. Looking about the darkened room, his eyes adjusted to the dim light as the sound of
the sea roared past outside.

Crates, sacks, and barrels held in place by thick webs of netting lined each wall, allowing little room for passage through.
On the floor, tossed to one side, was his armor and cloak. There
was no sign of his backpack or the Wolfshead blade, and he'd
been stripped bare-chested, left with only his breeches. Looking up he saw a metal grille some twenty feet overhead, where
he caught sight of booted feet walking past.

"Hello!" he cried out. "Can anyone hear me?" It was useless,
the thunderous sound of the sea and the creaking and groaning
of the timber walls obscuring his shouts. He checked himself
over, looking for wounds or injuries that Cane had inflicted
while he was unconscious, but found nothing. He shouted out
once more, his dry and parched lips cracking as he screamed.

Drew could feel the anger building inside. Who did they
think they were, locking him up like this, chaining him like an
animal? Well, he thought, if it was an animal they wanted it
was an animal they were going to get. Let's see how these kidnappers fared with a monster on their ship. He let his mind focus, channeling the Werewolf. The dark shape of the Wolf leapt
forward into his mind's eye, teeth flashing and claws slashing.
He felt his back arching, and took deep breaths as he brought
the animal forth.

Recoiling in fresh agony, he shook with tearing jolts of

pain as he felt the manacles cutting into his wrists. Foolishly he'd thought he could break his bonds, but he'd reckoned wrong. Blood streamed down his arms, midchange. Lurching and bucking with pain, Drew managed to pull the hook from the beam, but still the handcuffs threatened to tear the flesh and muscle from his arms. He dropped to the floor, rolling about in torment as he tried to refocus, tried to reverse his transformation. Thrashing, he kicked out, entangling his ankle in a loop of netting and bringing a procession of boxes and crates tumbling down on him with a crash. Spicy hot liquid poured over his eyes, into his face, into his mouth.

The blackout was instantaneous.

When Drew awoke for the second time, he found his accommodation had improved remarkably. He was lying in a bed and looking up at a chandelier that was swaying to and fro, the telltale sign that he was still aboard a ship. Looking down to his hands, he saw they were still manacled. But there were no fresh wounds and scars circling his wrists; instead they were healed and clean of scar tissue. How long had he been asleep?

He turned his head one way and then the other, loosening the muscles, then pulled himself gently upward to rest against the ornately carved wooden headboard. The room was handsomely furnished. A writing table was secured to the wall with a porthole directly above, and a richly upholstered red leather chair stood before it, the seat swinging lazily on its swiveled frame as the sea gently rocked the vessel. A door marked the exit and, easing himself out of the bed, he made straight for it. He grabbed the handle: locked. Drew hammered his fists on it, bound together as they were, shouting beyond for attention. When no one came he walked over to the porthole to peer out. The White Sea lay beyond as far as the eye could see, with no sign of land.

There was the sound of a key turning in the lock and Drew hastily picked up the only thing he could reach that resembled a weapon: a porcelain chamber pot from the foot of the bed. Raising it high he slipped behind the door as it opened inward, ready to strike down at his captor.

He was astonished to see Gretchen step into the room, looking about. She wore a finely tailored emerald green dress that was cut at the shoulder to reveal her smooth ivory skin.

"What?" he gasped in shock. "You're my *jailer* now?"

She spun about, obviously surprised to see Drew poised to strike her with the antique lavatory pot. Before she could speak she was shepherded farther into the room as three more figures entered. First came a short, wiry-looking man, who had a shortsword held cautiously forward in his hands now that he knew where Drew was hiding. Behind him came Hector, a wary look on his face as he stood by Gretchen's side. Finally, Captain

Cane entered the bedchamber, closing the door behind him with a confidence that said he didn't fear Drew in the slightest.

"You liar!" gasped Drew. "You gave us your word you wouldn't harm us, that you would deliver us safely to the Shanti Isles!"

"No," corrected the sea captain. "I gave you the word of Captain Cane, a man as fictitious as a child's fairy tale. He was a flight of fancy, nothing more. A whim, if you will. No, that fellow doesn't exist," he went on, tapping his forehead, "except in here."

Drew could feel the anger welling up inside him again.

"Steady, pup," said the man. "We really don't want another accident like we had in the hold now, do we? It took all your friend's know-how to ensure those pretty little paws didn't pop clean off your body. And while we're at it, you might want to put the pot down. That's an antique, you know."

Petulantly, Drew threw it against the wall, where it shattered into a myriad of magnificent pieces.

The captain shook his head wearily. "Is he always like this?" he asked Hector.

"Yes," replied Gretchen for her cousin.

"Who are you?" demanded Drew.

"He's Count Vega," answered Hector, "of the Cluster Isles."

"*Prince* of the Cluster Isles, if you will," corrected the sea captain.

"Pirate prince, you mean," said Gretchen.

"Oh, please," protested Vega, striding to the porthole to look out to the sea beyond. "I'm a businessman, an entrepreneur; I see opportunities and I take them."

"Like you took us?" challenged Drew.

"Yes," replied the man shortly. "You are a business arrangement, nothing more."

"And what do you intend to do with us?" asked Drew, glancing back to the door and a means of escape. Count Vega seemed to read what he was thinking.

"There really is nowhere to run, Drew. So long as those steel bracelets are firmly about your wrists you are of no threat to anyone. Unless you count yourself—one more attack of the wolfies and I shan't be letting your friend attend to your injuries. You can make do with two paws instead of four. You are both my guest *and* my prisoner."

"Where are you taking us?" Drew played catch-up as he tried to work out precisely what danger they were in.

"He's delivering the three of us to Highcliff," Gretchen said sadly. "You do realize, Vega, that you are banished from Highcliff under pain of death, don't you?"

"Ah, my lady," said the count, stepping forward to run a hand through her hair. She flinched, pulling away, and Drew felt himself step forward. "I believe that by delivering your pretty face and your kidnappers to the king I shall prove my loyalty to His Majesty and shall receive his gratitude in the process. Then I shall take back what is rightfully mine."

285

"You're a fool," said Gretchen.

"No," answered the count. "I am an opportunist. It is not every day that a trio of wanted therians lands squarely in my lap. I shall make the most of this while the sun shines and the seas surge." He made for the door, taking the handle and opening it wide. "Come, Figgis," he said, and the wiry old fellow, who had remained silent throughout, followed him. "My lords, lady, you have the freedom of the *Maelstrom*. Please enjoy your stay. And try not to break anything else." With that the two men strode from the room, leaving the door creaking open on its hinges.

Drew sat down on the bed, his head thumping with anger at their fresh predicament.

"What on earth happened?" he asked, finding it hard to believe what was going on. "We came so close to getting away—how could this be?"

"Well," the Boarlord said, "once Vega had drugged us he had us taken to this ship, the *Maelstrom*. And then he sent his men back to get Gretchen."

Drew looked to the Werefox, concern etched on his face. "Did they hurt you?" he asked.

"No," she said. "Although I hurt them. You'll see some of them still bear my claw marks when you get up on deck."

"They set sail that very night, by all accounts," continued Hector. "It appears we woke around the same time, you and I, because I heard all the commotion from my cabin."

"Am I the only one who they chained up?" asked Drew upon hearing Hector mention his cabin.

"It seems so," shrugged the Boarlord, slightly ashamed by the lack of perceived threat he'd posed to Count Vega. "Well, you should be proud, Drew. You caused all kinds of trouble in the hold. You'd brought down a crate of Spyr Oil flasks onto your head. When we got you clear, you were delirious, didn't know who or what or where you were. You've been under its influence for three days now, this being the first time you've fully and properly regained consciousness. If a normal man had taken a hit like you did, I imagine his brain might have exploded."

"Three days? How many days in the last month have I been comatose?" Drew almost laughed with the notion, but the humor couldn't quite break the surface.

"Gretchen cleaned you up. Between the two of us we've been looking after you."

"Thank you. Both of you," he said, making extra effort to extend his appreciation toward Gretchen. "Is he really taking us to Leopold?"

"I'm afraid so," said Gretchen. "We've spent these days in the count's company, talking with him over breakfast, lunch, and dinner, and he's immovable on the subject. He sees this as a way of getting his precious Cluster Isles back."

"What's the story with them?" asked Drew, still trying to get a handle on their situation.

287

"Well," began Hector. "Count Vega was one of your father's allies back in the campaigns. He was the youngest sea captain in the navy, and came from a long line of noble stock from the Cluster Isles. However, just when your father needed him most he betrayed him to Leopold when he saw the tide was turning. But after his victory, the new King Leopold said any man prepared to sell out his king for the promise of gold could not be trusted. The king sent a governor to the Cluster Isles, and since then Vega has been forced to wander the White Sea, privateering in the king's name, bringing loot to His Majesty and then heading out to sea again. With no home beyond the wooden frame of this ship, he's a drifter *and* a traitor."

Drew's head spun: who could he trust beyond Hector in this world of backstabbing, betrayal, and side-switching nobles?

"Have we really no hope of getting him to change his mind?" asked Drew. "Surely a lifetime of sailing the ocean, banished by this tyrant king, has brought some sense to the man? Why should he want to help him when he's clearly his enemy?"

"Vega genuinely believes he can be redeemed in the king's eyes, and thinks this is the way to do it," said Gretchen, interjecting. "This whole thing leaves my blood cold. I'm being bandied about like some rotten bag of bounty, handed over to the highest bidder. And neither of you, no matter how irritating I find you," she said directly to Drew, "deserves this fate."

"We could jump overboard," suggested Drew.

"And swim where?" asked Gretchen. "We're miles out at sea."

"Maybe we could steal a boat?" he chanced. "Do they have any rowing boats on deck?"

"They do," said Hector, "but we'd have no hope of finding land without the proper navigational equipment and maps. Plus we're on the *Maelstrom*, remember," he added.

"What's so special about the *Maelstrom*?" asked Drew. "Have I missed something?"

"Not that the man is averse to boasts," said Hector, "but if Count Vega told you that the *Maelstrom* was the fastest vessel in the ocean, he would be not be lying. It's legendary. He can outrun anything in this ship, and chasing down a small boat piloted by three fugitives would be next to no challenge at all."

As if he needed further evidence of how great a boat this was, Drew set off to the doorway to make his way up on deck. The other two followed, close behind him. Winding his way through a corridor, he walked up a flight of slatted wooden stairs and into the bright sunlight beyond.

The *Maelstrom* was indeed magnificent. Men raced around the rigging and decks, hurrying about their business, paying the three new arrivals no attention at all. Drew noticed that Gretchen had told no word of a lie—two of the sailors walked by with great scars across their faces, the skin still pink and sore from the passage of her sharp claws.

Three huge masts reached up into the sky, the tiny figure

of a boy in the crow's nest visible to Drew, silhouetted against the sun. Eight great sails were taut with a favorable wind at their back, urging the *Maelstrom* through the waves of the White Sea. Drew peered over the side of the ship toward the sea below, where white foam and spray erupted from the surface of the water. A row of cannons could be seen poking out of her side intermittently, the wind whistling musically over their open ends.

Drew looked up, dizzied by the size of the ship. Nobody challenged him, nobody paid him any attention, nobody saw him as a threat. He was a toothless wolf to these men. And there, standing proud on the deck of the ship, clutching the wheel, stood Count Vega, Pirate Prince of the Cluster Isles, Lord of All He Surveyed. He smiled at Drew, revealing those perfect white teeth, as the *Maelstrom* made for Highcliff and the king.

4

Talking to the Departed

ON THE SIXTH day at sea, the *Maelstrom* had dropped anchor just off the small island of Cutter's Cove. It was a minor but frequently visited port for those who sailed on the White Sea, providing a place to gather provisions as well as an opportunity to drop off goods to prospective business partners. Count Vega rarely missed an opportunity to stop there; the sea captain had explained that he had a crate of dates and fine wines to deliver to the island's governor. The three captives had overheard a different reason as to why the *Maelstrom* had stopped in the port, as some of the deckhands gossiped about Count Vega's relationship with the governor's wife.

Drew, Hector, and Gretchen remained on the ship, tantalizingly close to the relative freedom of Cutter's Cove. While there were hills and wilds on the island where they might seek sanctuary, it would only ever be temporary. The concerted efforts of a search party would soon find them, as the island was only about five miles across at its widest point. Their best hope would be to try to board another ship destined for the mainland, but the sea captain had left strict instructions in his brief absence. Not only were they to stay aboard the *Maelstrom*, but his crew was to watch them at all times, leaving no chance to make a break with a rowboat.

Drew had found himself more frequently in the company of Gretchen, as Hector locked himself away in his chambers to write and meditate. The Boarlord was frightened—Drew knew this—and for good reason. They were two days' away from Highcliff, and both knew what fate awaited them when the king finally received them. If Hector chose to spend this time in his own company, reflecting upon the decisions that had led him here, then Drew couldn't stand in the way of that. There was no harm in going to see him, though, in case the Boarlord wanted to get anything off his chest. Drew made his way into the belly of the ship and headed for his friend's bedchamber. He rapped his knuckles on the door.

"Hector," he called. "Are you there?" He tried the handle, but it was locked.

"Just one moment," his friend responded.

Drew heard movement from within the room and the sound of furniture being shifted. It took the Boarlord a while to open the door. What was he doing in there? When it opened, Drew found the cabin was dark, the curtain drawn over the porthole. The bed was still made, and Hector's satchel lay open on the bedspread, some of the contents within spilling out.

"What have you been up to?" asked Drew, walking past his friend and making for the window. He grabbed the curtain and pulled it back, letting the sun's rays stream into the room. Hector squinted at the harsh light, shuffling to sit on the bed.

"Just sleeping," said Hector. "I'm tired."

Drew looked at the bed again, unruffled and covered in the satchel's contents. *Not quite true,* he thought.

"I was worried about you," he said, sitting in a swiveled leather chair like the one in his own room. Papers littered the Boarlord's writing table, scribbled ink notes in a language Drew didn't recognize adorning each page. "You know, if you want to talk about anything, I'm here."

"I know," said Hector, stifling a yawn. "But, really, don't worry about me. I'm just a little weary." He stretched, his heels catching on the round rug at the foot of his bed, the edge of which was folded up. Drew could just make out a line of yellow powder that had been scattered on the floorboards beneath it. He jumped up and grabbed the rug, pulling it clear and causing Hector's feet to fly into the air.

"Drew, no!" he cried, but it was too late.

A circle of brimstone had been carefully traced onto the floor; within its center, smaller circles with wax symbols were melted into the grain of the boards. A black candle rolled out from where it had been stowed under the lip of the rug, proof if Drew needed it that his friend had been practicing magick.

"What have you been doing, Hector?" he demanded.

"Nothing," said the Boarlord, shaking his head. "Don't worry, please, Drew. I've caused no harm to myself or anyone on board the ship."

"But brimstone? The candle? Have you been communing with the dead?"

"Yes," said Hector, his head hanging shamefully.

"But why?" asked Drew. "You saw how dangerous it was last time. That shaman's corpse would have killed you if I hadn't been there. Why would you put yourself—and everyone else—in peril again?"

"But I know where I went *wrong* last time, Drew. I didn't pay the ceremony enough respect; I was careless. This time I haven't made the same mistakes. I've been careful," he said, striding to the table and picking up a clutch of papers. "These are my own notes on the ceremony, with revisions and safety measures in place to ensure I don't lose focus again."

"I don't like it," said Drew. "Not one bit. Have you been speaking to the shaman? What on Old Brenn's earth could he tell you? This is madness!"

"I've been speaking to my father," replied Hector in a quiet, tremulous voice. "I've been saying good-bye to him."

Drew fell silent. His shoulders sagged with heartbreaking

sympathy. He walked over to his friend and, in spite of the manacles that still bound his wrists, hugged him to his chest.

"Oh, Hector," he said, as the other started sobbing. "I am so sorry. I . . . I didn't realize . . ."

"You weren't to know," sniffed the Boarlord. "And yes, I am ashamed. But I needed to say good-bye, needed to know he was at peace. And he is, Drew. He is. He wants me to forgive my brother; can you believe that?"

"Well, I can see his point, difficult as it is to take. Vincent was only doing what he thought was best for your family."

"For himself," snapped Hector, not quite ready for forgiveness it seemed. He looked at Drew, his face pale, a sheen of sweat leaving him looking quite sickly.

"So how did you speak with him? I thought you needed the body to commune with? You said your time was limited, that the soul would depart before long."

"My father is different from the shaman—I don't require his body to commune with his spirit. Two factors aided my reaching him; we share the same bloodline, plus he was a magister in life."

"How does the fact that he was a magister aid you?"

"His spirit is rich in magicks and remains in the living world longer than that of other humans and therians." Hector smiled as he thought of the dear old Boarlord before continuing.

"I climbed into the circle this time. It's not dangerous

when communing with a loved one. It's only when the line is broken and you're contacting a dark spirit that you put yourself in danger. I do not fear my father's ghost. He can sleep now, Drew. He can be at peace." Hector rubbed at the dried wax on his left palm, peeling it off in great clumps. The black mark still remained there, Drew noticed, larger now thanks to the new burns.

"And will you be at peace now, Hector?"

"I don't know what you mean," he replied sheepishly.

"You've had a lot to deal with lately, my friend. You've lost everything, and in no small part thanks to me."

"Drew," said Hector, placing a hand onto his shoulder and giving him a reassuring squeeze. His eyes suddenly lit up, his voice strong and sure. "You have to understand, whatever I've lost and however I've suffered, it pales into insignificance compared to your lot. What you've been through—and survived— it makes my head spin. I couldn't have done it. I don't think you realize just how important you are, Drew."

Drew began to shake his head, but Hector continued.

"The Seven Realms of Lyssia are in pieces thanks to Leopold, crushed by his greed and cruel rule. I know you wanted none of this, Drew, but even as a reluctant hero, look what you've done for folk."

"I've done nothing."

"You saved the lives of a scout and his apprentice. You showed the people of Oakley that they could make a stand. You vanquished the Wereserpent, defeated her Wyldermen, and saved Gretchen's life. And you helped a cowardly Boarlord find a backbone too. You have an effect on everyone you come into contact with. There's a ripple effect, Drew, and your influence is spreading. Just imagine what you could have achieved if you'd had a *plan*."

"A plan?"

"Yes—you've let fate bring you this far and cast you into these predicaments. The people of Lyssia are crying out for a hero, someone who will stand up to the king. Until your arrival it never looked like that would happen. I read the history books and prophecies in Redmire's library. Those writings are littered with predictions for this, 'the Age of the Catlords'—dragons waking, the dead walking, brothers battling, a great werewar— who knows how many will come true? But most magisters share the belief that one was certainly true. The old scriptures spoke of a Champion of Light, who would make a stand against the Dark. I think that champion is you, Drew."

Drew smiled but Hector wasn't joking. He spoke earnestly, sniffing only occasionally as he wiped away the tears. Drew was shocked to hear the Boarlord speak so passionately. He seemed slightly delirious; perhaps he'd spent too long in the spirit circle.

"Light and Dark?"

"That's right. The writings say that when the Seven Realms are broken there will be a great battle of day versus night, the Light against the Dark."

297

"So the Dark is the king?"

The Boarlord shrugged without a definitive answer.

Drew continued: "Hector, you have an overactive imagination. No offense, but I don't really believe in prophecies. I'm a fool farm boy who has fallen into the hands of my enemy with embarrassing ease. I couldn't have made things simpler for Leopold if I'd turned up in Highcliff and knocked on the door for him."

"Fate's a funny thing. Perhaps you're *supposed* to arrive in Highcliff. Everything happens for a reason."

"I think you've spent too long 'communing,' my friend. Perhaps you need to have a rest? You've been through a lot."

Hector ignored him, continuing to drive his point home. "I believe in you, Drew. I know things look grim, but I'm still convinced your story won't end in Highcliff at the hands of the king. I don't think destiny is done with you yet."

"I wish I shared your optimism."

A horn sounded on deck, breaking the conversation and signaling the return of Count Vega.

"Come," said Drew, moving the rug back over the markings on the floor. "Let's tidy all this away. I don't think it'd be good for the captain to find you've been practicing magicks on board his ship. Sailors are superstitious at the best of times; if they find you've been dabbling in the dark arts they're likely to throw you overboard as an offering to Sosha!" As Drew sorted the floor out, Hector grabbed all his papers, shoving them into his satchel. Drew handed him the long black candle.

"Thanks, Drew," said Hector, smiling and wiping away his tears. He was much calmer now, to Drew's relief.

"Please let this be an end to it, Hector?" asked Drew. "I couldn't bear to think of you wallowing in any more misery, and, as you said, you've said your good-byes now."

"I promise," replied the Boarlord with a sniff, stowing the candle in the bottom of his satchel.

5

THE CRIMSON SEA

ARRIVING BACK ON DECK, Drew joined Gretchen as she stood watching the count return in his rowboat. The crew of the *Maelstrom* had all gathered on one side of the ship to welcome their captain back on board. The short wiry man, Figgis, stood ready to throw a rope ladder over the side for the small boat. Six men rowed the craft, while the pirate prince sat at the back, looking very pleased with himself. They'd been ashore the whole morning, time enough for him to conclude his business with the governor. A large keg of spirits sat in the middle of the boat, payment for whatever nefarious services he had performed. The crew of the *Maelstrom* whooped with anticipation.

"He's a rogue," said Drew. "A villain."

"He is," Gretchen agreed. "And there isn't a shred of decency you can plead to within his heartless body."

Bound as his arms were, Drew leaned against her, and she didn't pull away.

"There might still be hope for you, Gretchen. Hector and I . . . well, I don't want to think what will become of us. But, please, don't let yourself be trapped by these people. Duke Bergan would help you, I'm sure."

"My place is in Highcliff, Drew. I am to be wed to Prince Lucas and there is nothing you or I can do about that. My life has been leading to this; he and I have been betrothed since childhood. Perhaps he can change."

"He'll never change, and you know it. He's a sadistic monster, just like his father, and he will only bring you misery and heartache. You will not be happy by his side."

She said nothing and rested her head against his shoulder, her tumbling locks of red hair soft against his jaw. He couldn't help but breathe in her scent, which reminded him of wildflowers in the woods, the smell of carefree times. What was he thinking? This was the spoiled little rich girl who disliked him almost as much as he disliked her. Now wasn't the time for such nonsensical thoughts. She'd probably kick him if she knew what he was thinking. He pulled his wandering thoughts away from where they'd meandered and looked back to the rowboat as it neared the *Maelstrom*.

Before the boat could reach the ship, Drew felt a tingling

sensation, a sense that something wasn't quite right. Had he heard something? A series of thunking noises like axes hitting wood. He looked at the crew, who was gathered around him, calling to their comrades as they neared the ship, eager to receive the keg. Behind him he noticed that the deck was empty. Every sailor was peering over the side of the ship. Drew stepped away from Gretchen.

"What is it?" she asked, watching as he filed between the men toward the unmanned starboard side of the ship. He looked down the length of the long wooden rail. Dotted intermittently along its course were the hooked metal spikes of grappling irons, with ropes attached to them, disappearing over the side. He peered over just as the first pirate leapt aboard, the knife that had been held between his teeth now firmly in his hand.

"Attack!" shouted Drew, and the deck erupted into activity. As the pirate lunged at him he could do nothing but leap clear, his hands still bound by his steel manacles. He danced back as the man proceeded to rush at him, jabbing wildly with the knife while his comrades joined him on deck. Vega's men ran straight into the melee, cutlasses and shortswords at the ready, engaging their enemies earnestly. Within moments the deck was a sea of screams and cries as swords and knives, cutlasses and clubs clashed with one another. Blood flew as the ferocity of battle grew.

Drew was still being harried by the pirate who'd first leapt aboard, his back now against the wall of the lower deck. With nowhere to retreat he leapt toward his attacker, deftly dodging the man's lunges as he brought both his fists down into the bandit's face. Drew heard the pirate's nose splinter as his forearms connected, sending the now unconscious man tumbling to the deck with a crunch. He looked about. There was no sign of Gretchen or Hector, which hopefully meant they were safe. Picking up the pirate's dagger he tried to find his way around the combat, but was soon singled out for attention.

A tall bare-chested man covered in tattoos advanced toward him, a shortsword in each hand. As he scythed in with both weapons, Drew was able to parry one but not the other, cold metal tearing into the flesh at his hip. Grimacing with the shooting pain, Drew bowled into the man, figuring close quarters were his best chance with his hands bound. The two fell to the deck, grappling. Instantly the man was biting Drew, his rotten teeth digging deep into the flesh of his neck. Drew almost passed out with the savagery of the pirate's attack and the efforts to control his rage, knowing he had to keep the Wolf away and fight this as a man. If he lost control now, it could be the death of him, the hard metal handcuffs reminding him of what he stood to lose. He swung his head about, butting the man in the face and causing him to loosen his grip. Drew pulled his neck free, a gout of blood erupting from the wound. Still clasping the dagger, he stabbed down, catching the man in the leg and causing him to retreat.

Nursing his bloodied throat, Drew looked up and saw a

flash of red hair in the crowd of fighting figures: Gretchen! She was being carried toward the grapples by a pair of pirates, held aloft over the sea of swords. She wasn't going easy. Gretchen was changing as she struggled, her face contorting as razor-sharp teeth sprang to the fore. Her fingers had transformed into claws and she lashed out indiscriminately, tearing bloody strips from the men's arms and faces. At that moment Count Vega boarded the *Maelstrom*, his rapier in his hands as he dashed into the fight.

"Unhand her!" he cried, charging forward and finding an enemy pirate with almost every thrust.

Drew was in awe momentarily; the sea captain was a swordsman of skill like he'd never encountered. Vega spun, parried, and lunged, each time bringing fresh wounds to his opponents and not once receiving a hit in return. Bodies fell in his wake, lifeless or injured, either way no longer a threat. Drew looked to where they were taking Gretchen, and spied a pirate standing on the rails, beckoning his men to bring her to him. He wore a large black hat covered in red ribbons that trailed in the wind like crimson seaweed.

"To me, boys!" he cried. "Bring the girl to me!"

They're here for Gretchen, thought Drew instantly. Word must have gotten out about what unique goods Count Vega was transporting aboard the *Maelstrom*. It seemed the Pirate Prince wasn't the only opportunist on the White Sea after all. But Drew couldn't alert him, a line of fighting men blocking his

way. Looking across the deck, the opposing captain in the rib-
boned hat spied Vega cutting a path through his men toward
him. Seizing Gretchen under his arm, he began to descend one
of his grappling lines, letting the rope zip through his hands at
an alarming rate as he hit his boat below in four bounds.

"Back to the *Hellfire*, lads!" he bellowed as the waiting men
snatched Gretchen from his arms.

Her deadly hands lashed out at her captors, but they were
too many, pinioning her and throwing her to the deck of the
rowing boat.

Vega strode on, dancing and stabbing, still graceful amid
the sound of ringing steel and the showers of blood. Figgis was
at his side, scarily efficient with a dagger and a shortsword in
either hand. He might have been old, but he was as nimble as
any of the *Maelstrom*'s deckhands.

Drew leapt up a short flight of stairs to the top deck, dashing over to the rails to look below. Already the attackers were
beating a retreat, three boats departing as their oars heaved
into the water. The remaining *Hellfire* pirates on board began
to dive over, swimming to their drifting boats as they escaped
from the combat. Two of them couldn't resist taking blows at
Casper, the *Maelstrom*'s ten-year-old lookout, as they passed,
one of them cutting a deep wound into his back as they leapt
clear. The young boy staggered forward to the edge of the ship,
before toppling over the rail.

Count Vega took three steps back from the edge of his ship,

casting his rapier to one side. With two huge strides he sprang up onto the rail and launched himself through the air, twisting into a perfect dive before cutting the water just yards from the boat with Gretchen on board. Judging by Vega's actions he had no intention of letting the Werefox go. Drew looked down and saw Casper bobbing in the water, sputtering for air as the blood wept from his back. Drew paused for a moment before making up his mind. He jumped in.

The water was freezing, icy like nothing he'd ever experienced. Surfacing he kicked about, searching through the bodies for the young lookout. He finally saw the boy as his head disappeared and his hand grasped out of the sea. Drew kicked forward, pulling at the water with his manacled hands while his legs propelled him on. Casper's hand slipped below the churning waves, and Drew dived down. He could see the whites of the boy's eyes flashing past in the dark water, as a stream of bubbles escaped his mouth, the current pulling him under. Drew snatched Casper's wrist then kicked for the surface, working his legs with all the energy he could muster. Sucking in a gulp of air, he hauled the young boy up the length of his body, pulling him onto his chest while he treaded water. Some deckhands dived overboard to help carry the lookout to safety, two of whom also grabbed hold of Drew, incapable of swimming properly as he was. Rope ladders were lowered and he was helped back up the side of the *Maelstrom*. He looked back into the sea for Vega and Gretchen as the sailors tended to their wounded.

The rival pirates' rowboat was being buffeted by some great force beneath the waves. Two, then three men tumbled overboard, losing their footing under the heavy assault, the sea suddenly churning red where they landed. Only the pirate captain remained on board now, standing over the prone body of Gretchen, his cutlass held out warily. The buffeting stopped. The crew of the *Maelstrom* lined up along the rail, watching for what would happen next.

It was quiet, but only for a moment.

The water erupted beside the rowboat as a monstrous figure leapt out of the water, crashing into the captain before disappearing over the other side, taking the doomed man with it. Drew had just enough time to recognize the monster as Count Vega, but a transformation had taken place. It seemed to have happened in slow motion as Drew took in every detail. Gone were his devilish good looks, gone was the graceful fencer who had whirled through the pirates aboard the *Maelstrom*. The smile of perfect white teeth had been replaced by a gaping foot-wide mouth, arcing around a wide gray head. Jagged serrated teeth jutted from the jawline, row after row, and his head had elongated to a pointed gray snout. The white shirt of the Pirate Prince clung to his torso, his muscled chest rippling as he grabbed the rival captain. Deathly black eyes twinkled as the creature's teeth closed around his victim's chest, blinking as they bit down through skin, flesh, and ribs, before the two disappeared into the White Sea, turning it red in an explosion of blood.

The crew of the *Maelstrom* cheered as they threw lines out to the row boat. One of the sailors brought a blanket for Drew, placing it over his shoulders and patting his back with thanks. Hector emerged from belowdecks where he'd been hiding, obviously relieved to see his friends were both safe. Gretchen was escorted back up a rope ladder and onto the ship, the men treating her courteously as she found her feet once more. She rushed to Drew and Hector, and the three of them embraced.

Count Vega was the last to return to the *Maelstrom*. He appeared over the side of the rails having sprang up one of the grappling lines, hurdling the wooden balustrade in a graceful bound. His white shirt still hung off his chest, dripping with water and stained pink with the blood from the sea. He had returned to normal now, the beast he'd changed into smoothing away. One of his crew members chattered to him, pointing at Drew and then to Casper, who was being treated on deck. Vega picked up his rapier and strode forward, the hard soles of his knee-high boots slapping against the wooden planks as he approached.

"It appears I owe you my gratitude," said the Pirate Prince, twisting his neck to one side as his bones finished falling back into place. He jutted his jaw as he turned his head from side to side, a cracking noise emerging when he relaxed his joints. Gretchen cringed.

"I'd have done the same for any comrade," said Drew, look-ing over to the injured boy. "Is he all right?"

"He'll live, Drew, thanks to you." Vega took another step forward, his usual pleasant demeanor replaced by a more seri-ous one. "Nothing's changed, though, boy. I still have to take you to the king. Business is business, you understand? Really, I'm sorry."

Drew nodded, already resigned to that fact. "What hap-pened out there?" he asked, although in truth he knew the an-swer full well. He'd just witnessed Count Vega the Wereshark, scourge of the sea, in all his glory.

The Pirate Prince raised his rapier and turned the shining blade like a mirror so he could see his mouth. He chortled, rub-bing his thumb across his teeth with a squeak, giving them a careful clean. They gleamed white once more.

"What?" he said. "You thought you were the only one with the parlor tricks, pup?"

PART VI

HIGHCLIFF

I

INTO THE LION'S DEN

THE WHIP CRACKED, the silver studs that peppered its length leaving another trail of torn flesh along Drew's back. His legs threatened to give way under him as he stumbled forward along the drawbridge, feet tripping over each other. The manacles had been replaced by a purpose-built set of wooden stocks that he wore around his neck and wrists like a yoke. Although not visible to any onlooker, silver rings were embedded around each of the three holes, encircling his throat and hands in a cold embrace. Soldiers of the Lionguard marched on either side of him as he was paraded across the bridge. Behind him, Captain Brutus was rolling up the whip once more, readying himself to send another lash to the Wolf's back. Drew peered up through tear-drenched eyes to see an enormous metal portcullis disappear over his head like the mouth of some great leviathan, as he vanished into Highcliff Keep.

They had arrived only an hour ago, a collection of frigates guiding the *Maelstrom* into the city's harbor. People had lined the street from the docks right up to the castle to see the Wolf brought to the Lion's door. Some had cheered, the most fervent supporters of the king throwing refuse and rotten fruit and vegetables at Drew. For the most part the crowd watched in a mixture of morbid curiosity and pity as he was dragged, whipped, and prodded up the steep streets to the castle.

The walls of the fortress were built into the sheer and deadly cliffs that thrust up from the sea below, allowing the structure to sit towering over Highcliff, separated from the city on all sides but for a drawbridge. Enormous gray walls encircled the keep, still a hundred feet high at their lowest point, impregnable to invasion and intimidating to onlookers. Flags fluttered from the crenellations and turrets, revealing the heraldic devices of all Seven Realms. More striking than any of the others was the giant red flag that billowed above the gatehouse; it bore the image of the rampant gold lion of Leopold, rising on one hind leg as it pawed, roaring, at the heavens.

Drew had been led through a large public arena, known as the High Square, to the front of the gatehouse, where scaffolding and platforms were being hastily erected. Hector was also being led, unchained, with a modicum more respect. Count Vega strode along by his side in all his finery, scarlet-lined black cape fluttering from his shoulders. On his right hip he carried Drew's Wolfshead blade to match his own rapier on the other. All the while he watched Captain Brutus as he worked his misery upon Drew. If he was feeling any remorse, he didn't show it. Gretchen had been whisked away by carriage as soon as they had arrived, spirited to her future home by the Lionguard. Drew still found time to hope she was well and would emerge from this hell unscathed.

As the last of the Lionguard disappeared into the castle, the portcullis slowly lowered, groaning as a team of eight men worked the giant mechanism, easing the huge wheels around as they maneuvered it into place. When its teeth hit the ground the earth seemed to shake through Drew's feet, sending reverberations up his legs until they took hold of his heart.

A circular courtyard opened up before them, and the soldiers proceeded up a flight of stone steps to two enormous doors. One of the doors groaned as it swung open, the guards within standing to one side to let them enter. The prison party walked in, but not before Brutus gave Drew a final taste of his whip at the top of the steps.

An entrance hall greeted them, thick red carpets lining the stone-paved floor, directing them toward a further pair of ornate wooden doors. A woodland scene was depicted upon them, revealing all the animals of the forest leaping and chasing one another between the trees. Drew noticed an image of a wolf at the heart of the scene, although its face had been hacked and disfigured by the blows of a sword.

The doors opened and they were ushered through.

Three tall stained-glass windows cast an ethereal light over the great hall within, and six towering marble pillars held a curving roof high above their heads. Gathered between the pillars on either side of the hall were the great and the powerful of Lyssia. Lords and ladies in their finery stood shoulder to shoulder, watching intently as the prisoner arrived. They were all shapes and sizes, and Drew could only wonder what creatures hid behind their faces. None gave anything away; they looked on with vacant expressions, occasionally glancing up to the throne end of the huge chamber as if to show their approval.

At the head of the hall stood a large stone dais, upon which three thrones were positioned. The left chair was empty, while on the right sat Prince Lucas, whose eyes flashed with delight as the captive Werewolf was paraded forward. Standing to the side of the prince's throne was Gretchen, dressed in a beautiful lilac gown that trailed about her feet. She wore a crown of holly, and her ladies-in-waiting were once more at hand, closing ranks about their mistress. Men of the Lionguard flanked her, standing at attention. The look she gave Drew was one of heartbreaking sadness, and it was all the young lycanthrope could do to hold his nerve, his raw emotions threatening to spring forth at any moment.

The king's throne in the center was instantly recognizable to Drew, an awesome carved stone seat with images in relief of serpents riding along its arms and up its sides, clashing in a crescendo of teeth and tongues at its height. Within the maws of the serpents' death embrace sat a ruby the size of Drew's head. Behind the throne stood a figure in a black robe, a wide and heavy cowl hanging over the face, obscuring the features within.

And in the seat, a great beaming smile playing across his broad chiseled face, was King Leopold, Lord of Lyssia and Defender of the Seven Realms. The king looked every inch the lion in his lair, lounging upon his throne like a great cat might bask in the sun. Not an inch of the man was wasted, his shoulders bursting with honed muscles beneath his fur-trimmed red robe. He wore an iron crown, a crude trinket compared with the opulent shows of wealth that littered the hall. An enormous two-handed sword leaned against the side of his throne, its blade shining bright and silver in the midday light.

Drew was dragged unceremoniously to the stone steps of the dais, two of the Lionguard crossing their longswords before him. The king rose from the throne as the whole chamber waited in apprehensive silence to see what he was going to do. Leopold was well over six feet tall, bigger than Bergan and more imposing, hard as that was for Drew to believe. All eyes were on King Leopold as he slowly stepped forward and lazily descended the stone steps to stand before Drew.

"So," he said, in a deep growling voice that reverberated throughout the hall, "you're the thorn that's been stuck in my paw, then?" Drew opened his mouth to speak but the king quieted him immediately. "You needn't answer, boy. I know full well who and what you are, and if you feel the need to grace my ears with your voice then I'll proceed to have your tongue cut out. Nod if you understand."

Drew nodded, his face pale and his eyes wide.

"And who else do we have here?" Leopold asked, striding past Drew toward Hector, who stood some yards away. He clapped the Boarlord on the shoulders. "Look at you, Hector! You're wasting away to nothing. I'm sure this vile hound has been thoroughly foul to you while he's had you under his spell. You have my condolences for the atrocities he committed upon your father and the noble house of Redmire." He glowered in Drew's direction, but the young Werewolf simply kept his head down, staring at the bottom step of the dais. Leopold turned back to the Boarlord. "My poor boy, you need a hearty meal in your belly, get some of that Boar fat back, eh?"

Drew glanced up from beneath his fringe. The audience laughed all around them as Hector stood completely still, obviously terrified at what the king might do next. Drew was shocked when the king pulled the Boarlord to his chest in an embrace. The crowd cheered, overjoyed to see such forgiveness from their monarch. However, through a gritted smile the king managed to whisper something in Hector's ear, spittle foaming on his lips. Drew could clearly see Hector blanch and for a moment feared his friend might collapse to the floor. Whatever the king had said was clearly intended to strike fear into the young man's heart. It had done its job. Leopold withdrew quickly, kissing the Boarlord's tear-stained cheeks before waving for silence once more.

The great doors at the end of the hall opened suddenly, and all heads spun around to see who had arrived. Even Drew was able to crane about in his yoke to catch a glimpse of Duke Bergan entering Highcliff Hall, marching up the red carpet toward the throne.

2

LORD OF MERCY

THE BEARLORD OF Brackenholme wore a thick green cloak that was lined with golden thread, highlighting a pattern of vines and leaves that decorated its edging. A horn bounced from his hip with each heavy stride, the head of his ax looming menacingly across the top of his broad shoulders. His traveling companions, all dressed in woodland green cloaks, remained at the open threshold to the hall. When Bergan got within twenty feet of the throne, he dropped to one knee, bowing low and remaining there for a moment while he addressed his king.

"Your Majesty," said the Bearlord, "I apologize for the lateness of my arrival, but we were caught unawares by your decision to bring the wedding forward. We have been on the road for three days in order to be at your side. I hope I may still be of assistance to you at this most marvelous time."

Drew looked up at Gretchen. By her astonished reaction it seemed they had forgotten to inform her of this change in plan.

"Arise, Duke Bergan," said the king, smiling. "My brother Bear! It is so good to see you again, and I am delighted you've arrived safely."

The Bearlord rose from his knee back to his full height, towering behind Drew. Not once did he glance his way.

"I have to say I was surprised to hear you had moved the date of the royal wedding, Your Majesty. My people are preparing a great celebration for next week and have had to busily rearrange their blessings and offerings. Was there a particular need to rush this through?"

"Rush this through?" rasped a deep voice from the front of the hall. The figure that had stood behind the king's throne stepped forward now, resting a hand on the head of a stone serpent. The black cowl still covered his face, but Drew could just about make out his mouth.

"Indeed, when word reached us that Prince Lucas's future wife had been saved from the Wolf, we saw no need to delay the glorious day any further. It seems with villains like this," he gestured to Drew, "wandering our realms, there could be any number of miscreants who might want to stop this marriage. By ensuring that the royal wedding happens tomorrow we can see to it that no more . . . mishaps . . . befall this blessed union. Surely you don't doubt our king's judgment, Bergan of

Brackenholme?" The king turned at this to look at the Bearlord, throwing him a challenging glare.

Bergan glowered at the man in black, irked by the way he'd been addressed. The build of the hooded figure reminded Drew of Vankaskan, the prince's merciless companion on that terrible journey through the Dyrewood. Indeed a heavy chain of office hung on his chest, bearing the silver skull of a rat on it.

"Not at all, Lord Chancellor," replied Bergan. "I only worry that rushing such a historic event might tarnish the occasion for posterity."

"Don't concern yourself about such details," said the lord chancellor, sarcasm heavy in his voice as he retreated into the shadows. "Let me worry about that."

Duke Bergan bowed once more and took his place among the other Werelords, nodding acknowledgments as he joined a group of proud-looking men in gray winter cloaks. He glanced back down the hall to the rest of his traveling party. They bowed their heads briefly in the Bearlord's direction before disappearing from the doorway.

King Leopold walked back up to his throne, stopping at the top of the dais to turn and address his court. "Friends and brethren, you are my honored guests for the duration of your stay in Highcliff. There shall be a great feast tonight as you toast your future royal couple, and I promise you festivities the like of which you have never seen in any corner of Lyssia.

"In addition," he went on, reveling in their attention, "we

also thank Old Brenn himself for delivering unto us this most foul, wicked, and treacherous individual." At this he raised a damning finger toward Drew, letting it waver while a murmur rushed around the hall. "This illegitimate child of Wergar the Wolf, this conniving offspring of a vile and corrupt king, comes here, into my realm, to usurp the very throne that you good people bore me to. He had already planted the foul seed of rebellion in some of the more unruly quarters of our lands, where ignorant peasants speak of him as some kind of savior. Savior!" He laughed. "Savior of what?

"He has crawled out of the Dyrewood, killing indiscriminately as he prowls through our lands and raising hysteria in his wake. As a blessing to my son and his future wife, and as Old Brenn is my witness, I shall personally see this monster, the last in the line of the wicked wolves, put to the sword on the morrow!"

With these words there was a clamor of activity in the great hall, as gasps were drawn, voices were raised, cheers were unleashed, and naysayers cried out. This revelation came as no surprise to Drew; he'd known the king's intentions ever since he was bundled into the wagon back in Brackenholme. The king raised his hand, calling for the noise to quiet, but it didn't. Duke Bergan stepped forward, joined by one of the men in the gray cloaks.

"Your Majesty," he cried, "do not kill the boy. He is no danger to you, to any of us. Hand him over to me and I shall guarantee that he remains in chains for the rest of his life, imprisoned in my woodland fortress, unable to harm others. We need not spill his blood on a day of peace and prosperity!"

The man by his side, a tall, long-faced fellow with gray hair that gathered at the top of his cloak, almost blending into the winter furs, added his support.

"Your Majesty," he called, "this goes against the teaching of our kind. One Werelord shall not kill another, except upon the field of battle. That is our oldest and most ancient law. I implore you to reconsider!"

The king stared down his opposition, raising his hands in a show of negotiation, but still the broad smile remained there, indicating he was steadfast in his plans.

"Bergan of Brackenholme and Manfred of Stormdale, I hear your objections. But you do not see the wider picture. Challenging me as he has in his desire to win my throne from me—murdering his way across my kingdom, killing Baron Huth and Brenn knows who else—surely these are acts of treason?" At this Lady Gretchen made a move to step forward, to correct the king, wanting to cry out that it was a lie, but the Lionguard at her side took a firm grip of her arms, holding her back. Vankaskan had appeared out of nowhere, joined by one of his black-robed cohorts as he squared up against Bergan and Manfred of Stormdale.

"By challenging me," continued Leopold, "he has declared war upon the people of the Seven Realms. That, my friends, is the battlefield, and that is why I am justified in having him executed."

Still the crowd shouted, scuffles threatening to break out between supporters of the king and those who sought a peaceful solution.

"Silence!" cried the lord chancellor from behind the throne, as the king sat down, satisfied that he'd said his piece. "Or do you also challenge our king? Do you align yourself with the *Wolf*?" At this the room fell silent as each and every Werelord remembered his and her place, biting their lips and fighting with their thoughts as they quieted. One voice broke the silence. It was Count Vega.

"Your Majesty," he said, stepping forward from where he stood behind Hector, "if I may?"

The king waved a hand to allow him to approach, looking at the Pirate Prince with cold, calculating eyes.

"Count Vega," he said. "Yes. I almost forgot about you. What an unexpected pleasure for us all to see you in the Court of Highcliff."

Drew held his breath. Was there something the count might be able to do, some kind of deal he could strike that would save his life? Drew had shown a disregard for his own life by jumping to the aid of the count and his men on the *Maelstrom*; maybe this had counted for something. Perhaps Vega's conscience had been pricked. He listened on with a glimmer of hope in his heart.

"Although I have been outcast from this court for more

years than I care to remember, I have come to you a man re-born. I am, and always have been, your most loyal and loving subject, and hope that the recovery of Lady Gretchen and the delivery of Drew of the Dyrewood go some way to restoring any faith you had lost in me. By reclaiming my rightful posi-tion as Lord of the Cluster Isles, I shall be your obedient ser-vant of the ocean. I shall marshal the White Sea for you like no other man alive, ensuring all who sail it know the great and glorious deeds and kindness of our one and only true king."

Drew's glimmer of hope flitted out of existence. Bergan growled from the sides, unable to hide his contempt for the Pirate Prince. The king stroked his jaw, considering the Were-shark's words.

"In safely bringing me my future daughter you have in-deed repaired your tarnished reputation, Vega," he said. "Fur-thermore your gift of this wretch has not gone unnoticed."

Count Vega stood still, the shark smile spreading expec-tantly across his face.

"However, you remain untrustworthy, Prince of Pirates. I cannot have you in my company, worrying when the rapier might strike into my back. You may join the other guests for the feast and the wedding tomorrow, but must return to the *Maelstrom* by nightfall. Show me your loyalty by bring-ing more bounty to our people; take from the thieves of the sea and deliver their ill-gotten loot to Highcliff, so it may be better distributed among my faithful subjects. Then I may consider granting you your little islands once more."

Drew could see that Vega was crestfallen, but the captain of the *Maelstrom* tried to hide it. From the buzz that went around, everyone in the room recognized the smack in the face the Wereshark had just taken. He smiled, bowing low, before retreating into the crowd.

"Now," said the king, "I shall retire to spend some time with my family ahead of tonight's meal. Consider this the greatest of all feasts, with my loyal Werelords and their noble households gathered here as they are. Tonight, my friends, we dine together, at one table, to one purpose, all equal, all faithful."

He rose to a chorus of obedient cheers from the court, descending the steps to walk down the great hall, the cloaked lord chancellor on one side and Prince Lucas on the other. Gretchen looked despairingly to Drew as the guards who stood by her side, their hands still on her arms, escorted her away after the king.

Another whip crack sounded and Drew felt the skin over his spine tear. He staggered forward into the stone stairs, cracking his head as he fell to the floor. Stars fluttered in front of his eyes as he saw the faces of Hector and Bergan looking down, concern etched on their desperate faces. The Boarlord scratched at the palm of his left hand furiously, a mess of fear and nerves. Count Vega loomed into view beside him, chewing his nails as he stared down at the boy. Drew's final vision before he blacked out was of Captain Brutus's booted foot as it was brought down in a kick to his temple.

3

CONDEMNED

THE COCKROACH SCUTTLED along the edge of the wall, belly low to the ground, hugging its well-traveled path as it avoided its mortal enemy. Its antennae tested the path in front, searching for any scent that might reveal one of the beasts to it. Noises echoed around the chamber, bouncing down the corridor outside, human voices that cried out in pain or sobbed for mercy, but these alien cries meant nothing to the insect. Darting out to the rim of a tin plate it jumped over the side and to its prize.

The moldy crumbs from a crust of bread were a banquet for the tiny creature. It fed hungrily, eating as much as its small stomach could handle, conscious at all times that it was out in the open, visible to its predator.

A sudden movement from the shadows, large and dark. And swift. The beetle stopped gorging, preparing to take flight. But it was too slow.

The rat pounced, hitting the metal dish and sending the cockroach spinning onto the hard flagstones, helpless on its back. Scuttling forward, its pink fleshy tail flicking in anticipation of its own feast, the rat bore down on the beetle. Before it could strike, it felt the bare human foot connect with its ribs, sending it hurtling through the air to bounce off the wall and crumple to the ground. It limped away, injured, though not mortally, disappearing into a small hole in the wall. The cockroach seized its chance, grateful for whatever power had intervened. Flicking its wings out from its hard carapace it flew up to the tiny barred window and into the fresh night air to its freedom.

Drew watched the beetle as it disappeared and wished for all the world he were a bug right now. He stared up at the window, helpless. Even if he could reach it, he still had the stocks firmly fixed around his neck and wrists, pinioning him in their silver grip. He was going nowhere. He settled back down to the floor of his prison cell, leaning his back against the roughly hewn wall.

The sounds of the shouting prisoners in other cells had dashed any hope he'd had of sleep. Exhausted and injured as he was, the wailing of men driven mad by years of solitary confinement chilled his blood to the bone. He winced as he tried to get comfortable, the cuts on his back still painfully sore. The silver studs in Captain Brutus's whip had ensured that these wounds weren't going to heal in a hurry. These were scars for life, what little remained of it.

He was amazed that the king had allowed his men to arm themselves with weapons that had been treated with silver. How many of them, like Brutus, were equipped with implements that could kill a Werelord stone dead? Drew figured a privilege of being king was that Leopold could rewrite the rule book to suit himself. He doubted the other Werelords were aware, and Hector would be foolish to alert them and jeopardize his lucky reprieve.

There was a noise at the door. Another guard come to put the boot in? Three of them had taken it in turns to work Drew over the minute he'd been delivered to them, beating and battering him with sick abandon. He'd curled up on the floor as best he could, hampered by the wooden frame around his upper body. At least those wounds had already begun to heal—he could feel his ribs knitting themselves back together. Whatever happened now, they weren't going to kill him tonight; King Leopold wanted to save that pleasure for himself in the morning.

A key turned in the lock. Drew placed the right end of the stocks on the ground, using it to raise himself to his knees and then his feet as he struggled to stand. They could come in and fight him, but he'd be fighting back. His legs could still kick, and he could swing the yoke with some power if need be. He readied himself, gritting his teeth, his heart pumping. *Keep the Wolf at bay, Drew,* he told himself. *Don't die like this.*

The door opened and the light of a lantern lit up the room. Drew squinted. He saw a figure shimmering in the doorway, holding the lantern before her in a tentative hand, horrified at the thought of what she might find. His eyes slipped into focus as he saw Gretchen illuminated before him. She stepped in quickly, and the guard closed the door behind her, locking it.

She rushed to Drew, stopping only briefly to place the lantern on the floor. Throwing her arms around him, she hugged him tight. He winced, his ribs still on fire, stifling a cry. The Werefox recoiled, looking down at the patchwork of mottled blues, purples, and reds on his torso, every inch of his skin alive with livid marks.

"I'm so sorry! I didn't realize!" She stared again at his wounds, tears springing to her eyes. "What have they done to you?" she whispered.

"Nothing I wasn't expecting," he said. "Don't worry; they won't kill me. Not for a few hours yet." He managed a brave chuckle. His black humor was wasted on Gretchen.

"You shouldn't be here," she said. "But I have the king's ear. You must know—you have allies here, all at work, trying to secure your life."

Drew shook his head. He didn't want to hear such things.

"Duke Bergan, Duke Manfred the Werestag," Gretchen continued. "They appealed again to the king this evening. If anyone can convince him that your life should be spared, it is the three of us."

"Gretchen," Drew said, and then stopped. He smiled sadly. "My lady," he corrected himself. "You bring hope where there is none. You need to understand—I die tomorrow. It's what has to happen. Leopold will not allow me to live. He killed Wergar to take the throne. I'm a loose end that needs tying up, and what better platform to make an example of me than when every Werelord from Lyssia is gathered in Highcliff? Please, my lady, don't dwell on this. I don't want to hear it. It hurts more than any boot, whip, or blade. It breaks my heart." He lowered himself back to the floor.

She sighed. "You've made quite the impression on everyone, Drew of the Dyrewood. It seems that the great and the not-so-good of the Seven Realms are assembled upstairs, and the last thing that's on anybody's lips is this wretched marriage. They're all talking about you, Drew. I don't know . . . I just thought . . ." She shook her head. "Duke Manfred and his brother, Earl Mikkel, are with Duke Bergan now. They're good men, trustworthy. And Bergan's children are here too: Lord Broghan, and Whitley also. I believe you know each other?"

"Goodness, he's *Bergan's* son?" gasped Drew. His head spun with the implications. "Well, that explains a lot. Yes, we ran into each other in the Dyrewood."

Gretchen's brow creased as he mentioned Whitley. She was more than a little surprised to hear Drew describe Whitley as a "he," but she let it go; there were more pressing matters. The Werefox sat down beside him, spreading her green dress about her on the cold stone. She put a hand to his forehead and brushed the hair delicately from his eyes.

For a moment Drew was transported back to the Ferran farm and his mother's arms. He closed his eyes, wanting to savor the sensation, the memory. He opened them to find Gretchen staring intently at him with her emerald eyes. She was the most perplexing girl he'd ever met, seemingly calculating, yet captivating at the same time. The two had been through an awful lot in recent weeks, but he still felt as if he'd only scratched the surface of who the Werefox was. Right now she seemed vulnerable, far more sympathetic toward him than ever before. But he knew from previous experiences that her mood could change in a heartbeat.

"How is it that Lucas has allowed you to visit me?" asked Drew warily.

Gretchen shrugged. "He seems very receptive to my requests," she said, twirling her red hair with a lacquered fingernail.

I can believe that, thought Drew. Gretchen was used to getting what she wanted, and he had no doubt that the young prince had fallen for all her charming and willful ways. Even so, she must have gotten deep under his skin for him to allow her to come and see Drew.

As if she could read his thoughts, she continued, "I told him I wanted a final word with the 'vile creature' who had put me in such peril." She smiled shyly.

Sitting beside Gretchen, Drew realized that he would never discover where this strange, volatile friendship might have led. Where *any* of his friendships might have led. Hector, Whitley . . . Would they remember him? He allowed himself to wonder what Trent was doing now. Perhaps he hadn't joined the army as Ma had always feared. Perhaps he was still on the farm, living a life that Drew would never again know. With the lambing season upon them it would be hard work without an-other pair of hands. He clung to the idea that deep down Trent knew Drew wasn't a murderer. His heart ached with despair.

"Tell me about Hedgemoor," he said suddenly.

Gretchen was clearly taken by surprise. "My home?"

"Yes," he said. "We've spent the last month squabbling and scrapping, and not once in that time did you tell me about your family."

She shuffled closer to him, leaning against his chest. Drew felt thrilled yet awkward at the same time. Why had it been necessary for him to be at death's door before she'd finally warmed to him?

"Hedgemoor is the garden of the Seven Realms," she said, speaking longingly of her birthplace. "It's quite removed from the hustle and bustle of somewhere like Highcliff, or even Brackenholme for that matter. Merrydale reminded me of home, and the Barleymow River too. There was a stream," she said, smiling, "that ran past my bedroom window. As a girl I would sneak out at night and take midnight paddles in its cold waters. My feet would freeze, and the tiny fish would come creeping out of the reeds to come and nibble my toes. I couldn't feel them as they jostled between my toes and around my ankles, my feet numb. . . .

"My father said my mother used to do exactly the same thing, you know? When they courted, the two of them would take midnight strolls up the stream, trying to find its source, but they never succeeded." She laughed. "They would return to Hedgemoor, bedraggled and shivering, to a firm telling off from my grandmother and the maids!"

"What was your mother like?" asked Drew, trying to shift so his chin could rest against her head, but the stocks blocked any chance of this.

"I never knew her," she said wistfully. "She died when I was only a baby."

"I'm sorry," said Drew.

"You've nothing to apologize for. As strong as my mother's spirit was, her heart was weak. They said it was hereditary, that such illnesses and diseases come as a consequence when cousins, however distant, marry. That, I suppose, is a danger to many of my kind, blue-blooded Werelords, and I think that was the appeal of bringing me into the House of the Lion."

"How so?" asked Drew.

"My mother and father were Werefoxes, related, but not closely. Many of the old houses have kept to their own down the years, keeping true to their bloodlines. But one cannot continue this way; the blood grows weak and the children sick sometimes. The Werefamilies marry across races more frequently now, mixing their stock and making for stronger, tougher offspring. King Leopold will be hoping for some strong, strapping leonine grandsons from me in the near future, I have no doubt of that," she said sadly.

"My ma was an angel," said Drew, trying to move the subject away from the future and back to the past. "I could spend hours with her, listening to stories about the family, about my pa when he was in the army, her life as a maid here in Highcliff, about her childhood in the country. I miss her so much. Now I don't even know if she was my birth mother, but it makes no difference to me. The biggest regret in my life is that I couldn't help her. She died in front of me, murdered by a monster."

"Oh, Drew," Gretchen said, sitting up. "I didn't know. What monster?"

Drew recounted in more detail the tale that he had told Hector. "It came to the farmhouse the night I fled, the night my life changed forever. A big black beast, all claws, tail, and fangs. And red eyes . . ." He shivered, involuntarily, his body betraying him. "I still see those red eyes whenever I close my own." He pointed to the three scars at his breast, still visible beneath the fresh lacerations. "It did this to me. It's never healed."

"A Wererat," Gretchen said quietly. "You describe a Wererat, Drew . . ."

"What?" he said. "Like Vankaskan?"

"Indeed, but it may not have been him."

"No," he said. "I tore at its face, pulled the flesh clean away. I was a monster myself, I was wild—it was the first time I changed. But I remember wounding it in a way that seemed almost impossible to heal, even as a therianthrope. Vankaskan couldn't hide a scar like that."

The Werefox went silent, deep in thought. She bit her lip, almost hard enough to draw blood.

"What's the matter?" he asked, concerned at her mood.

"They told us that Wergar had sired you by some wench on one of his campaigns, so your right to be a Werelord was refuted. But if the Wererat came after you then that isn't true. Your mother," she said. "Your birth mother. I think she's still alive."

"What?" he said incredulously, as if hit by a hammer blow.

"Your father was Wergar," Gretchen explained, sitting up. "So your mother was Queen Amelie."

The shock on Drew's face was clear. Finally he knew where he came from. He *was* a Werelord.

"Their children died in a great fire when Leopold took the throne," she continued, nervously. "You would have died also, I suppose, if someone hadn't spirited you away. Your 'Ma,' I guess, if she was a maid here in Highcliff. Leopold took the throne, declaring that the Wolves were all dead. And I'm guessing he thought that was true at the time."

"What did he do to her?" Drew asked, scrambling onto his knees to look Gretchen in the eyes. "Where is she?"

"She's here, Drew. In this castle. The king had to take a bride, had to build his own Werelord legacy." She held his face in both hands. "He married your mother, Drew. Leopold married Queen Amelie."

No sooner had she said that than the keys turned in the lock. Gretchen snatched her hands away from Drew's face and jumped up as the door swung open. Drew crouched on the ground in his stocks, jaw slack, eyes flitting and blinking with tears as the full realization of what Gretchen had just said began to dawn on him. A figure stood in the doorway: Prince Lucas.

"My dear," the boy prince said, holding an elegant hand out. "That is time enough. I have indulged you with this wedding present, but we have guests to attend to." He smiled at the sight of Drew's tears. "I see you have given this wretched excuse for a man a fine sample of the Fox's bite, as you'd wished. Now come, my lady; we have a busy day tomorrow."

"You are correct, my darling," she replied, trying to control her voice. "I have said everything that I wish to say, and I thank you for this opportunity to unburden myself. He will not forget it."

Gretchen looked down at Drew as he knelt, putting the

pieces together as she'd handed them to him. The queen, Amelie, was his mother? And she was *alive*! Surely that could save him? Surely she could call upon her husband to show forgiveness?

"My lord," said Drew desperately, shuffling forward on his knees across the cold stone paving. It suddenly dawned on Drew that Lucas was his half brother, not that such information would sway the young Lion. If he could have put his hands together to plead, he would have done so. "I need to speak with the queen. May I send a message to her? May I speak with her?"

Lucas struck him so hard a tooth spun clean out of Drew's mouth, sending his head recoiling before he clattered to the ground. The prince shook the back of his hand in the air, willing the blood flow through it as he nursed it.

"How *dare* you speak of my mother, the queen, in such familiar tones. If my father didn't want to kill you himself tomorrow I would run you through this very moment." The prince leaned over and spat at Drew as he trembled on the ground, a mess of shock and distress.

"Come," said Lucas, snatching Gretchen by the arm and picking up the lantern. "We're leaving." With that the two of them strode from the room, the boy prince leading his future wife roughly into the corridor. She looked back, her face contorted with emotion, at her shivering friend on the floor, as the jailer closed the door with a violent, ominous slam.

4

DISSENTING DISCUSSIONS

WITH A DRUNKEN CLASH, the two golden goblets crashed into each other at the table in front of Bergan, their bearers cheering as the honey mead showered them. The Bearlord tried to hide his disdain by taking a long sip from his tankard. The king's guests had gathered within the banquet hall of Highcliff Castle; mercenary merchants, petty nobles, and loyal men of office had gathered in the keep, keen to take advantage of this rare show of generosity from the Werelion. Bergan noticed how some brought their wives, adorned in gaudy jewelry and garish costumes, while others left them at home, looking to indulge themselves with whomever they could find at the feast. Three enormous tables ran the length of the hall from the head of the room where the main table was situated. Food and wine from all over the realms cluttered the tables, an over-the-top show of indulgence by the king. Wealthy guests who were held in special favor by Leopold tore at the food, elbows flying and goblets clattering as wine flowed freely. Small dogs lingering beneath the tables fought for any dropped scraps they could scavenge.

Before the guests' tables, jesters, jugglers, and dwarves performed tricks and grotesque acts for their amusement. Musicians stood to one side, playing a bawdy tune at a rollicking pace. Billowing red and gold curtains bearing the coat of arms of Leopold rose to the high-vaulted ceiling behind each table, while one enormous drape towered like a flaming standard behind the king.

The head table was reserved for the wealthiest and most influential people of the Seven Realms. Forty of the continent's greatest Werelords were seated here, made up of numerous noble families, in various states of celebration. Bergan was one such honored guest. The king sat at its center, a smaller, less ostentatious throne than that in the great hall supporting his weight. At any point there was a courtier or two vying for his attention, begging for his ear and a moment of his time. To the left of him sat Queen Amelie, a picture of quiet elegance, the only wolf Leopold could bear to be close to. Perhaps the fact that she was a winter wolf, from the distant Sturmish city of Shadowhaven, was the only thing that had stayed his hand years ago. It was the gray wolves of Wergar's line that the king had so feared and despised.

She wore a long black dress, as had become her tradition, and her long white hair was tied back, held in place by a thin crystal tiara. Bergan hadn't failed to notice that she was not drinking, was not feasting; she seemed to be caught in some quiet contemplation. His heart ached for her. He'd known her in happier times, when she'd been the life and soul of Highcliff's banquets, the epitome of the elegant and entertaining hostess. The figure sitting there this evening was a shadow in comparison. She'd never recovered from Wergar's death.

On the other side of the king sat Prince Lucas, freshly returned to the huge table with his bride-to-be. While the boy prince was enjoying himself tremendously—laughing with those guests who approached the main table to give their blessings—the same could not be said for the Werefox. Much like the queen, Lady Gretchen had no appetite, sitting in silence, speaking to nobody. One more miserable soul for whom Bergan felt the weight of responsibility.

At one end of the long table sat the Ratlords. The lord chancellor and his four brothers were gathered here in their modest black robes, each one wearing matching heavy, silver chains of office around their necks. They appeared content to sit back and watch the guests go wild, their dark costumes seeming to intensify the shadows about them. From the opposite end of the table they were all but invisible, but Bergan and his companions never took their eyes from them. They kept their voices low, all too aware that the Ratlords' ears could be anywhere even though the noise in the hall was tremendous.

"I'm appalled," muttered Manfred the Staglord of Storm-dale, pushing the untouched food around his plate. "In all my years on this earth, I've never seen such a web of corruption. That boy they dragged in is an innocent; any fool can see that. The only thing he's guilty of is being the son of Wergar, and there was a time when such a curse would have been seen as a blessing. It's hardly a crime."

"He won't rest until he's seen the last of the wolves put to death," said his brother Mikkel, who sat at his side. Both of the brothers shared the same striking faces, deep brown eyes that seemed just a touch too far apart, their mouths set in stern grimaces at the bottom of their long faces. The gray-haired Manfred was ten years his brother's senior, but the younger earl was his equal in both wisdom and intelligence. Both had sat with Duke Bergan in Wergar's Council of Elders, and both clearly shared the Bearlord's dismay at the current king's actions.

"You know," said Bergan, leaning closer, the others craning their necks to hear him, "I knew when I first laid eyes upon him that he was Wergar's son. The king and I were like broth-ers; we grew up together. It was as if his ghost had wandered into Brackenholme. Still chills me just thinking about it," he said, shaking his head. "And I let him down, when I might have done more."

"What more could you have done, old friend?" asked Manfred. "We heard about the prince's party being ambushed by bandits, Bergan," he muttered, his dark eyes twinkling mischievously. "The boy had a chance to escape and took it. It's poor luck that he was caught in the end. But don't let that weigh on your conscience."

"I can't help it," replied the Bearlord. He laughed and raised a tankard to toast a passing Werelady. They had to look as if they were enjoying themselves, for fear of being singled out by the king and his allies. He glanced to the next table where his own son and daughter sat in the company of other future Werelords. They were both resplendent in their finery, far removed from the kinds of outfits they wore back home in the Dyrewood. His son, Broghan, was the image of him, and Bergan grew more proud of the young man with every passing day. The Bearlord had schooled Broghan to take his place when the time came, and he was happy in the knowledge that at his passing, Brackenholme would be left in safe hands.

His daughter, Whitley, was a less obvious success, but she had her own strengths and talents, combined with a will of her own. He had to admit that he had felt proud of her exploits in the forest with Hogan, which had probably saved the old scout's life. And it seemed that her encounter with Drew had acted as a catalyst for her confidence. This was the first time his daughter had left the woodland realm since that night, and he'd allowed her to ride alongside Broghan on the way to Highcliff.

He shook his head again. "I should have done more. I owed that much to his father."

The other two Werelords said nothing at this. In private company, down the years, they'd listened to the Bearlord berate himself for leading King Wergar back into Highcliff, and no amount of remonstrating had ever changed Bergan's opinion that he'd betrayed his king. Their constant reminders of how he'd genuinely believed he was brokering an amnesty, helping the family of the Wolf get out of Highcliff safely and in one piece, fell on deaf ears. The bloody chaos that had followed couldn't have been predicted, not by anyone, bar those within Leopold's closest circles of confidence, they pointed out.

"Could the boy really be one of Wergar's children, though?" asked Mikkel. "All the king's children died in the fire, remember."

"They may have burned in the fire, but they were dead before the flames touched them," said Bergan grimly. "He's the king's son all right. The likeness is uncanny. Wergar had two brothers but both died before they came of age. Wergar was the last of the Wolves, Mikkel. There's no doubting that."

"Maybe," chanced Manfred, "and this might stick in your craw as it does in mine. . . . Maybe Wergar had relations with some nameless woman on one of his campaigns, as Leopold suggested?"

"No," replied Bergan without hesitation. "The love the king had for Amelie was absolute. Not once in all my years at his side did I witness him stray, ever see his head turn."

Silence fell between the men as they pondered the logic. "Then he's her son," agreed Mikkel, won over by the Bearlord's reasoning. "And judging by his age that would make him the youngest—Willem. But that doesn't explain how he ended up parted from his brethren, how he never died in the fire."

"Pardon me, gentlemen, but would you mind if I joined you in conversation?" came a voice from behind Bergan's shoulder. "I'm struggling to find company this evening, which is hardly a fitting way to treat the savior of the realms."

It was Count Vega, smiling down at them roguishly. He leaned on the back of Bergan's chair with an unwelcome familiarity, swishing a goblet of red wine in his hand absently while he stared at each of them in turn.

"Keep walking," said Bergan. "I shan't be accountable for my actions if you remain here. I don't dine with traitors," he snarled.

"Forgive me, my fellow lords, but I disagree," whispered the count, leaning in. "I couldn't help but overhear your conversation, no matter how low-key you've tried to keep it. If such talk is not traitorous, then what is it?"

The Bearlord had to wonder how long the Wereshark had been standing there, listening in. Manfred growled, the Werestag's hand moving instinctively to his sword. Bergan moved quickly to stay it, as the Wereshark's eyes widened in pretend shock.

"Take a seat, Count Vega," said the Bearlord between gritted teeth. Perhaps it was best to keep this enemy close for the time being. The pirate pulled up a chair, straddling it in reverse so that he leaned forward onto its back. "So you've picked up the talent of eavesdropping as well since we last met. You're really moving up in the world."

"I hear and see things," said Vega, sipping at his goblet. "I believe all four of us, and others at this table, share misgivings over our king's actions."

"The only misgiving you have is that he didn't give you back your precious Cluster Isles," spat Mikkel, staring at the Wereshark coldly. "You don't share our feelings, don't pretend to for one minute, you snake."

"Shark," corrected the count. He swigged at his wine, glancing about to check he wasn't being watched. "I have information that will solidify your assumptions regarding the boy's parentage." Any hint of mischief or malice was gone from the rogue Werelord now, as he whispered earnestly what information he knew. They listened intently, occasionally laughing or smiling to passers-by to remove any clouds of suspicion.

Vega told them of the journey on the *Maelstrom*, of Drew's heroism in the face of grave danger when they were attacked, pulling the injured lookout from the sea. He told them of the raw strength of the youth, of how he nearly put a hole in the side of his ship when he'd "gone wolf" in the hull. And he recounted what Hector had told him of the boy's background, of his origins.

"With that behavior I would bet the *Maelstrom* he's a pureblood. It seems that our boy was raised by a scullery maid who was once in the service of the king and queen. The boy told the Boarlord that he'd been raised on a farm, that his father had fought in the Wolfguard, and that it was in Highcliff his parents had met." The Wereshark revealed the pommel of the boy's sword, hidden at his hip beneath the red lining of his cape. "He told the Boar that Ferran is the family name."

Bergan's brow furrowed as he cast his mind back. He'd never been particularly good at names. The Wolfguard had been manned by strong, loyal, and faithful men who would have died for the king. Sure enough, the boy had carried the Wolfshead blade, proof enough of a connection to the king's most loyal soldiers. He looked about the room at the assembled Lionguard. They lined the walls of the chamber, watching silently, a host of armored guardians.

"Can we believe then," asked Manfred, "that this scullery maid stole the boy away, rescued him from the fire? Does the queen even know one of her sons still lives?"

None of them could answer this. They looked over to her, a pale imitation of the young queen who had been so full of love, life, and laughter at the side of King Wergar many moons ago.

"If there were more of us here," whispered Mikkel, "we could have made a stand, could have challenged the king. Bergan, where is your cousin, Henrik of Icegarden? What a Werelord could do with Sturmland steel in his hand! Where is Lorimer the Horselord? There are so few at the feast."

"No," said Bergan. "The time to challenge was back when we were still an alliance. We should have done what was right when he seized power." Again he smiled as a serving girl walked by, topping up their goblets. "We are fractured now, broken, weakened by mistrust and our individual troubles. The Seven Realms are separate, all held down by the Lion. My cousin you speak of, the White Bear, I haven't spoken to him for fifteen years. He's never forgiven me for what happened back then, and I can't say I blame him either."

"There are some we could have called upon, if circumstances had been different," said the Bearlord. "Lady Gretchen's father, Gaston, would have stood by our side in times like this. He would turn in his grave to see what fate has befallen his daughter."

The suspicious death of Earl Gaston had caused great unrest among the noble households of the Seven Realms. Leopold had already started to move his troops into Hedgemoor alongside those of the late Earl Gaston. The once peaceful vale was now a foothold for the king's army along the edge of the Great West Road. The only thing missing from the equation was the marriage of his son to the heiress, Lady Gretchen, and that would be concluded within hours of this feast.

"And Baron Huth," offered Count Vega. "They say that Drew killed him, but I've spoken with the three witnesses who saw the old man's demise, and it was by the sword of that captain of the Lionguard, Brutus."

"By sword?" said the Werestag earl. "You know yourself that no mortal can kill a Werelord with a simple sword."

The count waggled his finger, correcting the Werestag. "He can be killed if that sword has been blessed with silver."

The others gasped, quickly regaining their composure as they remembered where they were. What Vega had said chilled Bergan to the bone, but he couldn't be allowed to let his mask slip.

"Drew saw it with his own eyes," continued Count Vega quietly. "The runes were lit with silver. Amazing what one can find out when one has guests aboard a long sea journey."

Bergan's stomach rolled with nausea. Silver had been outlawed in the Seven Realms for hundreds of years. The mining of the precious metal was a crime that brought with it the death penalty, and in each of the Seven Realms the ownership of the element was enough to guarantee one a lifetime behind bars. The news that Leopold was now permitting its use in the hands of his most brutal soldiers was incomprehensible. From where was he acquiring it? Who was in league with him? And who else had the poisonous metal hidden on his Lionshead blade? He looked again at the soldiers around the room as they suddenly became more threatening to the Bearlord. This would change everything if it were true.

"This is an outrage," spluttered Manfred under his breath, also glancing nervously at the ranks of Lionguard. "The king is arming his elite soldiers with weapons that can slay a Werelord in the blink of an eye? What other intentions does he harbor? Who else might he kill in order to retain power? Is it not enough that he has put an end to the wolf's line?"

"That's if we can believe our salty cousin," said the Werestag's younger brother, an arched eyebrow of suspicion jutting over his brow. "We have only his word for it."

"Ask the Boarlord's son, Hector, if you don't believe me. Oh, no, wait. You can't. He languishes in some cell for the night, not welcome at the king's table. I've no doubt they'll wheel the poor boy out to see the king's justice firsthand in the morning, but that's the last anyone will see of him, mark my words," said the Wereshark, rising from the table. "I return to the *Maelstrom* tomorrow and will be away from this godforsaken mass of rocks by the evening. It's been enlightening," he concluded, raising his goblet in a toast to the three. "Just one word of warning, though. Don't be fools. It's bad enough one Werelord should be killed in the morning. Don't make it four." He smiled, bowed, and walked away.

"That fellow is a troublemaker," said Mikkel, watching Vega as he sidled up to a trio of ladies-in-waiting. They immediately went giddy as he flattered and flirted with them. The count looked back just once before returning his attention to the girls. "I don't trust him."

"Then why would he tell us all that he has? What does he stand to lose? He has nothing, and we know how he feels about the king," said Manfred.

"All the more reason to distrust what he says," argued Mikkel. "He could be fueling us with ammunition where there is none, leading us in a merry dance that will get us all killed!"

"We can't stand idly by while they kill Drew, surely to Old Brenn?" said his brother, looking to Bergan. "Friend, I have two hundred of my men camped north of the city. I could send word to them this very minute if need be. Have you not brought your own guard with you from Brackenholme?"

"I have," said Bergan. "Indeed, many of them are lodging in Highcliff this evening. But the bulk of them are camped some distance outside the city; they are not at hand. Nor do they match the number of the Lionguard, even combined with your troops, assuming I was willing to call upon them. It would mean certain death for all of them." The Bearlord was still thinking, still casting his mind back to the old campaigns.

"Then there is no hope," said Manfred. "There is none who can help us."

Bergan clenched his fist suddenly, raising it as if he were about to strike the table, then remembering himself immediately. He lowered it beneath the table, and patted Manfred's leg, his eyes staring straight ahead across the room toward the rows of loyal Lionguard. He polished off the contents of his goblet, looking about the hall, smiling once more at the evening's revelers. He caught the eye of King Leopold, who was looking down the table to the end where they sat. At his side crouched the lord chancellor, his cowl still raised, muttering and murmuring while the party raged all around him. Bergan bowed, and the two Werestags followed suit. The king nodded his head slightly, smiling, his distrustful eyes upon them. Maybe he already knew what they were thinking. Maybe he was putting a plan of his own in motion that would tie up further loose ends.

"There is one who might be able to help," the Bearlord whispered to his friends as he rose from the table. He clapped the Werestags on their shoulders and paced away, his stride full of purpose, his head hatching a plan.

5

THE SWORD OF JUSTICE

GRETCHEN STOOD ON the castle balcony, alone with her thoughts. She watched the city of Highcliff coming to life below from her lofty vantage point. The sun rose in the eastern sky, casting dark, haunting, midmorning shadows over the length of High Square. A crowd had begun to gather before first light, mainly made up of citizens eager to see Drew put to death. People made their way to the square to see if this was indeed the ghost of the Wolf or the son of Wergar, people who had known their old king from long ago and never feared him. For all the rabble-rousing of those who had clamored for front seats, the masses who gathered behind seemed of a quite different mind-set. They clearly didn't share the carnival atmosphere that their more ignorant neighbors were creating.

Gretchen was under no illusions as to the generosity of King Leopold. Yes, they were at peace, there was no war, but the taxes increased each year and the poor grew poorer.

There was a time when the people of Highcliff looked upon the soldiers of the king as their army, their men, manned by brothers, fathers, and sons. Soldiers of Earl Gaston's army in Hedgemoor used to frequently join the Lionguard, but that was a thing of the past. The king's elite protectors held no such connection to the good folk of Highcliff or indeed of anywhere else in the Seven Realms. It was intentionally assembled from men-at-arms from the world over. Some of the old Wolfguard and their sons had joined their ranks, but they were few and far between. Before his death, Gretchen's father would tell her that in Wergar's time there was an openness between king, army, and civilians. This understanding had been all but forgotten since the rise of the Lion.

Gretchen had a lot to thank her late father for. He had taken it upon himself, with his daughter being his only heir, to school her in the politics of Lyssia, and she'd dutifully paid attention. She was all too aware that people dismissed her as a frivolous, haughty, spoiled young woman, and, for the most part, this had never bothered her. She knew that when the time came and she had to step up to her responsibilities, she would do so effortlessly, remembering all her tutelage and training. She would face ignorance, chauvinism, and belittlement from others, but those who dared to challenge her would be underestimating the Werefox at their peril. If her time came as queen, she would do what was best for the people of Hedgemoor, what was best for the people of the Seven Realms. Enduring Prince Lucas was tolerable if it meant she could fulfill that dream.

She'd heard the stories about the soldiers of the king, but up until very recently had chosen to ignore them as rumor and nothing more. Yet her time in the company of Drew and Hector had opened her eyes to what was really going on within Highcliff, and how far-reaching the implications were. She was also aware of the unpleasant rumors about her father's death in the king's court. Having a gaggle of gossiping ladies-in-waiting provided her with tidbits of information on many an occasion, even when they thought their whispers were out of her earshot. If the king had been responsible for her father's death she was left wondering who her real allies were. Duke Bergan and Hector were the only two she truly trusted. Them and Drew.

In a matter of hours Drew would be dead, and she would be married to Prince Lucas. She could aspire to have some influence on the people's affairs, but for herself she sensed only a life of sadness and misery ahead.

Within the courtyard of Highcliff Keep she could see the very best of the Lionguard regimentally marching through their drills, alert and attentive to their captain's orders. Beyond the walls the remainder of the Lionguard—far less recognizable as a respectable fighting unit—managed the city's crowds. Some of the old soldiers and campaigners from Wergar's army had remained, but they were fossils and out of step with the new blood. Mercenaries and swords for hire made up the bulk of their number, and they oversaw the people of Lyssia with an iron fist. The few uprisings that had occurred in recent years had been quickly and ruthlessly quelled, with stories about how the king's justice had been dealt floating away as silently as dead bodies down the Redwine. There was unrest in Westland, and now Gretchen knew why. The rumors, everything she'd heard, everything she'd chosen to ignore—it was all true.

Her ladies-in-waiting called her from within her bedchamber. It was time to make her way to the pavilion in the royal enclosure. Gretchen clutched the stone balustrade of the balcony, suddenly gripped by a dreadful fear that she might fling herself from it. Taking a deep breath, she watched the people below. They were going to be her people one day, and she had to hold on to that sliver of hope that when all the horrors of the morning had played out she might be able to do some good, no matter how small. They would depend on her. For the most part the people of Highcliff loved their families, they loved their city, and they loved their country more than any king or queen could wish or hope. And many of them had long memories of times of old, before a Lion sat on the throne.

Drew looked up at the midmorning sun as it rolled by overhead, wincing under its unforgiving glare. The wheels of the open horse-drawn cart groaned as they rattled over the giant timbers of the drawbridge from Highcliff Castle. Drew struggled to remain upright where he knelt in its center, hands bound behind his back by a rope laced with silver thread.

Lines of townsfolk thronged the path as the procession made its way to the scaffold, the Lionguard forming a cordon along the route, keeping the crowd back with pikes and swords drawn. A deathly quiet had fallen over the city, which hours earlier would have been hard to imagine. At sunrise the sound of bells ringing had heralded this great and momentous day, drawing people up from their beds at an ungodly hour to gather obediently in the High Square. Word was firmly out as to what the king's intentions were. The crowd had gathered to see the demise of the last of the line of the Wolves, at the hands of the Lion himself. Stalls had been set up by quick-thinking traders, some offering food and drink, but others trying to sell crude drawings of slain wolves etched onto slates and parchments. Drew smiled grimly at the entrepreneurs; business seemed slow for them.

An open scaffold took center stage in the square, a raised platform proudly displaying a large slab of stone: the executioner's block. A hemp basket sat neatly before it, ready to receive its grisly offering. The jailers had removed his manacles, throwing Drew a clean white tunic for his execution, more likely because it would cover his injuries rather than to make him appear respectable. Though his bruising had faded slightly there were still telltale red marks showing through the shirt's back where the wounds from his flogging remained open and angry. Drew's stomach heaved now as he was drawn ever closer, his fate stark and clear before him. Still, he tried not to show his fear, instead thinking back to Duke Bergan's words in Brackenholme. *No more tears. Give them nothing.*

Standing beside the block was the cloaked and cowled lord chancellor, talking at length with a scribe who was busy taking notes in a journal, nodding as the other spoke. The Lionguard stood at attention along the scaffold's edge, facing the crowd to look for signs of trouble. The spectators kept a respectable distance from the sinister scaffold.

As Drew was wheeled toward the scaffold, the faces of hundreds of strangers watched him pass. Some were shouting, baiting him, hurling abuse as the wheels rattled over the cobblestones. For the most part the faces were solemn and downcast; it appeared there was an overwhelming feeling of grief for his situation, regardless of how the king and his advisers had spun the story.

The cart rolled past the royal enclosure, a long wooden structure that had been erected to house the king, his companions, and the various Werelords who were in attendance. Drew looked up, catching sight of Duke Bergan, Count Vega, and the familiar face of his good friend Hector. The Boarlord was standing at the end of the platform, a guard on either side of him. Whereas most of the king's guests were in their finery,

Hector was drawn and haggard, wearing the same clothes that he'd been traveling in with Drew. His hair was unkempt, and he looked like he'd been receiving some special attention of his own. With his head down, chin resting on his chest, he looked broken.

The cart turned and pulled up in front of the scaffold. The driver jumped from the front, leading a team of four waiting soldiers around to manhandle Drew down. He was led roughly up the wooden steps onto the platform as the more zealous members of the crowd began shouting anew. Pushed into the middle of the wooden decking he was forced to his knees, the stone executioner's block within touching distance. He looked over his shoulder, where he knew the lord chancellor was standing, talking to his scribe.

"Eyes down, dog," hissed the Wererat.

Drew turned away, letting his gaze settle over the crowd. There were hundreds in the square, row upon row of witnesses to his death. Where they couldn't find room in the street they could be seen hanging out of windows at the back of the plaza, or perched upon rooftops for a better view of the spectacle. Drew looked back down the road to the castle gatehouse and saw two regal carriages making their way across the draw-bridge, splendid golden vehicles with footmen riding at the rear of each and teams of colorfully dressed drivers holding the reins.

The lord chancellor stepped forward in front of Drew, his robes brushing against the young man as he passed. There was a sweet sickly smell to the Wererat that spoke of decay and rot, instantly making Drew gag where he knelt.

"Your king arrives," shouted the lord chancellor, his voice carrying to the spectators in the distance. "This is the most important of days, where we witness our prince entering into matrimony. Nothing but your most fervent support for the monarch is expected. Do not disappoint His Majesty, or me for that matter!"

The crowd roared as one, the Wererat's prompting clearly providing the extra incentive that they needed. Drew could see soldiers milling among them. While one of the carriages pulled up at the royal enclosure, the other came to a halt before the scaffold. Footmen ran forward to open the doors swiftly as the king disembarked to a chorus of cheers. Trumpets sounded as he stood for a moment in the carriage doorway, his long red robe shining like a fiery beacon, his smile beaming as he waved to his people. Stepping down, he made the brief walk to the scaffold, lingering to wave at onlookers and shower them with his thanks and blessings before pacing slowly up the steps on to the wooden deck.

Drew watched him reveling as the center of attention, sup- posedly adored by his cheering masses. At no point did Leop- old look his way, taking an inexorable amount of time to make his way center stage. He waved, laughed, pointed, and cheered, as flowers were thrown forward, bouncing off the shields and armor of the regiments of Lionguard.

"My people," he cried, raising his hands to them in a show of appreciation, "such warm affection you show me on this most remarkable of days! I thank you from the bottom of my heart that you have turned out in such great numbers to witness this blessing for my son, your prince, and his bride-to-be. Your unwavering love and loyalty bring fresh joy to my soul with each passing day." At this the most devout in the crowd roared once more, a round of applause rattling through the throng like a volley of arrows. The king gestured to the royal enclosure where Prince Lucas, Lady Gretchen, and Queen Amelie had just taken their seats.

"But please," he went on. "Today is not for me; it is for my son, Lucas, and his enchanting fiancée!" More cheering erupted. Drew looked over. The boy prince rose to wave, grateful for the compliment from his father and the crowd's attention. Gretchen sat by his side wearing a silver gown, impeccably dressed and decorated. Her face was as still as a statue. She stared ahead as if in a trance, her demeanor directly mirroring that of Queen Amelie's. This was the first time Drew had laid eyes on the woman who was his mother, and his heart skipped a beat as he prayed she would look his way. Her long white hair was piled on her head, nestling within a crystal tiara. She was beautiful, just as he imagined a queen should be, but there was an emptiness to her face, as if great sadness was hidden just behind her eyes, locked away from the people. She wore a black dress, in contrast to Gretchen, and if she did know that

Drew was her son she showed no acknowledgment. She sat apparently motionless, as if she'd witnessed the coming savagery a thousand times before. Drew's stomach lurched again as he discovered new depths of misery.

"We shall bear witness to the joining of the House of the Lion and the House of the Fox, reaffirming our age-old allegiance to one another, while heralding the dawning of a bright new age ahead. My dear queen has joined us also, disregarding her ailments to be present at this blessing, such is the love she has for her family and her people." More excitement rose up from the crowd.

Drew had to wonder what he meant by ailments. Was she ill? The king turned to Drew finally.

"And here," he said, pointing at the boy who knelt before him, "is the man who would bring death and disorder to our fair realms. This is the creature who has wandered through our lands, terrorizing our people, causing chaos and treachery wherever he treads. This beast was born from the Wolf, some half-breed Wylderman who thinks that being the illegitimate offspring of a cruel and barbaric tyrant makes him the rightful King of Lyssia. What do you say, people? Is this your king?" he yelled, casting his hand toward Drew in a sweeping motion. The fervent crowd at the front of the cordon of guards booed and hissed, screaming obscenities while threatening to surge forward. The soldiers held them back, pushing with shield and pike shaft, maintaining their distance.

The king nodded, his face a mask of mock outrage and concern, his mood apparently as appalled as that of his subjects. He walked behind Drew, letting the crowd's noise build, letting the misguided hatred wash over the scaffold. He spoke to Drew, quiet enough that only the young Werewolf could hear him.

"You hear that, dog?" he said. "You hear the people? *My people!* Hear how they call my name and mock yours? Your father would be spinning in his grave to see the sniveling wretch I see before my eyes, that's if we hadn't burned his rotten corpse to ashes." Drew's eyes stung as tears began to well. He gritted his teeth, holding them back.

"To think," muttered the king, "that my own son shares the same blood as you. I feel sick to think that a dog like you was born into this world by my queen."

"Then you admit it," said Drew, not looking up. "The queen is my mother. How can you deny her the chance to know this?" he cried. "What kind of monster are you?"

The king didn't reply, instead a heavy boot at his back forced him slowly forward. He struggled against the pressure, but it was unrelenting as the Lion drove Drew toward the cold stone block. He looked down at the basket in front of him where bloated black flies buzzed inside, feasting on the remnants of some previous justice the king had dealt out.

Leopold pulled his sword free from its scabbard, holding the great blade up high over his head for the whole crowd to see. The screams from the front of the crowd reached new levels of raucousness, urged on by their performing king. The sword glittered as the sunlight danced across the wide blade. Embedded silver runes like those on Captain Brutus's longsword flashed across it, ensuring that the blow to come would be fatal. He crouched down beside Drew, who lay in submission at his feet.

"I am the Lion. I am the king of all the Seven Realms and the only lord and master these people will ever know," he whispered, saliva hitting Drew's cheek. "You are the Wolf. You are an outcast, a dead breed, a relic of a time long gone that shall never return." The hatred that the man held for Drew was palpable. Every word he threw at the boy was laden with contempt and disdain.

"You were born here and you die here. How fitting."

Leopold rose to his full height, swinging the sword up into the air with both hands high over his head. Drew could see the Lion's shadow cast long before his eyes, a perfect silhouette of the executioner. The king still had one more taunt for him.

"I'll give you this," he hissed finally, starting to swing the great sword down. "You put up more of a fight than your brothers and sisters did."

By the time the sword had finished its journey it was sending showers of sparks off the empty granite block in a deafening clash. The crowd gasped in shock and confusion. Where was the rolling head and the shower of blood? Drew was on his back in front of the king, his movement so swift as he dodged the blow that it had surprised even Leopold. The Werelion's face contorted with rage, his eyes glowing as his teeth sprang forth.

"No!" shouted Drew where he lay, hands still behind his back. "Know this!" he yelled to those in the crowd who might hear his voice. And his voice carried. "I am the son of Wergar and of Amelie, last in the line of the Werewolves of Lyssia, and the Lion is a thief and a murderer!"

"Silence!" roared Leopold, standing over him and raising the sword so its point aimed down at Drew's chest.

The crowd surged once more, and the Lionguard seemed to break in places, struggling to hold back the sea of bodies. The royal pavilion sprang into activity as the royal family and Werelords stood up as one from their seats and rushed forward to see what was happening. Queen Amelie had risen from her chair, a look of pained bewilderment upon her face. Gretchen rushed to her side, taking her hand tightly in her own and squeezing it. On the scaffold, before all of Highcliff, the Lion closed in to kill the Wolf.

"I want to look at you as you kill me," mouthed Drew to the enraged king, a strange, serene smile spreading across his face. He was at peace. The sword descended.

6

SACRIFICE

BEFORE LEOPOLD'S SWORD could connect with Drew's chest, there was a flash of movement as three members of the Lionguard crashed into the king, knocking him to the hard decks of the scaffold. A fourth soldier appeared above Drew, where the king had been just seconds before. He couldn't make the man out, the sun behind him casting his whole body into shadow, but the uniform of the Lionguard was unmistakable. As chaos erupted all around them, the man dropped to one knee, flipping a startled Drew onto his stomach. He felt a knife working hard at the unnaturally tight silver bonds that held his wrists together.

"Who are you?" Drew shouted over the din, but he received no response. He looked across the execution stage as the decking thundered under the sound of rushing booted feet, and the ringing of swords on shields shook his skull. He could see men of the Lionguard fighting one another, swords drawn, brother apparently attacking brother. In a flash of detail he noticed that a number of them had pulled their tabards away, revealing tattered old ones beneath, the image instantly searing itself on his brain—a silver wolf's head silhouetted against black. There weren't many of them, they were vastly outnumbered by others in the ranks of loyal men, but they had rushed toward the scaffold, forming a loose line of defense while the soldier behind him worked at his rope cuffs. He glanced behind, just in time to see three of the four men who had rushed the king fly high into the air, launched skyward as Leopold rose from the melee in all his glory.

As the soldiers' bodies landed with bone-crunching clatters, the Werelion let out a bloodcurdling roar. He was at least nine feet tall, his cloak flapping in the midmorning breeze, tattered by the sword blows that the men had delivered. His head was fully transformed, a snapping jaw of inch-long teeth gnashing at the air. A golden mane framed his broad head like a halo, and one of his huge clawed hands was still clutching the pommel of his sword, which now looked far more in proportion to his body than moments earlier. One soldier still held on to his back, sword raised, and plunged the blade into the Lion's shoulder. With a swift paw Leopold grabbed hold of the man across his back, reaching and finding his throat as he tore it loose in one savage motion. The body fell to the floor, lifeless.

Before the soldier cutting the last of Drew's bonds could finish, he was bowled out of the way by the king. A sweeping uppercut from Leopold's clawed hand sent the man skittering across the stage, a shower of blood trailing in his wake. Drew rolled over, channeling all of his strength into the change, risking everything in the hope that the soldier had cut enough of the silver bindings. Resisting at first, the ropes finally snapped as Drew felt muscle and raw energy rush through him.

The deck splintered beside his head as the king's sword smashed down, cleaving through the six-inch timbers like a knife through butter. Drew sprang to one side, keeping moving as the king followed him, the sword arcing through the air where the Werewolf's head had been a moment earlier.

Stay alert, thought Drew. *Remember Gerard's lessons: keep your legs moving, don't let him in.*

Again the sword flew down, crashing into wood as Drew jumped aside. With each evasion of the Lion's sword Drew could feel the Wolf growing stronger. His arms were now transformed, the white shirt no longer loose but straining across bulging muscles. Steel gray hair raced over his body as he let loose everything he had left. His dark clawed hands scrabbled at the decking as he stayed on all fours, bounding clear of the enraged Werelion time and time again. His jaw snapped, dislocating as the beast inside him rearranged his restrictive human features, thrusting a snarling muzzle outward while dark fur shot across his flesh. His amber eyes stayed on his enemy at all times, his senses becoming sharper as he let the Wolf loose.

For all the power, speed, and strength Drew now had at his disposal, he was still no match for the Werelion. As Drew found himself back where he'd originally lay bound, his right leg slipped through the timbers splintered by the Lion's earlier attack. It caught, just for a second, but it was long enough for the king to connect with both steel and claw. His silver-laced sword tore across Drew's shoulder, ripping a ragged hole, while his hand lashed up from below. He caught the Wolf on his jaw and sent him flying through the air to land in the middle of the warring soldiers.

Immediately a circle cleared around him, affording Drew a chance to look about. The royal pavilion was alive with activity—Werelords in various states of change engaging with soldiers and one another. He saw Prince Lucas pulling Gretchen by the hand as she lashed out at him. His mother, Queen Amelie, stood behind the Werefox, arms around her hips, trying to stop her son from taking Gretchen. Hector was standing beside a heavily built fellow whose canine head was covered with black and white fur. There was nothing comedic about the sight of the Werebadger, one of the lesser lords, as he defended the young Boarlord from the savage blows of Captain Brutus.

The crowd raged all around the square, inspired by the fight, rushing against the oppressive Lionguard as they noticed the colors of the Wolfguard dotted about the scaffold. Before

Drew could make out any more details, he felt a sword hack against his flank, then another, as two of the Lionguard dealt him raking blows. The bodies of men from both the Wolfguard and the king's soldiers littered the decking as Drew traded blows with the two attackers. Seeing their king heading for Drew, they fell back, reengaging other opponents.

Leopold paced toward Drew, huge chest heaving, his monstrous maw moving as he spoke. "No running, dog," he growled, his voice deep and booming, eclipsing the noise of the surrounding chaos. "Fight me! Coward!"

Drew knew he couldn't keep on running. He was already wounded and had nowhere to retreat to. Now was the time to make his stand. The Lion was about to shout something else, but the words never left his lips. Drew leapt from where he squatted on the ground, springing across the stage like a cannonball of claws and fangs. He hit Leopold square in the chest before he could raise his sword in defense, and the two hit the decking, howling and roaring, claws ripping, teeth clashing.

Drew could feel his claws connecting, ripping at the Lion's chest and flanks. He broke past the king's paws with his teeth to bite at the beast's neck, teeth closing and grinding at the skin. But Leopold was tough, his flesh hard and leathery, the Wolf's teeth only breaking the surface of the Lion's throat and causing superficial damage. All the while Drew tore and bit, the king continued his own assault, to greater and bloodier effect. He brought his back legs into the battle, his boots now in tatters as additional paws curled up from below, the razor-sharp claws digging and tearing at the young Wolf's unprotected belly. His arms kept a grip on Drew's back, holding him close in a death embrace, all the while pulling at his flesh. And his teeth came down again and again, biting into Drew's exposed shoulders and neck, fur flying as the softer, younger skin put up less resistance than his own.

Drew could feel his energy fading, his whole torso a mess of blood and torn flesh. He held on to his enemy—he had no choice—trading blows with the Werelion but losing the battle as time wore on. Within moments he could sense his body failing him, the contest edging ever nearer its grim conclusion. There was an earth-shaking crash, the whole decking threatening to collapse as a great weight landed upon it. A mighty horn blew, deafeningly loud, pealing out over the whole of Highcliff.

"Leave the boy alone!" bellowed a monstrous voice as further thunderous noises descended onto the scaffold. The king looked up as Drew struggled to pull free. Duke Bergan stood on the platform, himself changed into his therian form, the old Bear towering over everybody, even the giant beast that was the king. He lowered his horn to his hip, his ax at the ready. To his side stood another changed Werelord; the three-foot antlers that emerged from his long snorting skull came to wicked points, a full head of deadly daggers, as Manfred of Stormdale lowered his brow menacingly. Behind the two of them leapt Count Vega, still for the most part in his buccaneering human form, but with a smile full of sharp and savage teeth. The king held on to Drew, refusing to let go.

"And if I don't?" he growled. All the fighting on the scaffold had ceased, either through victory on one side or sheer disbelief at the sight that confronted the men.

"You kill him. We kill you. It ends here, now," said Bergan, his great shaggy head motionless as he stood ready to rush the king.

"Or," said Duke Manfred, "you leave, now, with your life, never to come back. Something you never allowed Wergar to do."

The Werelion looked at the boy in his grasp, the deep growl that emanated from his chest rattling its way through Drew's body like an earthquake. Standing suddenly, the Lion brought a clawed hand up to Drew's head, taking a grip of the Wolf's mane of dark black hair. The crowd booed, baying at him, calling for him to stop. He looked around the square, surveying the situation, horrified at how quickly his people had turned against him. A further figure bounded onto the stage, this one standing by his side: the lord chancellor.

"Your Majesty," whispered the Wererat, who was still in his cloaked human form, "I think it might be prudent if we make a retreat."

"Listen to Vanmorten," snarled Bergan. "They're the first words of wisdom that have ever slipped from the Rat's mouth."

The Wererat hissed from inside his hood, putting a hand on his master.

"My Lord," he said, "this is not a surrender. We have the castle. We have our army. We still have the city. These fools are now prolonging the inevitable. Give them the dog if it allows us to regroup, and then we shall strike back and lay waste to these traitors and their petty realms. We have allies. Remember?"

The king growled once more. The lord chancellor's words were hitting home, but the king was a proud man, and he'd never walked away from a fight in his life. The castle was a good idea, but it would be on his terms. He shifted his grip on the great sword in his other hand, his knuckles tightening about the scalp of the Wolf.

Before he could move, Count Vega had flung something through the air. It whirled across the stage as Drew reached out and snatched it with his right hand, not stopping its momentum. The Wolfshead blade landed smoothly in his grasp and he turned it toward his attacker. The sword hit the Lion square in his exposed torso, its razor-sharp edge finding purchase between the king's muscled ribs. In it went, clean through the Lion, right to the hilt and out the other side. The Lion lifted Drew by the hair, the sword sliding free from his chest, and sent him flying across the stage to land in a heap among the other bodies. The blow would not be fatal—the Wolfshead blade was untreated by silver—but such an attack would incapacitate the Lion.

"Protect the king!" roared Vanmorten, and a squad of Lionguard rushed to Leopold's side and dragged him away. Many of the men in the Wolf's colors lay dead, dying, or injured on the platform as the king and his soldiers retreated. Bergan did not follow—there was still business to attend to. The main force of the Lionguard remained in the square and was approaching the bloodied scaffold.

Drew rolled over where he lay, coming face-to-face with the helmeted head of the guard who had cut him free. The man's red tabard had been torn wide open by the king's attack, fully exposing the long-lost Wolfguard symbol beneath. This, too, had been sliced apart, and the steel armor of his breastplate had provided little resistance against the Werelion's deadly claws. The man's stomach was bleeding heavily. With his energy sapped, Drew could feel his body start returning to normal, his heart aching at the sight of the savior who had paid for Drew's life with his own. The man sputtered, and Drew reached with torn fingers to remove his helmet. As the armor came away Drew came face-to-face with Mack Ferran, his father.

"Pa?" Drew cried out, clutching the man's face in both hands. What was he doing here?

Mack Ferran's eyes were clouding over, and blood caked his mouth and teeth. His gauntleted fingers were holding his stomach in place, but it was a futile effort. "Son . . ." He coughed, but the effort was too great.

"No, Pa," said Drew, tears rushing free now. "Don't speak. We'll get you healed. Get you better."

"Drew, we have to move," shouted Duke Bergan, who stood

beside Manfred and Vega. Along with the remaining Wolf-guard, they kept the king's soldiers at bay as best they could. "They are too many! We need to go!"

The soldier in Drew's arms sputtered, bloody bubbles frothing in his mouth.

"Can't heal now, lad," he said. "Too late for that. The king, Drew. He killed your real family. Slaughtered 'em and burned 'em up. Your mother, she took you as her own." He coughed again, closing his eyes. "Your mother . . . I thought . . . thought you'd done that. Thought you'd turned on her. Turned on us."

Drew shook his head, sniffing. "No, never, Pa. I loved her. I love you all. It was a monster. A Wererat, they say. She died in my arms. . . ." he finished, realizing the same thing was happening all over again, this time with his father.

"I'm sorry, son," Mack Ferran whispered quietly, the air from his lungs escaping with these last words.

"I forgive you," returned Drew with a kiss to his father's cheek, but he was already dead.

"Drew!" shouted Count Vega, his rapier flashing out into the red-cloaked Lionguard, their ranks swelling all the while as soldiers rushed to their comrades' side. The king might have retreated, but this was still the Lion's city and all those who disputed that were still the enemy. "Move yourself! There are too many of them!"

Drew rose from the decking, shockwaves coursing through him, limping and staggering as he looked about. He could see the royal pavilion where a few remaining Werelords still held their ground. When he saw Hector in the middle of them, he felt a glimmer of relief. The Boarlord gestured desperately, beckoning him over, but got no response.

Manfred followed Drew's gaze. "To the pavilion!" he shouted, rushing up to Drew and taking him by the elbow. He was ushered down the steps of the scaffold, as three of the Wolfguard ran before them, pushing the crowds aside as they tried to force their way through. From the rear of the square the first wave of the men of Brackenholme was surging forward, accompanied by those from Stormdale. Drew saw Lord Broghan, the Bearlord's son, leading the way, swinging his ax through the king's men. They were still a great distance from the Werelords, fighting against a dedicated mass of Lionguard, but their sheer presence filled Drew's heart with hope. The tide might just turn.

The Lionguard at the scaffold seemed to sense the arrival of their enemy in force. From their vantage point they suddenly appeared to be disengaging, pulling back from direct combat. Drew heard the captains barking out orders to their men as they fell into units, guarding one another with shield and sword. As they retreated, some of the braver cityfolk began shouting at them—the few who had supported the king had fallen silent, either fleeing the scene of battle or being dispatched by their neighbors. Now the Lionguard weren't just facing the allies of Duke Bergan, but the very people they were sworn to "protect." A hail of stones and bricks showered forward, smashing and clattering against the soldiers' armor. The tide was indeed turning.

Drew was pushed and jostled through the crowd in the direction of the pavilion. His head swam with nausea as he looked down at his hands, still slick with the blood of his father. He turned them over and over again, back and then palm up, looking as their color slowly shifted from gray back to pink. The Wolf was retreating. Lights speckled in front of his eyes, tiny eruptions of dizziness as he tried to grasp what had just happened. He looked up to see Gretchen high in the pavilion, hugging Hector in triumph. To the other side of her was Queen Amelie, and her face was a mask of tears and joy.

Mother, thought Drew. *My mother.*

His head swam with confusion, his lycanthrope body numb to the great damage he'd sustained. Lightheaded and floating through the crowd, he looked over the sea of heads toward the castle. Vega and Bergan were close behind, the Wolfguard closing ranks around them as the Lionguard continued their retreat across the drawbridge. Drew snapped back into himself, like a drowning man gasping at air. The words of Leopold and Mack Ferran flooded back to him. The queen's children—his brothers, his sisters—butchered by the Lion, murdered and then burned. Who did the king answer to? What justice was there in this world if they let him go free?

Revived by his sense of duty, he broke away suddenly, unexpectedly. Transforming quickly from his Wolf form, he had slipped free from Manfred's grasp before the Werestag had a moment to react. He was gone into the throng in a moment, no longer the Werewolf but a man once again, blending in with the crowd.

"Where is he?" shouted Bergan across the crowd to Manfred. "Where's he gone?"

"He was here a second ago," called the Lord of Stormdale, looking about the crowd. Bergan followed his gaze, searching for the young man. The crowds held back from the Werelords, so monstrous and terrifying in appearance, and the panic about them caused even greater confusion as they searched for the escaped Werewolf.

"Drew!" roared Bergan into the crowd, but, bear or not, his voice didn't carry far into the tumult.

"There!" shouted Vega suddenly, pointing toward the castle as the drawbridge was raised. "Sosha, what is he *doing*?" he cried.

"No!" the three of them shouted in unison, Hector and Gretchen screaming the same pleas as they spied their friend, but it was too late.

Bergan could see Drew scrambling for purchase on the end of the drawbridge, one bloodied arm hooked over the edge as his legs dangled below. It was halfway up now, a great forty-foot bridge of the thickest timbers, rising to close against the stone wall of the gatehouse. A yawning chasm opened up below, a natural canyon that disappeared down the castle's cliff-face walls, ending where they met the sea in a mass of rocks and crashing waves. If the boy fell . . . Bergan didn't want to think of what the drop might do to him. Nor would he entertain the thought of what fate awaited him if he made it into the keep.

Exhausted, tattered, and torn, Drew scrambled to throw his leg over the edge of the drawbridge, his heel finally finding a grip as he pulled his aching body over. His ears were ringing as he readied himself on the end of the rising bridge. He wiped his blood-smeared hand across his brow, trying to clear his vision.

The last the assembled Werelords and crowds saw of Drew was the image of him raising the Wolfshead blade above his head as he disappeared down the other side of the bridge.

7

UNFINISHED BUSINESS

DREW LANDED WITH a sickening crunch on the cobbled ground beneath the gatehouse. Jagged pains shot up his left leg, and he looked down to see his foot twisted into an impossible position. He felt the bones inside his ankle grating against one another, tearing against the flesh within. The pain woke him from his fevered state, the clouds of confusion parting as he pulled himself together. Standing upright he held the sword point down, using it as a crutch, as he squinted into the courtyard beyond. His heart sank with dread realization. What was he doing here?

The courtyard was packed with the Lionguard, hundreds of Leopold's elite soldiers moving as one to see who had followed them into Highcliff Castle. The look of disbelief spread among them like wildfire, the men incredulous that the Wolf had pursued them. Drew turned around and saw the drawbridge disappearing into the darkened recesses of the gatehouse, his way of escape firmly blocked. He was under no illusions. This really was the end.

The sound of one man clapping slowly echoed across the courtyard over his shoulder. Drew's head dropped. He didn't want to, but he knew it was time to face his enemy. The bravado he'd felt lying before the executioner's block had escaped him now, evaporating like morning mist on a hot summer's day. Some headstrong, dazed compulsion had led him here, brought him to his death when he'd been in touching distance of freedom. He hopped about and made his way toward the king. The ranks of soldiers pulled back, their swords drawn, still wary of him initially. But as the wounded figure stumbled out of the shadows on one leg, they saw him for what he now was—defenseless and quite harmless. Leopold continued to clap as he came forward to meet Drew, his red-cloaked men parting before him like a tide of blood.

Drew felt a twinge of satisfaction: the king was still injured. Now he was back in his human form, it would be some time before his therianthropy began to work its magic on his stomach wound. Already one of his men had bandaged him around the middle, a long roll of white cloth mottled dark red where Drew's sword had impacted. The king was bedraggled and disheveled, as far from noble as Drew could imagine. He looked awful, but Drew knew he looked worse. The Werelion stopped clapping when he came within ten paces of Drew, clasping his hands together as if in prayer to Old Brenn.

"Thank you," he said, "for following me here. You would not believe what joy you've brought to your dear king's heart."

"You're not my king," said Drew. "Be done with it. Kill me now," he said, wincing and shifting his weight onto the Wolfs-head blade as he let his broken ankle hang loose.

The king stood there, looking the youth up and down. Then he slowly walked around Drew, inspecting him like he was a piece of meat hung in a butcher's shop, until he returned to face him. Beyond the king, Drew could see other members of the king's court, four of the five Rat King brothers standing as one. He couldn't see Vankaskan or Lucas, and could only hope that they'd been injured or worse in the earlier battle.

"I have a better idea," replied Leopold eventually. "Van-morten," he called, raising a finger to beckon the lord chancel-lor. The cowled man walked slowly forward, past his brothers, who watched with wide and excited eyes. Beyond the walls of Highcliff Castle they could all hear the shouts and jeers of the crowd. The people had revolted.

If any good can come from my death, let it be that, thought Drew. *Let these people be free from tyranny.*

The robed Wererat stood beside King Leopold. "Your Majesty," he said, bowing.

"I believe you and the boy are already acquainted?"

"We've never met," cut in Drew, before the Wererat could respond. "I know your brother Vankaskan, though, and I'm sure you're as sick as he is." Drew had nothing to lose and saw no harm in mouthing off to the king and his lackey. What more could they do to him now?

"Your memory fails you, boy," said Leopold. "It wasn't that long ago, surely?"

A feeling of unease gripped Drew. What were they playing at?

"My dear Lord Chancellor," continued Leopold. "Consider this a gift, my old friend, and a lesson. Never leave any loose ends. Always finish the task at hand."

The Wererat stepped closer, raising a clawed black hand to point at Drew's chest.

"Those scars," he said, flicking his claws against one another so that they clicked skeletally. From within the darkness of the cowl his red eyes glinted malevolently. "They look old. Fancy some fresh ones?"

Drew's jaw fell slack as he glanced at his chest. There were fresh wounds decorating his torso, but he knew what the Wererat was talking about. He looked at the three old scars across his breast, a badge that would forever remind him of the death of Tilly Ferran, the woman he would always love as his mother.

Vanmorten stopped in his tracks, raising a clawed hand to his hood. He tugged it back, revealing himself to Drew. The man was bald, his skin pasty and sickly, and his ruby eyes glowed with cruelty. Most shocking was the huge portion of flesh that was missing from the right side of his face. He was grotesque, his bare skull on show from his temple down to his jaw. The sweet stench of decaying flesh rolled off the unhealing wound in waves. He trailed his monstrous hand to the bleached bone of his face, scraping a black claw under the exposed eye socket.

Drew felt fresh nausea assailing his body. The farmhouse, his mother, the monster—it all rushed back. He hobbled backward toward a flight of stone steps that wound up along the length of the inner wall, ending on the battlements. The king laughed, clapping his hands cheerily as the Wererat stalked forward. The men of the Lionguard joined in raucously, waving and calling taunts to him as he retreated. Drew turned to struggle up the flagged stone steps, baskets and crates skittering out of his way as he tried to put distance between himself and the Wererat. He was on his hands and knees, the Wolfshead blade clattering along beside him as he pulled himself up the stairs on his stomach. He'd often dreamed of this moment—encountering the murderer who had killed his mother—and imagined what it would be like to take the life of the monster. Faced with the opportunity now, terror seized him and his nerves were failing. He was gravely injured, unprepared, and drowning with despair. The Wererat kept advancing, up the staircase, ever closer to him.

Vanmorten wasn't the tallest Werelord by any means, well

under six feet. However, Drew remembered all too clearly the creature he'd faced at the homestead. There had been nothing small about him. Both of the Wererat's arms were part changed now, thick, wiry black hair covering his forearms down to the horrible clawed hands. Drew, on the other hand, could feel his own insides twisting in on themselves, guts knotting and clenching as his own transformation spasmed and faltered. Tears rolled down his cheeks as he struggled on, gripped with fear. His memories were racing; he could *taste* the monster's blood in his mouth, back in the farmhouse.

"What a shame," said the Wererat. "I would have thought that you'd have ironed out those awful growing pains by now." He tutted, shaking his misshapen head. "Vankaskan warned me about you. Said you were a wild dog, a mongrel. I have to say you're doing your reputation proud, crawling away on your belly."

Drew arrived atop the battlements, the Wererat just behind him. He stood over Drew, towering and in complete control.

"I recognized you for the spawn of Wergar when we first met," he said, his voice grating like nails on a blackboard. "Living with that traitor in a windswept farmhouse. It makes perfect sense now. Stole you away from the Wolf's court, did she? I spent over a decade searching for that woman. I never let the scent go cold. It was unfinished business that needed to be taken care of." He ran a clawed finger under his throat in a slashing motion. "And it was."

"That was my mother!" cried Drew. "She never harmed anyone; she was innocent. She was no traitor." He pointed to the three scars on his chest. "You did that to me, I'll give you that. But I believe I had a hand in your spoiled good looks," he said, smirking at Vanmorten.

The Werelord's eyes glazed over with a furious red fire. He arched his back violently and his robes tore to shreds, falling to the floor as black oily hair spread over his body. Drew retreated into a towering stack of boxes and barrels, freshly delivered from the *Maelstrom* by a winch with rope and pulley that now dangled idle in the wind. Drew's ankle was on fire with pain, but he tried to push past it, pulling himself up on one foot, taking hold of a tall iron brazier that was full of burning coals for support. Below him in the courtyard he could see the king's soldiers massed, looking up, waiting for the kill. He looked the other way, beyond the walls, and saw rooftops of the city stretched out. In High Square the crowd was pointing up at him, craning to see Drew as he balanced on top of battlements. But between him and the safety of the city was the sheer drop that had loomed beneath him on the drawbridge.

He did his best to stand his ground, but as the Wererat changed he could feel his legs weakening again. *Stay strong, Drew*, he told himself. *Think of Ma.*

A long, black tail whipped out toward Drew, sending him

toppling sideways in the direction of the edge. Within the walls, the soldiers cheered. Arms raised high over his head, the Wererat leapt at him, jaws wide open and teeth snapping. Drew ducked and tumbled clear as Vanmorten smashed into the tower of stacked barrels and boxes, sending them crashing down on top of him.

King Leopold appeared at the top of the staircase, accompanied by the other three Rat King brothers. The Werelion watched with interest as all three Wererats hissed, stepping closer, their red eyes starting to glow.

"Back," snarled Vanmorten, climbing out of the splintered barrels. "The dog is mine, my brothers," he said in a low guttural growl. His voice was almost incoherent, the monster taking over. Vanmorten dived. Clearing the distance between them in one bound, the Wererat bowled into Drew, sending the two of them smashing into the crenellated stone wall. More barrels and boxes clattered down around them, their broken contents bouncing off them as they wrestled with each other. Drew tried again to call the Wolf, but he had no energy for the transformation, his hands doing all they could to hold back the Rat. Vanmorten was fast and wiry, squirming from Drew's grip every time he tried to fend him off. His fight with the Lion haunted Drew anew, and he knew the end was close, but with no chance of rescue this time.

Snatching the youth up, Vanmorten held him aloft triumphantly before hurling him over the side of the parapets to his doom. Screams flared up from the city below. Before he was clear of the wall Drew threw his left hand out desperately, catching hold of the winch, sending it spinning wildly about, rope and tackle rattling as it whirled. He held on with a white-knuckled grip, his other limbs flailing and the Wolfshead blade flashing through the air as he clutched it tightly. Both boy and crane smashed into the tall metal brazier, then back into the fray, sending burning coals scattering across the stone walk-way and over Vanmorten, flames leaping among the broken crates and barrels.

The three Wererat brothers now whooped and hissed excitedly, itching to pounce and join the fight. Drew was un-der no illusion: even if he were to somehow beat Vanmorten, another would leap into his place. The Wererat shook the hot coals from his greasy hide.

Drew and Vanmorten circled each other, scrambling over the broken crates and upturned cargo. The fire was now all around them, devouring anything it came into contact with. Flames licked across the battlements, out of control, leaping onto the precious crates of goods that still lined the castle walls. Drew hobbled past the staircase and the Wererat's snarl-ing brethren, keeping his back covered whenever possible. Still the king watched on, fascinated by the spectacle. All the while Vanmorten closed the distance between them.

The spirit of Mack Ferran loomed on Drew's shoulder, watching, judging. Is this how he, an elite soldier of the Wolfguard, would have fought a battle? On the retreat, backtracking, prolonging the inevitable? Was that how Drew should fight? Was that the way of the Wolf?

His mind set, Drew leapt into the fray.

8

THE FALL OF THE WOLF

THE TWO CHALLENGERS met in a whirlwind of sword and claw as the soldiers cheered. This was what they wanted to see. But it wasn't a lycanthrope that engaged Vanmorten. Ordinarily the Werewolf might have stood a chance, a toned and perfect killing machine. But this was Drew the young man who wrestled the beast, the Wolf within now spent. He lunged with the Wolfshead blade, striking at the Ratlord repeatedly, occasionally connecting but for the most part missing. Drew was ravaged with injury and only hoped he might take Vanmorten with him before he died.

The Wererat's jaws snapped in a blurred fury, lashing out blindly and tearing into the young man's stomach. He grabbed Drew's sword hand, crushing his grip until he dropped the

Wolfshead blade with a clatter. Vanmorten strained to get to Drew's underbelly, to bury his teeth in his softer flesh. Drew writhed, trying to get clear, but he was unprepared for the ferocity of the Wererat's attack. Each time he tried to pull back his head, Vanmorten's jaws closed around his hands and forearms, bringing up fresh gouts of blood with each bite.

Drew's chest screamed with pain as the Wererat tore a strip of flesh clean off his ribs. With his left hand he tried to prize the creature clear, his fingers hooking under razor-sharp teeth. Pulling with what little strength he had left, he succeeded in throwing Vanmorten back briefly but at further cost. As the Wererat sprang back for a moment, the bare side of his skull shimmering in the light of the fires, he spat something at Drew that bounced off the boy's chest. Drew gazed at the floor, horrified to see one of the bloody fingers of his left hand lying there. The Wererat chuckled as his brothers hollered with appreciation at the top of the stairs.

"Eat you," he said, chest heaving with the excitement and thrill of the combat. "Bit. By. Bit."

Drew felt sick to the core. He was lost—it was a massacre, and the monster was playing with him. His chest was carved with claw marks and his body was soaked with sweat. On his left hand a steady pulse of blood dripped from the wound. He fumbled with his right hand for the Wolfshead blade on the floor, tugging at the pommel before holding it up defensively.

"Look at the poor Wolf," said the mocking voice of King

Leopold from the staircase. The Ratlords joined him, screaming and clapping hysterically. "The pup has a sword?" he wheezed, a hand on his stomach where Drew had stabbed him.

Drew's vision blurred as his head swirled. He put pressure on his left leg, feeling his ankle crunch where it was broken, and let loose a scream of pain. Wiping his forearm across his brow, he only succeeded in smearing fresh blood in his eyes. Temporarily blinded he let out a roar as he felt claws rip into his right flank. He spun, lashing out, trying to clear his vision with rapid blinks. The Wererat was behind him now. Drew slashed forward with his sword, all coordination failing him, all of Gerard's lessons forgotten. He staggered dangerously close to the edge once more, only warned of his peril by the screams of the masses below. His sword smashed into another brazier on the wall, fresh coals flying. Again, claws raked through his skin, this time down his back as Vanmorten maneuvered about him. This would not be a quick death after all.

More laughter rang across the battlements as Drew collapsed against the broken boxes for support. He could feel his life beginning to fade. The Wererat snatched the blade from his shattered grip. Drew was a fool. He didn't belong here in this castle, fighting some monster. He was a farm boy, a simple shepherd. Was this how he was going to die? Wiped out of existence by the same tooth and claw that had started his nightmare?

"Kill him," said the king quietly. The Wererat turned to Drew.

Vanmorten gripped the boy's head in a clawed hand, knotting his black knuckles into his hair. Drew winced as the beast lowered his lips to his ear. "Now die, last Wolf," he spat in his ear, breath hot and foul. "Die like a dog." He loosed his grip and Drew heard the tip of his father's Wolfshead blade scrape along the floor as Vanmorten prepared to use it against him. In the midst of the raging fire Drew's gaze settled on a familiar-looking clay flask that lay in the jumble of broken goods. He recognized it from his time in the belly of the *Maelstrom*. Drew tore free, leaving clumps of his hair in the monster's clawed hand, snatching at the flask as he collapsed onto his back, hurling it up into the air at the Ratlord.

With unerring accuracy the clay jar hit the Wererat clean on the jaw, exploding and sending Spyr Oil showering over Vanmorten's face and torso. It was the lord chancellor's turn to be temporarily blinded as the thick, spiced oil stung his red eyes. Drew brought his good leg back, knee up to his chest, and with all the strength he could muster kicked up and out. His foot connected with the Wererat in the pit of his groin, sending him wheeling backward, snatching at thin air along the top of the wall as he reeled back into the fire.

With a screeching whoosh the Spyr Oil ignited, racing over Vanmorten's body with ravenous urgency. The Wererat wailed in agony as his oily hair went up in flames and burned at his flesh. His thick tail whipped in a frantic blur as he thrashed around in the fire. Drew scrambled forward, throwing his own hand into the fire as he reached for the Wolfshead blade. He grabbed the blistered claw of the Wererat. The heat was intense, the pain unbearable for Drew as he felt the fire race up his own arm, hair frying and skin blazing. Through the flickering flames he could just discern Vanmorten's furious red eyes locked on his own as the Wererat feebly held on to the sword. With a final tug it came free and Drew tumbled away from the fire, his arm charred and the sword a smoking brand in his grip.

Stumbling onto his good foot, he winced as he touched his left down for balance, looking through the fire. He could make out the wailing figures of Vanmorten's brothers, arms raised in fury beyond the wall of heat. They were beginning to change, dark hideous shadows flickering into life in the orange glow. He saw Leopold, roaring in dismay, screaming at the rest of the Ratlords to attack. Drew backed up toward the edge of the wall, the low crenellations bumping against his thighs as he hopped.

The inferno was raging now, out of control, as the fire devoured everything on the walkway. Fresh flasks of Spyr Oil exploded, sending many of those who gathered into retreat. But the brothers remained. Drew looked up to see three large, black shapes bound through the fire toward him. The Wererats snapped at one another as they advanced, bickering over who would get to tear the Wolf apart. He dared a glance over his shoulder, finding only air at his heel, ready to take him down to the White Sea below. He looked back to the flames. The biggest of the three brothers had muscled his way to the front. The air was thick with the smell of burned fur and smoking flesh. The hulking Wererat opened his mouth, letting sticky globs of drool fall from his maws. Drew knew he could back up no farther, his broken heel hanging over the lip of the battlements. He wavered for a moment, holding the Wolfshead blade toward the assembled monsters.

Then, in the blink of an eye and with a suddenness that took the Wererats and the king by surprise, Drew lowered his smoking sword and simply fell backward into the void.

Before he lost consciousness, his last memory was of the raging Wererats he'd left behind on the battlements disappearing into the distance, silhouetted by the inferno at their backs.

9

DREAMS AND DESTINY

DREW DREAMED HE was in his mother's arms. She was rocking him, soothing him, singing a lullaby. Was he a baby or a young man? He couldn't tell. He was warm and he was safe, that much he knew. The familiar scent of meadows and bluebells surrounded him, freshly picked from the lane that led to the Ferran farm. He could hear another voice, possibly his father working in the woodshed, calling dimly beyond his senses. The distant cry of gulls was clear enough, sending his mind racing back to his childhood when he chased the birds from the freshly plowed fields. All the while his mother rocked him in her arms, singing gently.

More noises began to creep into his dream, at odds with the surroundings. He could hear bells ringing, and the sound of water as waves rolled across his subconscious. Still the voice sang to him, soft and tender, his mother lovingly caressing his brow. There was a rising sense of discomfort that worked its way through his body, starting with his feet, then legs, and coursing through his whole frame. He tried to open his eyes, squinting at the harsh, bright light that filled his vision. A hand pushed down on his chest, holding him in place as he moved fitfully, writhing as the pain overtook him.

The smooth lip of a polished wooden cup touched his broken lips. A sweet-tasting nectar poured gently down his throat, instantly warming him and dulling the pain. Still the voice sang, never wavered, never ceased, as he drifted back into a surreal sleep.

When Drew finally awoke, he rubbed gingerly at his eyes before taking in his surroundings. He was back on board the *Maelstrom*, recognizing instantly the room Count Vega had kept him in on the last leg of their journey to Highcliff. He lay in the bed, blankets and quilt holding him firmly and cozily in one place, as the rocking motion of the ship sent the bright lantern above his head swinging this way and that. A chorus of bells could be heard ringing loud and clear, joined by the sound of distant singing and cheering. The rocking, the bells, the light—all things he began to remember from his dream.

Gretchen lay curled up in a leather armchair, her legs

tucked under her chin and her arms wrapped protectively around them. She looked exhausted but at peace, the red curls of her hair fluttering over her lips as she breathed. To her side, reclining in a wooden captain's chair, sat Hector, a book open in his lap as his head hung back, mouth wide open and snoring contentedly. Drew smiled, trying to pull himself up. His legs shot with pain, stiff and unmoving, angry jolts coming from his shattered bones.

He tugged the sheets loose, pulling them back to find that broad wooden splints had been attached to each leg with bandages and leather strips. They were bruised, blackened, and broken, lumps rising over their surface like discolored mountain ranges, but he knew they would mend. His chest and arms were also dressed with a patchwork quilt of bandages and dressings. On his left hand a bandage was wrapped around where he'd lost his little finger, and his right arm was coated with a slick, sweet oil that was working its magic, healing his burns. Hector's satchel lay open on the floor, many of his salves and ointments visible to Drew, and once more the young Werewolf was grateful to his friend. A shadow passed over Drew as somebody else came to crouch beside him.

"Drew of the Dyrewood," said a familiar voice. "Can't say I ever expected to see you again."

Drew moved to sit upright again with shock and surprise, until his wounded body screamed out in protest. He stifled a cry as the figure put a hand to his chest, easing him back into the bed. He blinked once, twice, with disbelief.

"Whitley?" he gasped. "Is that . . . you?"

He had very real doubts. The figure kneeling beside the bed did indeed at first glance appear to be the scout's apprentice he'd met so long ago in the Dyrewood, but there'd been a startling transformation. The face was undeniably Whitley's, but the outfit and appearance caused Drew a great deal of confusion. His friend was wearing a fine ivory dress, the hem, collar, and sleeves of which were decorated with an embroidered green ivy motif. A brown apron was tied around his middle, possibly to keep his dress clean, and his long brown hair was braided back from his brow, running halfway down his back. Drew's head swam.

"But . . . you're dressed as a girl," he whispered, as if trying to keep this revelation between the two of them.

"That's because I *am* a girl, stupid," said Whitley, pouring a mead-like liquid from a jug into a glass for him. "Here, drink this," she said, handing it to Drew. He gulped it down tentatively, choking as the realization finally sunk in.

"But you were pretending to be a boy when we met."

"I wasn't, Drew," said Whitley, taking the empty glass with a smile. "You assumed I was a boy, that's all. Maybe I was guilty of not correcting you, for which I might owe you an apology."

"What were you doing with Master Hogan?"

"Oh, I was his apprentice all right. Still am, I suppose, although he's still not well enough to return to the forest. I'm completing my training in the field, so to speak—that's why I accompanied my father to Highcliff."

"Your father—Duke Bergan, right?"

"That's correct." She smiled, rising and straightening the brown apron over her dress.

The door opened suddenly and a large figure bent low to enter from the dark corridor beyond. It was the Bearlord himself, who, upon taking one look at Drew sitting up in the bed, let a warm smile fill his bearded face.

"Ha!" he cried noisily, turning to lean back out of the door and call up the corridor. "He's up!"

Gretchen and Hector awoke instantly with a start, delighted by the sight of their risen friend in his bed. Both leapt from their chairs and rushed over to Drew, who gingerly held his arms out as they embraced him. Whitley stood to one side, smiling.

"You're awake!" Gretchen gasped, echoed by Hector's: "You're better!"

"Indeed I am," replied Drew. "Good of you to notice!"

Hector immediately started to take Drew's vital signs, checking his temperature and pulse, and looking over his wounds.

"He's fine, Hector," said Whitley. "I checked him while you were napping. Please don't worry yourself."

"You've been out cold all afternoon, since they fished you out of the harbor," said Hector, unable to stop himself from checking that the bandages were still taut.

"The harbor?" asked Drew. "I remember falling and then nothing."

"You might have died, lad," said Bergan, moving to sit in the leather armchair that Gretchen had vacated. "You can thank the Sharklord for thinking fast and diving in to rescue you. Mind, you'd swallowed so much of the White Sea I wasn't convinced there was much left to save."

Drew was amazed by the news, by all that was happening around him. He'd leapt from the battlements to deny the Were-rats the satisfaction of killing him. He hadn't expected to survive the fall; indeed, he thought the strange dream he'd been having was heaven, so vivid and rich had it been. He looked about the bed suddenly.

"My sword," he said. "Where's the Wolfshead blade?"

"Lost, I'm afraid," replied Hector. "It's somewhere in the harbor, I guess, or halfway across the White Sea by now. Sorry, Drew."

Drew felt great pain at the loss of the one thing that held a connection to the man he'd called his father, who had died so valiantly for him. He hoped they could find his body in the carnage of the scaffold, to give him the hero's send-off he deserved. All those Wolfguard soldiers deserved that much.

"The soldiers," said Drew, "why did they leap in to fight? How did they have Wergar's colors still?"

"That would be my doing, lad," said Bergan. "I knew Mack Ferran fought in the Wolfguard, and it nagged at me, trying to remember him. I recalled that some of the Wolfguard had returned to Highcliff's service after they had been disbanded. A number of those who guarded the king used to serve the Wolf, you see. So a thought occurred to me. I would ask about; find out if any of the Lionguard knew him. Sure enough they did. It was a greater shock to find that the man who raised you had rejoined the army."

Drew was astonished. "Why would he join with the Lion?"

"He told me straight enough. Said he thought you were the enemy. Held you directly responsible for killing his wife. His life fell apart that night, Drew. It was only when I explained what had actually happened to you, how a beast had killed your mother, that he realized what a fool he'd been. Seems he had time, no matter how brief, to try to make amends. And some old but still loyal men helped him. It was a selfless sacrifice Ferran and those soldiers made for you; never forget that."

Drew fell silent as he considered the situation. Mack Ferran had always harbored suspicions and mistrust with regard to Drew. Drew had known that throughout his childhood. Mack looked at him differently from how he looked at his birth son, as if he was waiting for him to put a foot wrong, to slip up. It was what any man would do, knowing his family could be at risk from Drew's lycanthropy when he came of age. In many ways he'd been right. And Trent? What had become of him? Drew resigned himself to the fact that he'd probably never know. He could only hope that if he ever did return to the Ferran farm he'd find his brother waiting for him, a daft grin spread across his face. He could only hope.

Drew heard the waves from his dreams beyond the wooden walls of the *Maelstrom* splashing lazily against the hardened hull. He could still taste the salty seawater in his mouth, in his stomach.

"I thought I'd died," he whispered. Whitley reached around him to plump up the pillows, now that he was sitting upright. She pulled the blankets back up where he'd kicked them loose, tucking them into place.

"So did we," said Gretchen, gently nudging Whitley out of the way to give Drew another embrace, wrapping her arms around his back tenderly. He raised his bandaged hand to hug her back, his body still aching as broken bones worked busily to knit themselves back together. Whitley watched, arching an eyebrow with a wry smile.

"You'll be out of action for a while, my friend," said Hector. "That fall fractured or broke just about every bone in your body. You're lucky you're blessed with lycanthropy, or you'd be fish food by now."

Drew looked to the porthole by the side of his bed and could see the night sky beyond, silver stars twinkling high overhead. The *Maelstrom* was anchored just off the coast of Highcliff and the city was also shining brightly in the darkness. Still the bells rang out in the city. He reached for the brass handle that held it shut, but it was stiff and wouldn't open.

"May I get some fresh air?" he asked.

"You've to stay in bed for a couple of days," said Hector. "You'll be back on your feet before you know it."

Drew sighed restlessly. "I dreamed while I slept, you know," he said, to none of them in particular. "Thought I was back home at the farmstead. My ma was nursing me, rocking me, looking after me. Singing to me." He shook his head. "Oh, I should have known I was dreaming. The rocking was the motion of the *Maelstrom*, and the bells, the water outside, even the lamp above my bunk, they all made appearances. Seems the only thing that I really imagined was my mother."

Hector looked at Gretchen, who in turn stared at Bergan. The old Bear scratched his head. A door closed in the corridor and Drew could hear footsteps approaching.

"I can see how you might have imagined that, lad," said Duke Bergan, rising from the chair and heading toward the door. "It's not as foolish as it sounds. She always did have a lovely singing voice."

Joining him as he waited by the open door was a lady in a long gray dress. Her white hair was worn long, falling around her face and down her back in wavy locks. Her face, though tired, was warm and soft, and her brown eyes shone as she looked at Drew. She wasn't Tilly Ferran. She might have changed from her regal robes and removed the crystal tiara, but she was unmistakable to him, to anyone. It was Queen Amelie.

Duke Bergan dropped to one knee and bowed, while Hector jumped from the bed to join him. Gretchen hurriedly rose and curtsied beside Whitley, both spreading their dresses wide before them as they sank down to the wooden floorboards. The whole thing was surreal to Drew as their shadows danced around the room under the swaying lantern light. Was he supposed to bow as well? He pulled the blankets loose again and moved clumsily to throw his legs over the side of the bed. The queen's quiet elegance was spoiled instantly as she rushed forward.

"What on *earth* are you doing?" she exclaimed, gently pushing his legs back on the bed. "It's far too soon for you to be getting up. You're not well. You need to rest!" She lowered him back into his pillows, fluffing them herself in the process and fussing as any mother would do for her child. She stopped as she pulled the quilt back up.

"Willem," she said, her face full of love.

"Pardon, Your Highness?"

"Willem," she repeated. "That was the name I gave you, although Drew sounds nice too. Tilly knew a good, strong name, didn't she?" Her smile started to fade. "I'm so sorry, Drew, for all that life has put you through."

"Your Highness," mumbled Drew, his cheeks hot and flushed. "Please don't apologize."

"You have to start by not calling me that," she said. "I know I'm not the lady who brought you up, who raised you and looked after you, and I wouldn't begin to try to replace that poor, kind soul. I knew your mother, Drew; she was a friend to me beyond class and position. A loyalty that is made even clearer to me now. I wish I could thank her." Tears welled in her sad, brown eyes. "I would, however, like the chance to try to start anew with you," she said. "I've spent years mourning the death of all my children, all my babies, only to discover that one of them still lives."

"Your High—er ... Queen Amelie?" Drew said. She brushed her hands at his choice of words dismissively, but nodded for him to speak. "You have another son, Prince Lucas. You raised him, didn't you?"

"I brought him into this world," she said, "out of duty to his father, and I love him in my way. It pains me that he is growing into the image of Leopold, a man who has kept me in a drugged despair for too many years. This is the man who con-vinced me that my children died in a fire. And now I hear ... now I discover ..." She sobbed, bringing her hands to her face. "My dear Drew, I can allow nothing to happen to you now, do you understand? You are your father reborn before my very eyes!"

"I'm not my father, though," he said, taking her hands in his own battered grasp. "And this is not a world where I feel comfortable. You ask me to be with you, which I would love more than anything in Lyssia, but this life doesn't suit me," he said, shaking his head. "I'm a shepherd boy, not the son of a king. I like to be outdoors, with the seasons on my face. Responsibility does not sit easily with me."

"Duke Bergan," the queen said. "Please speak with him. Tell him."

"Tell me what?" asked Drew, looking to all four of them.

"The life you knew before, Drew, you can't go back to it," said the Bearlord. "The Seven Realms are in pieces. Leopold remains at Highcliff Keep, a prisoner within his own castle. The forces of Brackenholme and Stormdale lay siege to the Lion, and the people of this great city are thankful. However, there is a storm on the horizon. Word of what has happened here will soon reach every corner of the continent and beyond. Armies will march to the city in the coming weeks, as claims to the throne are made and allegiances are offered. There is a vacuum, Drew, and you need to fill it."

"No," said Drew firmly. "I know nothing of politics or people and I can't be a pawn in some Werelord power play. Let me disappear, Duke Bergan. You take the throne, you rule the Seven Realms. I'll find a boat, cross the White Sea, head south, anywhere. But don't make me stay. I would only disappoint you."

"You would not, Drew," said the queen. "When the people see that the Wolf is here, only the foolhardy would make a challenge, and if they did you would not be alone. You will have

Lords Bergan and Manfred and others to call upon. Their allies are your allies. You have Lord Hector, here, and I'm sure I speak for Lady Gretchen when I say that the Foxes of Hedgemoor will support you." The Werefox nodded in total agreement. "And you have me, my son," she said. "I would die for you." She held his hands and squeezed them gently beneath her thin fingers.

"Don't you see, Drew?" said Gretchen, her green eyes blazing with a passionate fire. "This is your moment, now. This is where we can start to make things right."

Drew looked out of the porthole again, into the night. He sighed.

"Please," he said to them. "May I take some air? It is stifling down here and I need to clear my head." It was no word of a lie—the news they brought him was graver than he could have expected. When he awoke in the bed, he thought he would be able to drift off into the shadows, fall away from the intrigue that had dogged his life since his time in Brackenholme. Leopold had been defeated and the likes of Duke Bergan could set the world straight again. And even if he were to aid them in some small, inconspicuous way, at the back of his mind he had hoped for an opportunity where he might be able to escape, slip away from all these dramas. But his heart now told a different story. Could he really let the people in this cabin down? Or indeed the people in the city and beyond, if they believed in him as the queen said?

Duke Bergan bent to lift him up, raising Drew's left arm

over his shoulder before carrying the young man through the door. The Bearlord walked up onto the deck, and the others followed behind. The *Maelstrom* was alive with activity, illuminated by scores of lanterns that hung from the railings. Not only were sailors busy with their own duties, but nobles, captains of the guard, and other notables milled about, deep in negotiations, forming plans of action and then arguing over the details. Drew couldn't see the ship's captain. Count Vega was no doubt back in the port enjoying his newly restored celebrity status after his noble actions earlier that day. The sound of the bells in the city was louder now, joyous and celebratory as it echoed around Highcliff and its harbor. Drew caught sight of hundreds of people lining the piers, jetties, and promenade of the town, lanterns and torches held aloft as music played and the city folk reveled.

Hector joined him at his side. "Marvelous, isn't it, Drew?" said Hector. "My father said this day would come, when the people would rise up against the Lion."

"It would have happened with or without me, though," replied Drew.

The small figure of the lookout boy, Casper, wound his way carefully between the crowds on the *Maelstrom* before spying Drew suddenly. Immediately the boy dropped to his knee in a clumsy bow. Those around him noticed the young boy's actions and saw in turn that Drew had been brought up on deck. Like dominoes they toppled over into swift bows that passed over the ship in a wave of formality. Even though the queen's presence had been noted, too, this was clearly aimed at Drew. He was about to tell them to get up, to stop the charade, when he heard a splash and a wet thump, as something hauled itself out of the water onto the decking.

It was Count Vega. He was bare-chested and wore nothing but his leather breeches. Some of the noble ladies looked away, a little flustered. Even Gretchen and Queen Amelie averted their gazes, so striking did the Pirate Prince look. He winked at Whitley, and Drew felt Bergan's grip tighten around him with irritation.

Vega held a long stick wrapped in trails of green and brown seaweed in his hand. He strode up to Drew and gave him the briefest of courteous nods—they were aboard the Wereshark's ship, and he clearly didn't feel the need to pay his respects to anybody when he was at sea. He offered the seaweed-wrapped stick to Drew.

"It's taken longer than I thought," he said, breathing heavily and shaking his hair like a wet dog. Showers of salt water sprayed over all of them. "You should be more careful in future, my lord."

Drew, still cradled in Bergan's arms, took the stick from Vega in his free hand and was surprised by its weight, though he quickly recognized it. He held it at one end, tipping it so that the watery plants all tumbled away into a coiled heap on the deck. The Wolfshead blade gleamed in the moonlight.

A great cheer went up from along the harbor front. The people were suddenly waving furiously, throwing hats and flowers in the air.

"What are they doing?" Drew asked Bergan.

"Can't you see?" said the Bearlord. "Can't you hear?"

"Put me down for a moment," said Drew.

Hector stepped up to warn against this, but Gretchen took him by the forearm, holding him back. If anyone knew what Drew's remarkable body was capable of, it was the Wolf himself. Delicately, Duke Bergan let the young man place his bare feet on the cold planks. Drew wobbled for a moment where he stood, feeling as if his ankles were made of twigs and not bone. With the splints keeping his legs straight he hobbled over to the long rail that ran along the side of the *Maelstrom*, collapsing against it for support.

Hector and Gretchen joined him on either side, putting their arms around him. Duke Bergan stepped up behind the friends, taking Whitley's pale hand in his own. He smiled at his daughter, and she returned it with pride. He placed his other hand on Drew's shoulder; the youth felt the weight of the Bearlord's pawlike grip, ever so gently giving him a reassuring squeeze. Alongside them Queen Amelie smiled proudly, a genuine display of happiness that hadn't been witnessed by her people in many years.

The city was bustling. Drew didn't know what time of night it was, but judging by the position of the full moon in the night's sky it was the early hours of the morning. Elevated over the city, Drew could make out the lit arena of High Square and the troops assembled there, laying siege to the castle. And way up on the fortress walls, the battlements still smoked, flames leaping occasionally from the scene of his escape. He wasn't entirely sure, but he thought he heard the sound of roaring, deep within its walls.

"What is it?" asked Drew. "What are they chanting?"

"It's your name, Drew," said Hector to his left.

Indeed they were; Drew picked it out clear enough, but they were shouting something else as well.

"They're calling for the Wolf," said Whitley.

He turned to look at her. She nodded.

As he turned back to Highcliff, he felt Gretchen's lips brush against his ear, her breath warm on his skin, as she whispered, "They're chanting for their king."

Read an excerpt from the sequel,
Wereworld: Rage of Lions

I

OUTRIDER

AS THE BELLS of Brenn's Temple rang out, the young man rose from his chair and looked out over the Tall Quarter of the city of Highcliff. From his lofty vantage point he could have seen all of Westland's capital sprawling out before him, but for the dark clouds that filled the night's sky. The moon was obscured, just as they'd predicted. The third chime that marked the hour was his signal to go. Picking up his backpack from the foot of his bed, he checked it over once more. A thin bedroll was stowed in the bottom. Reaching a hand into the folds of material he felt around, his fingertips searching until they connected with the hard edge of the scroll case. Content, he removed his hand, patted the bedroll down and strapped the pack tightly shut.

1

He double-checked his weapon belt once more, tugging the buckle tight and shifting his scabbard around his left hip. The sword hilt and pommel, wrapped in dirty cloth, disappeared into the dark recesses of his cloak as he hefted the backpack over his shoulders. Stepping up to the window he deftly lifted the latch before swinging the window out. Cool night air rolled in, the smell of the sea riding the wind up from the Low Quarter. The streets were empty, although those avenues closer to Highcliff Keep glittered with torchlight. The encampment of military tents surrounding the castle effectively cordoned it off from the rest of the city under the watchful eye of Lord Bergan and his allies. The man glanced down—two floors below, the creaking wooden sign of the Halfway House inn swung to and fro in the breeze. If he were to slip, it would be a swift plummet to the cobbles four stories down and, doubtless, death.

The man reached up over his head and took a firm grip on the gutter. Turning his back to the street, he stood on the window ledge before hauling himself up to the roof. A dozen buildings separated him from the stables, with a handful of alleys and treacherous drops added for good measure. He set off, staying low and hugging the shadows. Up one slope and skidding down the next, each of his steps threatened to dislodge a shingle and send it crashing to the cobbles. Guards patrolled the streets every evening since the uprising, ensuring the curfew was maintained and nobody but the military was out after dark. As he approached a gap in the rooftops, he didn't slow to look down—if he had he might have had second thoughts. Instead he flung himself across the gap, landing with as much grace as his frantic heart allowed.

On only one occasion did he see any of the City Watch, but, worst luck, it was on the street corner nearest the stable block. At such a late hour they were quite relaxed, chatting as they walked the quieter avenues of the Tall Quarter. According to the Lord Protector, the curfew was simply a precaution in case hostilities recommenced. It was a good way for the allies' men to keep their attention focused on the deposed King Leopold the Lion without the distractions that the daytime brought. There was nothing for them to fear at their backs, and consequently the farther one moved away from the center of the city, the slacker security became. Four weeks of relative inactivity since the uprising had led the Lord Protector's men to think the battle was won. Nevertheless, the gates remained locked through the night, while by day they were heavily manned. Rumor had it that the guards had arrested at least thirty of the Lionguard who had tried to slip away from the city in the crowds, and they now languished in the cells of Traitor's House, awaiting trial.

The young man watched as the soldiers moved on. He counted thirty breaths before trusting his life to the rusty drainpipe that wound its way down to the street below. Dropping the last few feet, he ducked back into the shadows, glancing up and down the street to make sure nobody was about.

The stables backed up to Hammergate, one of the smallest entrances into Highcliff, traditionally used by the wealthier merchants who wanted to avoid the congested Mucklegate and Kingsgate. It cost a few bronze more to enter Highcliff via Hammergate, and consequently many of the townhouses in the Tall Quarter were home to Westland's most successful citizens. The man looked at the stables, lips dry with anticipation. There was bound to be a good horse or two to choose from in there.

Having scouted Hammergate thoroughly over the last two days, he knew exactly what to expect here. Indeed he'd chanced coming out over the rooftops the previous night to see what the numbers were like. Two soldiers manned the gate after dark, and they'd remained in their guardhouse for most of this time, stepping out only once to speak with their colleagues as they passed on patrol. The stable block was right beside the gate, making access directly from it and out of Hammergate relatively simple. If the gate was open. If . . .

Scampering across the street, the man hit the shadows on the opposite side, on the corner of the stable block that was blind to the guardhouse. He glanced round the corner. Dim voices and laughter could be heard from behind the glowing window of the guardhouse. Bending low once more he slipped round the corner and up to the gate. It was pitch black in the gate alcove, but he could just make out the wooden beam that held the gate shut. Taking hold of it he lifted it from its moorings and slid it back into the wall until one side of the gate was free. He held his breath all the while, heart thundering as he listened for the guards, but their easy banter continued unabated. He eased the left side of the gate forward, and it swung smoothly on its hinges to a point that was wide enough for him and a horse to get through.

Backing up, the young man disappeared into the stable block. Stalls lined the walls on either side, the gentle sounds of horses moving lightly in their sleep emanating from each of them. He looked quickly into them as he passed, left and right, trying to find a likely candidate. Halfway down the corridor he did a double take—there was a chestnut brown thoroughbred, the kind favoured by the cavalry. Stabled up here, it no doubt belonged to a merchant's courier. The decision was too easy.

Lifting the latch, he slipped inside as the horse suddenly started at a stranger's presence. He stepped up and smoothed his hands over the horse's neck and back, quickly putting it at ease.

"Good girl," he whispered, bringing his face round to hers and blowing on her nose. She seemed lively, which would be good. It had been so long since he'd worked with a horse that he found himself smiling. He reached ahead and began to untether her from a stone ring that held her close to the wall. Distracted, he didn't notice the rising glow of lamplight behind him.

"Who are you?"

The young man turned quickly, but it was too late to hide. An old man stood in the doorway, a hooded lantern held up so he could better see the intruder.

"I'm Goodman Wake's courier," he said, thinking quickly. He squinted into the light, unable to fully make out the old man's features. "Just come to check on my horse."

"Never heard of no Goodman Wake, and I'm sure as houses that ain't your mare." He stepped closer, moving the lantern forward. "You know there's a curfew on, don't you, boy?"

There was no time for games. He moved quickly, instinctively. Reaching into his cloak, he drew out his sword, and the stablehand began to stagger backward. The old man swung the lantern defensively, and the metal casing caught on the swaddled pommel, tearing free the materials that covered it. As the cloth fluttered to the ground, there was no mistaking the lionshead that shone in the lantern light, golden and roaring. The old man opened his mouth to cry out, and the attacker moved fast, swinging the sword round and bashing him across the temple with the pommel. A ragged gash appeared across his brow as he tumbled to the ground.

The young man had to work fast. He snatched down a saddle and threw it over the horse's back, hastily tying it off.

"Sorry," he said to the prone stablehand as he stepped over him, the horse following and doing likewise. Once out of the stall he hauled himself up into the saddle with ease.

"Stop him!" cried the old man. "Thief!"

The young horseman needed no more prompting. He kicked the horse's flanks, causing it to rear up before charging for the stable doors. He burst out into the street to find the soldiers out of their guardhouse and standing in his way, fully to attention, their pikes raised before them.

"Halt!"

Beyond them he could see the open gate, freedom so tantalizingly close. The guards were unaware of this situation at their backs. To be stopped now, so near escape—he grimaced, turning the horse and batting back the pikes with his lions-head blade. He could hear the sound of more guards running now as they charged down the street to their kinsmen's aid.

"Halt, I said," repeated the soldier. "In the name of the Wolf!"

That was the spur the rider needed. With another hard kick he urged his mount forward, charging the pikemen; roaring, wild. They looked terrified, wavering momentarily as the mad-man rushed them. A moment was all he needed. He swung the sword furiously, slashing down on his right side and knocking the pike from one guard's hand, before kicking out to the left and connecting with the second soldier's head. In a flash he was between them, past them and hurtling through Hammergate.

The guards didn't give chase. The man was just another coward who had served the Lion, desperate to get away from the Lord Protector's justice. They'd caught more than their fair share on the gates—so what if this little one got away? They watched him disappear into the darkness, the sound of hoof-beats fading, before eventually closing the gate.

They would forever remain oblivious to the importance of his mission.